"After having worked through the Gospel accounts in the writing of this book, I am less convinced of my own ability to *understand* God ... but even more convinced of the potential of every human being to *know* Him."

"We learn how to live with a person in direct proportion to how well we know that person. God became a human being in Jesus of Nazareth for more reasons than we will ever comprehend, but one of them *had* to be because he *understood* us — understood that we needed to know something of what his heart is like before we could trust him fully. The man or woman who is learning to live adequately in our common, troubled world, is learning something more every day about the God with whom it is our consummate privilege to live on this earth.

"I know of no better place to learn how to live than from the four provocative Gospel accounts of the earthly life of the God who loved us enough to become one of us."

— Eugenia Price

EUGENIA PRICE
LEARNING TO LIVE

A JOVE BOOK

This Jove book contains the complete
text of the original hardcover edition.
It has been completely reset in a typeface
designed for easy reading, and was printed
from new film.

LEARNING TO LIVE

A Jove Book / published by arrangement with
J. B. Lippincott Company

PRINTING HISTORY
Learning to Live is a one-volume edition of J. B. Lippincott Company's
Learning to Live from the Gospels (1968) and
Learning to Live from the Acts (1970).
Two previous printings
Jove edition / February 1986

ISBN: 0-515-08460-3

Jove Books are published by The Berkley Publishing Group,
200 Madison Avenue, New York, N.Y. 10016.
The words "A JOVE BOOK" and the "J" with sunburst
are trademarks belonging to Jove Publications, Inc.

PRINTED IN THE UNITED STATES OF AMERICA

TABLE OF CONTENTS

Learning to Live
from the Gospels

PREFACE

Learning to Live from the Gospels was written for men and women who, like myself, need to unlearn some of the static concepts acquired from years of religious conditioning. Men and women who need to begin to learn, not how merely to be theologically acceptable to their particular groups, but how to live adequately in today's world. Perhaps it isn't a very different world, but it seems more confusing, more complex. Different reactions are required from us. Old resting places must be relinquished, old horizons pushed up and out, if we are to function creatively within the framework of our swiftly evolving society. Our basic Christian absolute must remain (if we are to keep our sanity), but the attitudes of our hearts and the doors of our minds need to swing open to what God is saying for *now*.

If we believe, as I most certainly do, that the written-down Word of God is as relevant today as it has always been, surely the Bible is the one source of continuing light. To "worship" the Bible *or* to debunk it is wasteful, egocentric. We need be neither bibliolaters, idolizing the written words of the Scriptures, nor swinging radicals bent on demythologizing. Both approaches feed the already outsized human ego. The balanced Christian way to learn from the Bible is to study it through our knowledge of the always contemporary person of Jesus Christ—God himself—as he is discoverable to anyone in the pages of the New Testament.

You will find little or no information here concerning who wrote and who did not write the Gospels as we know them. You will find no scientific verification for the miracles—not even a defense of them. God's activities need no defense from us. There are no scholarly apologetics, no exegeses of the more obscure passages of Scripture. I do not know how to do any of this. I find it enough to attempt to learn how to live by the passages I do understand. Having

8

met Christ when I was well along on my earthly journey, what has held my interest from the beginning of my life with him has not been how to analyze or criticize the Bible, but *how to learn to live from it.*

My mail continues to show that people all over the world are still being confused, disturbed, shaken by some of the current Scripture debunking on which many of our learned men are spending their energies. We need to be shaken up now and then, but if faith in the eternal Christ can be destroyed by a mere book, that faith needs to take a fresh running start anyway. My mail also shows a growing unrest, even angry rebellion at the frequently dishonest, unrealistic rigidities of the religious legalists who fight to keep God in a box, using the Bible to justify their dogmatism, to give simplistic answers to the profound issues it raises. There is room, as I see it, between those two extremes, for people like us who have no axes to grind, but who know we need to learn to live our ordinary daily lives with God. Jesus was crucified by men who violently disagreed with him, who were driven to murderous extremes by the quiet, unshakable, revolutionary Authority of the Son of God. Among the silk-robed Pharisees and scribes were both the legalists and the debunkers, but they, alone, did not crucify Jesus. We were there, too, those of us who need to learn how to live.

In my opinion, most of us who honestly try to understand something of what God is saying to us in the Scriptures have never been attracted either to the rigid rules and regulations of extreme orthodoxy or to the abstract diffusion of radical theology. My prayer for us all is that we will soon come to see that there is only one absolute, one polestar—Jesus Christ, as God's own revelation of himself. I could become lost in the quagmire of existentialism without the one eternal starting place on which I can depend—the Saviour God. When we begin with him, we are free to move ahead, sure of our direction. Of course, we need each other. We need the products of our shared thinking and knowledge, but I believe we are to follow—to be truly influenced *only* by—the Christ of the Gospels.

After having worked through the Gospel accounts in the writing of this book, I am less convinced of my own ability to *understand* God, but even more convinced of the potential of every human being to *know* him. We learn how to live with a person in direct proportion to how well we know that person. God became a human being in Jesus of Nazareth for more reasons than we will ever comprehend, but one of them *had* to be because he *understood* us—understood that we needed to know something of what his heart is like before we could trust him fully. The man or woman who is learning to live adequately in our common, troubled world, is learning something more every day about the God with whom it is our consummate privilege to live on this earth.

I know of no better place to learn how to live than from the four provocative Gospel accounts of the earthly life of the God who loved us enough to become one of us.

EUGENIA PRICE

St. Simons Island, Georgia
May, 1968

SAINT MATTHEW

CHAPTER 1
vv. 21, 23
*. . . thou shalt call his name JESUS: for he shall
save his people from their sins. . . . they shall call his
name Emmanuel, which being interpreted is, God
with us.*

Even in the half-light of the Old Testament period,
Isaiah knew that the people needed God to be *with them.*
When the prophet told of the coming of the Messiah, he
said his name would be called Emmanuel—God with us.
Even then, Isaiah saw the people's need to have God with
them. Not remote and distant—*with them.* Surely, when
the Messiah did come, he fulfilled Isaiah's prophecy and
more. He was God with us, Emmanuel, but his name was
called *Jesus.* And this is one of the most clarifying verses in
the New Testament: right at the beginning of the first Gospel account, we are told that the Messiah's name would be
called *Jesus.* God has come in Jesus, to be with us—to be
Emmanuel—but our great need, as only God knew, was to
be saved from our sins. Jesus means Saviour. As the New
Testament completes the message of the Old, so the two
names given the Messiah complete each other. God cannot
freely be with a man without saving him from his sins. This
is the *nature* of the redeemer God. We are saved by an always present God, because of *what he is like*—not by acceptance of a certain doctrine or the performance of a
ritual.

CHAPTER 3
v. 17
*And lo a voice from heaven, saying, This is my be-
loved Son, in whom I am well pleased.*

The Father was saying more than the human mind can

11

ever comprehend when he declared that Jesus was his beloved Son, who pleased him.

One thing he must have meant was that he could *trust*
his Son completely. God alone knows how trustworthy
anyone is. The glory-filled moments after his baptism,
when Jesus actually saw "the Spirit of God descending like
a dove, and lighting upon him," must have brought an in-
describable feeling of exhilaration—both human and divine. But the Father, knowing the Son as he did, knew
there was in Jesus far more than feeling: There was in him
complete, uncluttered trustworthiness.

CHAPTER 4

v. 1

*Then was Jesus led up of the spirit into the wilder-
ness to be tempted of the devil.*

Jesus did not go off into the wilderness to be tempted in
order to prove his own advanced spirituality. He did not
wander off alone in an ascetic daze, seeking a still more exhilarating spiritual sensation: He was "*led* up of the spirit.
. . ." The Father deliberately led him into his time of conflict and agony of soul because the Father knew he could
trust his Son utterly.

Jesus' temptation in the wilderness was, in a definite
sense, a preliminary part of his Passion—his Cross Experience. Here, he was giving himself to us and for us just as
surely as he gave himself during the bright-dark hours
through which he hung on the Cross. The Father did not
lead his Son into temptation to prove his trustworthiness,
his inner strength, his ability to resist the tempter. The Father already knew. Jesus was led into his wilderness time
for our sake. *So we would know.*

vv. 3, 6

*. . . If thou be the Son of God, ... If thou be the
Son of God, . . .*

Until now, I have thought that the first two temptations
of Jesus were peculiar to him. Twice, his very identity as
the Christ was challenged: "If thou be the Son of God, . . ."
"If thou be the Son of God, . . ." This seemed always to

mean that only Jesus could have been tempted on this point, since only he is the divine Son of God. I now believe this is only part of it. It's true that he was challenged here in a way in which only he could have been challenged, but aren't *our identities* as forgiven, Spirit-filled sons of God challenged too by temptation? Doesn't the world look at us in the face of fresh trouble or criticism and ask: "If Christ lives in you as you claim he does, why should you go down under this thing?"

vv. 8, 9
Again, the devil taketh him up into an exceeding high mountain, and sheweth him all the kingdoms of the world, and the glory of them; And saith unto him, All these things will I give thee, if thou wilt fall down and worship me.

God does not want us to be naïve. In Jesus' wilderness experience we are told what to expect of ourselves: an overwhelming tendency to worship secularism. Christians seem to fail at this point more than at any other. Even the most doctrine-minded among us can rationalize an act if it inflates our bank accounts.

vv. 19 through 22
. . . Follow me, . . . And they straightway left their nets, and followed him. . . . and he called them. And they immediately left the ship and their father, and followed him.

Straightway. Immediately. Peter and Andrew "straightway left their nets, and followed him." James and John "immediately left the ship and their father, and followed him."

None of these men wasted time with doubt, self-analysis, cost-weighing. They didn't ask for proof that Jesus was born of a virgin or if miracles were myths. They didn't pin him down to find out whether or not he believed the Scriptures were inspired. They asked no questions about his political leanings. There was no indecision whatever. Not one of the four wrote a ten-page letter to anyone asking for advice. They simply went with him—straightway and immediately.

CHAPTER 5
vv. 1 through 12a

And seeing the multitudes, he went up into a mountain and when he was set, his disciples came unto him:

And he opened his mouth, and taught them, saying,

Blessed are the poor in spirit: for theirs is the kingdom of heaven.

Blessed are they that mourn: for they shall be comforted.

Blessed are the meek: for they shall inherit the earth.

Blessed are they which do hunger and thirst after righteousness: for they shall be filled.

Blessed are the merciful: for they shall obtain mercy.

Blessed are the pure in heart: for they shall see God.

Blessed are the peacemakers: for they shall be called the children of God.

Blessed are they which are persecuted for righteousness' sake: for theirs is the kingdom of heaven.

Blessed are ye, when men shall revile you, and persecute you, and shall say all manner of evil against you falsely, for my sake.

Rejoice, and be exceeding glad: ...

These verses, called the Beatitudes, sound like madness or, at best, wishful thinking to those still dwelling in darkness. Christians have been so tormented by failing in their foolish attempt to follow the Beatitudes as rules laid down for living the adequate life that some have even invented dispensations—little chopped-up sections of time—which conveniently put the Beatitudes in another era. Any other time—but not now. Once more, God has provided a great simplification: If one thinks at all, it is obvious that what Jesus did not do was lay down a list of "how-to" regulations. He was *describing* the inevitable *result* of the Spirit-filled life. *If* we have begun to permit God to live his life in us, these are the ways we will be: never proud spiritually;

willing to admit our heartbreaks and our griefs—i.e., we will be realistic about life; never complaining, but rejoicing when we hunger for more righteousness—when we see our need; always merciful—willing to stand in the other person's shoes; always pure in heart—possessing unmixed motives; never relishing the role of troublemaker, willing to move out toward peace; never falling into the trap of self-pity when we have been wronged for Jesus' sake—for being a way we know it is right to be, regardless of the cost to us.

We are to rejoice and be exceeding glad when we see any of these divine family traits showing up in us in our daily round. The Beatitudes could, I suppose, be called a kind of check list—but never a set of rules. Jesus is declaring: This is the great potential for all of you.

v. 13
Ye are the salt of the earth: but if the salt have lost his savour, wherewith shall it be salted? it is thenceforth good for nothing, but to be cast out, and to be trodden under foot of men.

If Christians are the salt of the earth, why do we have such a flavorless world? Jesus was not wrong. Perhaps we have just refused to realize how utterly singular—how unique—salt is. As he said: If the flavor has gone out of the salt—what is going to "salt" the salt?

v. 20
For I say unto you, That except your righteousness shall exceed the righteousness of the scribes and Pharisees, ye shall in no case enter into the kingdom of heaven.

Unless we exhibit a kind of love and understanding and wisdom that *exceeds* that demonstrated by those who are dead certain they have it all figured out, we have in no way learned the nature of the atmosphere of the Kingdom.

vv. 22, 28, 32, 34, 39, 44
But I say unto you, . . . But I say unto you, . . . But

I say unto you, . . . But I say unto you, . . . But I say unto you, . . . But I say unto you, . . .

Jesus came saying (verse 18) that he was not here to discount what was tried and true of the *old*. "But *I* say unto you, . . ." We need to dwell on that often repeated phrase of his: "But I say unto you, . . ." He did not come to obliterate anything—he came bringing it all, making it all available in himself. This is what is *new:* The day for rules and regulations is past. Grace and truth have come in Jesus Christ—and with him, the whole life. *It is all in him.*

v. 45
   That ye may be the children of your Father which is in heaven: for he maketh his sun to rise on the evil and on the good, and sendeth rain on the just and on the unjust.

We will know that we are the children of the Father when it begins to seem right and natural to us to *want* the sun to rise on both the evil and the good; when we *care* that the rain falls on the just and the unjust. God is love, and he loves *every man* and *every woman*—good and evil, just and unjust. This is difficult for us to accept, feeling as we do, that somehow he owes us more love because we have been driven by our own desperate need to receive his forgiveness.

v. 48
   Be ye therefore perfect, even as your Father which is in heaven is perfect.

This simple statement of Jesus' has caused great frustration and confusion. People unwisely try to whip themselves up into what they consider God's perfection. This is nonsense. God is God and we are we. We are to live up to the limits of our capacities—*where we are* on our journey. We are to give out to the extent of our love—as much as we have learned about love. We are being "perfect" as the Father is perfect when we live all the love we know.

CHAPTER 6
vv. 4, 6
. . . thy Father which seeth in secret. . . . . . . thy Father which seeth in secret. . . .

The phrase ". . . thy Father which seeth in secret. . . ." is repeated three times in the first part of this chapter (also verse 18). It is *implied* many more times in what Jesus is saying. *God is a realist.* He does not bother with outward appearances, with loud, lengthy prayers, with broadcast charity. He does not bother because he does not need to bother. These are, in reality, irrelevant. "The Lord looketh on the heart." God sees motives, not performances. He sees reactions first, then actions. How much more *rest* and how much less *waste* there would be if we realized this.

vv. 14, 15
For if ye forgive men their trespasses, your heavenly Father will also forgive you: But if ye forgive not men their trespasses, neither will your Father forgive your trespasses

Jesus is not implying here that we should bargain with God; certainly not that God bargains with us. It is simply that as long as a human heart is hardened toward anyone, i.e., refusing forgiveness for any reason, it is also closed to God. He never invades. He waits for the open heart. God is always willing—eager—to forgive. But we must be in a condition to receive his forgiveness.

v. 23
. . . If therefore the light that is in thee be darkness, how great is that darkness!

Could this be at least partial explanation for the strange, often cruel personalities of men and women who profess Christ (have perhaps settled, for themselves at least, all doctrinal problems!) but whose "light" is so lacking in love, it is full of darkness?

v. 24
. . . Ye cannot serve God and mammon.

Neither can we love God and harm one of his loved ones.

v. 33
...seek ye first the kingdom of God,...

If we seek God first—give him our full attention—everything else falls into place. If we are style-conscious, the designers have us. If we are money-conscious, we are owned by our bank accounts. If we are self-conscious, we insist upon self-ownership. But if we are God-conscious, the way is clear. We are off our own hands. What gets our attention gets us.

CHAPTER 7
v. 5
Thou hypocrite, first cast out the beam out of thine own eye; and then shalt thou see clearly to cast out the mote out of thy brother's eye.

Not only are we blinded to how to help our brother, if we have left the "beam" in our own eye, we are also squinting and peering fuzzily at the very nature of God—unable to see him clearly either.

vv. 21 through 23
Not every one that saith unto me, Lord, Lord, shall enter into the kingdom of heaven; but he that doeth the will of my Father which is in heaven. Many will say to me in that day, Lord, Lord, have we not prophesied in thy name? and in thy name have cast out devils? and in thy name done many wonderful works? And then will I profess unto them, I never knew you: depart from me, ye that work iniquity.

If "God is love," then isn't his will always centered in the inclusive necessity to love? Will only those who have dropped the art of self-defense in favor of the willingness to love enter into the Kingdom? Will he give admittance into the Kingdom for skillful expounding of the prophecies and doctrines of the Christian faith? For good deeds well done? For thrashing the devil? No. Our *Father seeth in secret*, where the heart is, where love is or isn't. And only he knows.

v. 29

For he taught them as one having authority, and not as the scribes.

Jesus was not just another writer of spiritual truths. He was God become Man, possessing both the Authority of God and the Authority of Man.

CHAPTER 8
vv. 8 through 10

The centurion answered and said, Lord, I am not worthy that thou shouldest come under my roof: but speak the word only, and my servant shall be healed. For I am a man under authority, having soldiers under me: and I say to this man, Go, and he goeth: and to another, Come, and he cometh; and to my servant, Do this, and he doeth it. When Jesus heard it, he marvelled, and said to them that followed, Verily I say unto you, I have not found so great faith, no, not in Israel.

Jesus marveled because one man understood his Authority and acted on his clear understanding. There is enormous simplification here. And great urgency for us to begin to think of how we complicate faith. We need only to recognize who God is, and begin to act on what we have recognized.

vv. 19, 20

And a certain scribe came, and said unto him, Master, I will follow thee whithersoever thou goest. And Jesus saith unto him, The foxes have holes, and the birds of the air have nests; but the Son of man hath not where to lay his head.

He made no promises of material security. If a man follows Jesus, he must not follow him for where they may be going together, but for one reason only: to be with him.

vv. 21, 22
*And another of his disciples said unto Him, Lord,
suffer me first to go and bury my father. But Jesus
said unto him, Follow me; and let the dead bury their
dead.*

Jesus was not being cruel here. He was simply saying:
Up ahead is *life.* Follow me, and your attention will be
riveted forever upon life.

CHAPTER 9
vv. 10 through 13
*And it came to pass, as Jesus sat at meat in the
house, behold, many publicans and sinners came and
sat down with him and his disciples. And when the
Pharisees saw it, they said unto his disciples, Why eateth your Master with publicans and sinners? But
when Jesus heard that, he said unto them, They that
be whole need not a physician, but they that are sick.
But go ye and learn what that meaneth, I will have
mercy, and not sacrifice: for I am not come to call the
righteous, but sinners to repentance.*

"Go ye and learn what that meaneth, . . ." In rebuking
his critics, the shallow-thinking Pharisees, Jesus did not
say, "Get out a book about love and learn what I mean."
He said, "*Go ye* and learn. . . ." He knew they, who already had life decided and analyzed both intellectually and
doctrinally, needed to take an *active step* in love. But he
did give them one potent clue as to how to do it: "I will
have mercy, and not sacrifice." The time for ceremonial
sacrifices ended when the Lamb, himself, came on the
scene. Spiritual arrogance cannot live in his presence.

v. 36
*But when he saw the multitudes, he was moved with
compassion on them, because they fainted, and were
scattered abroad, as sheep having no shepherd.*

If we would remember this reaction of Jesus as we read
magazines and newspapers, or walk our crowded streets,

we would find ourselves forgetting how to be merely shocked.

CHAPTER 10

v. 13

And if the house be worthy, let your peace come upon it: but if it be not worthy, let your peace return to you.

If we offer peace and good will in a situation and they are not received—if we are scorned, laughed at, "cut down to size" for our efforts—we have obeyed Jesus anyway. And if it has been real peace we offer, with no mixed motives, only peace can come back to us. Even if it is slammed back in our faces, we are still the recipients of peace. The same is true of love.

v. 16

Behold, I send you forth as sheep in the midst of wolves: be ye therefore wise as serpents, and harmless as doves.

Where I live there are both snakes and doves. This admonition of Jesus has taken on fresh meaning: We are to be as wise as serpents, but without their bite or venom. We are to be as harmless as doves, but without their voracious appetites or their stupidity. The dove, though beautiful, seems to be a rather stupid, uncertain bird, but surely its intentions are harmless. Otherwise it would not announce its arrival with such a whistling of its wings. The snakes in the woods around my house are silent.

vv. 19, 20

But when they deliver you up, take no thought how or what ye shall speak: for it shall be given you in that same hour what ye shall speak.

For it is not ye that speak, but the Spirit of your Father which speaketh in you.

When we are utterly frightened and helpless and at a loss for words, God's Spirit can get through to us far more easily.

v. 26

Fear them not therefore: for there is nothing covered, that shall not be revealed; and hid, that shall not be known.

One day the cover will be removed and there will stand God, obviously in full charge. And all those who cannot now believe will see him as having always been just that— God in full charge of his creation. And at that time, ". . . every knee shall bow."

vv. 29 through 31

Are not two sparrows sold for a farthing? and one of them shall not fall on the ground without your Father. But the very hairs of your head are all numbered. Fear ye not therefore, ye are of more value than many sparrows.

Now and then a bird flies accidentally against the screen on my back porch and breaks its neck. The Father knows. He is the only Person alive who can give full attention to every living being every minute. He is not only the only one who *can* do this; he is the only one who wants to.

vv. 34 through 37

Think not that I am come to send peace on earth: I came not to send peace, but a sword. For I am come to set a man at variance against his father, and the daughter against her mother, and the daughter in law against her mother in law. And a man's foes shall be they of his own household. He that loveth father or mother more than me is not worthy of me: and he that loveth son or daughter more than me is not worthy of me.

Jesus, of course, did not mean to imply that he had come to break up families. Invariably, he used the sharp illustration—what we now call "attention grabbers." And yet beneath this harsh-sounding statement is truth. Anyone who permits even a member of his family to cause him to drift away from Christ, from love, is heading for trouble. Jesus did not come to bring an easy peace. He came to bring *lasting* peace. Every form of indulgent sentimentality must be cut away before anyone can follow the Christ of Calvary. But when indulgent sentimentality is gone, *love* can replace it.

CHAPTER 11
vv. 2, 3

Now when John had heard in the prison the works of Christ, he sent two of his disciples, and said unto him, Art thou he that should come, or do we look for another?

John the Baptist was a God-centered man of enormous faith. And yet, when Jesus did nothing to bring about John's release from prison, but went out teaching and preaching, John—quite understandably—began to doubt. Plainly, he began to doubt that Jesus was the One he, John, had been heralding for so long. John, by the standard of human accomplishment, was the greatest religious leader of his time. Jesus said of him: (verse 11) ". . . Among them that are born of women there hath not risen a greater than John the Baptist: . . ." Still, here was this great prophet of God *doubting* the very heart of the message God had given him to preach to the people. If John, the messenger of God, harbored doubts, how ridiculous that *we* are surprised, shocked when we also doubt! Are we greater than John? Do we have more spiritual depth? More spiritual perception? These are irrelevant questions. The relevant question is: Do we have the *humility* of John? *Authentic humility can afford to admit doubt.* John made no attempt to hide his uncertainty. He sent two of his own disciples to Jesus to ask him point-blank—two men who had followed John for all the days he had gone about preaching. Even before his followers, John's humility stood up. He cared more about discovering the truth, having his doubts put down, than he cared about his own reputation as a religious leader. To doubt is not necessarily un-Christian. To lack humility *is*.

vv. 4, 5

Jesus answered and said unto them, Go and shew

*John again those things which ye do hear and see:
The blind receive their sight, and the lame walk, the
lepers are cleansed, and the deaf hear, the dead are
raised up, and the poor have the gospel preached to
them.*

In answer to John's question, Jesus said simply that the
disciples of John were to tell the Baptist what they had seen
there: The blind were seeing again, the lame were walking,
the lepers were being healed, the deaf heard, the dead lived
and the good news was being given to those who so desperately needed it. He did not send John's two friends back to
their teacher in prison with a carefully set forth theological
treatise. He sent them with one fact: Creativity is taking
place! Nothing is being torn down that has stood from the
beginning. Everything is only being strengthened, made
new, restored.

v. 6
*And blessed is he, whosoever shall not be offended
in me.*

Jesus sent word to John entirely sufficient to end John's
doubt, but being Jesus, he went a step farther. Jesus did not
admonish John in this statement; he encouraged him. To
me, it was as though Jesus were saying *more* than "Yes,
John, I am the One who fits, according to your message,
into the divine plan." He was also saying, "I supersede even
the divine plan! Even in prison, John, you will find peace if
you do not lose your faith in *me*. Not merely in my mission
on earth, but in *me*."

v. 11
*Verily I say unto you, Among them that are born of
women there hath not risen a greater than John the
Baptist: notwithstanding he that is least in the kingdom of heaven is greater than he.*

Jesus praised John the Baptist. He went so far as to declare there had never been a man born of woman who was
greater. *But,* and this is the key: As great as John was, the
most insignificant person who is *born into* the Kingdom

would be greater! This in no way denigrates John. Rather,
it clarifies Jesus' set of values: the very values of God himself. No one was more loyal than John, no one more sacrificial, no one expended his energies more recklessly. But
these, valuable as they are, are not the qualifications for entering the Kingdom of God. There is but one: faith in Jesus
Christ.

v. 12
    *And from the days of John the Baptist until now
    the kingdom of heaven suffereth violence, and the vio-
    lent take it by force.*

This is a difficult passage. I have never been entirely satisfied with the explanations I have read concerning it. The
words "violence" and "force" have been distorted for us by
current news coverage. So, perhaps a look at a newer translation is needed. J. B. Phillips translates verse 12 this way:
"From the days of John the Baptist until now, the Kingdom of Heaven has been taken by storm and eager men are
forcing their way into it." The Amplified: "And from the
days of John the Baptist until the present time the kingdom
of heaven has endured violent assault, and violent men
seize it by force [as a precious prize]—a share in the heavenly kingdom is sought for with most ardent zeal and intense exertion." Other versions give similar light. At this
point in my own thinking, I believe that at least part of
what Jesus was saying had to do with the sudden *availabil-
ity* of the Kingdom to the common man. Until John the
Baptist, the people had to depend upon their priests. The
holy of holies was closed to them. Suddenly, it was no
longer closed. And they plunged into God's presence. How
have we so diminished the wonder of the open door that
men no longer attempt to rush into the Kingdom of God?

vv. 16 through 19
    *But whereunto shall I liken this generation? It is
    like unto children sitting in the markets, and calling
    unto their fellows, and saying, we have piped unto
    you, and ye have not danced; we have mourned unto
    you, and ye have not lamented. For John came neither
    eating nor drinking, and they say, He hath a devil.*

*The Son of man came eating and drinking, and they
say, Behold a man gluttonous and a winebibber, a
friend of publicans and sinners. But wisdom is justified of her children.*

Jesus' irony here is, as always, more than attractive, it is
profound. He is saying in a highly colorful manner that
there is no pleasing the public! The immaturity of the
masses of people sticks out all over: If you don't dance
when I play my pipes or mourn when I want to play funer-
al, I won't play. The same irony permeates the sharp comparison he made between himself and John the Baptist. He
said in effect; "John was bred to austerity, to the lonely life,
to the aesthetic way, and you said he had a devil. I come
being utterly and warmly and joyfully human, 'eating and
drinking' and enjoying myself and enjoying you. So, you
tack a label on me. I'm a glutton and I'm a winebibber.
There is no satisfying the public. But wisdom—the wisdom
of God available to anyone who will take it—is justified, is
proven only by her actions. You're all talking too much!"

vv. 25, 26
*At that time Jesus answered and said, I thank thee,
O Father, Lord of heaven and earth, because thou
hast hid these things from the wise and prudent, and
hast revealed them unto babes. Even so, Father: for
so it seemed good in thy sight.*

Jesus had just finished upbraiding the sinfulness and ma-
terialism and immorality of cities where he had attempted
to make his purpose clear. They would be far less fortunate
in the judgment than the wicked, ancient cities of Tyre and
Sidon—even Sodom. Jesus Christ had not come to them,
but the people of Chorazin and Bethsaida and Capernaum
had been exposed to him, had seen his love in operation,
had heard his message. They had had a chance—firsthand
—to see their need of repentance.

And immediately following this caustic statement, it is as
though he sighed, reminding even himself—with thanksgiv-
ing—that the Father had dared to be clear and simple. Had
not settled for revealing himself to the "wise and prudent"
—the scholarly intellectuals—but had made himself clear

in such a way that even children could grasp his identity.
There is no indication anywhere in the Bible that we need
to be brilliant or clever or learned in order to know God.
There is every indication that all of us, even the brilliant
and the clever and the learned, *must be childlike*. This was
"good" in the Father's sight because only the unsuspicious,
open heart, with no false confidence in itself, *can trust*. The
Father is always realistic about both things and people.

vv. 28 through 30
*Come unto me, all ye that labour and are heavy
laden, and I will give you rest. Take my yoke upon
you, and learn of me; for I am meek and lowly in
heart: and ye shall find rest unto your souls. For my
yoke is easy, and my burden is light.*

Jesus' strong warning to Chorazin and Bethsaida and
Capernaum (vv. 20 through 24) is followed by his strongest claim to the Authority of God (v. 27). But here, he dif-
fers from so many of his well-meaning servants who settle
for ending with a tirade against the sinfulness of man:
Jesus never settled merely for convicting a man of his sin;
he always offered freedom, rest, peace. "Come unto me, all
ye that labour and are heavy laden, and I will give you
rest." When he blazed out at sinfulness, he did not direct
his fire at the sinner. They received the full force of his
love! Condemnation cannot bring rest. Guilt cannot bring
rest. Jesus was never about the business of causing anxiety.
He was about his Father's business, and this was to bring
sinful man back into the restful, creative relationship of
Eden.

Anxious, restless Christians are a contradiction of the
Gospel of Christ. "Because of who I am," he declared, "I
will rest you—if you will only come to me and give me a
chance." As always, he took the time and expended the effort to explain—if an explanation was really necessary. The
idea of rest in the deeps of the human spirit in the midst of
any trouble required explanation and he made it. "Take my
yoke upon you, and learn of me. . . ." We have read at
length about the fact that Jesus understood the value of
yokes, that he made them with his own hands in Joseph's
carpenter shop. But too often, we stop with the yoke. He

did not. In the very same sentence, he gave us the most important instruction even he ever gave: ". . . *learn of me.* . . ." Discover for yourselves, he told us, something of the true nature of this God who longs over you. Find out what he is really like in his heart, his plane, his dreams for the people he loves. Don't settle for a secondhand notion of God. Learn of him firsthand by learning of Jesus Christ, his one complete, uncluttered, clear revelation of himself. Rest comes no other way. Through Christ, it can come to everyone. With him, no one is left out.

CHAPTER 12
v. 7
I will have mercy, and not sacrifice, . . .

For all the years until Jesus came clarifying God, man had depended upon his own ability to make a suitable sacrifice. It is clear now, if we will only see, that mercy outshines any sacrifice we could imagine. God would rather see us showing mercy than writing large checks.

v. 13
Then saith he to the man, Stretch forth thine hand. And he stretched it forth; and it was restored whole, like as the other.

God does not require nor want our sacrifices. The supreme sacrifice has already been made on Calvary. But there is a part for us. God is not interested in mere manipulation of the human heart. Jesus healed the man with the withered hand, but the man had to "stretch forth (his) hand." The healing became useful to him when he had done his human part. God always desires *our* participation.

v. 19
He shall not strive, nor cry; neither shall any man hear his voice in the streets.

Jesus did not come making a display of himself, shouting at the top of his lungs; he did not walk the earth blowing trumpets or setting up high-pressure organizations for purposes of newspaper coverage or promotion. He sent out no four-color brochures, no flyers for store windows. He did not thump a pulpit nor cry into a microphone. "He shall not strive, nor cry; neither shall any man hear his voice in the streets." He worked sanely, quietly, profoundly, with the dignity of love. Notice specifically that he did not "strive." His work was exhausting, constant, but his inner peace held. Jesus was crucified on a Cross. He did not drop dead from striving to do in his human strength what only the supernatural God could do.

vv. 31, 32

Wherefore I say unto you, All manner of sin and blasphemy shall be forgiven unto men: but the blasphemy against the Holy Ghost shall not be forgiven unto men. And whosoever speaketh a word against the Son of man, it shall be forgiven him: but whosoever speaketh against the Holy Ghost, it shall not be forgiven him, neither in this world, neither in the world to come.

In my opinion, these two verses have caused more unnecessary heartache and inner misery than any other in the entire Bible. Surely, I do not know all their meaning. But Jesus Christ never caused unnecessary confusion. He still does not. "God is *never* "the author of confusion."

At least once a month I receive one or more letters from some trembling, anxious person who is sure he or she has committed the unpardonable sin against the Holy Spirit. Stop and think: If a human heart cares enough one way or the other to be distraught with worry and concern over a thing like this, doesn't it make sense that that person could not possibly have committed such a sin? In the first place, one has to *believe* in the Holy Spirit before one cares at all about sinning against him! Doesn't the very question answer itself? Do you fear you have committed the unpardonable sin against the Holy Spirit? I don't think I understand all of what that sin might be, but if you are worried about it, you certainly have not!

vv. 46 through 50

While he yet talked to the people, behold, his mother and his brethren stood without, desiring to speak

*with him. Then one said unto him, Behold, thy mother
and thy brethren stand without, desiring to speak with
thee. But he answered and said unto him that told
him, Who is my mother? and who are my brethren?
And he stretched forth his hand toward his disciples,
and said, Behold my mother and my brethren! For
whosoever shall do the will of my Father which is in
heaven, the same is my brother, and sister, and
mother.*

Jesus was not *excluding* his mother or his brothers. He
was *including* us.

CHAPTER 13
vv. 54 through 58

*And when he was come into his own country, he
taught them in their synagogue, insomuch that they
were astonished, and said, Whence hath this man this
wisdom, and these mighty works? Is not this the carpenter's son? Is not his mother called Mary? and his
brethren, James, and Joses, and Simon, and Judas?
And his sisters, are they not all with us? Whence then
hath this man all these things? And they were offended in Him. But Jesus said unto them, A prophet is not
without honour, save in his own country, and in his
own house. And he did not many mighty works there
because of their unbelief.*

Jesus' visit to his home town was not publicized. He
came home quietly, being himself. He hadn't maneuvered
any honorary degrees, nor bought any time on any com-
munications media. He just came home the way he left,
being the Son of God, *being himself.* The home-town folk
were not impressed. They knew his mother and father as
their neighbors. They knew all Jesus' brothers and sisters
by name. They had no more faith in him than in any other
home-town young man. As a consequence, he "did not
many mighty works there because of their unbelief."

In this startling sense, we *do* control the "mighty works"
of God!

CHAPTER 14
vv. 10 through 14

And he sent, and beheaded John in the prison. And his head was brought in a charger, and given to the damsel: and she brought it to her mother. And his disciples came, and took up the body, and buried it, and went and told Jesus. When Jesus heard of it, he departed thence by ship into a desert place apart: and when the people had heard thereof, they followed him on foot out of the cities. And Jesus went forth, and saw a great multitude, and was moved with compassion toward them, and he healed their sick.

Jesus loved John the Baptist. They were not only cousins; they had been united in the purpose of God. They shared the same goals. We are not told in detail of their personal relationship, but there can be little doubt that the two were close, or that John's ignominious death grieved Jesus. He tried to get away alone in order to cope with his loss. It was impossible to get away. The crowds followed him, and the sight of their crippled legs and blind eyes and empty souls caused his compassion to overcome his grief. He did what he had to do: He showed them his heart.

v. 27

. . . Be of good cheer; it is I; be not afraid.

After Jesus had fed the multitudes toward whom he had shown compassion, he sent his disciples away in a ship and dismissed the people—still longing, needing to be alone with the Father. By evening, he had managed some time for himself, for healing of his grief, for new strength. But his disciples were out on the sea in their small ship when a storm began to whip up gigantic waves, tossing their boat dangerously. "He was there alone," but he was also God, and he knew his men were afraid without him. Once more, he relinquished his much needed solitude and ". . . went unto them, walking on the sea." Of course, the disciples were terrified. To their minds, the sight of a man coming toward their plunging boat across the black fury of the stormy water, had to be a spirit—an apparition! They ". . . cried out for fear." And then Jesus said a most important, many-dimensioned thing: "Be of good cheer!" he called out to them. "It is I; be not afraid."

I have always been struck by the fact that he said "Cheer up" first. He is still calling out to us when the wind turns our normally quiet waters into a whirlpool of fury that can suck us under or batter us to our knees in abject fear. I have known his call to change entire lives. As I write this, at a time that could bring me fear, I hear his call to me: "Cheer up! Don't be afraid—it is I!"

He is in every blast of trouble, every moment of panic, every time of pressure, of fear, of grief. of confusion. And he is not an apparition—this call to us from the very heart of God is not a mere phrase to stiffen our spines—it is reality. "It is I." *He is in it.* And where he is, fear vanishes and the courage of good cheer returns.

vv. 32, 33
And when they were come into the ship, the wind ceased. Then they that were in the ship came and worshipped him, saying, Of a truth thou art the Son of God.

When Jesus and poor human Peter climbed aboard the tossing ship, "the wind ceased." And the disciples said: "Of a truth thou art the Son of God." There is no better way to be certain of that than to have had him sweep one's fear away.

CHAPTER 15
v. 14
Let them alone: they be blind leaders of the blind. And if the blind lead the blind, both shall fall into the ditch.

Good advice. When one is struck full in the face by Pharisaism, don't complain, don't attack, don't try to change them—let them alone.

CHAPTER 16
vv. 11, 12
How is it that ye do not understand that I spake it not to you concerning bread, that ye should beware of

*the leaven of the Pharisees and of the Sadducees?
Then understood they how that he bade them not be-
ware of the leaven of bread, but of the doctrine of the
Pharisees and of the Sadducees.*

We should not wonder at the wild array of fringe cults
among people who seek God. Without the teaching of
Jesus, made clear to us (as he promised) through his Holy
Spirit, it is no wonder at all that men become confused.
Look at the very men who lived and slept and ate and
worked with Jesus when he was on earth! Read these verses
with the idea of seeing how "far out" they were much of
the time in their understanding.

Jesus said, "Take heed, and beware the leaven of the
Pharisees and of the Sadducees." The disciples, their minds
on the fact that they forgot to bring any bread along,
missed his point entirely. Shaking his head, perhaps, he
asked them if they had forgotten so soon that he had fed—
not only the five thousand when there was no food, but a
short time later—seven thousand. His reminder that it
would be utterly ridiculous for him to worry about forgotten bread when he had himself made bread for thousands
finally cleared their muddled minds a little. And they saw
that he was warning them about "doctrine clutchers." Not
the leaven of bread—the leaven of the hypocritical spirit.
This leaven grows inside a man's heart in no time. It flat-
ters his ego to feel himself right above all men. It is tempting.

vv. 13 through 18
*When Jesus came into the coast of Caesarea Philip-
pi, he asked his disciples, saying, Whom do men say
that I the Son of man am? And they said, Some say
that thou are John the Baptist: some, Elias; and others, Jeremias, or one of the prophets. He saith unto
them, But whom say ye that I am? And Simon Peter
answered and said, Thou art the Christ, the Son of the
Living God. And Jesus answered and said unto him,
Blessed art thou, Simon Bar-jona: for flesh and blood
hath not revealed it unto thee, but my Father which is
in heaven. And I say also unto thee, That thou art*

*Peter, and upon this rock I will build my church; and
the gates of hell shall not prevail against it.*

Although I have written many times on Peter's sudden
declaration that Jesus was the Christ, the Son of God, I
confess some uncertainty as to the sequence of realization
among Jesus' disciples. We have just noted in Matthew's
Chapter 14, verse 33, that when Jesus got into the boat
with them and the wind subsided, *they* called him the Son
of God. And yet, Peter said: "Thou art the *Christ,* the Son
of the living God." There is little doubt that this was the
first time anyone had experienced and voiced the *entire
truth* about his identity. The dawn of full truth broke slowly and gradually upon the men and women who followed
him during the years of his earthly life. Even though the
men in the boat—his close, intimate associates—declared
him to be the Son of God, the use of the name *Christ*
meant that Peter knew the Messiah had come! The fact
that when, on the sandy coastal road at Caesarea Philippi,
Jesus asked: "Whom do men say that I am?" showed that
he, Jesus, was well aware of the confusion in men's minds.
The fact that his own disciples mentioned that people were
hinting that he was John the Baptist returned from the
dead, or Elijah or Jeremiah, indicates the talk going
around. Talk, full of questionings and theories. Peter nailed
it down for all time, and Jesus blessed him and assured him
that this all important flash of truth came straight from the
Father. There had apparently been no gossip that he was
the Messiah. No man had told Peter. The Father was able
to get through to Peter and Jesus said, "Blessed art thou,
Simon Bar-jona. . . ." And Jesus, because Peter had
grasped this central truth, the rock beneath all other truth,
changed Simon's name to Peter, which meant "rock." Peter
had, by the grace of God, set his feet on the Rock—the
fact that Jesus of Nazareth *was* the Christ, the Son of the
living God. On this Rock—this truth and this truth alone—
did Jesus feel safe in building his church.

vv. 21 through 23
*From that time forth began Jesus to shew unto his
disciples, how that he must go unto Jerusalem, and
suffer many things of the elders and chief priests and*

scribes, and be killed, and be raised again the third
day. Then Peter took him, and began to rebuke him,
saying, Be it far from thee, Lord: this shall not be
unto thee. But he turned, and said unto Peter, Get
thee behind me, Satan: thou art an offence unto me:
for thou savourest not the things that be of God, but
those that be of men.

Here the first dark cloud appeared in the exhilarating,
clear sky of the men who followed Jesus. Immediately after
Peter declared him to be the Christ, the Son of the living
God, Jesus began to tell them of the tragedy ahead. He
made sure, first, that they knew his true identity, and then
he spoke of his planned journey to Jerusalem, his suffering
and betrayal, his death and resurrection. It seems doubtful
that they heard the word "resurrection," so stunned were
they that he was going to walk knowingly into his death. At
least Peter rebuked him and told him nothing like that
should ever happen to *his* Master. Here again, Peter was
being his old impulsive self. He had just uttered the truth
central to all human fulfillment, and in a matter of minutes,
he was on his own again, saying a foolish thing. So foolish,
so beside the point, that Jesus called the same man he had
just blessed and complimented, "Satan!" Now, of course,
he was not calling Peter names. He was, as always, speaking truth. ". . . thou savourest not the things that be of
God, but those that be of men." Peter was impatient for a
materialistic, earthly kingdom in which he would have a
prominent place. Just another reason why Jesus would not
have planned to build his church on Peter, a mere man. On
any man.

vv. 24 through 28

Then said Jesus unto his disciples, If any man will
come after me, let him deny himself, and take up his
cross, and follow me. For whosoever will save his life
shall lose it: and whosoever will lose his life for my
sake shall find it. For what is a man profited, if he
shall gain the whole world, and lose his own soul? or
what shall a man give in exchange for his soul? For the
Son of man shall come in the glory of his Father with
his angels; and then he shall reward every man ac-

cording to his works. Verily I say unto you, There be
some standing here, which shall not taste of death, till
they see the Son of man coming in his kingdom.

From here on, the sky grows darker, the sayings harder
—not only to hear, but to understand. Talk from the Master of self-denial, of each man taking up his own cross.
Talk that smacked only of defeat and failure. Even when
he spoke of himself as coming "in the glory of his Father
with his angels" to reward them for their good works, his
meaning must have fallen flat around them. Talk of his im-
pending death had frightened and discouraged them, had
stultified their minds. They felt anxious and uncertain
about their own future. They had learned to love him as
both Master and Man—intimate Companion, Leader—
what would life be without him? Their own anxious hearts
and confused minds blinded and deafened them to what he
was saying. They were deaf to what he said about his own
Cross and about the crosses they were to take up for his
sake. Verse 28. "Verily I say unto you. There be some
standing here, which shall not taste of death, till they see
the Son of man coming in his kingdom." How this must
have confused them! Wasn't he already there? Did he mean
not to set up his kingdom right there in their land *for
them?* How many interpretations have you read of this
strange verse? As many as I have, no doubt, but is it wrong
to think that this was true? That most of the men standing
there in the road at Caesarea Philippi with Jesus that day
did not taste death until he came in his kingdom? Judas
tasted death by his own hand, but didn't the King come
back in his own Kingdom *at Pentecost?* It's worth thinking
through.

CHAPTER 17
v. 3
*And, behold, there appeared unto them Moses and
Elias talking with him.*

One provocative thought about the appearance of Moses
and Elijah on the mountain when Jesus was transfigured
before his three disciples, Peter, James and John: In spite
of their utterly human frailties, *he saw their potential.*

These three men were the ones he trusted to *see* him transfigured. They were the three he felt he could trust (once his Spirit indwelt them) with having experienced this brilliant sight.

And just now, I am struck for the first time with the *nearness,* the proximity of those who have left this earth in physical death and have begun living in the Eternal: *In a moment,* Elijah and Moses were there, recognizable as Elijah and Moses!

Those who are out of our sight here are not far away. They are close.

v. 5
... This is my beloved Son, ...

Once more, the Father speaks of his son. How he loved him! How pleased he was with him. "This is my beloved Son, in whom I am well pleased." The same words he spoke about Jesus at his baptism in the beginning of his earthly ministry. Now, near the end, the words again: "This is my beloved Son, in whom I am well pleased." Did the Father say this to him on the Cross? More. He did more then than speak words to his beloved Son. *He held him.* And loved us through him as he hung there.

CHAPTER 18
v. 1
At the same time came the disciples unto Jesus, saying, Who is the greatest in the kingdom of heaven?

Peter, James and John had just come down from their high spiritual experience on the Mount of Transfiguration and joined right in with the others to ask: "Who is the greatest in the kingdom of heaven?"

Well, Pentecost had not happened yet. Visions and high moments are not enough to keep us spiritually sane or humble.

v. 11
For the Son of man is come to save that which was lost.

Pity those who think he came for any other reason.

vv. 12, 13

How think ye? if a man have an hundred sheep, and one of them be gone astray, doth he not leave the ninety and nine, and goeth into the mountains, and seeketh that which is gone astray? And if so be that he find it, verily I say unto you, he rejoiceth more of that sheep, than of the ninety and nine which were not astray.

Does this mean Jesus is more pleased to have us go astray and return than to have us remain loyal to him? Ridiculous thought. And yet, early in my own Christian life, when I was wound up like a tight spring and speaking of nothing except *my* conversion, *my* forgiveness for the sin in *my* life, some mixed-up souls asked me this question. God is simply extra joyful to see one of his loved ones saved from self-destruction, and he can't help rejoicing. The ninety and nine had caused him no anguish. The *one* did. Even God rejoices when he is relieved of anguish. Either way, God loves everyone.

vv. 19, 20

Again I say unto you, That if two of you shall agree on earth as touching any thing that they shall ask, it shall be done for them of my Father which is in heaven. For where two or three are gathered together in my name, there am I in the midst of them.

This is not merely a prayer technique. It is a fact.

CHAPTER 19
vv. 23, 24, 26

Then said Jesus unto his disciples, Verily I say unto you, That a rich man shall hardly enter into the kingdom of heaven. And again I say unto you, It is easier for a camel to go through the eye of a needle, than for a rich man to enter into the kingdom of God. . . . but with God all things are possible.

Jesus had nothing against rich men. God has nothing

against rich men now. It is simply true that God is a realist. He and he alone knows how hard a thing is for a man to do in that man's particular circumstance.

v. 30
But many that are first shall be last; and the last shall be first.

We're going to be very, very surprised one day.

CHAPTER 20
vv. 15, 16
Is it not lawful for me to do what I will with mine own? Is thine eye evil, because I am good? So the last shall be first, and the first last: for many be called, but few chosen.

God has rights. And he alone merits them. He knows. This is why judgment was put into the hands of Jesus Christ. And God's judgment and God's justice can never, never be measured by what *we understand* of judgment or justice. For this I am grateful.

vv. 17, 18, 19
And Jesus going up to Jerusalem took the twelve disciples apart in the way, and said unto them, Behold, we go up to Jerusalem; and the Son of man shall be betrayed unto the chief priests and unto the scribes, and they shall condemn him to death, And shall deliver him to the Gentiles to mock, and to scourge, and to crucify him and the third day he shall rise again.

The sky darkens still more. They are on their way to Jerusalem. For the second time he tries to make them understand that he will die and rise again. His patience is unbelievable, *until* we know him better.

vv. 20, 21
Then came to him the mother of Zebedee's children with her sons, worshipping him, and desiring a certain thing of him. And he said unto her, What wilt thou?

*She saith unto him, Grant that these my two sons may
sit, the one on thy right hand, and the other on the
left, in thy kingdom.*

For the second time he has told them of what lies ahead.
He will be scourged, he will be betrayed, he will be mur-
dered. And almost at once the mother of Zebedee's children, James and John, pops her impudent question: She
wants *her* two boys in the choice seats in Christ's earthly
kingdom. Evidently no one was listening to him. As too
many of us do not listen. We, like Zebedee's wife, Jesus'
relative, are too preoccupied with our own ambitions.

CHAPTER 21
v. 10
    *And when he was come into Jerusalem, all the city
was moved, saying, Who is this?*

When Jesus comes on the scene, people are *moved,* And
always there is the question: Who is he? "Who is this?" His
identity goes on being the key.

v. 15
    *. . . and the chidren crying in the temple, and say-
ing, Hosanna to the son of David; . . .*

The children knew who he was.

v. 22
    *And all things, whatsoever ye shall ask in prayer,
believing, ye shall receive.*

Neither is this a prayer technique. It is also a fact.

v. 23
    *By what authority doest thou these things? And
who gave thee this authority?*

His identity again. "By what authority . . .?" Until one
knows *who he is,* understanding is not possible. Faith is *less*
possible.

CHAPTER 22
v. 15
Then went the Pharisees, and took counsel how they might entangle him in his talk.

Sound familiar? He was not entanglable!

v. 34
But when the Pharisees had heard that he had put the Sadducees to silence, they were gathered together.

The Pharisees were so pleased that he had silenced their rivals, the Sadducees, they " . . . gathered together." They had a committee meeting and tried new tactics.

CHAPTER 23
v. 3 (Read vv. 1 through 10.)
All therefore whatsoever they bid you observe, that observe and do; but do not ye after their work: for they say, and do not.

This is an astounding passage when it is read thoughtfully. Jesus instructed his disciples to conform—that is, not to be known as renegade rebels. And yet, in the plainest of language, he warned them not to imitate the *attitudes* of those scribes and Pharisees in charge of their formal worship! "They are sayers and not doers," he declared. "They will load you with burdensome rules and laws and not move a finger to help you bear them!" They (the scribes and Pharisees—you know them today) are people-pleasers, "spiritual" exhibitionists, showoffs. They love the best rooms, the front seats in church. They revel in being called Rabbi, Rabbi—or as we might say today—leader. "But don't yearn to be known as a leader," he admonished them. There is only one leader—Christ. Just as there is only one Father in heaven.

Much of this may seem contradictory. He is urging us to go along with those who "sit in Moses' seat"; that is, go to church, join the fellowship, obey those who lay down the rules, but do not *be* like them! Shun *being as they are.* How few of us dare to suspect that our Lord was willing to trust us to such difficult extents. To suggest that such delicate balance would be possible among mere mortals. But he did. And it is, because he indwells us now. *Pentecost has happened.* We can be guided by his very mind within us.

vv. 11 through 13, 37

But he that is great among you shall be your servant. And whosoever shall exalt himself shall be abased; and he that shall humble himself shall be exalted. But woe unto you, scribes and Pharisees, hypocrites! for ye shut up the kingdom of heaven against men: for ye neither go in yourselves, neither suffer ye them that are entering to go in. . . . O Jerusalem, Jerusalem, thou that killest the prophets and stonest them which are sent unto thee, how often would I have gathered thy children together, even as a hen gathereth her chickens under her wings, and ye would not!

Be courteous and obey the rules of your church, even if among the deacons or officials of that church, *you know* for a fact that there are "scribes and Pharisees." But remember, *they* are not the greatest in the kingdom of God, no matter how important their committee appointments. They love their positions and their robes of authority, but "he that is greatest among you shall be your servant. And whosoever shall exalt himself shall be abased; and he that shall humble himself shall be exalted." The glorious, relieving paradox of God!

Note: If possible, read this entire chapter carefully in *several* modern translations, particularly *"Good News for Modern Man"* (American Bible Society).

"But woe unto you, scribes and Pharisees, hypocrites!" I know of no other place where Jesus spoke at such length, or with such severity *against* anything. He did not launch into thoughtless tirades. He spoke with reason and logic, and his teaching is always more thought-provoking than emotion-arousing. This blast is not an emotion-arouser, either. It is hard fact about the attitude of heart which obviously is the most repugnant to God! The attitude of heart which is at the opposite pole from what God intended. The pharasaical heart, the hypocritical heart is anathema to God. Twice Jesus showed anger, fury at what he saw on earth—here, in this scathing denunciation and when he drove the money-changers from the Temple. Both outbursts hit at the same evil—hypocrisy. He did not blaze away at Mary Magdalene or Judas, he blazed at the Pharisees, the "impostors" in the Kingdom of God. *But* for a redemptive reason: *Everything he did and everything he said always led directly toward the potential of redemption.* In verse 37, he demonstrated the Father heart, the attitude of God toward everyone, including the hypocrites, by a shattering outburst of compassion toward the city where the scribes and Pharisees and Sadducees ruled: "Oh Jerusalem, Jerusalem, . . . how often would I have gathered thy children together, even as a hen gathereth her chickens under her wings, and ye would not!"

He condoned nothing that was not holy, but his heart, his God-heart, could not close toward anyone, even the "impostors" in the Holy City.

CHAPTER 24
vv. 34 through 36

Verily I say unto you, This generation shall not pass, till all these things be fulfilled. Heaven and earth shall pass away, but my words shall not pass away. But of that day and hour knoweth no man, no, not the angels of heaven, but my Father only.

This chapter is an enigma to me. There are scholars and nonscholars who write entire books on it. I would not dare try. In verse 34, Jesus said: "This generation shall not pass, till all these things be fulfilled." Was he wrong about the end? The consummation of life on earth? Some authorities believe he was. At least one school of scholarship contends that this is one "proof" that Jesus was merely a human being who *achieved* the closest of all relationships with the Father through faith and obedience. I am not swayed by this. Neither am I swayed by those who "specialize" in the Second Coming—even by those who "wait" for it and, with every new generation, find the "definite signs" which convince them that the end is near. Jesus said his "words shall not pass away" and he also said that all judgment had been placed in his hands by the Father. This is enough for me. I can trust his judgment concerning the end of things, just as I can trust his love to redeem and keep me. He also

said, ". . . of that day and hour knoweth no man, . . ." But
the Father does know, and this is more than enough. We
can trust him with all of it. After all, he is "the beginning
and the end." Whatever God does will be right and fair and
creative. If I have trusted him with the beginning, I can
trust him with the end.

CHAPTER 25
vv. 34 through 40

*Then shall the King say unto them on his right
hand, Come, ye blessed of my Father, inherit the
kingdom prepared for you from the foundation of the
world: For I was an hungred, and ye gave me meat:
was thirsty, and ye gave me drink: I was a stranger,
and ye took me in: Naked, and ye clothed me: I was
sick, and ye visited me: I was in prison, and ye came
unto me. Then shall the righteous answer him, saying,
Lord, when saw we thee an hungred, and fed thee? or
thirsty, and gave thee drink? When saw we thee a
stranger, and took thee in? or naked, and clothed
thee? Or when saw we thee sick, or in prison, and
came unto thee? And the King shall answer and say
unto them, Verily I say unto you, Inasmuch as ye
have done it unto one of the least of these my
brethren, ye have done it unto me.*

I feel the same about this chapter. The only part of it in
which we have control are these verses. We can learn from
them something—enough, surely—of the key to God's
judgment of us. We are to *love*, and to show our love in
concrete ways. The rest we can leave in his hands. Either
we trust him or we don't. Beware of the trap of having to
decide with our minds about what God has planned.

CHAPTER 26
vv. 3 through 5

*Then assembled together the chief priests, and the
scribes, and the elders of the people, unto the palace
of the high priest, who was called Caiaphas. And con-
sulted that they might take Jesus by subtilty, and kill
him. But they said, Not on the feast day, lest there be
an uproar among the people.*

Doesn't this sound familiar? The religious "authorities" who "have it all figured" get together to decide how to "cut their man down to size" by *subtlety*. "Let's not do anything rash," they insist. "Nothing that will bring criticism to our own fine spirituality and prestige. Let's get rid of him, by all means, but in a subtle, careful way so it will appear that *he* and not *we* are in the wrong. We will be clever and let him hang himself! Not on our feast day, mind you, because this would cause the people to rise up against *us*."

I have been gotten rid of "by subtlety." Perhaps so have you. I know of at least a dozen of my close friends who have also been given the "subtle" treatment just before they were put out of their "religious" jobs or their "religious" organizations, were even pushed out of their churches. God tells us, in effect: "Don't be surprised that this happens to you. It also happened to me. Part of the reason I permitted it to happen to me is so you would be able to identify with me when your time comes and so that you would know that I also know how you feel!"

v. 11 (Read vv. 6 through 13.)
For ye have the poor always with you; but me ye have not always.

Jesus is not here saying that nothing matters but the spiritual. He is not suggesting that we are to ignore the poor because they are always with us. He is saying something far deeper: Love comes first. Love of God, as he really is, will bear the kind of fruit that takes care of the human needs of man. He is showing us here that there is a right sequence: Love God and then we will automatically love man.

v. 25
Then Judas, which betrayed him, answered and said, Master, is it I? He said unto him, Thou hast said.

Jesus did not say "Yes" when Judas asked: "Is it I?" He did not need to. He knew that Judas knew. There is a clue here to the ridiculousness of some of our prayers when we pray: "Lord, *if* I have sinned, forgive me." He created right into us an antenna that picks up our sin for us. We know about our sin, *if* we are living near the Source of all goodness.

vv. 31, 32

Then saith Jesus unto them, All ye shall be offended because of me this night: for it is written, I will smite the shepherd, and the sheep of the flock shall be scattered abroad. But after I am risen again, I will go before you into Galilee.

He gave them ample warning of the trouble ahead. He also gave them ample confidence: "But after I am risen again, I will go before you into Galilee." He would meet them at their familiar place, where they would be at home again with him. Safe. As with all he said, there is a dimension here for us, too. We all have trouble up ahead. No one is immune to the sudden shock, the quick tragedy, the bitter failure. At those times it seems almost certain that God is dead for us. He and his disciples lived out the drama— the familiar drama that has always haunted man. Trouble strikes, God seems dead, and then, if we trust him, he always, by some means, sees us through it. He is risen now forever. As I write this, I am living through a trouble spot *knowing*, reckoning on the fact that he has gone before me into *my* Galilee, where things will somehow be right again. The problem may not be solved, but he will be there waiting for me. That is always enough.

vv. 33 through 35

Peter answered and said unto him, Though all men shall be offended because of thee, yet will I never be offended. Jesus said unto him, Verily I say unto thee, That this night, before the cock crow, thou shalt deny me thrice. Peter said unto him, Though I should die with thee, yet will I not deny thee. Likewise also said all the disciples.

I have just now noticed that the incident of Peter's boasting claim to eternal loyalty follows the passage in which Jesus promised to be there waiting for them after their trouble struck. This, too, is for us. It is glib of us, as it was glib and superficial of Peter, to insist that we know how we

are going to react in any circumstance. Jesus knew what
Peter would do before the cock crowed the third time. He
knows what we will do. This knowing does not change his
love. He will still be there up ahead, in our Galilee waiting
for us.

vv. 38, 40
*Then saith he unto them, My soul is exceeding sor-
rowful, even unto death: tarry ye here, and watch
with me. . . . What, could ye not watch with me one
hour?*

Little should be said here. Much should be thought, taken
in, absorbed, allowed to become a part of us, as our very
breath is a part of us. Jesus Christ, the Son of God, *needed*
his friends.

vv. 43 through 45.
*And he came and found them asleep again: for
their eyes were heavy. And he left them, and went
away again, and prayed the third time, saying the
same words. Then cometh he to his disciples, and
saith unto them, Sleep on now, and take your rest: behold, the hour is at hand, and the Son of man is betrayed into the hands of sinners.*

The men kept falling asleep when he needed them to be
with him. For a moment, his humanity took over, as he
came back to where they slept, almost begging them to
wake up and help him. When they did not, he settled it
alone with his Father, the only way anyone can really settle
anything. It is human to run to our friends. Jesus did. He
does not condemn us for this, but waits for us to do as he
did, go finally to the Father alone and transact business on
the ground of his love. Jesus' suffering was still up ahead,
but once he had done this, he could walk again to where
the disciples slept and tell them to go on and get their rest.
His heart had grown quiet in the ugly face of what lay just
ahead.

vv. 48, 49
Now he that betrayed him gave them a sign, saying

Whomsoever I shall kiss, that same is he: hold him fast. And forthwith he came to Jesus, and said, Hail, master; and kissed him.

Judas is pictured as the essence of evil. People hate him, consider his sin the supreme sin. I wonder. I don't know, but I wonder. It has always seemed to me that at least we should think on the possibility that Judas was driven by impatience and ambition. Could it be that, like some of us, he thought he could coerce his Master into plunging ahead to establish that kingdom on earth so that he, Judas could take his place in it as a valued minister? Aren't there men and women who follow Christ, as Judas followed him, believing that by deciding *for* God, they will reap their reward? And when it does not turn out that way, as it did not for Judas, they turn against God in deed or at least in reaction?

vv. 63 through 65

But Jesus held his peace. And the high priest answered and said unto him, I adjure thee by the living God, that thou tell us whether thou be the Christ, the Son of God. Jesus saith unto him, Thou hast said: nevertheless I say unto you, Hereafter shall ye see the Son of man sitting on the right hand of power, and coming in the clouds of heaven. Then the high priest rent his clothes, saying, He hath spoken blasphemy; what further need have we of witnesses? behold, now ye have heard his blasphemy.

Even against the array of false witnesses, *Jesus held his peace.* He "considered the source" and found it unworthy of self-defense. How much injury we would avoid if we could only learn the value of considering the source of our injury.

The high priest dared him to say he was the Christ, the Son of God. He said even more, and immediately there went up the cry of "blasphemy." What Jesus said went directly against what they had staked their success upon. They *had to be right,* and when he proved them wrong, he had to be a blasphemer. In just one more deliberate way, he walked into their trap for our sakes. If he had not, we could not believe in him. He was considering us then as he is considering us now.

v. 75
And Peter remembered the word of Jesus, which said unto him, Before the cock crow, thou shalt deny me thrice. And he went out, and wept bitterly.

No wonder Peter wept. He had just gotten the first clear look at himself as he really was. I believe Peter honestly thought he would not deny Jesus, no matter what happened. He was not consciously bluffing. He just didn't know himself. Like many of us, he had to learn the hard way.

CHAPTER 27
v. 2
And when they had bound him, they led him away, and delivered him to Pontius Pilate the governor.

How ridiculous and self-revealing of them to bind him! He had offered not one gesture of resistance. His persecutors were being driven to extremes by the very strutting sin which he was about to blot out on his Cross. For them too, it was blotted out. Love can go no further than he went.

vv. 3 through 5
Then Judas, which had betrayed him, when he saw that he was condemned, repented himself, and brought again the thirty pieces of silver to the chief priests and elders. Saying, I have sinned in that I have betrayed the innocent blood. And they said, What is that to us? see thou to that. And he cast down the pieces of silver in the temple, and departed, and went and hanged himself.

Judas repented, but he repented in the presence of the helpless priests and elders—helpless to *forgive* him. He had managed things his own way and by that very management had shut himself off from the presence of the only One who could have forgiven him. We have no way of knowing that Jesus did not hear his repentance; he "heard" many

things that were not even spoken, and perhaps Judas was
forgiven. He would be forgiven if he repented, even after
what he did, or my whole concept of God's forgiveness is
wrong. But Judas had maneuvered Jesus' arrest. If the
Master forgave him, Judas was too far·away to hear. Jesus
was bound and being led away to Pontius Pilate. And not
knowing, Judas threw away the thirty pieces of hated silver
and killed himself.

v. 19
*When he was set down on the judgment seat, his
wife sent unto him, saying, Have thou nothing to do
with that just man: for I have suffered many things
this day in a dream because of him.*

New light into the *limitless reaches of God's love* is
shown me in that, through his wife's dream, God was giving even Pilate a chance to act on the truth he was hearing
straight from the lips of the Son of God. Pilate listened to
the people instead.

v. 25
*Then answered all the people, and said, His blood
be on us, and on our children.*

We wonder at the frenzy, the uncontrolled anger and
outright stupidity of mob action. We say we can't understand how demonstrations can turn to riots, how men and
women whipped into rage can burn buildings and throw
stones and snipe from rooftops with rifles. It's all here, in
its wildest, most destructive form. We have not changed.

vv. 28 through 30
*And they stripped him, and put on him a scarlet
robe. And when they had platted a crown of thorns,
they put it upon his head, and a reed in his right hand:
and they bowed the knee before him, and mocked
him, saying, Hail, King of the Jews! And they spit
upon him, and took the reed, and smote him on the
head.*

The violence and injustice poured upon him—even the

spitting and the jeering—paled alongside his inner certainty. Selfish, sinful men go wild in the presence of holiness. Holiness stood, unmoved, unstained in their midst.

vv. 45, 46
Now from the sixth hour there was darkness over all the land unto the ninth hour. And about the ninth hour Jesus cried with a loud voice, saying, Eli, Eli, lama sabachthani? that is to say, My God, my God, why hast thou forsaken me?

Darkness fell over the land because man was trying to put out the only true Light forever. And, as he hung on his Cross, because he was human as well as divine, there came —even for Jesus—one lightless moment: The total realization of the full load of mankind's sin so crowded his heart that he felt cut off from the Father, and cried: "My God, My God, why hast thou forsaken me?" He did not cry: "*Hast* thou forsaken me?" *He felt forsaken.* His consciousness that the Father was with him, sustaining him, had held him through the Garden of Gethsemane, the betrayal, the mock trials, the scourgings, the humiliation, the desertion by his disciples, the first hours of agony on the Cross. But there came that moment, when he was unable not to cry *with a loud voice;* unable not to ask *why.* We have no record to my knowledge that Jesus had ever asked *why* of the Father before. He had asked that if it be possible, he might avoid the Cross. But he did not ask *why* his Father had not thought of another way to show us his redemptive love. No one knows fully the reason for his cry in that one black moment. But surely, we can receive some help in our own moments of agony when our loud cries push up through broken hearts to form themselves into that same helpless word: Why? If Jesus went this far in order to make identification with me in my sufferings, in order to let me know that he knows how I feel, some of my own pain drops away. At least, a light breaks into my darkness. A ray of light for me straight from his black moment on the Cross.

vv. 57 through 61
When the even was come, there came a rich man of Arimathaea, named Joseph, who also himself was

*Jesus' disciple: He went to Pilate, and begged the
body of Jesus. Then Pilate commanded the body to be
delivered. And when Joseph had taken the body, he
wrapped it in a clean linen cloth. And laid it in his
own new tomb, which he had hewn out in the rock:
and he rolled a great stone to the door of the sepulchre, and departed. And there was Mary Magdalene, and the other Mary, sitting over against the
sepulchre.*

Not until now do we have any record that the rich man,
Joseph of Arimathea, had taken any public step to show
that he was a disciple of Jesus. Perhaps he had only then
come to believe in him. At any rate, he did what he could
do because of his influence and his wealth. He was powerful enough to gain an audience with Pilate and to persuade
him to give him the body of his dead Master. He was
wealthy enough to have his own fine sepulchre ready. We
are told that Joseph himself took the body and wrapped it
in clean linen and laid it in his own sepulchre. But then he
went away. The women who had loved Jesus for so long
and had ministered to his needs up and down the dusty
roads of Galilee and Judea did not leave. They could not.
At the end, when Joseph of Arimathea had walked away,
two of these women were still there, sitting beside the
sepulchre and one of them was Mary Magdalene.

v. 66
*So they went, and made the sepulchre sure, sealing
the stone, and setting a watch.*

How ludicrous that they imagined a mere stone could
keep him inside. He, who had created the stone itself.

CHAPTER 28
vv. 1 through 7
*In the end of the sabbath, as it began to dawn to-
ward the first day of the week, came Mary Magdalene
and the other Mary to see the sepulchre. And, behold,
there was a great earthquake: for the angel of the
Lord descended from heaven, and came and rolled
back the stone from the door, and sat upon it. His*

*countenance was like lightning, and his raiment white
as snow: And for fear of him the keepers did shake,
and became as dead men. And the angel answered and
said unto the women, Fear not ye: for I know that ye
seek Jesus, which was crucified. He is not here: for he
is risen, as he said. Come, see the place where the
Lord lay. And go quickly, and tell his disciples that he
is risen from the dead; and, behold, he goeth before
you into Galilee; there shall ye see him: lo, I have told
you.*

Their grief must have been so mingled with the horror
they had experienced watching him die on the Cross that
much of what he had said to them was erased from their
memories. Each time he had told them he would be crucified, he had also told them he would rise again. Shock and
tragedy do this to us. Still, early on the first day of the week
at dawn, the two Marys were there. At least they would be
near his mutilated body, even though the big sepulchre
stone separated them. According to Matthew, the angel did
not come to roll the stone away until the women arrived.
Everything God does is done *for people*, never only to display his power to an empty universe. It is beyond me to
imagine the new shock and the new kind of joy and wonder
that must have flooded these women's hearts as the angel of
the Lord told them their beloved Master had risen as he
said he would. And, oh, we must *never* miss God's marvelous continuity: The angel of the Lord used the very same
words Jesus had used with them when he said he would *go
before them into Galilee* and meet them there. Not only is
God the master of perfect continuity, he never fails to
make his promises accessible to us. Have you ever noticed
that the promises of God in the Scriptures are always plain
and understandable? The difficult portions seldom contain
promises. *His promises are clear.* He knows we have trouble understanding when we are grieved, or ill, or weary, or
defeated. The angel spoke in *Jesus' own words* to the
Marys as they stood beside the open, empty tomb that first
Easter morning. They were to go quickly and tell the men,
his closest friends, who had deserted him in his need. God,
in the face of their weakness, made sure he sent the women
to let the fainthearted men know that he *had* risen as he

said. ". . . Go quickly, and tell his disciples. . . ." They had
run away, but he wanted them to know, too. He wanted
their faith restored.

vv. 9, 10
*And as they went to tell his disciples, behold, Jesus
met them, saying, All hail. And they came and held
him by the feet, and worshipped him. Then said Jesus
unto them, Be not afraid: go tell my brethren that
they go into Galilee, and there shall they see me.*

And as the women ran to tell, Jesus himself met them.
The risen Lord, giving them his own triumphant greeting.
The Williams translation says he called: "Good morning!"
The Emphasized New Testament translates the King
James' "All Hail!" as "Joy to you!" Somewhere I have read
one footnote that translated it: "Oh, joy!" J. B. Phillips in-
terprets it as "Peace be with you!" I like them all. Whatever his actual words, they had to be words of joy, the very
joy of God that now, it *was* all finished! The way back into
the Garden of Eden was open forever to all people who
would come home. And as the women fell to their knees,
holding his feet and worshiping him in their great joy, he
reminded them once more that they were to go tell his
frightened brothers that he would be waiting for them all in
Galilee.

v. 20
*Teaching them to observe all things whatsoever I
have commanded you: and, lo, I am with you alway,
even unto the end of the world. Amen.*

Back in Galilee together, *with some of the brothers still
doubting,* Jesus went right on and made the statement that
should be enough for us all forever: ". . . lo, I am with you
alway, even unto the end of the world." In *Discoveries,* the
first book I ever wrote, I recently came upon this line: "I
find that as long as I am aware of his presence, I am adequate for any event." I had known him less than two years
when I wrote it. Now, almost twenty years later, it is still
true. As long as we are aware that God has said he will
never leave us, we are adequate to anything.

SAINT MARK

CHAPTER 1
vv. 12 through 14
And immediately the spirit driveth him into the wilderness. And he was there in the wilderness forty days, tempted by Satan; and was with the wild beasts; and the angels ministered unto him. Now after that John was put in prison, Jesus came into Galilee, preaching the gospel of the kingdom of God, . . .

In two short verses (12, 13) Mark covers the temptation in the wilderness. And no one can say it is not covered. The word "immediately" moves us from the baptism to the temptation. Mark sees no need for detail. If Jesus (verse 14) went directly from the wilderness experience into Galilee, "preaching the gospel of the kingdom of God," obviously he had overcome his tempter!

v. 22
And they were astonished at his doctrine: for he taught them as one that had authority, and not as the scribes.

The word "astonished" sets the tone for his entire ministry. Mark himself seems astonished. We should be, too.

vv. 30, 31
But Simon's wife's mother lay sick of a fever, and anon they tell him of her. And he came and took her by the hand, and lifted her up; and immediately the fever left her, and she ministered unto them.

When Jesus raised Simon's mother-in-law from her sickbed, he did more than heal her body. He healed her to begin ministering to those around her.

v. 33
And all the city was gathered together at the door.

What better way to describe the magnetism of Christ?
Simon's mother-in-law was not a famous woman. Neither
was Simon. But Jesus was there!

v. 45
*But he went out, and began to pubish it much, and
to blaze abroad the matter, insomuch that Jesus could
no more openly enter into the city, but was without in
desert places: and they came to him from every
quarter.*

Here is an instance of Mark's interesting choice of
words. When Jesus had healed the leper and charged him
not to tell anyone so that his ministry could go on without
the constant deterrent of more and more crowds, Mark
writes: "But he went out, and began to publish it much,
and to blaze abroad the matter. . . ." Jesus needed to cover
a wider territory, to expose more and more people to himself. His compassion was not in short supply, but his time
was. Still, the man *blazed abroad* the news of his healing
and "they came to him from every quarter." Jesus did not
wander leisurely about the countryside robed in spotless
garments, raising his hand in slow, studied gestures, speaking only gentle words. He was *besieged* by the crowds because his fame began to be blazed abroad. His was the
most active of lives, the roughest in many respects, the
most strenuous. And much of his energy was spent in trying to dodge the multitudes in order to get away alone to
pray for strength and wisdom. In the other three Gospel
accounts, there is less indication of this tightly packed,
pressure-filled schedule. We need to be aware of it. Mark
makes certain we are.

CHAPTER 2
vv. 5, 7
*When Jesus saw their faith, he said unto the sick of
the palsy, Son, thy sins be forgiven thee. . . . Why doth
this man thus speak blasphemies? who can forgive sins
but God only?*

Back in Capernaum, it is once more noised around that Jesus is there and the crowds grew so large that four friends, unable to get in, tore a hole in the roof of the house and lowered their palsied friend at Jesus' feet. Here, we see him moving toward the central reason for his coming to earth: He forgave the sick man of his sins! Jesus did not come primarily to heal sick bodies and open blind eyes and deaf ears. *He came to save people from their sins.* Of course, when he mentioned this his real trouble began. To show the relationship between the spiritual and the physical, he healed the man, also. But first, he forgave him of his sins.

vv. 13, 14
And he went forth again by the sea side; and all the multitude resorted unto him, and he taught them. And as he passed by, he saw Levi the son of Alphaeus sitting at the receipt of custom, and said unto him, Follow me. And he arose and followed him.

I like Levi. Looking from the viewpoint of the average churchgoer, Levi would be the last man on earth Christ would call to become one of his intimate disciples. He was a publican, a tax collector—money-hungry, materialistic, expedient—a real worldling. Jesus knew this, and so he saw to it that, when Levi first glimpsed him, he was being followed by a multitude. This would impress Levi! Jesus loved him, wanted him, and so he called him in the one way Levi could understand. Jesus knew he could change the man once they were living together.

vv. 16, 18
. . . How is it that he eateth and drinketh with publicans and sinners? . . . Why do the disciples of John and of the Pharisees fast, but thy disciples fast not?

Here Mark begins his account of the succession of tricky questions thrown at Jesus morning, noon and night. The Master's wit and brilliant mind fairly crackle in these verses. But seldom, if ever, did he resort only to humor or satire. "They that are whole hath no need of a physician, but they that are sick. . . ." That much is humor, genuine wit. But he did not stop there: ". . . I came not to call the righteous, but sinners to repentance."

When they attempted to trick him on the question of fasting, reminding him that John's disciples fasted and his did not (inferring a piety in the disciples of John the Baptist and a lack of it among his), he answered with a humorous remark about a bridegroom's presence with the "children of the bridechamber." Then, a profound thrust broke into his humor: "But the days will come, when the bridegroom shall be taken away from them, and then shall they fast. . . ." While he was with them, while they were all together and working, Jesus believed utterly in joy and good times. Time enough when they took him away for sadness and fasting.

CHAPTER 3
vv. 1 through 5

And he entered again into the synagogue; and there was a man there which had a withered hand. And they watched him, whether he would heal him on the sabbath day; that they might accuse him. And he saith unto the man which had the withered hand, Stand forth. And he saith unto them, Is it lawful to do good on the sabbath days, or to do evil? to save life, or to kill? But they held their peace. And when he had looked round about on them with anger, being grieved for the hardness of their hearts, he saith unto the man, Stretch forth thine hand. And he stretched it out: and his hand was restored whole as the other.

Here, Jesus is turning the tables on his questioners. And he does it dramatically, commanding the man with the withered hand to, "Stand up and come out here in front!" (Phillips). Then Jesus turned to the hecklers and asked the question (verse 4): "Is it lawful to do good on the sabbath days, or to do evil? To save life, or to kill?" When they refused to answer, it angered and hurt him. He was not angered by their stubbornness, rather by the hardness of their hearts. He then asked the crippled man to stretch out his hand, and when he did, it was made whole. Never did

Christ separate his truth from his love. He healed as he
taught and he taught as he healed.

v. 6

*And the Pharisees went forth, and straightway took
counsel with the Herodians against him, how they
might destroy him.*

In one quick sentence Mark begins the movement toward the Cross. "Straightway," when they saw Jesus heal a
man on the Sabbath, they began to make their plans to get
rid of him.

CHAPTER 4
v. 41

*And they feared exceedingly, and said one to anoth-
er, What manner of man is this, that even the wind
and the sea obey him?*

When Jesus had quieted the storm, perhaps for the first
time his disciples began to realize that their Master was different from all other teachers on earth. Up to now, it is
quite possible they followed his attractive human personality, reveled in his wit, his keen perception, were captivated
by the type of pungent, astute wisdom reported in the first
part of Chapter 4. Now, they feared exceedingly, and said
one to another, What manner of man is this, that even the
wind and the sea obey him?"

CHAPTER 5
v. 6

*But when he saw Jesus afar off, he ran and wor-
shipped him, . . .*

Even this demented, tormented, animal-like man found,
down deep in his twisted being, a response to the Son of
God.

vv. 15, 17

*And they come to Jesus, and see him that was pos-
sessed with the devil, and had the legion, sitting, and
clothed, and in his right mind: and they were afraid.*

*... And they began to pray him to depart out of their
coasts.*

The people had become so accustomed to the wild mach-
inations of the insane Gadarene, they were more afraid
of him when Jesus returned him to his right mind than they
had been before!

This was too much for them. Too much goodness and
power to let loose. "And they began to pray him [Jesus] to
depart out of their coasts."

vv. 18 through 20
*And when he was come into the ship, he that had
been possessed with the devil prayed him that he
might be with him. Howbeit Jesus suffered him not,
but saith unto him, Go home to thy friends, and tell
them how great things the Lord hath done for thee,
and hath had compassion on thee. And he departed,
and began to publish in Decapolis how great things
Jesus had done for him: and all men did marvel.*

This is a most interesting point. Up to now, Jesus had
asked those he healed not to tell. When the grateful Gadarene begged to go with Jesus, Jesus refused him, but told
him to go "tell them how great things the Lord hath done
for thee, and hath had compassion on thee." He does not
trust us according to our abilities or our education or our
connections with the right people. He trusts us with his
work according to what he knows he has been permitted
to do for us.

Evidently, according to verse 20, the Gadarene did a
good job for him.

vv. 27, 28
*When she had heard of Jesus, came in the press be-
hind, and touched his garment. For she said, If I may
touch but his clothes, I shall be whole.*

We do not have to beg God to take some action toward
us. This woman touched him and he had not even seen her
until he looked around for her. If we have learned something of his true nature, have formed the habit of knowing

there is healing in his very person, we can often just reach out and receive what we need. His gifts are always ready to our hand.

CHAPTER 6
vv. 1, 2, 3

And he went out from thence, and came into his own country; and his disciples follow him. And when the sabbath day was come, he began to teach in the synagogue: and many hearing him were astonished, saying, From whence hath this man these things? and what wisdom is this which is given unto him, that even such mighty works are wrought by his hands? Is not this the carpenter, the son of Mary, the brother of James, and Joses, and of Juda, and Simon? and are not his sisters here with us? And they were offended at him.

Back in his own home town of Nazareth, instead of pride in his great works and his marvelous teaching, his old friends and neighbors "were offended at him." Evidently even the members of his immediate family were not with him, either, because he said: "No prophet goes unhonored —except in his native town or with his own relations or in his own home!" (verse 4, Phillips). This is true, and just as too much adulation from strangers can smother, lack of caring and faith from our loved ones can wound us.

v. 14

And king Herod heard of him; (for his name was spread abroad:) and he said, That John the Baptist was risen from the dead, and therefore mighty works do shew forth themselves in him.

Poor old Herod, still guilty over having been talked into killing John the Baptist, doubtless felt every good man or prophet *could* be John coming back to haunt him!

v. 42

And they did all eat, and were filled.

Everyone always is when God does the providing. "He will fill the hungry with good things."

v. 56
... as many as touched him were made whole.

As many as touch him will always be made whole. But we are not to sit back idly and wait. We are to exercise our wills and *touch him*.

CHAPTER 7
vv. 6 through 9
He answered and said unto them, Well hath Esaias prophesied of you hypocrites, as it is written, This people honoureth me with their lips, but their heart is far from me. Howbeit in vain do they worship me, teaching for doctrines the commandments of men. For laying aside the commandment of God, ye hold the tradition of men, as the washing of pots and cups: and many other such like things ye do. And he said unto them, Full well ye reject the commandment of God, that ye may keep your own tradition.

God is far less interested in what we say and do than in what *we are*. He is not impressed with traditionalists, yet he is not against tradition; rather he is *for originality:* newness of spirit.

v. 13
Making the word of God of none effect through your tradition, ...

Man is to worship the living God, not tradition.

vv. 15 through 23
There is nothing from without a man, that entering into him can defile him: but the things which come out of him, those are they that defile the man. If any man have ears to hear, let him hear. And when he was entered into the house from the people, his disciples asked him concerning the parable. And he saith unto them, Are ye so without understanding also? Do ye

*not perceive, that whatsoever thing from without en-
tereth into the man, it cannot defile him; Because it
entereth not into his heart, but into the belly, and
goeth out into the draught, purging all meats? And he
said, That which cometh out of the man, that defileth
the man. For from within, out of the heart of men,
proceed evil thoughts, adulteries, fornications, murders,
Thefts, covetousness, wickedness, deceit, lascivious-
ness, an evil eye, blasphemy, pride, foolishness: All
these evil things come from within, and defile the man.*

Read these verses carefully. How has it happened that so
many sincere, well-meaning Christians have reversed this?
Have so reversed what Jesus said that in some Christian
schools and organizations a pledge not to do this or that or
the other must be signed before a student can matriculate
or an employee be hired? Doesn't it seem a dangerous thing
to reverse the order of God?

CHAPTER 8
vv. 3, 8, 9
*And if I send them away fasting to their own
houses, they will faint by the way: for divers of them
came from far. . . . So they did eat, and were filled:
and they took up of the broken meat that was left
seven baskets. And they that had eaten were about
four thousand: and he sent them away.*

He was not only interested in his crowds as long as they
were listening to him, (as long as the "meeting" was in
progress). He was concerned about them on the way home
too.

vv. 34, 35
*And when he had called the people unto him with
his disciples also, he said unto them, Whosoever will
come after me, let him deny himself, and take up his
cross, and follow me. For whosoever will save his life
shall lose it; but whosoever shall lose his life for my
sake and the gospel's, the same shall save it.*

Two things come to me here. Jesus, who usually had

trouble avoiding crowds, *this time,* because of the importance of what he was about to say, "called the people unto him with his disciples also, . . ." Could it be that he was attempting to show the disciples (his close twelve) that what he had to say to them was not theirs exclusively? Could it be, too, that because this is one of his most difficult teachings, he was putting them on their mettle—before outsiders? His reason is not important, I suppose, but it is interesting that he called the people for this particular message and did not keep it exclusively for his immediate helpers. One other point: The twelve must have been shocked by what he said. After all, they believed they had been following him all along! Now, he was saying they, along with everyone else, had to pick up a cross in order to follow him. That they had to lose their lives in order to save them. The twelve had been following Jesus, sure that their doing so would give them a special spot in his kingdom. They loved him humanly speaking, but he was their key to success too. And here he is saying there is only self-denial up ahead.

CHAPTER 9
vv. 2 (Read through v. 8.)
And after six days Jesus taketh with him Peter, and James, and John, and leadeth them up into an high mountain apart by themselves: and he was transfigured before them.

So much is here in these seven verses. First of all, Peter and James and John must have been stunned by the sudden transfiguration of their familiar Master. His ordinary clothing became more radiant and dazzling than any earthly bleaching could have made it. And then, before their eyes appeared Elijah and Moses, who began a direct conversation with Jesus. We do not know that the three disciples understood the conversation. They were undoubtedly too appalled by what they saw. Peter was so beside himself with awe and fright, he "really did not know what to say" (Phillips). But, being Peter, he had to say something and so in the midst of the supernatural conversation, he blurted: "Master, it is wonderful for us to be here! Shall we put up three shelters—one for you, one for Moses and one for

Elijah?" (Phillips). Then God handled their confusion for them: ". . . there was a cloud that overshadowed them: and a voice came out of the cloud, saying, This is my beloved Son: hear him."

Was God saying that the day of Elijah and Moses had passed? Important as it had been, was it now (for purposes of the spiritual life of man) history? Surely, he pointed them directly to his Son and commanded that they "hear *him*." And my favorite part of the incident: ". . . suddenly, when they had looked round about, they saw no man any more, save Jesus only with themselves."

Peter was going to build houses for everybody. God said no. *Look at my Son only.*

How is it that so many serious students of the Bible fall into the trap of controversy concerning events in the Old Testament when the Lord of the Scriptures has made this whole thing so clear in Jesus Christ? What we don't understand we can put aside and look only at Jesus.

vv. 20 through 24

And they brought him unto him: and when he saw him, straightway the spirit tare him; and he fell on the ground, and wallowed foaming. And he asked his father, How long is it ago since this came unto him? And he said, Of a child. And ofttimes it hath cast him into the fire, and into the waters, to destroy him: but if thou canst do any thing; have compassion on us, and help us. Jesus said unto him, If thou canst believe, all things are possible to him that believeth. And straightway the father of the child cried out, and said with tears, I believe; help thou mine unbelief.

Jesus here made a definite effort to involve the sick child's father, too. First, he asked a question about the child's history. Then he told the man that the child could be well again if he, the parent, believed it. "And straightway the father of the child cried out, and said with tears, Lord, I believe; help thou mine unbelief."

More than once I have been thankful that this verse is in the New Testament. The man believed just enough to trust Christ to help him believe fully. I am in this predicament often. We all are, if we admit it. And there is rest and

strength and an opening for more faith just in the saying:
"Lord, I believe—help thou mine unbelief!"

vv. 38 through 40

*And John answered him, saying, Master, we saw
one casting out devils in thy name, and he followeth
not us: and we forbad him, because he followeth not
us. But Jesus said, Forbid him not: for there is no
man which shall do a miracle in my name, that can
lightly speak evil of me. For he that is not against us is
on our part.*

When one looks around at various smug religious
groups, one can only wonder if those people have read
these verses. The disciples were smug in their position as
his followers. *They* lived and traveled with him. What right
did an outsider have to cast out demons in the name of
their Master? Jesus set them straight. At least he tried. We
are to *include*, never *exclude*.

CHAPTER 10

v. 17 (Read through v. 24.)

*And when he was gone forth into the way, there
came one running, and kneeled to him, and asked
him, Good Master, what shall I do that I may inherit
eternal life?*

Jesus knew, the minute the rich young man came asking
his question, what the outcome would be. It once seemed to
me that Jesus was splitting hairs when he admonished the
young man not to call him "good." Now, I see He knew the
boy would try flattery first—anything to manage the answer he hoped for. Anything to cause the Master to forget
to tell him he would have to let go of his money god. Jesus
knew he would not win the rich young ruler, but he must
have shared with his disciples later how he felt about the
boy: He loved him. He wanted him as a follower, but not
on the young man's terms. Only God's terms work. Another thing I see now is that Jesus did not high-pressure him.
He permitted the saddened young man to walk away. Until
he could put his trust in God and not in his riches, there
was no point in detaining him.

vv. 25 through 27

It is easier for a camel to go through the eye of a needle, than for a rich man to enter into the kingdom of God. And they were astonished out of measure, saying among themselves, Who then can be saved? And Jesus looking upon them saith, With men it is impossible, but not with God: for with God all things are possible.

No man can talk a rich man out of his faith in his riches into faith in God. But God can do even this! ". . . I, if I be lifted up . . . , will draw *all* men unto me" (John 12:32).

vv. 28 through 30

Then Peter began to say unto him, Lo we have left all, and have followed thee. And Jesus answered and said, Verily I say unto you, There is no man that hath left house, or brethren, or sisters, or father, or mother, or wife, or children, or lands, for my sake, and the gospel's, But he shall receive an hundredfold now in this time, houses, and brethren, and sisters, and mothers, and children, and lands, with persecutions; and in the world to come eternal life.

Too often we feel that everything Jesus said to his disciples was hard. Peter reminded the Master that they had left all to follow him. Jesus agreed and told them their reward would be great. The disciples seemed so slow to learn every word of commendation from him must have been worth all the riches in the world to them. There was one thorn in his commendation, though, his promise of riches: He said they would receive "an hundred fold now in this time, houses, and brethren and sisters, and mothers, and children, and lands, *with persecutions;* and in the world to come eternal life." There is always the cost of discipleship, but it is not always material poverty. Few of God's true disciples are ever for long in real material want. Success is not promised, nor is material wealth promised, but the normal mind indwelt by the Spirit of God is a balanced, adequate mind—adequate to earn a living and adequate to suffer want and persecutions. Adequate to live life as it really is.

v. 32 (Read through v. 45.)

*And they were in the way going up to Jerusalem,
and Jesus went before them: and they were amazed;
and as they followed, they were afraid. And he took
again the twelve, and began to tell them what things
should happen unto him.*

Read verses 32 through 34 carefully. He is giving the
disciples a detailed description of what is ahead for him. As
they walk toward Jerusalem, they are not walking in ignorance of what to expect. He knows the agony in store for
him, even to the humiliating detail of the spitting. Then
read verse 35: John, the "beloved disciple," and his brother
James seemed to let all the Master said run off like water
off a duck's back! He is telling them of his sufferings to
come and they ask if he will do for *them* right then whatever they ask of him. Both men wanted choice seats in his
"glory." The day their Master mounted the throne of the
earthly kingdom they still believed he would set up, these
two wanted to be on his left and his right. It seems not only
crass, insensitive, but totally selfish. Only Jesus knows exactly what their motives were. Perhaps their motives, like
many of ours, were mixed. Perhaps they wanted to sit in
those places to be near him—perhaps. At any rate, he did
not scold them. He used their self-centered request, as he
always did, to teach them all.

CHAPTER 11
vv. 8 through 10.

*And many spread their garments in the way: and
others cut down branches off the trees, and strawed
them in the way. And they that went before, and they
that followed, cried, saying, Hosanna; Blessed is he
that cometh in the name of the Lord: Blessed be the
kingdom of our father David, that cometh in the name
of the Lord: Hosanna in the highest.*

The crowds were strewing his path with branches and
shouting "Hosanna in the highest!" But I doubt that he was
fooled. I think of him riding along on his little colt, almost
unaware of the empty adulation. He knew it was empty. In

a few days some of the same celebrants would be shouting
"Crucify him!"

v. 25

*And when ye stand praying, forgive, if ye have
ought against any: that your Father also which is in
heaven may forgive you your trespasses.*

Here again, this is not just another "prayer technique."
When "we stand praying" we know when our prayers are
amiss. And remember, only when we forgive those who
trespass against us do our hearts open to the forgiveness of
God.

vv. 27 through 33

*And they come again to Jerusalem: and as he was
walking in the temple, there come to him the chief
priests, and the scribes, and the elders, And say unto
him, By what authority doest thou these things? and
who gave thee this authority to do these things? And
Jesus answered and said unto them, I will also ask of
you one question, and answer me, and I will tell you
by what authority I do these things. The baptism of
John, was it from heaven, or of men? answer me. And
they reasoned with themselves, saying, If we shall say,
From heaven; he will say, Why then did ye not believe
him? But if we shall say, Of men; they feared the people: for all men counted John, that he was a prophet
indeed. And they answered and said unto Jesus, We
cannot tell. And Jesus answering saith unto them, Neither do I tell you by what authority I do these things.*

The old scribes and the chief priests and the elders, his
faithful hecklers, were after him once more, as he walked
in the temple. After him again with their everlastingly
tricky questions. *His authority was still bothering them.* By
what authority did he do the things he did? Who gave him
this authority? I can imagine Jesus sighed wearily, but his
mind was razor sharp: "I am going to ask you a question,"
he replied, "and if you answer me I will tell you what authority I have for what I do. The baptism of John, now—
did it come from Heaven or was it purely human? Tell me

that" (Phillips). The learned men argued with each other, figuring a way out: If they said John's baptism came from Heaven, they knew Jesus would say, "Then, why didn't you believe in him?" They knew if they said John's baptism was only humanly devised, their answer would infuriate the people who still believed that John was a true prophet of God. They settled for a noncommital, safe answer: "We don't know."

Of course, Jesus won the skirmish, but their determination to be rid of him once and for all increased. He was not protecting himself in any way at any turn.

CHAPTER 12
vv. 28 through 31
And one of the scribes came, and having heard them reasoning together, and perceiving that he had answered them well, asked him, Which is the first commandment of all? And Jesus answered him, The first of all the commandments is, Hear, O Israel; the Lord our God is one Lord: And thou shalt love the Lord thy God with all thy heart, and with all thy soul, and with all thy mind, and with all thy strength: this is the first commandment. And the second is like, namely this, Thou shalt love thy neighbour as thyself. There is none other commandment greater than these.

This chapter is one long series of trick questions aimed at causing the Lord to "hang himself." As always, he used them creatively—to instruct, to reveal. This is one of the more provocative examples: One clever scribe, figuring that if he could get the Master to favor one Commandment given to Moses over another, he would trap him. Jesus answered by quoting a scripture familiar to them (Deuteronomy 6: 4, 5), which boils all the Commandments down to two which are inclusive. He remained true to what he knew to be fact and still met them on ground where they could feel familiar.

vv. 32, 34
And the scribe said unto him, Well, Master, thou hast said the truth: . . . And no man after that durst ask him any question.

This is a marvelous passage! Marvelous in its succinctness. In its possible hidden meanings. The clever scribe commented upon Jesus' definition of the true Commandments of God this surprising way: "I am well answered . . . You are absolutely right when you say that there is one God and no other God exists but him; and to love him with the whole of our hearts, the whole of our intelligence and the whole of our energy, and to love our neighbors as ourselves is infinitely more important than all these burnt offerings and sacrifices" (Phillips).

Jesus must have looked deeply into the scribe's heart for a moment, because he said to him: " 'You are not far from the kingdom of God!' After this, no one felt like asking him any more questions" (Phillips). Why didn't they? Jesus had struck a nerve. He had won in the manner of love, not of conquest. What he said had struck the man's inner being. *No one dared risk such exposure after that.*

I can't help wondering how closely this interesting passage has been studied, especially by those who insist upon a confession of sin in a man *before* he can be considered close to the Kingdom of God. Jesus seemed to use the opposite approach. Certainly here. He saw a spark of hope in this man and fanned it. He not only accomplished what had seemed impossible, i.e., to silence his questioners, but he deftly nudged a man toward hope.

CHAPTER 13
v. 11

But when they shall lead you, and deliver you up, take no thought beforehand what ye shall speak, neither do ye premeditate: but whatsoever shall be given you in that hour, that speak ye: for it is not ye that speak, but the Holy Ghost.

Jesus never hesitated to tell them things that were spiritually "over their heads," beyond their current experience. It seems to me he counted heavily on *some* of his words, at least, falling into their subconscious minds, to be brought up and used later. As he warned them of their trials ahead, he told them (as though they had been already taught concerning the work of the Holy Spirit) that they were not to worry about what they would say to the authorities, "for it is not ye that speak, but the Holy Ghost." *Remember, Pentecost had not yet occurred.* Jesus knew it *would* occur, though, and that you and I would be reading his words long after.

CHAPTER 14
vv. 6, 7

And Jesus said, Let her alone; why trouble ye her? she hath wrought a good work on me.

For ye have the poor with you always, and whensoever ye will ye may do them good: but me ye have not always.

Mark, in spite of his brevity, has clarified something here. In his version of the Gospel account, Marks reports that Jesus did not settle for saying merely that the poor we always have with us. Mark adds: ". . . and whensoever ye will, ye may do them good: but me ye have not always."

". . . whensoever ye will ye may do them good: . . ." We are always able to help the poor. Most of us don't think so, but if we believed what Jesus said here, we would not only stop fighting poverty programs, we could begin to make them unnecessary!

v. 8

She hath done what she could: she is come aforehand to anoint my body to the burying.

"She hath done what she could: . . ." One of the Lord's tenderest statements. I try sometimes to imagine how this woman felt when he defended and encouraged her, appreciated her, said she would be memorialized "wheresoever this gospel shall be preached. . . ." Her heart had directed her to do a beautiful and good thing, and God noticed.

vv. 30, 31

And Jesus saith unto him, Verily I say unto thee, That this day, even in this night, before the cock crow twice, thou shalt deny me thrice. But he spake the

*more vehemently, If I should die with thee, I will not
deny thee in any wise. Likewise also said they all.*

It is interesting that Mark writes that even after Jesus
told Peter he would deny his Master three times before the
cock crowed, Peter argued with him. Mark also reports,
"Likewise also said they all." Peter, apparently, was not the
only disciple who lacked self-knowledge.

v. 40
*And when he returned, he found them asleep again,
(for their eyes were heavy,) neither wist they what to
answer him.*

They must have sat up blinking at him, totally unable to
think of a word to say for themselves.

vv. 50 through 52
*And they all forsook him, and fled. And there fol-
lowed him a certain young man, having a linen cloth
cast about his naked body; and the young men laid
hold on him: And he left the linen cloth, and fled
from them naked.*

It is said that this young man who lost his cloak was
John Mark, the author of this Gospel. Tradition says that
the disciples and Jesus ate their Passover supper together in
the upstairs room of John Mark's mother's house. It all fits
together. Even though Mark was a young man, he experienced the shame of that flight for more than one reason!
We know from this, though, that he saw the arrest. His telling is firsthand.

v. 54
*And Peter followed him afar off, even into the pal-
ace of the high priest: and he sat with the servants,
and warmed himself at the fire.*

Dear, miserable Peter. He fled, too, but not far. At least
he followed Jesus at a safe distance. Not commendable, but
he did follow; he did stay around.

v. 69
And a maid saw him again, and began to say to them that stood by, This is one of them.

Do you like it said of you that you are "one of them?" How do you react to it? When this was said of Peter, he was "warming himself," protecting himself. Why are we embarrassed to be called "one of them"—Christian? For the same reason, perhaps, that Peter was ashamed? Because he resembled his Master so little? We need to be perceptive here. We will none of us ever *act like Jesus* on this earth. Shouldn't we accept the joy of being known as "one of them"? And not cringe, directing attention to our inadequacies?

v. 72
And the second time the cock crew. And Peter called to mind the word that Jesus said unto him, Before the cock crow twice, thou shalt deny me thrice. And when he thought thereon, he wept.

Mark throws extra light here: "And when he *thought thereon*, he wept." If only we *thought* more.

CHAPTER 15
vv. 3, 4, 5
And the chief priests accused him of many things: but he answered nothing. And Pilate asked him again, saying, Answerest thou nothing? . . . But Jesus yet answered nothing; so that Pilate marvelled.

Jesus' silence finally caused Pilate to marvel. The strength of God was in it.

v. 15
And so Pilate, willing to content the people, . . .

Pilate, like many of us today, was simply "willing to content the people." We brush over this weakness. It is a serious sin, no matter what our work or calling. It, more than anything else, goes on delivering Jesus into the hands of his enemies.

SAINT MARK   75

v. 21
*And they compel one Simon a Cyrenian, who
passed by, coming out of the country, the father of
Alexander and Rufus, to bear his cross.*

Wouldn't you like to know if Simon, the Cyrenian, *willingly* helped Jesus bear his cross?

v. 31
. . . He saved others; himself he cannot save.

Himself he *would* not save. We were all too important to him.

v. 39
*And when the centurion, which stood over against
him, saw that he so cried out, and gave up the ghost,
he said, Truly this man was the Son of God.*

Do you ever wonder why the centurion began to believe
Jesus was the Son of God from having heard his last, loud
cry when he "gave up the ghost?" Was it something in that
voice? Perhaps a ring of triumph? Triumph mingled with
the ending of a creative human life? Even as Jesus died, he
drew this man to him. I learn from thinking on this one
seldom-mentioned incident in the Great Enactment of love.

vv. 44, 45
*And Pilate marvelled if he were already dead: and
calling unto him the centurion, he asked him whether
he had been any while dead. And when he knew it of
the centurion, he gave the body to Joseph.*

It is interesting to realize that it was the centurion whom
Pilate called to make sure Jesus was dead. The centurion's
job, apparently, was to watch the Crucified closely. He became a believer by doing it.

CHAPTER 16
vv. 4, 5
And when they looked, they saw that the stone was

*rolled away: for it was very great. And entering into
the sepulchre, they saw a young man sitting on the
right side, clothed in a long white garment; and they
were affrighted.*

Matthew says the angel rolled away the stone. Mark says
it was already rolled away when the women came to care
for his body. No matter. The important thing is that the
tomb was empty. Jesus did not have to wait for the stone to
be rolled away in order to walk out.

vv. 9 through 11
*Now when Jesus was risen early the first day of the
week, he appeared first to Mary Magdalene, out of
whom he had cast seven devils. And she went and told
them that had been with him, as they mourned and
wept. And they, when they had heard that he was
alive, and had been seen of her, believed not.*

Did Mary Magdalene run ahead and so meet Jesus, the
risen Lord, first? I like to think she did. He had done so
much for her. Her need had been so great, her love drove
her to hurry back to him "at the rising of the sun." She
must have gotten there first and she must have been the
first to run, breathless, to tell his disciples. But she was, to
the men, merely a talkative woman. They did not believe
her.

vv. 12, 13
*After that he appeared in another form unto two of
them, as they walked, and went into the country. And
they went and told it unto the residue: neither believed they them.*

The disciples' lack of faith was not altogether due to the
fact that Mary of Magdala was a mere woman. The "two
of them" to whom Jesus appeared (Luke's Gospel) on the
road to Emmaus were men. They told the other disciples
and were also doubted.

vv. 14, 15
Afterward he appeared unto the eleven as they sat

at meat, and upbraided them with their unbelief and
hardness of heart, because they believed not them
which had seen him after he was risen. And he said
unto them, Go ye into all the world, and preach the
gospel to every creature.

As he had always done, Jesus did what he had to do. He
went straight to the disciples, (locked up safely in a room,
eating) and upbraided them for their little faith. But *he*
went, longing for them to be comforted, to know. And the
fact that they had been hard to convince did not stop him
from giving them his great commission: "Go ye into all the
world and preach the gospel to every creature." He has
never waited for us to "advance" to a particular spiritual
state before sending us out. This false idea is behind our
silly disillusionment when a "Christian leader" falls on his
or her face. God does not send "supreme beings"; he sends
faulty men and women—like the eleven who deserted him
in his hour of greatest need. If he waited for our "perfection," there would be no one to go!

SAINT LUKE

CHAPTER 1
v. 6
And they were both righteous before God, walking in all the commandments and ordinances of the Lord blameless.

It must be realized that both Zacharias and his wife, Elisabeth, were righteous people before God; considered by God to be "blameless." This is important to the impact of the next considered verses.

vv. 8, 11, 13 through 17
And it came to pass, that while he executed the priest's office before God in the order of his course, . . . there appeared unto him an angel of the Lord . . . the angel said unto him. Fear not, Zacharias: for thy prayer is heard; and thy wife Elisabeth shall bear thee a son, and thou shalt call his name John. And thou shalt have joy and gladness; and many shall rejoice at his birth. For he shall be great in the sight of the Lord, and shall drink neither wine nor strong drink; and he shall be filled with the Holy Ghost, even from his mother's womb. And many of the children of Israel shall he turn to the Lord their God. And he shall go before him in the spirit and power of Elias, to turn the hearts of the fathers to the children, and the disobedient to the wisdom of the just; to make ready a people prepared for the Lord.

When the angel of the Lord came to Zacharias, he spared no effort to make himself understood. He even encouraged the old priest by reminding him that he and his elderly wife would "have joy and gladness." He explained the mission of the son to be born to them in their declining years. Nothing was omitted. God knew it would come as a

shock to them both, since they were too old to have a child.
And so he went the whole way to explain.

v. 18
*And Zacharias said unto the angel, Whereby shall I
know this? for I am an old man, and my wife well
stricken in years.*

In spite of God's care to make himself clear, in spite of
the fact that Zacharias was considered "blameless" before
God, the old man's first question was riddled with doubt.
He did not ask "How can this happen?" as Mary asked
when told by the angel that she would bear a son by the
Holy Spirit. Zacharias had not accepted what the angel said
as fact at all. He asked: "Whereby shall I know this?" Not
"How can this be?" But, "How am I to know what you say
is true?"

vv. 19, 20
*And the angel answering said unto him, I am Ga-
briel, that stand in the presence of God; and am sent
to speak unto thee, and to shew thee these glad tidings. And, behold, thou shalt be dumb, and not able to
speak, until the day that these things shall be performed, because thou believest not my words, which
shall be fulfilled in their season.*

The angel Gabriel identified himself as one who stood in
the presence of God, and immediately informed the doubting Zacharias that he would be unable to speak one more
word until the day his son would be born. There are those
who believe God struck the old priest dumb as punishment
for his doubt. Others theorize that such deep and sudden
doubt can silence a man's tongue. Still others (and I tend
toward this) feel the shock was too much for the old man's
emotional make-up. He had a psychosomatic reaction to
the stunning news. I lean toward this theory simply because
I do not believe God punishes in such ways. I believe he
punishes by love and that is, in the long run, more severe
and brings more lasting results. On the other hand, I can
accept the fact that God gave Zacharias a temporary res-
pite from speech—not so much as a punishment—but so

that he would not be able to discourage his equally ancient
wife, Elisabeth. After all, she had the difficult time ahead,
and doubt caught from her husband could make it still
more difficult. Elisabeth needed desperately to be free from
doubt, to be able to receive the rest and strength that come
from complete trust in God. Perhaps God was merely
guaranteeing her peace of mind by keeping Zacharias'
mouth shut. The fact of his inability to speak could also be
the convincing factor for Elisabeth that he had truly seen
and talked with the angel of the Lord. As with so many
other provocative passages in the Bible, it is a waste to permit oneself to be sidetracked into controversy. Too much
of life-changing importance is about to happen!

vv. 26 through 34

*And in the sixth month the angel Gabriel was sent
from God unto a city of Galilee, named Nazareth, To
a virgin espoused to a man whose name was Joseph,
of the house of David; and the virgin's name was
Mary. And the angel came in unto her, and said, Hail,
thou that art highly favoured, the Lord is with thee:
blessed art thou among women. And when she saw
him, she was troubled at his saying, and cast in her
mind what manner of salutation this should be. And
the angel said unto her, Fear not, Mary: for thou hast
found favour with God. And, behold, thou shalt conceive in thy womb, and bring forth a son, and shall
call his name Jesus. He shall be great, and shall be
called the Son of the Highest: and the Lord God shall
give unto him the throne of his father David: And he
shall reign over the house of Jacob for ever; and of his
kingdom there shall be no end. Then said Mary unto
the angel, How shall this be, seeing I know not a man?*

Six months later, when Elisabeth was well along in her
pregnancy, the same angel, Gabriel, appeared to her young
cousin, Mary, in the hill town of Nazareth with news so
startling that a much older and wiser woman might understandably have fainted or flown into hysterics. Not Mary.
Of course, she was perturbed, unable to imagine what such
a lofty message could mean. After all, she was only an in-

significant young girl, about to be married to Joseph, the kindly carpenter. How could *she* be singled out to be addressed as "blessed . . . among women"? What Gabriel was really saying was that the Messiah was coming and that he would be *her* child. Now, Jewish women for years had been praying and hoping for this signal honor. I doubt that Mary had done this. In her estimation, she would be the last person God would choose. Yet, here was the angel telling her that even before she had known a man, she would conceive a child who would be called "the Son of the Highest"! But, in all her shock and confusion, Mary remembered the angel had said, "The Lord is with thee." For Mary, whose simple faith had never wavered, *this was enough*. So, her first question was full of trust: "How shall this be, seeing I know not a man?" She did not ask, as Zacharias had asked, how she could know this was the truth. *She asked for no proof.* Just how was it going to happen? A logical question. In effect: "I believe you, but please tell me how this will take place."

vv. 35 through 38

And the angel answered and said unto her, The Holy Ghost shall come upon thee, and the power of the Highest shall overshadow thee: therefore also that holy thing which shall be born of thee shall be called the Son of God. And, behold, thy cousin Elisabeth, she hath also conceived a son in her old age: and this is the sixth month with her, who was called barren. For with God nothing shall be impossible. And Mary said, Behold the handmaid of the Lord; be it unto me according to thy word. And the angel departed from her.

And the angel told her carefully, clearly. He also explained about her elderly cousin, Elisabeth; that she was in her sixth month with child. He did not go into the purpose of John's birth. God knew this would be too much for the young, awe-struck girl to take in. Rather, Gabriel told her about Elisabeth more to assure her that ". . . with God nothing shall be impossible." For Mary this was enough. Her answer to Gabriel holds the key to releasing God's power for us all: "Behold the handmaid of the Lord: be it unto me according to thy word." Phillips translates her words this way: "I belong to the Lord, body and soul . . . let it happen as you say."

vv. 39, 40 (Read through v. 45.)

And Mary arose in those days, and went into the hill country with haste, into a city of Juda; And entered into the house of Zacharias, and saluted Elisabeth.

Mary, needing someone to share her awe and her joy, hurried, as soon as possible, to Elisabeth's home. Elisabeth would understand. Her old cousin, too, was shut away from the unknowing world by the miracle of God taking place in her. No one but Elisabeth could possibly know how she felt. And when Mary reached her cousin's house, even before she had a chance to tell what had happened, Elisabeth's baby leaped for joy within her and God verified his plan to them in a moment of intense joy and praise. Before his birth, Elisabeth called Jesus her Lord!

These two women needed each other and God saw to it that they could share the wonder together. He is always aware that there are times when his glory is too much for us. This, of course, is why he permits only occasional glimpses of it. We could not bear the wonder otherwise.

vv. 62 through 64

And they made signs to his father, how he would have him called. And he asked for a writing table, and wrote, saying, His name is John. And they marvelled all. And his mouth was opened immediately, and his tongue loosed, and he spake, and praised God.

As soon as Zacharias had agreed with Elisabeth that the angel of the Lord had named the baby John, instead of Zacharias, the old priest could speak again. And he really spoke! In words inspired by God himself, he prophesied the future life of his son and his role in announcing the coming of the "dayspring from on high"—Mary's child, not yet born.

CHAPTER 2
vv. 1 through 7

*And it came to pass in those days, that there went
out a decree from Caesar Augustus, that all the world
should be taxed. (And this taxing was first made when
Cyrenius was governor of Syria.) And all went to be
taxed, every one into his own city. And Joseph also
went up from Galilee, out of the city of Nazareth, into
Judaea, unto the city of David, which is called Bethlehem; (because he was of the house and lineage of
David:) To be taxed with Mary his espoused wife,
being great with child. And so it was, that, while they
were there, the days were accomplished that she
should be delivered. And she brought forth her first-
born son, and wrapped him in swaddling clothes, and
laid him in a manger; because there was no room for
them in the inn.*

Matthew has explained the turmoil in gentle Joseph's
heart when he learned that Mary was "great with child" before he had known her. Joseph took the way of love and
boldly went to his native city of Bethlehem with his expec-
tant wife, to be taxed. The gossip back in Nazareth must
have made the air crackle! But God had spoken to them
both, had acted within them both, and they went on without fear. Not only did Joseph show his strong faith in God,
his quality of character; he showed only the greatest tenderness toward Mary. She was going to be as comfortable
as a woman could be in a stable, when her son was born. I
am sure Joseph left nothing undone that could be done for
her. And God, as always, was making creative use of even
the crude, makeshift surroundings. It was a chilly night; the
houses and inns were poorly heated. But Mary had the
warmth of the bodies of the animals near her in the stable.
God wastes nothing. Not even our hardships.

vv. 8 through 18

*And there were in the same country shepherds abid-
ing in the field, keeping watch over their flock by
night. And, lo, the angel of the Lord came upon them,
and the glory of the Lord shone round about them:
and they were sore afraid. And the angel said unto*

them, Fear not: for, behold, I bring you good tidings
of great joy, which shall be to all people. For unto you
is born this day in the city of David a Saviour, which
is Christ the Lord. And this shall be a sign unto you;
Ye shall find the babe wrapped in swaddling clothes,
lying in a manger. And suddenly there was with the
angel a multitude of the heavenly host praising God,
and saying, Glory to God in the highest, and on earth
peace, good will toward men.

And it came to pass, as angels were gone away
from them into heaven, the shepherds said to one an-
other, Let us now go even unto Bethlehem, and see
this thing which is come to pass, which the Lord hath
made known unto us. And they came with haste, and
found Mary, and Joseph, and the babe lying in a
manger. And when they had seen it, they made known
abroad the saying which was told them concerning
this child. And all they that heard it wondered at those
things which were told them by the shepherds.

God did not come into the world as a Man, with enormous advance publicity and noisy fanfare. But neither did
he make his entrance among us with no signs of confirma-
tion. It would have done little good if he had announced
his arrival elaborately to the world. The world did not understand him, would not have grasped his meaning. And
so, God spread the word that the Saviour was here, that redemption was at hand, by the same means he still uses:
through the few people who live close enough to him to understand something of his purposes. God made his an-
nouncements to those who believed in him. First, Zacharias
and Elisabeth, who spread the word concerning the mission
God had planned for their son, John. Then, Mary and Joseph. Now, in these verses, he is telling the simple shepherds on the hillside outside Bethlehem. They were all believers, who took him at his word. The "remnant" as Bible
scholars say. And to the shepherds, God made his joyful
announcement in a heavenly choral concert! Were these
plain, working men the only ones who were able to hear the
celestial chorus that night? I wonder. At any rate, once
they heard and saw, the shepherds "made known abroad
the saying which was told them concerning this child." God

did not come unannounced. He simply made his announcement only to those who could and would hear.

v. 19
But Mary kept all these things, and pondered them in her heart.

Mary apparently talked little about what had happened. She didn't need to. God did not choose her to spread the glad news, he chose her to bear his Son. I try at times, but I can't imagine what she "pondered in her heart." Oh, we can know some of it, I suppose. "Mother things" certainly. This was God's Son, but it was her son, too. At any rate, Mary had too much to think about to talk.

v. 30 (Read vv. 22 through 33.)
For mine eyes have seen thy salvation, . . .

God evidently was making his announcement directly to the hearts and minds of other devout Jews, too. I have always loved this passage concerning old Simeon, waiting to die, but knowing he would not die until he had seen the Lord's Christ. Mary and Joseph were not famous people. I doubt that anyone but God knew they were in the temple that day, but he knew, and he sent old Simeon there *to see Jesus*. The most meaningful part of this incident to me is what Simeon said when he took the Baby in his arms: "Lord, now lettest thou thy servant depart in peace, according to thy word; *for mine eyes have seen thy salvation*." He could have said: ". . . for mine eyes have seen the Christ." *The words are interchangeable*, but how seldom we think of them that way! We have compartmentalized, as is our dear, foolish delight. Most of us think of our "salvation" as a *thing*, a *process*, a *happening*. Jesus Christ himself *is* our salvation! When one sees him, one sees salvation. Surely, this thoughtless compartmentalizing is the reason so many sincere, fearful Christians speak of "losing their salvation." Can one "lose" God? Didn't he say he would be with us always? That he would never leave us or forsake us? "Salvation" cannot die because God cannot die. Old Simeon had it straight, and Mary and Joseph marveled. I don't blame them.

v. 49 (Read vv. 42 through 52.)

And he said unto them, How is it that ye sought me? wist ye not that I must be about my Father's business?

Luke wrote this episode of Jesus' conversing with the learned men in the temple with great skill. Mary must have told him about it. I can almost hear her: "He had always been such a good boy, so considerate. In all his twelve years, I hadn't had a moment's worry over him until that day. Joseph and I were frantic! We searched everywhere. Because Jesus had always been such an obedient and thoughtful little boy, we were sure something dreadful had happened to him. And then we found him, sitting right there in the midst of those learned doctors, both answering their profound questions and asking his own of them! As calm and mature as you please. And they were treating him as though he were a respected adult. Dr. Luke, they were *all* astonished at his learning! I was proud of him, of course, but I couldn't help scolding him a little. We had been so frightened. And when I asked him why he had worried us so, he answered in the strangest words. Oh, he wasn't sharp with me. His voice was quiet and gentle, as though he were praying that I would somehow understand: 'How is it that ye sought me? Wist ye not that I must be about my Father's business?' Well, I can tell you, neither Joseph nor I understood at all, but after that, we all went home together and never again was he anything but what he had been before—a good, thoughtful, obedient boy." You can be sure Mary never forgot the incident, but evidently she said no more about it then. She just kept all his "sayings in her heart." Jesus grew up in a typical hill-country town, in healthy surroundings, close to nature—away from the dirt and bustle of Jerusalem or Bethlehem. How like God to arrange this. He wanted him to be reared in naturalness, sensitive to the sky and the sea and the olive trees and the grapevines and the wheat fields. He worked in his earthly father's carpentry shop with his hands. It was hard, manual work, but creative. Surely, God chose the right earthly father for him. Joseph was a kind man, strong, full of faith, and gentle. And the Boy Jesus was the Son of God. It is no wonder he "increased in wisdom and stature, and in favour with God and man."

CHAPTER 3

vv. 1 through 6 (Read through v. 18.)

Now in the fifteenth year of the reign of Tiberius Caesar, Pontius Pilate being governor of Judaea, and Herod being tetrarch of Galilee, and his brother Philip tetrarch of Ituraea and of the region of Trachonitis, and Lysanias the tetrarch of Abilene, Annas and Caiphas being the high priests, the word of God came unto John the son of Zacharias in the wilderness. And he came into all the country about Jordan, preaching the baptism of repentance for the remission of sins; As it is written in the book of the words of Esaias the prophet, saying, The voice of one crying in the wilderness, Prepare ye the way of the Lord, make his paths straight. Every valley shall be filled, and every mountain and hill shall be brought low; and the crooked shall be made straight, and the rough ways shall be made smooth; And all flesh shall see the salvation of God. . . .

Luke has set his scene well again. We know who is in political power; we know the date and something of the times. At the end of Chapter 1, Luke had written of John: "And the child grew, and waxed strong in spirit, and was in the deserts till the day of his shewing unto Israel." John, born of aged parents, had grown up in very unnatural conditions compared with the childhood of Jesus. He was, according to Mark, "clothed with camel's hair, and with a girdle of a skin about his loins; and he did eat locusts and wild honey. . . ." John was a totally dedicated man with a mission straight from God. No man on earth had been given such responsibility, and John fulfilled his calling. But he was considered an eccentric, an aesthete, and compared with Jesus, he was. This is in no way a deprecation of John. Unless a man is the only begotten Son of God, as Jesus was, such a mission would so occupy him that he would have no energy left for the normal pursuits of life! John the Baptist has

intrigued me as a human being for years. I admire him, I
pity him, I'm sure I would have found him uncomfortable
socially. His life was so taken up with his mission (most of
which was new to him) that there was no time to learn social niceties, to enter into comfortable human relationships.
As it appeared to him, he had no choice but to deny himself all these things and live alone in the desert, trying
every minute to learn more of what was expected of him.

So here is John, as a grown man, in Luke's graphic account, mingling with throngs of people, away from his beloved desert and his privacy, embarked on his mission at
last, still pouring himself out for God. And doing so with
power and insight and enormous vigor. Stretching himself,
as it were, across the wide gap between the semidarkness of
the Old Testament toward the bright light of the New. Utterly convinced of the power of the living God. Shouting
to the crowds that thronged around him that "God is able of
these stones to raise up children unto Abraham!" Using
foreshadowings of the kind of practical, Christian teaching
that concerns human behavior, relationships. (See verses
11, 12, 13, 14.) Proclaiming that "one mightier than I
cometh, the latchet of whose shoes I am unworthy to un-
loose." As God planned it, Elisabeth's son was announcing
the coming of Mary's Son, who would make the crooked
straight and the rough ways smooth.

vv. 19, 20
But Herod the tetrarch, being reproved by him for
Herodias his brother Philip's wife, and for all the evils
which Herod had done, Added yet this above all, that
he shut up John in prison.

Just before Jesus appeared to take his place in line to be
baptized by John, Herod (because of John's condemnation
for the King's love affair with his brother's wife) was being
pressured by his mistress to shut John up in prison. The
Baptist baptized Jesus, the Holy Spirit led Jesus into the
wilderness to be tempted and tried, and John was silenced
—shut away from the sky and the wind and the sun he
loved so much—by four close, thick, damp stone walls,
never to be free again in this world.

CHAPTER 4
vv. 14, 15

*And Jesus returned in the power of the Spirit into
Galilee: and there went out a fame of him through all
the region round about. And he taught in their synagogues, being glorified of all.*

After his baptism by John in the Jordan, after John's imprisonment by Herod, after his own temptation-filled forty
days in the wilderness alone, Jesus "returned in the power
of the Spirit into Galilee." His earthly ministry had begun,
and it is interesting to observe that in these early days, he
was "glorified by all." His tormentors had not yet started
their pursuit of him.

vv. 16 through 21, 28 through 30

*And he came to Nazareth, where he had been
brought up: and, as his custom was, he went into the
synagogue on the sabbath day, and stood up for to
read. And there was delivered unto him the book of
the prophet Esaias. And when he had opened the
book, he found the place where it was written, The
Spirit of the Lord is upon me, because he hath anointed me to preach the gospel to the poor; he hath sent
me to heal the broken-hearted, to preach deliverance
to the captives, and recovering of sight to the blind, to
set at liberty them that are bruised, To preach the acceptable year of the Lord. And he closed the book,
and he gave it again to the minister, and sat down.
And the eyes of all them that were in the synagogue
were fastened on him. And he began to say unto them,
This day is this scripture fulfilled in your ears. . . .
And all they in the synagogue, when they heard these
things, were filled with wrath, And rose up, and thrust
him out of the city, and led him unto the brow of the
hill whereon their city was built, that they might cast
him down headlong. But he passing through the midst
of them went his way.*

Apparently his troubles did not begin until he went back
to his home town of Nazareth. Even here, for the first moments of his teaching in the familiar old synagogue—his

audience made up of his friends and neighbors and relatives—things went rather well. But as he bore in upon their precious traditions, as he began to shake their *status quo*, they turned on him and attempted to push him headlong over a cliff! "But he passing through the midst of them went his way."

CHAPTER 5
v. 4 (Read through v. 11.)
Now when he had left speaking, he said unto Simon, Launch out into the deep, and let down your nets for a draught.

This is a story none of the other Gospel accounts tells. Its impact to me is in the fact that Jesus uses whatever is at hand, whatever is familiar, most understandable, to draw his disciples to him. Peter and Andrew and James and John "understood" about fishing.

vv. 36 through 39
And he spake also a parable unto them; No man putteth a piece of a new garment upon an old; if otherwise, then both the new maketh a rent, and the piece that was taken out of the new agreeth not with the old. And no man putteth new wine into old bottles; else the new wine will burst the bottles, and be spilled, and the bottles shall perish. But new wine must be put into new bottles; and both are preserved. No man also having drunk old wine straightway desireth new: for he saith, The old is better.

Jesus had grown up simply, knowing about grapes and harvest and the making of wine and the use of leather wine bottles. He did not grow up in luxury. Putting patches on worn garments was no new thing to him.

CHAPTER 6
v. 12
And it came to pass in those days, that he went out into a mountain to pray, and continued all night in prayer to God.

The burden of his days was so heavy, even Jesus could not have managed without longer and more frequent times of prayer with the Father than most of us ever experience.

vv. 41, 42

And why beholdest thou the mote that is in thy brother's eye, but perceivest not the beam that is in thine own eye? Either how canst thou say to thy brother, Brother, let me pull out the mote that is in thine eye, when thou thyself beholdest not the beam that is in thine own eye? Thou hypocrite, cast out first the beam out of thine own eye, and then shalt thou see clearly to pull out the mote that is in thy brother's eye.

His humor is keen here, but beneath it—truth. Isn't it really ridiculous for a gossip to condemn a man for drinking too much?

CHAPTER 7

v. 9 (Read vv. 1 through 10.)

When Jesus heard these things, he marvelled at him and turned him about, and said unto the people that followed him, I say unto you, I have not found so great faith, no, not in Israel.

This is a strong story. And with a surprise twist at the end. Not the healing of the beloved servant. When Jesus healed, it was no surprise. The surprise is that Jesus, for once, had a chance to marvel at something! Here was a man—a pagan centurion—who understood authority and obedience. The centurion's marvelous simplicity here merits much attention.

CHAPTER 8

vv. 1, 2, 3

And it came to pass afterward, that he went throughout every city and village, preaching and shewing the glad tidings of the kingdom of God: and the twelve were with him, And certain women, which had been healed of evil spirits and infirmities, Mary called Magdalene, out of whom went seven devils, And Joanna the wife of Chuza Herod's steward, and

*Susanna, and many others, which ministered unto him
of their substance.*

Most of us think only of Mary of Magdala when we
think of the woman from whom Jesus "cast seven devils."
Mary would, I'm sure, be the first to admit that it was she.
But evidently he was followed and minstered to (from their
own resources) by other women, some of whose needs had
been as great and as shocking as the Magdalene's. One of
these was Joanna, the wife of Herod's steward. Another
was an otherwise anonymous woman named Susanna—all
of whom were anything but anonymous to Jesus.

v. 9

*And his disciples asked him, saying, What might
this parable be?*

Whatever the full meaning of the parable of the sower
might be (and here Jesus gave his men an interpretation),
it is evident that he knew as he worked (and accepted the
fact) that all the seed he dropped would *not* fall on good
ground. We can learn from this acceptance. Jesus was
never anxious, he never pressured anyone into the Kingdom. His is a much wider view than ours can be, but perhaps we should accept his seeming relaxation in the midst
of his labors by faith, and make it our own.

CHAPTER 9
vv. 1, 2

*Then he called his twelve disciples together, and
gave them power and authority over all devils, and to
cure diseases. And he sent them to preach the kingdom of God, and to heal the sick.*

I never cease marveling at the chances God takes. These
twelve men seem to have caught on so slowly; their faith
appears so weak, their love so limited. And yet he sent
them out in his name to cast out devils and cure diseases!
As he sends us. We tremble in fear for the reputation of
God. Certainly, his view is infinitely broader than ours, infinitely more liberal, because God goes right on taking
these bad risks.

v. 9

And Herod said, John have I beheaded: but who is this, of whom I hear such things? And he desired to see him.

Eventually Herod got his chance "to see him," but under very different circumstances (Luke 23: 8, 9).

vv.10, 11

And the apostles, when they were returned, told him all that they had done. And he took them, and went aside privately into a desert place belonging to the city called Bethsaida. And the people, when they knew it, followed him: and he received them, and spake unto them of the kingdom of God, and healed them that had need of healing.

When the disciples returned from their first trip without the Master, of course, they were full of stories of the wonders that had happened because of the authority he had given them. Jesus attempted to take them away where they could be alone and rest and pray—to give them a much needed recharging for what he knew lay ahead. But, as usual, the crowds came with their needs and were met, as usual, with his compassion, his attention, his healing. *And* the miracle of the multiplied food for their hunger.

v. 18

And it came to pass, as he was alone praying, his disciples were with him: and he asked them, saying, Whom say the people that I am?

At last he is alone with his disciples at prayer. And Luke tells us it is in the midst of prayer that he asks the one vital question: "Whom do men say that I am?" Perhaps Peter's answer could be, in part, correct because of the wonders he had just experienced through the authority given him by this Man who could not be like any other man on earth. Who *had* to be "The Christ of God."

v. 36
*And when the voice was past, Jesus was found
alone. And they kept it close, and told no man in
those days any of those things which they had seen.*

The three who went with Jesus to the Mount of Transfiguration were growing. It must have been very difficult
for them to "keep it close," to tell no man what they had
seen there. It would have been easy to boast. After all, they
were the three he chose to witness it. We have no record
that they did anything but keep still about it.

v. 51
*And it came to pass, when the time was come that
he should be received up, he stedfastly set his face to
go to Jerusalem.*

Another "transfiguration" must have appeared in his
face. The quality of flint showed. His whole will was
"steadfastly set" to walk directly into his agony, even to the
Cross. If one has not seen the stern side of the face of Jesus
Christ, one has not yet seen him.

vv. 52 through 56
*And sent messengers before his face: and they
went, and entered into a village of the Samaritans, to
make ready for him. And they did not receive him,
because his face was as though he would go to Jerusalem. And when his disciples James and John saw this,
they said, Lord, wilt thou that we command fire to
come down from heaven, and consume them, even as
Elias did? But he turned, and rebuked them, and said,
Ye know not what manner of spirit ye are of. For the
Son of man is not come to destroy men's lives, but to
save them. And they went to another village.*

When they came to the Samaritan village en route to
Jerusalem, they were turned out. No one would receive
them. The seven-hundred-year-old antagonism between the
Samaritans and the orthodox Jews still held. The Jews de-
spised the Samaritans as aliens who claimed the privileges
of Israel. The despising worked both ways. Just knowing

Jesus was on his way to Jerusalem (the city they hated) was enough to cause the Samaritans to refuse him shelter. James and John, whom Jesus had rightly surnamed Sons of Thunder, thundered! They were so angry they wanted to burn up the village, using Elijah (II Kings 1:10) as their authority. Jesus rebuked them. They were now living under *his* authority! And "the Son of Man is not come to destroy men's lives, but to save them." Weary as they were, they plodded on to another village for the night. We had better not use even Scripture to back up our anger, if it seems unlike Jesus.

vv. 57, 58

And it came to pass, that, as they went in the way, a certain man said unto him, Lord, I will follow thee withersoever thou goest. And Jesus said unto him, Foxes have holes, and birds of the air have nests; but the Son of man hath not where to lay his head.

This man obviously was not a disciple, but wanted to be. Jesus wanted him to count the cost first. He would have to be willing, as the Master was, to enjoy fewer privileges than foxes enjoy.

vv. 59 through 62

And he said unto another, Follow me. But he said, Lord, suffer me first to go and bury my father. Jesus said unto him, Let the dead bury their dead: but go thou and preach the kingdom of God. And another also said, Lord, I will follow thee; but let me first go bid them farewell, which are at home at my house. And Jesus said unto him, No man, having put his hand to the plow, and looking back, is fit for the kingdom of God.

These are hard sayings. And yet, we must never lose sight of the fact that only Jesus knew these men as they really were. Perhaps if the one had gone off to bury his father, he would never have come back. The same may have been true of the man who wanted to go home for a tearful farewell to his family. The family pull may have been

stronger than the pull toward Christ. Jesus knew in detail.
He *still* knows in detail.

CHAPTER 10
vv. 1 through 3
*After these things the Lord appointed other seventy
also, and sent them two and two before his face into
every city and place, whither he himself would come.
Therefore said he unto them, The harvest truly is
great, but the labourers are few: pray ye therefore the
Lord of the harvest, that he would send forth labourers into his harvest. Go your ways: behold, I send
you forth as lambs among wolves.*

The time was growing short. His missionary enterprise
had to be enlarged. Seventy disciples went out this time—as
before, *two by two.* Jesus, even in the face of the enormity
of his still unfinished task, bothered to think of the men's
need of companionship. Especially since they were being
sent "as lambs among wolves."

v. 25 (Read through v. 37.)
*And, behold, a certain lawyer stood up, and tempt-
ed him, saying, Master, what shall I do to inherit eternal life?*

Luke enlarges this episode most helpfully. It is almost as
though his lawyer is a different man from Mark's. This is,
of course, because two writers see him in differing aspects.
All of which can be enlightening rather than confusing to
us. Luke includes the parable of the Good Samaritan to en-
large our view and stretch our understanding of loving
one's neighbor. Jesus induces the scribe to answer his own
question: Who is my neighbor? We see that our neighbor is
anyone who needs us. The Good Samaritan story gives the
provocative feeling that Jesus was looking ahead to our
world of troubled race relations. Remember, the Jews
hated the Samaritans and the Samaritans hated the Jews.

CHAPTER 11
v. 33
No man, when he hath lighted a candle, putteth it

in a secret place, neither under a bushel, but on a candlestick, that they which come in may see the light...

It is good to think on the Lord's plain common sense.

v. 34

The light of the body is the eye: therefore when thine eye is single, thy whole body also is full of light; but when thine eye is evil, thy body also is full of darkness.

If we have eyes only for God, we do not miss the needs of the world he loves. "The light of the body is the eye." *We become what we look at.* What gets our attention, gets us. And this includes a steady diet of TV and gossip. If Christ has our attention, we are full of light. His light.

v. 35

Take heed therefore that the light which is in thee be not darkness.

Does this make you think of the tight-mouthed, doctrine-clutching Christians who put their own religious concepts before love? Their doctrine may be perfectly "correct"; to the best of their knowledge, their faith is in Jesus Christ. But he warned, "Take heed therefore that the light which is in thee be not (as) darkness."

The same is true, of course, of the sort of liberal who bends every effort to "show love" to the needy, but who ignores the necessity for redemption in every human heart. The same warning applies: "Take heed therefore that the light which is in thee be not [as] darkness."

Chapter 12
vv. 8, 9

Also I say unto you, Whosoever shall confess me before men, him shall the Son of man also confess before the angels of God: But he that denieth me before men shall be denied before the angels of God.

Jesus is not bargaining here. Not making deals. He is speaking realistically, as always. If we do not confess him

as being ours, he cannot confess us as being his. He would
be lying if he did.

vv. 27, 28

*Consider the lilies how they grow: they toil not,
they spin not; and yet I say unto you, that Solomon in
all his glory was not arrayed like one of these. If then
God so clothe the grass, which is to day in the field,
and to morrow is cast into the oven; how much more
will he clothe you, O ye of little faith?*

I have heard people complain, "Yes, but I'm not a lily. I
can't be expected to stand rooted in one spot!" This is not
the point. Our western minds are so literal. The lily and the
grass merely meet the conditions of growth and they grow.
Is this asking too much of us as human beings?

v. 32

*Fear not, little flock; for it is your Father's good
pleasure to give you the kingdom.*

One of the dearest verses in the New Testament. In the
whole Bible for that matter. It is seldom used as a verse of
comfort. But, how comforting it is! It relaxes me to be
thought of by God as one of his "little flock." And to think
it is our Father's "good pleasure to give us the kingdom!"
Surely, only the unduly troubled mind, the anxious heart,
the misinformed, the darkened insight could insult such a
Father by *pleading* for what Jesus says gives him "good
pleasure."

CHAPTER 13

vv. 10 through 17

*And he was teaching in one of the synagogues on
the sabbath. And, behold, there was a woman which
had a spirit of infirmity eighteen years, and was bowed
together, and could in no wise lift up herself. And
when Jesus saw her, he called her to him, and said
unto her, Woman, thou are loosed from thine infirmity. And he laid his hands on her: and immediately she
was made straight, and glorified God. And the ruler of
the synagogue answered with indignation, because that*

Jesus had healed on the sabbath day, and said unto the
people, There are six days in which men ought to
work: in them therefore come and be healed, and not
on the sabbath day. The Lord then answered him, and
said, Thou hypocrite, doth not each one of you on the
sabbath loose his ox or his ass from the stall, and lead
him away to watering? And ought not this woman,
being a daughter of Abraham, whom Satan hath
bound, lo, these eighteen years, be loosed from this
bond on the sabbath day? And when he had said these
things, all his adversaries were ashamed: and all the
people rejoiced for all the glorious things that were
done by him.

Jesus himself called the woman with the bent back from
the audience in the synagogue this particular Sabbath day.
She did not come to him, *he called her* and healed her. And
yet, the infuriated ruler of the synagogue dared not berate
Jesus because the audience was so "with" him. Luke gives
us a contrast here to the usual heckling of the Master himself. This time the ruler shouted at the *people.*

vv. 18 through 22

Then said he, Unto what is the kingdom of God
like? and whereunto shall I resemble it? It is like a
grain of mustard seed, which a man took, and cast
into his garden; and it grew, and waxed a great tree;
and the fowls of the air lodged in the branches of it.
And again he said, Whereunto shall I liken the king-
dom of God? It is like leaven, which a woman took
and hid in three measures of meal, till the whole was
leavened. And he went through the cities and villages,
teaching, and journeying toward Jerusalem.

The Lord's feeling ran so deep after the incident with the
crippled woman he had healed, he seemed to be trying
harder and harder to make people understand that the
kingdom he preached was not an outer thing governed by
laws, but an inner, living organism capable of growth.
"What is the kingdom of God like? What illustration can I
use to make it plain to you?" And then he likened it to a
mustard seed. And again, "What can I say the kingdom of

God is like?" And then he likened it to the yeast a woman uses in making bread. We can feel his inner tension grow as he nears Jerusalem. Not for fear of what lay ahead, but for sorrow that the time was growing so short. He is expending his energies almost constantly these days, trying, trying to get through to his listeners.

CHAPTER 14
vv. 11 through 14
For whosoever exalteth himself shall be abased; and he that humbleth himself shall be exalted. Then said he also to him that bade him, When thou makest a dinner or a supper, call not thy friends, nor thy brethren, neither thy kinsmen, nor thy rich neighbours; lest they also bid thee again, and a recompence be made thee. But when thou makest a feast, call the poor, the maimed, the lame, the blind: And thou shalt be blessed; for they cannot recompense thee: for thou shalt be recompensed at the resurrection of the just.

Always the glorious paradox of the Gospel. Christ looks through the opposite end of the telescope and sees things and people as they are.

vv. 26, 27
If any man come to me, and hate not his father, and mother, and wife, and children, and brethren, and sisters, yea, and his own life also, he cannot be my disciple. And whosoever doth not bear his cross, and come after me, cannot be my disciple.

Jesus was not about the business of breaking up families. He was about the business of calling men to God, but always, always, he urged them to count the cost of discipleship. These words sound hard. Viewed from *his* vantage point—where the obstacles are *already gone*—they are only freeing.

CHAPTER 15

Note: In this entire chapter, in my opinion, Jesus is attempting, *as the high point of his teaching ministry*, to explain to the people something of the true nature, the seeking, loving heart of his Father. Jesus seems determined to unlock them from their old concept of a vengeful God. The Father *he* comes revealing is one capable of rejoicing when one lost person comes home.

vv. 1 through 7

Then drew near unto him all the publicans and sinners for to hear him. And the Pharisees and scribes murmured, saying, This man receiveth sinners, and eateth with them. And he spake this parable unto them, saying, What man of you, having an hundred sheep, if he lose one of them, doth not leave the ninety and nine in the wilderness, and go after that which is lost, until he find it? And when he hath found it, he layeth it on his shoulders, rejoicing. And when he cometh home, he calleth together his friends and neighbours, saying unto them, Rejoice with me; for I have found my sheep which was lost. I say unto you, that likewise joy shall be in heaven over one sinner that repenteth, more than over ninety and nine just persons, which need no repentance.

Oddly, but not oddly, at the moment of my own turning to Jesus Christ, the old song "The Ninety and Nine" came hauntingly to my mind. I had not heard it in more than twenty-five years. Not since I was a small child and had been popped up on a platform and permitted to sing all the verses. But there it was and there God was and there was I, convinced at last, that his heart had been longing over this one lost sheep. His is that kind of heart. God is not partial to sinners who need repentance over those righteous persons who do not. He is simply *concerned over human need.* And when need is met, he rejoices.

vv. 8 through 10

Either what woman having ten pieces of silver, if she lose one piece, doth not light a candle, and sweep the house, and seek diligently till she find it? And when she hath found it, she calleth her friends and her neighbours together, saying, Rejoice with me; for I have found the piece which I had lost. Likewise, I say

unto you, there is joy in the presence of the angels of
God over one sinner that repenteth.

Here again, the parable of the woman who lost one coin
points to the fact of the searching heart of God. For one
lost child, the Father will pour out his light, will sweep
away obstacles, will deligently seek until that lost child is
found. And, because of *what he is like,* he rejoices. The
woman's distress over the lost coin does not mean that she
did not value the ones she still had.

vv. 25 through 32
Now his elder son was in the field: and as he came
and drew nigh to the house, he heard musick and
dancing. And he called one of the servants and asked
what these things meant. And he said unto him, Thy
brother is come; and thy father hath killed the fatted
calf, because he hath received him safe and sound.
And he was angry, and would not go in: therefore
came his father out, and intreated him. And he an-
swering said to his father, Lo, these many years do I
serve thee, neither transgressed I at any time thy com-
mandment: and yet thou never gavest me a kid, that I
might make merry with my friends: But as soon as
this thy son was come, which hath devoured thy living
with harlots, thou hast killed for him the fatted calf.
And he said unto him, Son, thou art ever with me, and
all that I have is thine. It was meet that we should
make merry, and be glad: for this thy brother was
dead, and is alive again; and was lost, and is found.

Another parable—Jesus' strongest, most poignant, in my
opinion—to show the true nature of the Father's heart. He
is not giving advice to earthly fathers as to how to rear a
son. And although there is much, much here of spiritual
help for those who have strayed away from the Father's
house, for purposes of symmetry and clarity, we will look
only at the marvelously balanced structure of Luke's
Chapter 15: from beginning to end, a characterization of
the *seeking, rejoicing* Father. The ninety-nine sheep who
remained in the shepherd's fold could not argue that they
had been neglected while the shepherd hunted the one that

was lost. Sheep can neither argue nor complain. At least,
not in language to upset people. The nine remaining coins
did not show signs of jealousy because the woman swept
her house and searched until she found the lost coin. Coins
do not show signs. But the elder brother, in the third paral-
lel parable, flared at his father: "Look, how many years
have I slaved for you and never disobeyed a single order of
yours, and yet you have never given me so much as a
young goat, so that I could give my friends a dinner! But
when that son of yours arrives, who has spent all your
money on prostitutes, for *him* you kill the calf we've fat-
tened!" (Phillips). (Notice, when referring to the prodigal
the elder brother did not call him "my brother," but "your
son.") Jesus' fictitious father in the parable went right on
acting and being like his heavenly Father: "My dear son,
you have been with me all the time and everything I have is
yours. But we *had* to celebrate and show our joy. For this
is your brother: I thought he was dead—and he's alive. I
thought he was lost—and he is found." Is the Father really
like this? Yes, he is. Or his own Son was wrong about him.

CHAPTER 16
vv. 24 through 26
*And he cried and said, Father Abraham, have
mercy on me, and send Lazarus, that he may dip the
tip of his finger in water, and cool my tongue; for I
am tormented in this flame. But Abraham said, Son,
remember that thou in thy lifetime receivedst thy good
things, and likewise Lazarus evil things: but now he is
comforted, and thou art tormented. And beside all
this, between us and you there is a great gulf fixed. . . .*

Here we see the frightening consequence of man's stead-
fast refusal to consider the needs of his less fortunate fellow man. So locked was the heart of the rich man that he
was unaware of the beggar, Lazarus, until Lazarus ended
up at God's side and the rich man wallowed in the torment
inevitable to the condition of his selfish heart. The difference between these two men was like a "great gulf
fixed." And Jesus contended that nothing could have shak-
en the rich man from his self-love and indifference.

CHAPTER 17
vv. 5, 6

And the apostles said unto the Lord, Increase our faith. And the Lord said, If ye had faith as a grain of mustard seed, ye might say unto this sycamine tree, Be thou plucked up by the root, and be thou planted in the sea; and it should obey you.

It is not the amount of faith we have—even faith the minuscule size of a mustard seed will do. It's the object of our faith that matters. *Faith in God* can uproot things!

vv. 7 through 10

But which of you, having a servant plowing or feeding cattle, will say unto him by and by, when he is come from the field, Go and sit down to meat? And will not rather say unto him, Make ready wherewith I may sup, and gird thyself, and serve me, till I have eaten and drunken; and afterward thou shalt eat and drink? Doth he thank that servant because he did the things that were commanded him? I trow not. So likewise ye, when ye shall have done all those things which are commanded you, say, We are unprofitable servants: we have done that which was our duty to do.

This passage worried me for a long time. It seemed unlike the God of the parables of the lost sheep, the lost coin and the prodigal. Now, I see it only points up his grace! If this is the way we are, then isn't it all the more amazing that God could rejoice when an "unprofitable servant" comes home?

vv. 15, 16

And one of them, when he saw that he was healed, turned back, and with a loud voice glorified God, And fell down on his face at his feet, giving him thanks: and he was a Samaritan.

Luke must have had a special concern for race relations, for brotherhood. Have you noticed his tendency to point up the good characteristics of Samaritans? The other nine lepers seem to have been Jews. At least this is implied.

Luke calls our attention to the fact that a hated Samaritan was the only one of the ten who bothered to say thank you to Jesus.

CHAPTER 18
vv. 1 through 7

And he spake a parable unto them to this end, that men ought always to pray, and not to faint; Saying, There was in a city a judge, which feared not God, neither regarded man: And there was a widow in that city; and she came unto him, saying, Avenge me of mine adversary. And he would not for a while: but afterward he said within himself, Though I fear not God, nor regard man; Yet because this widow troubleth me, I will avenge her, lest by her continual coming she weary me. And the Lord said, Hear what the unjust judge saith. And shall not God avenge his own elect, which cry day and night unto him, though he bear long with them?

Except for the three clear ones in Chapter 15, to me, most of the parables are difficult. So far, I find myself reading them often and swiftly, attempting an over-all impression—a spiritual "idea" of what he is saying. I don't think Jesus was deliberately obscure. Perhaps it is the "spiritual idea" he wants to convey. Here, what I see is that if man, temperamentally loath to do his duty, does it for a friendless widow just because she is persistent, how much more willing is God to listen to the petitions of his children? He speaks in these chapters of apocalyptic mysteries which could frighten us all. I make no attempt to deal with them, but I do see Jesus reassuring us steadily, by sandwiching in these marvelously quieting concepts of God. Because of what Jesus shows God to be like, I can relax about the things I do not understand.

vv. 10 through 14

Two men went up into the temple to pray; the one a Pharisee, and the other a publican. The Pharisee stood and prayed thus with himself, God, I thank thee, that I am not as other men are, extortioners, unjust, adulterers, or even as this publican. I fast twice in the week, I give tithes of all that I possess. And the publican, standing afar off, would not lift up so much as his eyes unto heaven, but smote upon his breast, saying, God be merciful to me a sinner. I tell you, this man went down to his house justified rather than the other: for every one that exalteth himself shall be abased; and he that humbleth himself shall be exalted.

One fresh insight comes to me here (at least for me it is fresh). So much has been written about the Pharisee and the publican, but what I'd like to add is that all that is required with God is honesty. The publican was honest. The Pharisee was not; either he was not or he had missed the point of humility before God for so long that he had lost sight of what honesty really is. Perhaps he was so neurotic that he really did feel himself better than the publican. I've known men like that. Women too. True honesty before God brings self-knowledge. And self-knowledge in the presence of God brings peace.

CHAPTER 19
vv. 5, 6 (Read vv. 1 through 10.)
And when Jesus came to the place, he looked up, and saw him, and said unto him, Zacharias, make haste, and come down; for to day I must abide at thy house. And he made haste, and came down, and received him joyfully.

I love Zacchaeus. Many people do. I think Luke liked him. But this was far from the case with Zacchaeus' neighbors and the people of Jericho who lived when he lived. They hated him because he was a rich publican. The publican's opportunities to assess great wealth were due to the unjust extortion possible under the system by which the collection of taxes was farmed out to individuals. Zacchaeus was utterly, selfishly practical. He looked out for Zacchaeus. Even to climbing the tree for a better look at Jesus when he passed by. But somewhere in this man was the potential for a true response to love. Jesus sensed it, looked up in the tree where Zacchaeus was perched, and called out to him: "Zacchaeus, make haste, and come down; for today I must abide at thy house!" The insignificant, hated little rich man scurried down out of the tree and "received him joyfully." And Zacchaeus' practical sense did not desert him: even his repentance was practical. He did not just say "I'm sorry, Lord. I'll do better." He laid it on the line: "Behold, Lord, the half of my goods I give to the poor; and if I have taken anything from any man by false accusation, I restore it to him fourfold." With a glad heart and no reservations, Jesus could reply: "This day is salvation come to this house, . . ." The Saviour had come to save that which was lost. And Zacchaeus did not fool around. He was thoroughly lost, but then at the first glimpse of Jesus, he was thoroughly saved!

vv. 37 through 40
And when he was come nigh, even now at the descent of the mount of Olives, the whole multitude of the disciples began to rejoice and praise God with a loud voice for all the mighty works that they had seen; Saying, Blessed be the King that cometh in the name of the Lord: peace in heaven, and glory in the highest. And some of the Pharisees from among the multitude said unto him, Master, rebuke thy disciples. And he answered and said unto them, I tell you that, if these should hold their peace, the stones would immediately cry out.

Jesus is entering Jerusalem at last, on the colt, as was prophesied. How closely God stayed with the established Jewish pattern. How he longed over his chosen people, doing all possible to enable them to feel at home in the revolutionary new kind of Kingdom his Son came proclaiming. And as Jesus rode toward the Holy City, "multitudes of his disciples began to rejoice and praise God with a loud voice for all the mighty works that they had seen." Most of them, perhaps all, did not realize toward what agony he was riding. They were filled with joy and they let it be known in no uncertain terms. They were rowdy—yelling and cheering—and it irked the frustrated Pharisees who had not yet trapped him, so they demanded that Jesus rebuke them for their uncouth behavior. He refused, knowing *where the disciples were* in their understanding. They just had to cheer what they had seen with their own eyes!

There was no longer any point in repressing them. The forces against him were too strong to permit a bloody uprising. The time was too short. Let them cheer.

v. 41
And when he was come near, he beheld the city, and wept over it, . . .

He was near tears as they cheered, knowing what he knew—not about his sufferings ahead, but about the city he loved, the City of God, Jerusalem. There is a point on the road over the Mount of Olives where the city bursts into view. His disciples shouted and cheered, but "when he was come near, he beheld the city, and wept over it."

vv. 47, 48
And he taught daily in the temple. But the chief priests and the scribes and the chief of the people sought to destroy him, And could not find what they might do: for all the people were very attentive to hear him.

The chief priests and the scribes were "people pleasers" first. They were still after him, but they were hard put to it to find a way to destroy him without upsetting the people who were still "very attentive to hear him." Jesus knew this, and took full advantage of it.

CHAPTER 20
vv. 19 and 20
And the chief priests and the scribes the same hour sought to lay hands on him; and they feared the people: for they perceived that he had spoken this parable against them. And they watched him, and sent forth spies, which should feign themselves just men, that they might take hold of his words, that so they might deliver him unto the power and authority of the governor.

There could be no doubt even to the darkened minds of the chief priests and the scribes that Jesus directed this

stinging parable about the absentee vineyard owner at
them. Their only recourse was to double their efforts to
trap him. To double their watch on him. To increase the
number of spies who were to pass themselves off as "just
men" so that they might "deliver him unto the power and
authority of the governor." They were closing in on him
swiftly, time ran short, the questions became more astute,
trickier than ever before. In the presence of his majesty
and dignity, the questions became more superficial *seeming,* but each one bore barbs to hook him, to force him to
play into their determined hands.

vv. 45, 46, 47
*Then in the audience of all the people he said unto
his disciples, Beware of the scribes, which desire to
walk in long robes, and love greetings in the markets,
and the highest seats in the synagogues, and the chief
rooms at feasts; Which devour widows' houses, and
for a shew make long prayers: the same shall receive
greater damnation.*

He was walking steadfastly into their trap, but he was
still their judge! They did not know it, but he was still, as
he had been from the beginning, in charge of their souls.

CHAPTER 21
vv. 37, 38
*And in the day time he was teaching in the temple;
and at night he went out, and abode in the mount
that is called the mount of Olives. And all the people
came early in the morning to him in the temple, for
to hear him.*

From Sunday to Thursday of Holy Week, "in the day
time he was [still] teaching in the temple. . . ." He would be
about his father's business until the last minute. At night he
went, presumably with his disciples, to the Mount of Olives
to rest. But always, early the next day, the people were in
the temple waiting for him to begin teaching again. And to
the very last day, he was there.

CHAPTER 22
vv. 15 through 23

And he said unto them, With desire I have desired to eat this passover with you before I suffer: For I say unto you, I will not any more eat thereof, until it be fulfilled in the kingdom of God. And he took the cup, and gave thanks, and said, Take this, and divide it among yourselves: For I say unto you, I will not drink of the fruit of the vine, until the kingdom of God shall come. And he took bread, and gave thanks, and brake it, and gave unto them, saying, This is my body which is given for you: this do in remembrance of me. Likewise also the cup after supper, saying, This cup is the new testament in my blood, which is shed for you. But, behold, the hand of him that betrayeth me is with me on the table. And truly the Son of man goeth, as it was determined: but woe unto that man by whom he is betrayed! And they began to enquire among themselves, which of them it was that should do this thing.

He "desired" to eat this last Passover feast with them before he suffered. Judas had made his deal and Jesus knew it because he knew Judas. He would not eat again with them "until it be fulfilled in the kingdom of God." Before the cup and the bread, he *gave thanks.* By all he must suffer, he could be thankful because his act would usher in the Kingdom on earth, and his beloved disciples would benefit. How he loved them. A "new testament"—a new covenant from God—was at hand. This one eternal in the heavens and on the earth. He longed to be remembered by them when they would again repeat this supper after he was gone. And Judas was still at the table! *He loved Judas, too.* (Luke does not say Judas fled into the darkness, but, from the other accounts, we know Judas left soon after this.)

v. 24

And there was also a strife among them, which of them should be accounted the greatest.

This is difficult to believe, but in the midst of this deeply meaningful, sorrowful meal together, a wrangle broke out on the same old note: Who is going to be the greatest in the

kingdom? It is obvious that none of the men yet believed
Jesus would go through with death.

vv. 31, 32

*And the Lord said, Simon, Simon, behold, Satan
hath desired to have you, that he may sift you as
wheat: But I have prayed for thee, that thy faith fail
not: and when thou art converted, strengthen thy
brethren.*

In spite of their crassness, the Lord had messages of love
and caring for them. He knew the men had not been truly
converted to his way. Not yet. They loved him as their
Master, but even though he knew he had influenced their
thinking, a conversion that would last would not be possible without the power of the Holy Spirit within each man.
And Pentecost had not happened yet. He must suffer first.

vv. 35 through 38

*And he said unto them, When I sent you without
purse, and scrip, and shoes, lacked ye any thing? And
they said, Nothing. Then said he unto them, But now,
he that hath a purse, let him take it, and likewise his
scrip: and he that hath no sword, let him sell his garment, and buy one. For I say unto you, that this that
is written must yet be accomplished in me, And he
was reckoned among the transgressors: for the things
concerning me have an end. And they said, Lord, behold, here are two swords. And he said unto them, It
is enough.*

A warning to get ready for danger ahead. But *not* to re
sist it by force. His words "It is enough" dismiss the whole
idea of resistance. Two swords for the whole group would
be enough to protect them against unexpected danger from
wild animals, and so forth, but at the betrayal a short time
later, Jesus made it plain that he did not operate by the
sword.

vv. 50, 51

*And one of them smote the servant of the high
priest, and cut off his right ear. And Jesus answered*

and said, Suffer ye thus far. And he touched his ear,
and healed him.

Jesus healed the damaged ear, saying: "That will do!"
(Phillips). His was the way of peace, not the sword, where
resistance was concerned. (John says it was Peter who
drew his sword and cut off the servant, Malchus' ear.)

vv. 60, 61, 62
And Peter said, Man, I know not what thou sayest.
And immediately, while he yet spake, the cock crew.
And the Lord turned, and looked upon Peter. . . . And
Peter went out, and wept bitterly.

When the rooster crowed, Peter was still in the process
of denying Jesus for the third time. The words were not yet
out of his mouth. The sound of the cock crowing must
have been like a crash against his heart. And at the sound,
Jesus, who was being led past him, bound with ropes,
turned and *looked upon Peter*. He spoke no word of condemnation to his unstable disciple. *He just looked at him.*
There was no need for words. That look did it. Peter went
out and wept bitterly. Over his weeping, he could hear the
sounds of the mockery and the spitting and the crack and
slap of their hands as they struck his Master repeatedly in
the face. He was out of Jesus' sight, but he would never
forget that *look*.

CHAPTER 23
vv. 4 through 9
Then said Pilate to the chief priests and to the peo-
ple, I find no fault in this man. And they were the
more fierce, saying, He stirreth up the people, teaching
throughout all Jewry, beginning from Galilee to this
place. When Pilate heard of Galilee, he asked whether
the man were a Galilaean. And as soon as he knew
that he belonged unto Herod's jurisdiction, he sent
him to Herod, who himself also was at Jerusalem at
that time. And when Herod saw Jesus, he was exceed-
ing glad: for he was desirous to see him of a long sea-
son, because he had heard many things of him; and he
hoped to have seen some miracle done by him. Then

he questioned with him in many words; but he answered him nothing.

Jesus stands, a moral, mental and spiritual giant alongside Pilate and Herod. He dwarfs them in every way, showing Pilate as evasive and cowardly; Herod as downright silly, wanting to be entertained, hoping to see him perform a miracle!

v. 27
And there followed him a great company of people, and of women, which also bewailed and lamented him.

Only Luke mentions that the women who loved him walked the Via Dolorosa with him as he stumbled toward Calvary.

vv. 28 through 31
But Jesus turning unto them said, Daughters of Jerusalem, weep not for me, but weep for yourselves, and for your children. For, behold, the days are coming, in the which they shall say, Blessed are the barren, and the wombs that never bare, and the paps which never gave suck. Then shall they begin to say to the mountains, Fall on us; and to the hills, Cover us. For if they do these things in a green tree, what shall be done in the dry?

And as always, even on this last torturous walk, he was teaching and warning.

vv. 32 through 34
And there were also two other, malefactors, led with him to be put to death. And when they were come to the place, which is called Calvary, there they crucified him, and the malefactors, one on the right hand, and the other on the left. Then said Jesus, Father, forgive them; for they know not what they do. And they parted his raiment, and cast lots.

Two criminals went with him to their deaths, one hung on his right hand and one on his left. At this point perhaps the one criminal was silent, except for sharp cries of pain as the nails pierced his flesh and the long cry of unbelief at the amount of total pain when the weight of his body sagged against the nails. The other criminal hung there cursing and railing—not at his crucifiers, but at Jesus.

Jesus was praying for the forgiveness of his tormentors, and a manifestation of love like this evokes either curses or submission.

v. 35

And the people stood beholding. And the rulers also with them derided him, saying, He saved others; let him save himself, if he be Christ, the chosen of God.

His old antagonists, the rulers, were there too, enjoying their "victory" to the end. Still heckling him.

vv. 39 through 43

And one of the malefactors which were hanged railed on him, saying, If thou be Christ, save thyself and us. But the other answering rebuked him, saying, Dost not thou fear God, seeing thou art in the same condemnation? And we indeed justly; for we receive the due reward of our deeds: but this man hath done nothing amiss. And he said unto Jesus, Lord, remember me when thou comest into thy kingdom. And Jesus said unto him, Verily I say unto thee, Today shalt thou be with me in paradise.

The repentant thief followed no ritual, received no baptism, became a member of no church, memorized no Scripture verses, kept no regular quiet times. He just turned to Jesus with an open, contrite heart and asked to be remembered. Jesus' forgiving spirit, even on his Cross, had won the criminal's heart.

CHAPTER 24
vv. 6 through 12

He is not here, but is risen: remember how he spake unto you when he was yet in Galilee, Saying, The Son of man must be delivered into the hands of sinful men, and be crucified, and the third day rise

*again. And they remembered his words, And returned
from the sepulchre, and told all these things unto the
eleven, and to all the rest. It was Mary Magdalene,
and Joanna, and Mary the mother of James, and other
women that were with them, which told these things
unto the apostles. And their words seemed to them as
idle tales, and they believed them not. Then arose
Peter, and ran unto the sepulchre; and stooping down,
he beheld the linen clothes laid by themselves, and departed, wondering in himself at that which was come
to pass.*

Luke reports two angels at the empty tomb. No matter
the number. What they said to the grieving women is the
important thing: "Why seek ye the living among the dead?"
And then they reminded Mary of Magdala and Mary, the
mother of James, and their friends that Jesus had told them
he would be crucified and that on the third day he would
rise again. With this prod from the angels, they remembered his words! Suddenly it was all making sense to them,
and they ran to tell the eleven remaining disciples. Only
Peter gave enough credence to their "idle tales" to run to
the tomb to see for himself. (John writes that he ran with
them, but Luke does not report this.) Peter seems still a
touch skeptical. Unlike the women who believed, he merely
wonders. Did the disciples' egos, block their believing?
After all, *they* were the men whom he had chosen by name
to be his intimates. The women had followed Jesus of their
own accord, out of gratitude for what he had done for
them. There is no record that he cast any devils out of
Peter or James or John or any of the Twelve. He chose
them, and in their still unregenerate states, this must have
gone to their heads.

vv. 13 through 26
  *And, behold, two of them went that same day to a
village called Emmaus, which was from Jerusalem
about threescore furlongs. And they talked together of
all these things which had happened. And it came to
pass, that, while they communed together and reasoned, Jesus himself drew near, and went with them.
But their eyes were holden that they should not know*

*him. And he said unto them, What manner of com-
munications are these that ye have one to another, as
ye walk, and are sad? And the one of them, whose
name was Cleopas, answering said unto him, Art thou
only a stranger in Jerusalem, and hast not known the
things which are come to pass there in these days?
And he said unto them, What things? And they said
unto him, Concerning Jesus of Nazareth, which was a
prophet mighty in deed and word before God and all
the people: And how the chief priests and our rulers
delivered him to be condemned to death, and have
crucified him. But we trusted that it had been he
which should have redeemed Israel: and beside all
this, to day is the third day since these things were
done. Yea, and certain women also of our company
made us astonished, which were early at the sepulchre;
And when they found not his body, they came saying,
that they had also seen a vision of angels, which said
that he was alive. And certain of them which were
with us went to the sepulchre, and found it even so as
the women had said: but him they saw not. Then he
said unto them, O fools, and slow of heart to believe
all that the prophets have spoken: Ought not Christ to
have suffered these things, and to enter into his glory?*

These two disciples were not of the original Twelve, but
evidently, they were close, and present with the others,
when the women came to tell them the Lord was risen.
Their horror at what had happened to him must have
blinded their eyes. This and their own personal disappointment that they would not be among his intimates when he
set up his kingdom. They could never be now. Their king
had gone down to defeat. These few facts robbed them of
their little faith." Peter and John had not actually seen
Jesus when they ran to the Sepulcher to check out the
women's story, and the men had all accepted the fact of
defeat.

In verse 26 Jesus said a most revealing thing to them:
"Ought not Christ to have suffered these things . . .?" To
me, that is one of the most poignant and truest character-
izations of God! Wasn't he saying: "Could I, the Son of the
God who loves all of you so much, do *any less* than I did?"

vv. 27 through 32

And beginning at Moses and all the prophets, he expounded unto them in all the scriptures the things concerning himself. And they drew nigh unto the village, whither they went: and he made as though he would have gone further. But they constrained him, saying, Abide with us: for it is toward evening, and the day is far spent. And he went in to tarry with them. And it came to pass, as he sat at meat with them, he took bread, and blessed it, and brake, and gave to them. And their eyes were opened, and they knew him; and he vanished out of their sight. And they said one to another, Did not our heart burn within us, while he talked with us by the way, and while he opened to us the scriptures?

The disciples en route to Emmaus were not of the Twelve, but they had heard in detail of how he broke bread during the Last Supper and called it his body that would be broken for them. When he took the bread that night at dinner with them, and blessed it and broke it—they knew him. That was all he was after—*recognition*. Once they recognized him as their Lord, he vanished. Their hearts had burned within them as he opened the Scriptures on the way to Emmaus, but evidently that was not enough to cause them to know him. The broken bread did it.

vv. 33 through 43

And they rose up the same hour, and returned to Jerusalem, and found the eleven gathered together, and them that were with them, Saying, The Lord is risen indeed, and hath appeared to Simon. And they told what things were done in the way, and how he was known of them in breaking of bread. And as they thus spake, Jesus himself stood in the midst of them, and saith unto them, Peace be unto you. But they were terrified and affrighted, and supposed that they had seen a spirit. And he said unto them, Why are ye troubled? and why do thoughts arise in your hearts? Behold my hands and my feet, that it is I myself: handle me, and see; for a spirit hath not flesh and bones,

*as ye see me have. And when he had thus spoken, he
shewed them his hands and his feet. And while they
yet believed not for joy, and wondered, he said unto
them, Have ye here any meat? And they gave him a
piece of a broiled fish, and of an honeycomb. And he
took it, and did eat before them.*

Now, they were excited and hurried back to find the
other men. Together again, they all began comparing
stories, wondering, analyzing, theorizing. And as they
talked, Jesus himself stood there among them and said:
"Peace be unto you." And once more, he did all he could
do to dispel their doubts. Specifically, he ate something.
Would a mere spirit eat food?

v. 45
*Then opened he their understanding, that they
might understand the scriptures.*

I have always been struck with the mystery of this verse.
How did he open their understanding? It is not for us to
know; at least, it is not vital that we know. But we can suppose he did it as he does it now with us—through the Holy
Spirit. For that brief time with him, they must somehow
have had access to the Spirit from within, as they all had
after Pentecost. As we all have now.

vv. 49 through 53
*And, behold, I send the promise of my Father upon
you: but tarry ye in the city of Jerusalem, until ye be
endued with power from on high. And he led them
out as far as to Bethany, and he lifted up his hands,
and blessed them. And it came to pass, while he
blessed them, he was parted from them, and carried
up into heaven. And they worshipped him, and returned to Jerusalem with great joy: And were continually in the temple, praising and blessing God. Amen.*

Luke ends his Gospel on a continuing note. The end of
the written account is in truth, a beginning. Since Luke is
also the writer of Acts, he has made the link here. Jesus
promises them they will be "endued with power from on

high" if they will follow his instructions and tarry in Jerusalem—together. And leaving them, he led them out as far as their old familiar resting place at Bethany. He led them and blessed them and as he was blessing them, his hands lifted up, he was parted from them—back to his Father in heaven.

The disciples did not weep and wail and shout for his return. "They worshipped him, and returned to Jerusalem with great joy . . ."! And were continually in the temple, after that, praising God and rejoicing, their expectations high.

SAINT JOHN

CHAPTER 1
vv. 1, 2

*In the beginning was the Word, and the Word was
with God, and the Word was God. The same was in
the beginning with God.*

There is light from many of the newer translations on
these first two verses, but none equals the King James version in pure poetry. I am convinced no one will ever write
a more perfect sentence than the sentence we know as the
first verse of this Gospel. The second verse emphasizes
what has already been almost perfectly said, and to me, this
is the key to John's entire Gospel: He wants it made very,
very clear at the outset that *Jesus Christ is central.* That He
is not, in any way, less than God himself. There was Someone else there with the Father "in the beginning." The first
verse of the Gospel of John linked with verse 26 of the first
chapter of Genesis makes a totally believable whole. Look
at them together:

"In the beginning was the Word, and the Word was
with God, and the word was God" (John 1:1).
"And God said, Let *us* make man in our image, after
our likeness" (Genesis 1:26). (Author's italics.)

The two verses could have been written by the same person as far as the literary beauty and simplicity and phrasing
go. And to me, they are marvelously melded in meaning.
They do not explain redemption, but they put God within
reach by making it clear that there *was* Someone else there
"in the beginning" who could come to us in Person. Someone equal with God, the Creator.

v. 3

*All things were made by him: and without him was
not any thing made that was made.*

The poetry still stands up here: "All things were made
by him: and without him was not any thing made that was
made." There will never be a more musical sentence. But
most important, we are permitted, right at the very beginning of John's account, to rest everything we are on the
fact that this Man about whom he will be writing was *not*
just another great teacher. He was not only "with God," he
was God. And, what's more, he was the Creator God: ". . .
without him was not any thing made that was made."
Whatever this God-Man had to say was *truth*. Not because
of his undeniably superior intellect, but because of *who he
was!* John writes from the standpoint of Hebrew philosophy, beginning with the fact of God. With the Hebrew
mind there was no need to prove God, as with the Greek
mind. One either believes or does not believe in a Supreme
Being of some kind. John's purpose is not to prove God.
He begins with that premise as established. His purpose *is
to make it as clear as possible that God revealed himself as
he really is in Jesus of Nazareth.*

vv. 4, 5

*In him was life; and the life was the light of men.
And the light shineth in darkness; and the darkness
comprehended it not.*

The poetry goes on as John equates life with light. There
is no possible way to experience entire truth without this
"life" within us. Half truth, yes. Great learning, yes. But
not entire truth. This life of Christ "still shines in the darkness and the darkness has never put it out" (Phillips). It
can never be put out. John is offering absolute assurance:
There is the fact of God, the fact of Christ, and the fact of
the light he brings which no amount of human darkness
can extinguish.

vv. 6 through 18

*There was a man sent from God, whose name was
John. The same came for a witness, to bear witness of*

*the Light, that all men through him might believe. He
was not that Light, but was sent to bear witness of that
Light. That was the true Light, which lighteth every
man that cometh into the world. He was in the world,
and the world was made by him, and the world knew
him not. He came unto his own, and his own received
him not. But as many as received him, to them gave
he power to become the sons of God, even to them
that believe on his name: Which were born, not of
blood, nor of the will of the flesh, nor of the will of
man, but of God. And the Word was made flesh, and
dwelt among us, (and we beheld his glory, the glory as
of the only begotten of the Father), full of grace and
truth. John bare witness of him, and cried, saying, This
was he of whom I spake, He that cometh after me is
preferred before me: for he was before me. And of his
fulness have all we received, and grace for grace. For
the law was given by Moses, but grace and truth came
by Jesus Christ. No man hath seen God at any time;
the only begotten Son, which is in the bosom of the
Father, he hath declared him.*

Before John tells the story of the ministry of John the
Baptist, he nails down his premise of truth with long, shining nails. There was a man named John who came announcing the Light, but John was not the Light. The world
did not recognize this Light, the One who *was* this Light,
but he was already in the world—the Son of God *had* come.
And everyone who did recognize him was enabled to become a son of God also. Farfetched? John doesn't mind
that. He is declaring truth and truth will defend itself.
Truth will defend *Himself.* And in verse 14 (which to me
could follow 1 and 2 with perfect continuity) he tells us
who this was who was with God in the beginning. He iden-
tifies that Word who "was with God"—"who *was* God." It
would seem John had reached his crescendo when he de-
clares: "And the Word was made flesh, and dwelt among
us, (and we beheld his glory, the glory as of the only begotten of the Father,) full of grace and truth." Whoever this
was with God in the beginning had come to earth to live
among us! And he was full not only of grace, but of truth.
"And we beheld his glory, . . ." John, the writer, *saw* him.

John the Baptist was proclaiming him to be "before him" because he *was* "in the beginning" with God. It seems as though John, the author of the Gospel, is unable for a little while longer to launch into the actual narrative. "One more thing, I must tell you," he appears to be saying, "and that is that 'no man hath seen God at any time, but the only begotten Son . . . (this Jesus of Nazareth, my Master), *he hath declared him'!*" Another crescendo following a crescendo. There is no limit to them for John. He has *seen* Truth Himself—all the high barred gates have been flung open! The mounting crescendos can go on and on now, through eternity. His Master, Jesus Christ, has come to make God known to all men. Moses brought the law, but Christ has come to make it possible—by the very grace he brings—to keep that law. The lowliest man or woman can now *know* the God of Israel! Can know his intentions toward us, can know his heart, can begin to understand his ways.

vv. 29
The next day John seeth Jesus coming unto him, and saith, Behold the Lamb of God, which taketh away the sin of the world.

The climactic moment of the lonely, isolated, wholly dedicated life of Elisabeth's son, John, has come. He sees Jesus walking toward him through the crowd, and shouts: "Behold the Lamb of God, which taketh away the sin of the world"! No more need for sacrificial lambs on the altar of the Lord. Jesus has come; he who *has been* the sacrificial lamb since the foundation of the world. He who has been ". . . slain from the foundation of the world" (Revelations 13:8). It has all been in God's plan from the beginning. The sin of mankind came as no surprise to the Lord God. When he created, he already had redemption under way!

vv. 35 through 37
Again the next day after John stood, and two of his disciples; And looking upon Jesus as he walked, he saith, Behold the Lamb of God! And the two disciples heard him speak, and they followed Jesus.

Talking with two of his own disciples, John the Baptist, ". . . looking upon Jesus as he walked, . . . saith, Behold the Lamb of God!" Repeating himself for the sake of his own disciples, wanting so much for them to know the truth of what he had been telling them about the One who would come to save Israel from her sins. Wanting to impress upon them that he, their master, John, was *not* the Messiah, but that the Messiah, Jesus, was now among them. In those days, a teacher's reputation was mainly dependent upon the *loyalty* of the men who followed him. John risked this, so convinced was he of the *truth* God had taught him during those years alone in the wilderness. In verse 37, we see that John's two disciples left him to follow Jesus. Humanly speaking, this would be hard for a man to take. With John the Baptist, it meant he had taught his disciples well. They "heard him speak," they got his message and followed *Jesus.*

vv. 45 through 50

Philip findeth Nathanael, and saith unto him, We have found him, of whom Moses in the law, and the prophets, did write, Jesus of Nazareth, the son of Joseph. And Nathanael said unto him, Can there any good thing come out of Nazareth? Philip saith unto him, Come and see. Jesus saw Nathanael coming to him, and saith of him, Behold an Israelite indeed, in whom is no guile! Nathanael saith unto him, Whence knowest thou me? Jesus answered and said unto him, Before that Philip called thee, when thou wast under the fig tree, I saw thee. Nathanael answered and saith unto him, Rabbi, thou art the Son of God; thou art the King of Israel. Jesus answered, and said unto him, Because I said unto thee, I saw thee under the fig tree, believest thou? thou shalt see greater things than these.

John, the evangelist, writes of one provocative incident when Jesus is calling his disciples not mentioned in the other three Gospel accounts. The men are excited: Andrew ran to call his brother, Simon; Philip ran to call his friend, Nathanael. And when he learned from Philip that he had found "him of whom Moses in the law, and the prophets, did write" and that he was Jesus of Nazareth, the son of Joseph, Nathanael made what can be interpreted as a smart-alecky, sarcastic remark: "Can there any good thing come out of Nazareth?" In fact, this has, with usage, become a sarcastic question. Or perhaps it was considered so then. Still, Jesus said of Nathanael, "Behold an Israelite indeed in whom is no guile!" Nathanael's question did not sound one bit guileless. *But Jesus knew Nathanael.* The Master never acted or reacted on mere words. Always he looked beneath the words at the man. Evidently Nathanael *was* guileless. Nazareth was an obscure little hill country town. No one of any note had ever come from there. To me, Nathanael was simply asking a natural question.

In verses 49 and 50, we need to think ahead to Peter's declaration that Jesus was the Christ, the Son of God. Why is that given more importance—treated usually, as the first time any man really had the Lord's identity straight? It occurs to me that because of what Jesus replied to Nathanael when he declared him right away to be the Son of God, the King of Israel, that Jesus here is merely letting it be known that he *does* see into not only the heart, but the intelligence and judgment of a man. Obviously, he knew that his new disciple, Nathanael, was not only guileless, but impulsive. Jesus recommended that Nathanael wait a while and really see what was up ahead before jumping to conclusions concerning the Master's identity. The Lord is always interested in our believing with our *whole* hearts.

CHAPTER 2
vv. 8 through 11

And he saith unto them, Draw out now, and bear unto the governor of the feast. And they bare it. When the ruler of the feast had tasted the water that was made wine, and knew not whence it was: (but the servants which drew the water knew;) the governor of the feast called the bridegroom, And saith unto him, Every man at the beginning doth set forth good wine; and when men have well drunk, then that which is worse: but thou hast kept the good wine until now. This beginning of miracles did Jesus in Cana of Galilee, and manifested forth his glory; and his disciples believed on him.

The wine episode at the marriage feast in Cana has caused no end of confusion. That Jesus turned the water into wine is fact, and John emphasizes it. I think it is intended to be neither an aid nor a stumbling block for those who choose to fight the liquor interests. There is nothing so superficial here. I do not suggest that I understand all there is to understand about the use of this incident, but it is the first recorded miracle of Jesus in John and it should not be dodged. Troubling questions arise: Was it worthy of the Son of God that his first miracle should be the mere relieving of a social embarrassment at a wedding feast? Does it jibe with his usual reluctance to work miracles for the sake of working miracles? Was it sensible to have made *so much* wine? More than one hundred gallons? I don't think John invented the whole episode. I believe it happened as he told it. John was there. For me, the story has these values: It clearly demonstrates the difference between the attitude toward life Jesus held and the attitude toward life which John the Baptist held. Jesus' is the New Testament view, John's the Old. From this incident, we see that Jesus had come to mingle with men and women in the daily round, the ordinary events of their lives. It shows me in a remarkable way the gracious condescension of the Son of God. It is also true that in the Old Testament, wine symbolizes reconciliation with God (Isaiah 55:1): "Ho, everyone that thirsteth, come ye to the waters, and he that hath no money; come ye, buy and eat; yea, come, buy wine and milk without money and without price." And Isaiah 25:6: "And in this mountain shall the Lord of hosts make unto all people a feast of fat things, a feast of wines on the lees, . . ." Clearly, Isaiah is intimating the coming of a New Order. The New Order came with Jesus, and so the symbol of wine would have had definite spiritual meaning for the Jews at the wedding feast. It could well have been regarded as a sign that the Kingdom of God had come in the Person and activity of Jesus. I cannot help thinking too, of Jesus' use of wine as the symbol of his own blood to be shed. The time was coming, even though this miracle took place at the outset of his ministry, when Christ's atoning death would replace the ancient Jewish rites. The water of Judaism had been replaced by the wine of the Gospel. And

perhaps he made such a quantity of wine to show us that
with him no one was ever going to be stinted! Jesus came
to give *abundance*.

v. 15

*And when he had made a scourge of small cords, he
drove them all out of the temple, and the sheep, and
the oxen; and poured out the changers' money, and
overthrew the tables; . . .*

I don't even try to understand this incident in relation to
human anger. It wasn't. It was perhaps the only true righteous indignation ever experienced on the earth. The point
is not whether it is "kind" to do what Jesus did. We need
make no apologies. We need only to *try* to see at least
dimly, how man's desecration of the holy affects God.

CHAPTER 3
vv. 1 through 3

*There was a man of the Pharisees, named Nicode-
mus, a ruler of the Jews: The same came to Jesus by
night, and said unto him, Rabbi, we know that thou
art a teacher come from God: for no man can do
these miracles that thou doest except God be with
him. Jesus answered and said unto him, Verily, verily,
I say unto thee, Except a man be born again, he cannot see the kingdom of God.*

The learned man, Nicodemus, was all set to have a profound theological discussion with Jesus as one rabbi to another. Jesus made anything resembling a merely academic
conversation impossible by stating flatly, at the outset of
their talk, that until a man is born all over again, he cannot
even *see* the Kingdom of God!

v. 8

*The wind bloweth where it listeth, and thou hearest
the sound thereof, but canst not tell whence it cometh,
and whither it goeth: so is every one that is born of
the Spirit.*

As I write, the tassels of Spanish moss on the live oaks outside my room are hanging straight and motionless. There is no perceptible sign of any wind stirring. Half an hour ago, the moss was whipping wildly in a high wind off the ocean as the tide changed. Now, these few lines later, I can see one and then two strands of gray moss move, hang limp a moment, then move again. We can only tell the wind is blowing by the movement we see in its path. *There are no pat answers in the Kingdom of God.*

vv. 16, 17
For God so loved the world, that he gave his only begotten Son, that whosoever believeth in him should not perish, but have everlasting life. For God sent not his Son into the world to condemn the world; but that the world through him might be saved.

Dr. E. Stanley Jones called John 3:16: "The twenty-five most important words in history." They are. But I am seeing that we need verse 17 for clarity, for verification of verse 16. How far away we have wandered when our "religion" tends to cause us to look for faults, to condemn. Jesus reminded us constantly that the Son of God came, not to condemn the world, but to save it. Love never condemns. It does not merely condone, either. It saves.

vv. 18, 19
He that believeth on him is not condemned: but he that believeth not is condemned already, because he hath not believed in the name of the only begotten Son of God. And this is the condemnation, that light is come into the world, and men loved darkness rather than light, because their deeds were evil.

Man has already condemned himself by choosing darkness. He needs no further condemnation, but he does need saving love.

v. 35
The Father loveth the Son, and hath given all things into his hand.

This truth is the greatest relief I know.

CHAPTER 4
v. 4
And he must needs go through Samaria.

It is as though he had no choice. There was so much to teach *us* by going through Samaria.

vv. 6 through 8
Now Jacob's well was there. Jesus therefore, being wearied with his journey, sat thus on the well: and it was about the sixth hour. There cometh a woman of Samaria to draw water: Jesus saith unto her, Give me to drink. (For his disciples were gone away unto the city to buy meat.)

Jesus met the woman alone. His disciples had gone shopping. It is just as well. They could never have done what he did: place himself in the position of having to ask this outcast woman for a favor. "Please give me a drink" (Phillips).

v. 9
Then saith the woman of Samaria unto him, How is it that thou, being a Jew, askest drink of me, which am a woman of Samaria? for the Jews have no dealings with the Samaritans.

I don't think the Samaritan woman was dodging any issues yet. She was simply a woman who came right out and said what she thought, and it was unheard of for a Jew to ask a favor of or even to speak to a Samaritan. Our race barriers pale by comparison.

v. 10
Jesus answered and said unto her, If thou knewest the gift of God, and who it is that saith to thee, Give me to drink; thou wouldest have asked of him, and he would have given thee living water.

As always, Jesus took advantage of every opening to
prick the interest.

v. 11
*The woman saith unto him, Sir, thou hast nothing
to draw with, and the well is deep: from whence then
hast thou that living water?*

She may be hedging a bit here, but I don't think so.
Plainly, he had no bucket. How could he possibly give her
living water? Remember, this woman was—like too many
people—a literalist.

v. 12
*Art thou greater than our father Jacob, which gave
us the well, and drank thereof himself, and his children, and his cattle?*

She is sarcastic here, growing a touch uneasy.

vv. 13 through 15
*Jesus answered and said unto her, Whosoever drink-
eth of this water shall thirst again: But whosoever
drinketh of the water that I shall give him shall never
thirst; but the water that I shall give him shall be in
him a well of water springing up into everlasting life.
The woman saith unto him, Sir, give me this water,
that I thirst not, neither come hither to draw.*

She grabbed at his offer, but he did not settle for her impulsive request for the living water he spoke of. He knew
her motives were mixed. After all, she came regularly to
the well at a time of day when the other women were *not*
there. She had the kind of reputation that forces a woman
to avoid other women when possible. And *if* this strange
Man could give her water that would so satisfy her thirst
she would never have to come to the well again, it would
be fine.

vv. 16 through 24
*Jesus saith unto her, Go, call thy husband, and
come hither. The woman answered and said, I have no*

husband. Jesus said unto her, Thou hast well said, I have no husband: For thou hast had five husbands; and he whom thou now hast is not thy husband: in that saidst thou truly. The woman saith unto him, Sir, I perceive that thou art a prophet. Our fathers worshipped in this mountain; and ye say, that in Jerusalem is the place where men ought to worship. Jesus saith unto her, Woman, believe me, the hour cometh, when ye shall neither in this mountain, nor yet at Jerusalem, worship the Father. Ye worship ye know not what: we know what we worship: for salvation is of the Jews. But the hour cometh, and now is, when the true worshippers shall worship the Father in spirit and in truth: for the Father seeketh such to worship him. God is a Spirit: and they that worship him must worship him in spirit and in truth.

His abrupt change of subject must have startled the woman. Suddenly, he was hitting a nerve. He shocked her, caught her off guard, so that she blurted out the truth to him. And he must have seen her long subdued conscience, still alive and able to feel guilt—thereby able to receive help. But there was that one moment of openness, and then her defenses flew back up, as she parried: " 'I can see that you're a prophet! Now our ancestors worshipped on this hillside, but you Jews say that Jerusalem is the place where men ought to worship—' " (Phillips transates this as a broken speech, with Jesus interrupting her.) " 'Believe me,' returned Jesus, 'the time is coming when worshipping the Father will not be a matter of "on this hillside" or "in Jerusalem" . . . God is Spirit, and those who worship him can only worship in spirit and in reality' " (Phillips). It must have "gotten to her"; perhaps she felt included for the first time, when Jesus told her the Father was seeking those who would be willing to worship him freely in spirit and reality —*truth*.

v. 25
The woman saith unto him, I know that Messias cometh, which is called Christ: when he is come, he will tell us all things.

He touched a responsive place in her because immediately she mentioned the coming of the Messiah.

vv. 26 through 29

Jesus saith unto her, I that speak unto thee am he. And upon this came his disciples, and marvelled that he talked with the woman: yet no man said, What seekest thou? or, Why talkest thou with her? The woman then left her waterpot, and went her way into the city, and saith to the men, Come, see a man, which told me all things that ever I did: is not this the Christ?

His simple, profound reply is the only place in the New Testament to my knowledge where—in so many exact words—he says he is the Christ. Immediately, the sinful woman—the last person on earth the religionists would select to be an evangel—ran to tell that she had met the Messiah! Her light was pale; she believed in him only because he had told her about herself, *but she believed.*

vv. 39 through 41

And many of the Samaritans of that city believed on him for the saying of the woman, which testified, He told me all that ever I did. So when the Samaritans were come unto him, they besought him that he would tarry with them: and he abode there two days. And many more believed because of his own word; . . .

And many Samaritans believed because of her. The race barriers even went down so that they invited Jesus and his men—Jews—to stay two days with them! As with Mary of Magdala and the prodigal and all of us who know the immensity of our need, this woman's word held added weight. And once more there was rejoicing in heaven because a few more lost sheep came home. "Christ Jesus came into this world to *save* sinners. . . ." Not to condemn.

CHAPTER 5
v. 18

Therefore the Jews sought the more to kill him, because he not only had broken the sabbath, but said

*also that God was his Father, making himself equal
with God.*

What really stirred the Pharisees to fury was this hill-
country itinerant preacher who dared to make himself
equal with the God of Israel. Their conditioning had blinded their minds to receive any *new truth* about the God of
their father Abraham. Sound familiar?

v. 22
*For the Father judgeth no man, but hath committed
all judgment unto the Son:*

The Great Relief again. And how it must have rocked
the learned Jews! This "upstart" would be sitting in judgment upon *them?* To their ears, blasphemy, pure and simple. His pomposity must be brought to an end by any available means.

CHAPTER 6
vv. 14, 15
*Then those men, when they had seen the miracle
that Jesus did, said, This is of a truth that prophet that
should come into the world. When Jesus therefore
perceived that they would come and take him by
force, to make him a king, he departed again into a
mountain himself alone.*

When Jesus fed the multitude on this occasion, John tells
us that the crowd went wild. Not in so many words are we
told, but he tells us by way of Jesus' decision: "Then Jesus,
realizing that they were going to carry him off and make
him their king, retired once more to the hillside quite
alone" (Phillips). His time had not yet come. *And* an
earthly kingdom was *not* his purpose.

vv. 24 through 26
*When the people therefore saw that Jesus was not
there, neither his disciples, they also took shipping,
and came to Capernaum, seeking for Jesus. And when
they had found him on the other side of the sea, they
said unto him, Rabbi, when camest thou hither? Jesus*

answered them and said, Verily, verily, I say unto you,
Ye seek me, not because ye saw the miracles, but be-
cause ye did eat of the loaves, and were filled.

The people were determined to get at him. They followed him on foot and in boats. But (verse 26) he knew
their motives were mixed. They didn't want him for himself, they wanted him for what he could do for them.

vv. 32 through 35, 41

Then Jesus said unto them, Verily, verily, I say
unto you, Moses gave you not that bread from heav-
en; but my Father giveth you the true bread from
heaven. For the bread of God is he which cometh
down from heaven, and giveth life unto the world.
Then said they unto him, Lord, evermore give us this
bread. And Jesus said unto them, I am the bread of
life: he that cometh to me shall never hunger; and he
that believeth on me shall never thirst. . . . The Jews
then murmured at him, because he said I am the
bread which came down from heaven.

They taunted him with Moses and the manna, and when
he declared himself to be the bread of life, their fury grew.
They did not want *him.* He did not fit their concept of a
God who doled out to his people in a material sense.

vv. 48 through 52

I am that bread of life. Your fathers did eat manna
in the wilderness, and are dead. This is the bread
which cometh down from heaven, that a man may eat
thereof, and not die. I am the living bread which came
down from heaven: if any man eat of this bread, he
shall live for ever: and the bread that I will give is my
flesh, which I will give for the life of the world. The
Jews therefore strove among themselves, saying, How
can this man give us his flesh to eat?

His words were spirit and their questions were all materialistic!

vv. 53 through 61

*Then Jesus said unto them, Verily, verily, I say
unto you, Except ye eat the flesh of the Son of man,
and drink his blood, ye have no life in you. Whoso
eateth my flesh, and drinketh my blood, hath eternal
life; and I will raise him up at the last day. For my
flesh is meat indeed, and my blood is drink indeed. He
that eateth my flesh, and drinketh my blood, dwelleth
in me, and I in him. As the living Father hath sent
me, and I live by the Father: so he that eateth me,
even he shall live by me. This is that bread which
came down from heaven: not as your fathers did eat
manna, and are dead: he that eateth of this bread shall
live for ever. These things said he in the synagogue, as
he taught in Capernaum. Many therefore of his disciples, when they had heard this, said, This is an hard
saying; who can hear it? When Jesus knew in himself
that his disciples murmured at it, he said unto them,
Doth this offend you?*

He was not even slowed down by their anger. One can
feel the tension and tenderness and determination in his
voice when he repeatedly called himself the bread of life.
He was using a symbol common to everyone—everyone
likes bread in some form. It is needed for life. And yet they,
even some of his disciples, were so earth-bound and materialistic, they missed his point entirely.

vv. 65 through 69

*And he said, Therefore said I unto you, that no
man can come unto me, except it were given unto him
of my Father. From that time many of his disciples
went back, and walked no more with him. Then said
Jesus unto the twelve, Will ye also go away? Then
Simon Peter answered him, Lord, to whom shall we
go? thou hast the words of eternal life. And we believe
and are sure that thou art that Christ, the Son of the
living God.*

Some of his own turned and left him. And Jesus faced
the Twelve asking, perhaps wearily: "Will ye also go
away?" And Peter spoke a marvelous truth: "Lord, to

whom shall we go?" Being with Jesus had spoiled everything else for Peter. The Twelve had come this far. They
would stay with him.

CHAPTER 7
vv. 31, 32

*And many of the people believed on him, and said,
When Christ cometh, will he do more miracles than
these which this man hath done? The Pharisees heard
that the people murmured such things concerning
him; and the Pharisees and the chief priests sent officers to take him.*

Then, as now, the people were in varying stages of belief.
Some "believed on him" and expressed their belief this
way: "When Christ cometh, will he do more miracles than
these which this man hath done?" They did not yet have insight or courage to call *him* the Christ, but they were on
their way. And the scribes and Pharisees grew more
furious, more determined to kill him.

vv. 33, 34

*Then said Jesus unto them, Yet a little while am I
with you, and then I go unto him that sent me. Ye
shall seek me, and shall not find me: and where I am,
thither ye cannot come.*

Jesus knew well what lay ahead. He had told his disciples
repeatedly that he would be killed and now he said it to the
people in their varying stages of belief, giving them warning also.

vv. 37, 38

*In the last day, that great day of the feast, Jesus
stood and and cried, saying, If any man thirst, let him
come unto me, and drink. He that believeth on me, as
the scripture hath said, out of his belly shall flow riv-
ers of living water.*

Jesus made no effort to hide from his tormentors. At the
feast of the Passover, with thousands to hear, "Jesus stood
and *cried*, saying, if any man thirst, let him come to me,

and drink." His one burning passion was not to protect himself, but to make men hear and understand and follow him.

v. 39
(But this spake he of the Spirit, which they that believe on him should receive: for the Holy Ghost was not yet given; because that Jesus was not yet glorified.)

John, the author of this Gospel, here offers one of his several interpretative kindnesses. He explains that Jesus spoke of the Holy Spirit in v. 38, and that the Holy Spirit had not yet been given. As from the beginning of his account, John, too, longs for *our* understanding.

CHAPTER 8
vv. 3 through 6, 10, 11
And the scribes and Pharisees brought unto him a woman taken in adultery; and when they had set her in the midst, They say unto him, Master, this woman was taken in adultery, in the very act. Now Moses in the law commanded us. that such should be stoned: but what sayest thou? This they said, tempting him, that they might have to accuse him. But Jesus stooped down, and with his finger wrote on the ground, as though he heard them not. . . .When Jesus had lifted up himself, and saw none but the woman, he said unto her, Woman, where are those thine accusers? hath no man condemned thee? She said, No man, Lord. And Jesus said unto her, Neither do I condemn thee: go, and sin no more.

This is one of the most telling stories in any of the Gospel accounts. Two things strike me:

Jesus did not stand around posturing, attempting to look and act like Someone special. I have read that other authors feel he must have written something profound in the dirt at his feet. I doubt that. Of course, it wouldn't change anything for us if he did, but I think he was *doodling.* Much as one of us would doodle while waiting for some boring, dull tirade to end. He knew perfectly well that the scribes and Pharisees had brought the wretched adulteress to him—not to make certain that her punishment was just, but to trap *him*. He knew everything the old boys were going to say, knew their tricky motives, knew their tired old logic. *Only the woman was important to him.* He knew *she* could be redeemed. They could not be as long as they stayed locked up in their precious *status quo*. He stooped down and doodled on the ground for a while, as though hoping they would go away. When they didn't, he straightened up and said something that would send them scurrying while there was time.

And then he used the whole incident redemptively. Not only to forgive the woman's sins, but to point up once more that the Son of God did not come to condemn. One thing that comes to me which I have never thought of before, is that *she* waited.

vv. 21, 22
> *Then said Jesus again unto them, I go my way, and ye shall seek me, and shall die in your sins: whither I go, ye cannot come. Then said the Jews, Will he kill himself? because he saith, Whither I go, ye cannot come.*

They were really in the dark. Mixed up! Does this give any hint of how important it is for us that Pentecost *has* happened?

v. 58
> *Jesus said unto them, Verily, verily, I say unto you, Before Abraham was, I am.*

"In the beginning was the Word, and the Word was with God, and the Word was God!" (the exclamation point is mine.)

CHAPTER 9
vv. 1 through 3
> *And as Jesus passed by, he saw a man which was blind from his birth. And his disciples asked him, saying, Master, who did sin, this man, or his parents, that he was born blind? Jesus answered, Neither hath this*

*man sinned, nor his parents: but that the works of
God should be made manifest in him.*

Here is the old question which haunts so many shallow
thinkers. Is extreme suffering—say blindness—caused by
extreme sinning? Haven't you heard the "righteous" fortunate person click his or her tongue and declare: "Well,
look how he lived. God is punishing him with·this afflic-
tion!" Nonsense. Jesus does relate sin to suffering, but *not*
in specifics like this. He said: "Neither hath this man
sinned, nor his parents." God was about to be glorified in
the healing. (Not only the healing of the man's eyes, as we
shall see in the next passage, but his entire being.) Who
had sinned and who hadn't is beside the point. Why do we
insist upon generalizing everything Jesus said?

vv. 10, 11
*Therefore said they unto him, How were thine eyes
opened? He answered and said, A man that is called
Jesus made clay, and anointed mine eyes, and said
unto me, Go to the pool of Siloam, and wash: and I
went and washed, and I received sight.*

There begins an interesting *sequence of the birth of faith*
here: In these two verses, we see the man who had been
healed of his blindness giving Jesus the credit, but calling
him merely: "A *man* that is called Jesus. . . ."

v. 17
*They say unto the blind man again, What sayest
thou of him, that he hath opened thine eyes? He said,
He is a prophet.*

He has progressed a step. He is now saying: "He is a
prophet."

vv. 24, 25
*Then again called they the man that was blind, and
said unto him, Give God the praise: we know that this
man is a sinner. He answered and said, Whether he be
a sinner or no, I know not: one thing I know, that,
whereas I was blind, now I see.*

They press him again and he witnesses strongly. He has taken a further step.

vv. 27 through 32

He answered them, I have told you already, and ye did not hear: wherefore would ye hear it again? will ye also be his disciples? Then they reviled him, and said, Thou art his disciple; but we are Moses' disciples. We know that God spake unto Moses: as for this fellow, we know not from whence he is. The man answered and said unto them, Why herein is a marvellous thing, that ye know not from whence he is, and yet he hath opened mine eyes. Now we know that God heareth not sinners: but if any man be a worshipper of God, and doeth his will, him he heareth. Since the world began was it not heard that any man opened the eyes of one that was born child.

He witnesses again *and* preaches them quite a little sermon in the process. One can feel this young man's faith taking root!

vv. 33 through 38

If this man were not of God, he could do nothing. They answered and said unto him, Thou wast altogether born in sins, and dost thou teach us? And they cast him out. Jesus heard that they had cast him out; and when he had found him, he said unto him, Dost thou believe on the Son of God? He answered and said, Who is he, Lord, that I might believe on him? And Jesus said unto him, Thou hast both seen him, and it is he that talketh with thee. And he said, Lord, I believe, And he worshipped him.

When Jesus heard that the Pharisees had thrown the harassed young man out, *Jesus went looking for him and found him.* And the beautiful culmination of the birth of the boy's faith comes with the *personal encounter* with Christ. As soon as he realized that God loved him enough to seek him out personally, he believed. "And he worshipped him."

CHAPTER 10
vv. 1 through 5

Verily, verily, I say unto you, He that entereth not
by the door into the sheepfold, but climbeth up some
other way, the same is a thief and a robber. But he
that entereth in by the door is the shepherd of the
sheep. To him the porter openeth; and the sheep hear
his voice: and he calleth his own sheep by name, and
leadeth them out. And when he putteth forth his own
sheep, he goeth before them, and the sheep follow
him: for they know his voice. And a stranger will they
not follow, but will flee from him: for they know not
the voice of strangers.

John recounts few parables. This one is very simple—the
subject matter familiar to them all. It is merely a description of a sheepfold, its door, its shepherd, and a statement
of what they already knew: if anyone attempted to get at
the sheep through any but the main door, which would always be opened for the shepherd, that person would be an
intruder, possibly intent upon stealing the sheep. The Eastern shepherd, also, did not drive his sheep, he led them. He
went "before." And no flock of sheep would follow a
"shepherd" with a strange voice.

vv. 7 through 11

Then said Jesus unto them again, Verily, verily, I
say unto you, I am the door of the sheep. All that ever
came before me are thieves and robbers: but the sheep
did not hear them. I am the door: by me if any man
enter in, he shall be saved, and shall go in and out,
and find pasture. The thief cometh not, but for to
steal, and to kill, and to destroy: I am come that they
might have life, and that they might have it more
abundantly. I am the good shepherd: the good shep-
herd giveth his life for the sheep.

He is explaining to his disciples that he is **not** pointing
them merely to the right door, that he *is the door*. He is the
only possible way for a man to enter fully into relationship
with the Father. Anyone who claims to be able to give life

—new life—in any other name than the name of the crucified Saviour (who will lay down his very life for the sheep)
is a thief or a robber. I do not at all think, as I have read
elsewhere, that Jesus is saying that the Old Testament
prophets were false prophets. They prophesied his coming.
He refers to religious traditions other than the Judeo-
Christian here. He calls himself the "good shepherd," too,
and I doubt if any one of us has ever dwelt long enough on
that concept. Still, I am newly struck with his having called
himself "the door." "I am the door: by me if any man
enter in, he shall be saved, and shall go in and out, and find
pasture." Where I now live, I am more aware of the necessity of going out. As long as I was a city cliff-dweller, I
went out when I had to, but thought little of going out otherwise. Now, at almost every "pause in the day's occupa-
tions," I go outside. I see no rooftops, only vast stretches of
wide marsh and dense woods. My house is literally riddled
with windows, so I can see outside even when I'm in. In the
geographical location of my house, I have found new freedom. If *he* is the door, and if we can go in and out *by him,*
isn't he speaking of a new freedom here? Isn't he holding
out to us the potential of still more freedom than most of
us have conceived? The very freedom of knowing that even
when we are walking helplessly into trouble or out of
peace, he is still *the door?* And the good shepherd?

vv. 14 through 16
   *I am the good shepherd, and know my sheep, and
   am known of mine. As the Father knoweth me, even
   so know I the Father: and I lay down my life for the
   sheep. And other sheep I have, which are not of this
   fold: them also I must bring, and they shall hear my
   voice; and there shall be one fold, and one shepherd.*

Mention the name of Jesus and watch the blank looks on
some faces. They evidently do not know his voice. And of
course, do not know he is *their* shepherd, too.
   These blank looks don't follow the mention of God, only
the name of Jesus Christ. It is like an embarrassment. This
is no criticism of them—only of us who keep him a secret.
Real relationship—adequate living—is the inevitable result

when the shepherd who knows his sheep abides with the sheep who know their shepherd. It is as simple as that.

In verse 16, Jesus is not letting the disciples get by with their being exclusive. They tended to be, you know, as we do. The God of the New Testament is never, never exclusive. Always inclusive.

vv. 17 through 20
Therefore doth my Father love me, because I lay down my life, that I might take it again. No man taketh it from me, but I lay it down of myself. I have power to lay it down, and I have power to take it again. This commandment have I received of my Father. There was a division therefore again among the Jews for these sayings. And many of them said, He hath a devil, and is mad; why hear ye him?

He did not have to die, and he made that clear. He was pulling no punches now. The end was near. And the people thought he was mad! It seems strange to us, knowing that the Jews had been conditioned to the sacrifice for sins, that they did not catch his meaning. And yet I suppose it really isn't so strange. What he was about to do was so foreign to any concept man held of God, it must have been unbelievable. They had been accustomed to making their own sacrifices before God—it never occurred to them that God might make his own *for sheer love of them.*

v. 23, 24, 30
And Jesus walked in the temple in Solomon's porch. Then came the Jews round about him, and said unto him, How long dost thou make us to doubt? If thou be the Christ, tell us plainly. . . . I and my Father are one.

John here reaches another crescendo. The people asked Jesus point-blank if he was the Christ, and he answered them in a rising outburst of truth which culminated in the one claim which drove his accusers to a white-hot fury: "I and my Father are one." To claim equality with the Lord God of Israel was to them the ultimate blasphemy.

CHAPTER 11

vv. 5, 6

Now Jesus loved Martha, and her sister, and Laz-
arus. When he had heard therefore that he was sick,
he abode two days still in the same place where he
was.

We miss much of the value of this poignant narrative if
we don't have it straight that Mary and Martha and Lazarus were close, personal friends of Jesus. In recent
months, they had become like chosen members of his own
family. From Luke's narrative, we know something of the
intimacy of Jesus' relationship with the little family at
Bethany. He loved them and he knew them *as they were.*
He knew Mary to be more spiritually hungry than Martha,
but he knew Martha to be more responsible in her daily
round. Perhaps even fussy about it. He knew Lazarus as
their young brother, eager to learn, the man of the family.
Jesus was "at home" with the three. He went there often
because he chose to. He liked to. He loved them. They
could not be expected to understand a two-day delay. I
have read and heard endless theories as to why Jesus waited. Somewhere in an earlier book, I may have had a few
theories myself. Now, it seems unimportant for us to have
a specific reason. Couldn't it have been that Jesus was
merely waiting until he knew it was God's time? God was
going to be glorified in the urgent meeting with Mary and
Martha, and only Jesus would have known the appointed
time. God was going to be glorified in the raising of Lazarus from the dead *and* in the Crucifixion of Jesus. Going
back into Judea guaranteed that Crucifixion. He knew this.
The family at Bethany was prominent. There would be no
chance of keeping his visit a secret, even if he had wanted
to. He was walking *now* steadily toward the Cross.

vv. 23 through 27

Jesus saith unto her, Thy brother shall rise again.
Martha saith unto him, I know that he shall rise again
in the resurrection at the last day. Jesus said unto her,
I am the resurrection, and the life: he that believeth in
me, though he were dead, yet shall he live: And who-
soever liveth and believeth in me shall never die. Be-

lievest thou this? She saith unto him, Yea, Lord: I believe that thou art the Christ, the Son of God, which should come into the world.

Martha has run complaining to Jesus that if he had been there her brother would not have died. When he said: "Thy brother shall rise again," Martha answered, "Yes, yes, I know all about the resurrection on the last day, but—" Jesus stopped her with one of his most stunning claims: "I am the resurrection, and the life: he that believeth in me, though he were dead, yet shall he live; And whosoever liveth and believeth in me shall never die." Martha, up to that point, although she was a follower of Jesus, still clung comfortlessly to the old Pharisee doctrine of "the last day." She wasn't interested in "last days" now. She was concerned with today when her beloved brother lay dead in his grave. But then, Jesus must have looked at her, quieting her scattered, grief-stricken thoughts because when he asked her if *she* believed what he had said, the normally fussy, anxious woman replied unequivocally: "Yea, Lord: I believe that thou art the Christ, the Son of God, which should come into the world." Martha went further than he had asked her to go. Or perhaps she suddenly saw that believing that Jesus is *life,* is synonymous with believing that he is the Christ.

vv. 32 through 36

Then when Mary was come where Jesus was, and saw him, she fell down at his feet, saying unto him Lord, if thou hadst been here, my brother had not died, When Jesus therefore saw her weeping, and the Jews also weeping which came with her, he groaned in the spirit, and was troubled, And said, Where have ye laid him? They said unto him, Lord, come and see. Jesus wept. Then said the Jews, Behold how he loved him!

When Mary ran to meet Jesus, weeping, he was very different with her. He *knew* both sisters. With Mary, *he* wept too. And surely, it would be a mistake to eliminate human sorrow from verse 35: "Jesus wept." He loved Lazarus, too. He hated to think of the fine mind struck dumb by death, the once strong young body stiff and cold, beginning to decay in an airless tomb. He hated the grief he saw in the eyes of Lazarus' sisters. But I believe the storm of grief that tore through him, causing him to weep, was also his own soul trembling with hatred—*the holy hatred of God for anything that causes suffering among his children.* Every time he had performed a miracle during his earthly ministry, he must have struggled with all the dark powers that lay behind sin and death and destruction. He did not heal without cost to himself. When the woman with the "issue of blood" touched him—touched merely the hem of his garment—he felt virtue go out of him. It is as though some of this constant struggle were released here as he wept with Mary. He was on his way to Calvary to overcome these dark powers, but Calvary was not quite yet. And Jesus wept.

vv. 38 and 43

Jesus therefore again groaning in himself cometh to the grave. It was a cave, and a stone lay upon it. . . . And when he thus had spoken, he cried with a loud voice, Lazarus, come forth.

The great upheaval within Jesus kept him groaning in himself as he walked with Mary to the place they had buried Lazarus, his friend. After his prayer to the Father for the people's sake, and for his own, he cried with a loud voice: "Lazarus, come forth!" Jesus did not need to shout in order to raise Lazarus. It has meaning for me, at least, that his own human emotions were climaxed in what he *knew* he was going to accomplish.

v. 44

And he that was dead came forth, bound hand and foot with graveclothes: and his face was bound about with a napkin. Jesus saith unto them. Loose him, and let him go.

God had raised Lazarus, but Jesus, always wanting participation on our part, gave the people something to do: "Loose him and let him go."

vv. 53, 54

*Then from that day forth they took counsel togeth-
er for to put him to death. Jesus therefore walked no
more openly among the Jews; but went thence unto a
country near to the wilderness, into a city called
Ephraim, and there continued with his disciples.*

The die was cast for certain now, after the raising of Lazarus. The people were so impressed, his enemies knew
they had no choice but to be rid of him. And Jesus "walked
no more openly among the Jews"; but went to Ephraim
and spent time with his disciples, presumably still teaching
and healing.

CHAPTER 12

vv. 1 through 3

*Then Jesus six days before the passover came to
Bethany, where Lazarus was which had been dead,
whom he raised from the dead. There they made him
a supper; and Martha served: but Lazarus was one of
them that sat at the table with him. Then took Mary a
pound of ointment of spikenard, very costly, and anointed the feet of Jesus, and wiped his feet with her
hair: and the house was filled with the odour of the
ointment.*

Hatred toward him and love for him were at an all-time
high. Actively, his death was being planned in Jerusalem.
And his disciples were spending as much time with him as
possible, some, like Mary, the sister of Lazarus, showing
her adoration in every conceivable way. Lazarus sat at dinner with Jesus the night his sister, Mary, anointed her Lord
with a pound of ointment of spikenard and wiped his feet
with her hair. There is a variation here from the other Gospels, but whoever the woman was who anointed Jesus for
his burial, the motive is the same—*love for him,* and that is
what matters.

vv. 4 through 8

*Then saith one of his disciples, Judas Iscariot, Si-
mon's son, which should betray him, Why was not this
ointment sold for three hundred pence, and given to*

*the poor? This he said, not that he cared for the poor;
but because he was a thief, and had the bag, and bare
what was put therein. Then said Jesus, Let her alone:
against the day of my burying hath she kept this. For
the poor always ye have with you; but me ye have not
always.*

Judas Iscariot is tipping his hand. He does not care that
much for the poor, or so John believed, but he is constantly
exposing his impatient, materialistic nature. The nature
that drove him to betray his Master for thirty pieces of silver. Jesus is not suggesting that it does not matter about the
suffering of the poor. He is pointing out the difference between charity and adoration of God. One does not rule out
the other, but the two are not to be passed off as the same.
Both are essential.

vv. 12 through 16
*On the next day much people that were come to the
feast, when they heard that Jesus was coming to Jerusalem, Took branches of palm trees, and went forth to
meet him, and cried, Hosanna: Blessed is the King of
Israel that cometh in the name of the Lord. And
Jesus, when he had found a young ass, sat thereon; as
it is written, Fear not, daughter of Sion: behold, thy
King cometh, sitting on an ass's colt. These things understood not his disciples at the first: but when Jesus
was glorified, then remembered they that these things
were written of him, and that they had done these
things unto him.*

Jesus' fame spread like wildfire after he raised Lazarus
from the dead. It roared and crackled around his head
wherever he went. And of course, when the people learned
that he was coming to Jerusalem for the feast of the Passover, they cheered and threw flowers and shouted praises all
along his route to the Holy City. His disciples did not understand why he insisted upon riding into Jerusalem on an
ass's colt, but when he died, they realized it had been written of him. What a shocking time of realization those men
had up ahead.

vv. 32, 33

And I, if I be lifted up from the earth, will draw all men unto me, This he said, signifying what death he should die.

The depths of meaning which lie here in this brief, certain statement of Jesus', we cannot possibly know. No one can know all he meant. We can know, however, that he said if he is lifted up, he will draw *all men* unto him. Does this sound as though the Lord God has picked out a select few? Was Jesus wrong? Dare we believe that he will draw all men unto him? My heart shouts yes! And yet, I know the violence that is unleashed among the saints of God who seem to expect a sparsely populated heaven. I know that "no man cometh unto the Father except by" Jesus Christ. What did he mean by saying "I, if I be lifted up from the earth, will draw *all men* unto me?" John inserts one of his explanatory notes in verse 33: "This he said, signifying what death he should die." And yet, if that was all Jesus meant, he could have merely said: "I am to be lifted up from the earth on a Cross." But he added that when this occurred, he would draw all men unto him. One thing I know: If his love is truly motivating our lives, *we long* for God to have a more far-reaching, vastly wider plan than he has felt it wise to reveal to us.

vv. 44 through 46

Jesus cried and said, He that believeth on me, believeth not on me, but on him that sent me. And he that seeth me seeth him that sent me. I am come a light into the world, that whosoever believeth on me should not abide in darkness.

His words speak for themselves here, but I am enlightened by the fact that John tells us "Jesus cried and said . . ." This is his last chance at the multitudes. His longing over them caused him to cry aloud one more time, in one more valiant effort to get through to them.

CHAPTER 13
v. 1

Now before the feast of the passover, when Jesus

knew that his hour was come that he should depart
out of this world unto the Father, having loved his
own which were in the world, he loved them unto the
end.

". . . he loved them unto the end." Rieu translates this:
". . . and now he showed how utterly he loved them."

vv. 3 through 5

Jesus knowing that the Father had given all things
into his hands, and that he was come from God, and
went to God; He riseth from supper, and laid aside his
garments; and took a towel, and girded himself. After
that he poureth water into a bason, and began to wash
the disciples' feet, and to wipe them with the towel
wherewith he was girded.

Jesus was secure in his own identity. He could perform
this task, normally done by a slave, with perfect poise.
Nothing *could* demean him. There is a great truth here for
us: If we are secure in our identities as children of God,
neither can we be insulted, belittled, demeaned.

v. 30

He then having received the sop went immediately
out; and it was night.

Judas could no longer stay in the presence of the One he
had betrayed. I doubt that he was merely obeying his Master by leaving abruptly. It is true that Jesus had said: "That
thou doest, do quickly." But Judas *had* to run. Out of the
lighted room, out of the light of the Lord's presence—"and
it was night" where he ran.

vv. 33 through 35

Little children, yet a little while I am with you. Ye
shall seek me: and as I said unto the Jews, Whither I
go, ye cannot come, so now I say to you. A new com-
mandment I give unto you, That you love one anoth-
er; as I have loved you, that ye also love one another.
By this shall all men know that ye are my disciples, if
ye have love one to another.

"Little children, yet a little while I am with you." For he loved them. The time was very short now to be together in the old, familiar, intimate way. And he reminded them that (as he had told the Jews), they, too, would seek him, but where he would be, they could not follow. For this reason, he must say to them what he felt to be the most important thing he had ever said: *They were to love each other as he had loved them!* This would be the way men would know that they were the disciples of Jesus Christ—if they truly loved each other. He did not say men would recognize them as Christians if they attended church every Sunday, if they tithed their money, if they studied the Scriptures, if they prayed. He said men would know *if they loved*. And they were to love each other. A cross on the steeple and a Christian name on the church sign do not make a church *Christian*. Men will know a church is a church made up of the followers of Jesus Christ only if they show love *toward each other*.

vv. 36 through 38
Simon Peter said unto him, Lord, whither goest thou? Jesus answered him, Whither I go, thou canst not follow me now; but thou shalt follow me afterwards. Peter said unto him, Lord, why cannot I follow thee now? I will lay down my life for thy sake. Jesus answered him, Wilt thou lay down thy life for my sake? Verily, verily, I say unto thee, The cock shall not crow, till thou hast denied me thrice.

Peter, like so many of us, was hung up on a technicality. He missed what Jesus had to say about love because he was curious to know where Jesus was going!

CHAPTER 14
vv. 1 through 4
Let not your heart be troubled: ye believe in God, believe also in me. In my Father's house are many mansions: if it were not so, I would have told you. I go to prepare a place for you. And if I go and prepare a place for you, I will come again, and receive you

unto myself; that where I am, there ye may be also.
And whither I go ye know, and the way ye know.

Jesus did not humiliate Peter by ignoring his question
(end of Chapter 13). Even after he warned the big fisherman that he would deny him three times before the cock
crowed in the morning, he used Peter's question as a spring-
board for one of his most glorious statements. The disciples
were not to let their hearts be troubled because he was
going away. They were to trust him. "Do not be worried
and upset." *(Good News For Modern Man.)* "I am going
to prepare a place for you," he said, and added (I think
importantly) that if it were not so, *he* would have told
them! I have, through the years, formed the habit of adding
this assurance to all the statements of Christ and it is enormously strengthening and enlightening. For example: "I
and the Father are one. . . ." *If it were not so, I would have
told you.* "And I will pray the Father and he shall give you
another Comforter. . . ." *If it were not so, I would have
told you.* "I am the door. . . ." *If it were not so, I would
have told you.* "I am the good shepherd. . . ." *If it were
not so, I would have told you.* "Lo, I am with you always."
If it were not so, I would have told you. He is trustworthy.
And he was on his way that night to prepare a place for
them in his Father's house. For each one of them. If it
were not so, he would *have told them.*

vv. 5 through 7

*Thomas saith unto him, Lord, we know not whither
thou goest; and how can we know the way? Jesus saith
unto him, I am the way, the truth, and the life: no
man cometh unto the Father, but by me. If ye had
known me, ye should have known my Father also:
and from henceforth ye know him, and have seen him.*

Perhaps their fear of losing him muddied their memories. At least Thomas asked point blank: "Lord, we know
not whither thou goest; and how can we know the way?"
Jesus, once more, used an obvious, panic-induced question
to point up a central truth: "I am the way, Thomas. I am
the way. I am the truth. I am the whole of life!" (My own
interpolation.) In other words anyone can know the way by

knowing the One who himself *is* the way. And I am forever
grateful that he clarified further that he had come to make
the Father plain: "If ye had known me, ye should have
known my Father also: and from henceforth ye know him,
and have seen him." Anyone who has seen Jesus Christ has
a definite idea of what God is really like. It is unavoidable.

vv. 8 through 11
*Phillip saith unto him, Lord, shew us the Father,
and it sufficeth us. Jesus saith unto him, Have I been
so long time with you, and yet hast thou not known
me, Philip? he that hath seen me hath seen the Father;
and how sayest thou then, Shew us the Father? Believest thou not that I am in the Father, and the Father
in me? the words that I speak unto you I speak not of
myself: but the Father that dwelleth in me, he doeth
the works. Believe me that I am in the Father, and the
Father in me: or else believe me for the very works'
sake.*

John does a remarkable writing job here in helping us
once more through his remembered dialogue between Philip and the Master. After Jesus' explanation to Thomas, it
seems impossible that anyone could still have a question
concerning the Father. And yet we do, as Philip did, and
John, bless him, has further clarified.

v. 14
If ye shall ask any thing in my name, I will do it.

Add to this promise: "If it were not so, I would have
told you," and you will find it easier to act upon and to believe.

vv. 16 through 18
*And I will pray the Father, and he shall give you
another Comforter, that he may aibde with you for
ever; Even the Spirit of truth; whom the world cannot
receive, because it seeth him not, neither knoweth
him: but ye know him; for he dwelleth with you, and
shall be in you. I will not leave you comfortless: I will
come to you.*

Jesus promises them that God will send the Comforter, the Holy Spirit of God himself. He did not merely say "The Father will send you some form of comfort." He said *Someone* was coming! And then, to me *most meaningfully,* in almost the same breath, Jesus said: "I will come to you." The Holy Spirit, when he came, would not be a stranger to them. Jesus and the Father and the Holy Spirit are *one.* When the Spirit would come to live with and within the disciples, they would no longer be grieving and lonely and lost. I dare to believe that what Jesus was saying was that the same Spirit which they had seen in him, to which they had been so attracted, would then be with them forever. In a definite sense, he himself would be coming back to them. "I will come to you." The Book of Acts tells the story of his first return.

vv. 25, 26

These things have I spoken unto you, being yet present with you. But the Comforter, which is the Holy Ghost, whom the Father will send in my name, he shall teach you all things, and bring all things to your remembrance, whatsoever I have said unto you.

He was doing all he could to make things clear to them on their last night together, but he well knew they were getting almost none of it. Even to this, he said in effect: "Don't worry if you do not grasp all I say. This same coming Comforter will teach you what you need to know and bring it to mind for you when you need it." (My interpolation.)

CHAPTER 15
vv. 1 through 5

I am the true vine, and my Father is the husbandman. Every branch in me that beareth not fruit he taketh away: and every branch that beareth fruit, he purgeth it, that it may bring forth more fruit. Now ye are clean through the word which I have spoken unto you. Abide in me, and I in you. As the branch cannot bear fruit of itself, except it abide in the vine; no more

can ye, except ye abide in me. I am the vine, ye are
the branches: He that abideth in me, and I in him, the
same bringeth forth much fruit: for without me ye
can do nothing.

I see this now, almost twenty years after my own conversion to Jesus Christ, as the simplest possible teaching concerning the tremendous potential of productivity and rest available to us through the indwelling Holy Spirit. Did you ever hear of a branch *pleading* with its vine to send down more sap so that it could live and bear fruit? The branch merely stays on the vine—and *expects.*

vv. 8, 9

Herein is my Father glorified, that ye bear much
fruit; so shall ye be my disciples. As the Father hath
loved me, so have I loved you: continue ye in my love.

Jesus said God, his Father, was glorified *if* his disciples bear much fruit. How have we so distorted this as to mean that the Father is only glorified according to how many "souls we win?" I have never won a soul to Christ. None of us has. God does his own winning and the sooner we learn this the more rested and relaxed and natural we are going to be as children in the Kingdom. Jesus said, don't forget, that if he were lifted up he would do his own drawing. The fruit that glorifies the Father has been listed for us by Paul (Galatians 5:22). And soul winning is *not* on the list. These characteristics of Christ himself, *are* on the list: "Love, joy, peace, patience, kindness, generosity, fidelity, tolerance and self-control" (Phillips). Love heads the list! And as Jesus said: "Continue ye in my love."

v. 14

Ye are my friends, if ye do whatsoever I command
you.

Jesus was not merely being strict. Doing what he commands has nothing whatever to do with love *unless* we are obeying because we believe with all our beings that *he knows best.* Duty is not the point at all.

v. 15

Henceforth I call you not servants; for the servant knoweth not what his lord doeth: but I have called you friends; for all things that I have heard of my Father I have made known unto you.

When people write and preach about the necessity of *serving* the Lord, I wonder if they have forgotten what Jesus said that last night: ". . . the servant knoweth not what his lord doeth: but I have called you friends; for all things that I have heard of my Father I have made known unto you." A servant serves his master blindly. We are not living in the dark! Jesus Christ has chosen us to be his *friends*. It is far simpler to be a servant than a friend. I never think of how well or how poorly I am "serving" the Lord. I don't think in terms of service at all. Rather, *am I his friend?* Friends share. Friends make each other glad or sad or hopeful or hopeless. Friends support each other. Friends love. Do I love him? Do you? Friendship has to do with *being*. Service can be mere *doing*.

vv. 26, 27

But when the Comforter is come, whom I will send unto you from the Father, even the Spirit of truth, which proceedeth from the Father, he shall testify of me: And ye also shall bear witness, because ye have been with me from the beginning.

Once more, he promises that they will understand his meaning *after* the Comforter comes to them. They will feel at home with the Holy Spirit because he will testify to them of Jesus. They will feel familiar with him because they will be reminded of the very essence of the personality of their Master whom they loved so dearly. And they will bear witness to their comfort and peace with the Spirit, because they have been with Jesus from the beginning. In other words, the world will know they are *still* with Jesus! Their grief gone, their spirits elevated, their minds cleared, their courage high, their love strong.

CHAPTER 16

vv. 5 through 14, 20, 22

But now I go my way to him that sent me; and none of you asketh me, Whither goest thou? But because I have said these things unto you, sorrow hath filled your heart. Nevertheless I tell you the truth; It is expedient for you that I go away: for if I go not away, the Comforter will not come unto you; but if I depart, I will send him unto you. And when he is come, he will reprove the world of sin, and of righteousness, and of judgment: Of sin, because they believe not on me; Of righteousness, because I go to my Father, and ye see me no more; Of judgment, because the prince of this world is judged. I have yet many things to say unto you, but ye cannot bear them now. Howbeit when he, the Spirit of truth, is come, he will guide you into all truth: for he shall not speak of himself; but whatsoever he shall hear, that shall he speak: and he will shew you things to come. He shall glorify me: for he shall receive of mine, and shall shew it unto you. . . . and ye shall be sorrowful, but your sorrow shall be turned into joy. . . . I will see you again, and your heart shall rejoice, and your joy no man taketh from you.

He has given them the assurance of the Holy Spirit, but they are still blinded by their sorrow at losing him. (Of all people on earth, Jesus understands grief.) He tries reasoning with them, to show them that it will be far better for them if he returns to his Father, *so that* the Spirit may come to them. I imagine he "lost" them as he attempted to explain all the Spirit would do, but in verse 20, he found a response again when he said: . . . ye shall be sorrowful, but your sorrow shall be turned to joy." They could take his word for things; this they knew. I feel, at least, that had I been one of the disciples that night, I should have clung to the fact that he said my sorrow would somehow be turned to joy. "I will see you again, and your heart shall rejoice, and your joy no man taketh from you." The grief remains, but the sting is gone from death when we can really believe that "I will see you again."

v. 33

These things I have spoken unto you, that in me ye might have peace. In the world ye shall have tribulation: but be of good cheer; I have overcome the world.

He was always realistic with them. He is always realistic with us. Life is not going to be easy. There will be plenty of trouble ahead. No man is immune. But, the Lord said we were to "be of good cheer [because] I have overcome the world." He does not imply that he will see that everyone is kind to us, or that he will fill our storehouses with wealth. He said these things so we "might have peace" *in the midst of* tribulations, knowing nothing can ever change him. In this way, if our eye is single—filled with Jesus only—we can never be overcome because he has overcome the downpull of the world and we are *free in him.* "If the Son . . . shall make you free, ye shall be free indeed" (John 8:36).

CHAPTER 17

v. 3

And this is life eternal, that they might know thee the only true God, and Jesus Christ, whom thou hast sent.

Jesus gives eternal life because it is only through him that anyone can really know what God is like: *can know God.* And Jesus' own definition of eternal life is—*to know God.*

v. 4

I have glorified thee on the earth: I have finished the work which thou gavest me to do.

Nothing remained at this point, but the supreme revelation of God's own heart on the Cross. The Lamb had been slain before the foundation of the world. Jesus did not *change* the Father's heart toward us as he hung there. He was revealing it—supremely.

v. 5

And now, O Father, glorify thou me with thine own

*self with the glory which I had with thee before the
world was.*

We cannot know all of what he means here, but surely,
he is saying in part, at least: "Oh, Father, now let me come
home!"

vv. 6 through 11

*I have manifested thy name unto the men which
thou gavest me out of the world: thine they were, and
thou gavest them me; and they have kept thy word.
Now they have known that all things whatsoever thou
hast given me are of thee. For I have given unto them
the words which thou gavest me; and they have received them, and have known surely that I came out
from thee, and they have believed that thou didst send
me. I pray for them: I pray not for the world, but for
them which thou hast given me; for they are thine.
And all mine are thine, and thine are mine; and I am
glorified in them. And now I am no more in the world,
but these are in the world, and I come to thee. Holy
Father, keep through thine own name those whom
thou hast given me, that they may be one, as we are.*

How sensitive of Jesus to permit his disciples to hear his
own special prayer for them! This is one of life's truly en-
couraging and comforting experiences, to be permitted to
hear someone pray for us. I do not think Jesus was refusing
in any way to petition the Father in behalf of those who
were still not believers when he said: "I pray not for the
world. . . ." This was a particular time of fellowship and
prayer with and for his disciples—his chosen ones. Would
the Man who poured out his entire life for the multitudes
refuse to pray for them? This interpretation is superficial in
the extreme. He just wanted his men to know that *this
prayer* was especially for *them.*

v. 15

*I pray not that thou shouldest take them out of the
world, but that thou shouldest keep them from the
evil.*

He didn't want them to shut themselves away to lives of
"holy contemplation." He wanted them "in the world"
where the need was, but showing that their own needs had
been met in him.

v. 18
*As thou hast sent me into the world, even so have I
also sent them into the world.*

In fact, he is *sending* them into the world. He did not
stay in glory, remote from man's sin and suffering, so of
course, he did not want his followers to seclude themselves
with their own "spiritual experiences."

vv. 20 through 23
*Neither pray I for these alone, but for them also
which shall believe on me through their word; That
they all may be one; as thou, Father, art in me, and I
in thee, that they also may be one in us: that the
world may believe that thou hast sent me. And the
glory which thou gavest me I have given them; that
they may be one, even as we are one: I in them, and
thou in me, that they may be made perfect in one; and
that the world may know that thou hast sent me, and
hast loved them, as thou hast loved me.*

He prayed for us too that night.

v. 24
*Father, I will that they also, whom thou hast given
me, be with me where I am; that they may behold my
glory, which thou hast given me: for thou lovedst me
before the foundation of the world.*

And he prayed to be with his disciples and with us, Just
think: He wants to be with *us.*

CHAPTER 18
vv. 1 through 3
*When Jesus had spoken these words, he went forth
with his disciples over the brook Cedron, where was a
garden, into the which he entered, and his disciples.*

And Judas also, which betrayed him, knew the place:
for Jesus ofttimes resorted thither with his disciples.
Judas then, having received a band of men and offi-
cers from the chief priests and Pharisees, cometh
thither with lanterns and torches and weapons.

The familiar spot in the garden "over the brook Cedron," where Jesus and his disciples had gone together so
often, was, on this night, eerie with long, jumping shadows
from the torches and lanterns carried by the band of ap-
proaching soldiers. There was the clank and rattle of
swords and armor and the thud of boots as the heavily
armed company closed in on the quiet Galilean. The restful, joy-filled, stimulating hours they had known there in
the better days were gone; none of his men laughed now:
they cowered in fright and anger.

v. 4
Jesus therefore, knowing all things that should
come upon him, went forth, and said unto them,
Whom seek ye?

Jesus stepped quickly forward, poised, in full command
of the situation—the really ludicrous situation. "Whom
seek ye?" he asked before one of his enemies could collect
himself enough to speak.

vv. 5, 6
They answered him, Jesus of Nazareth. Jesus saith
unto them, I am he. And Judas also, which betrayed
him, stood with them. As soon then as he had said
unto them, I am he, they went backward, and fell to
the ground.

Finally someone said that they sought Jesus of Nazareth.
And when Jesus answered simply: "I am he," they all (presumably Judas, too,) fell back, surely in awe of both His
commanding presence and His courage. Some of them
even fell to the ground.

vv. 7, 8
Then asked he them again, Whom seek ye? And

they said, Jesus of Nazareth. Jesus answered, I have
told you that I am he: if therefore ye seek me, let
these go their way:

Even here, Jesus was offering himself in his disciples'
stead. "Take me. Let them go free." (My own interpolation.)

vv. 10, 11

Then Simon Peter having a sword drew it, and
smote the high priest's servant, and cut off his right
ear. The servant's name was Malchus. Then said Jesus
unto Peter, Put up thy sword into the sheath: the
cup which my Father hath given me, shall I not
drink it?

Peter, in his outrage, drew his sword and cut off one
man's ear. With the same authority and for the same basic
reason, he once said: "Get thee behind me, Satan!" Jesus
admonished him again: "Put up thy sword into the sheath:
the cup which my Father hath given me, shall I not drink
it?"

John does not describe Gethsemane, but this is its victory: ". . . shall I not drink it?"

v. 28

Then led they Jesus from Caiaphas unto the hall of
judgment: and it was early; and they themselves went
not into the judgment hall, lest they should be defiled;
but that they might eat the passover.

The self-righteous Jews led Jesus first to Annas, the
father-in-law of the high priest, Caiaphas, but they would
not lead him into the judgment hall of the gentile, Pilate,
for fear of contaminating themselves so they could not eat
the Passover Feast. God pity their blindness, and through
his Son, he did.

vv. 37, 38

Pilate therefore said unto him, Art thou a king
then? Jesus answered, Thou sayest that I am a king.
To this end was I born, and for this cause came I into

*the world, that I should bear witness unto the truth.
Every one that is of the truth heareth my voice Pilate
saith unto him, What is truth? And when he had said
this, he went out again unto the Jews, and saith unto
them, I find in him no fault at all.*

Jesus proclaimed truth to the pagan governor, Pilate,
and it appears that, for a fleeting moment, Pilate *thought*.
"What is truth?" he asked. But before Jesus could answer,
the expedient Pilate stopped thinking, turned abruptly and
went back outside to the Jews.

CHAPTER 19
v. 5
*Then came Jesus forth, wearing the crown of
thorns, and the purple robe. And Pilate saith unto
them, Behold the man!*

"Then came Jesus forth wearing the crown of thorns,
and the purple robe." Beaten, spat upon, bruised, blood
trickling from his head over his face. And Pilate said: "Behold the man!" Coming from Pilate, this could have
meant: "Look here, this is the battered, helpless creature
you would crucify! This is the bruised, harmless man you
are afraid of!" John, however, seems to want to read into
Pilate's words a deeper truth. He makes no explanation
here, but his phrasing indicates it to me. And who knows
that Pilate did not speak from the conflict in his own soul?
After all, he had been with Jesus!

vv. 21, 22
*Then said the chief priests of the Jews to Pilate,
Write not, The King of the Jews; but that he said, I
am King of the Jews. Pilate answered, What I have
written I have written.*

Is Pilate here unconsciously testifying to the truth?

vv. 26, 27
*When Jesus therefore saw his mother, and the disci-
ple standing by, whom he loved, he saith unto his
mother, Woman, behold thy son! Then saith he to the*

*disciple, Behold thy mother! And from that hour that
disciple took her unto his own home.*

The Son of God was *demonstrating* the very *heart* of his
Father on the Cross—his arms stretched wide to embrace
the whole world of lost men and women. But he took note
of individual human need even as he suffered for all mankind: He gave his mother to his beloved disciple, John, and
he gave John to his mother.

v. 30
*When Jesus therefore had received the vinegar, he
said, It is finished: and he bowed his head, and gave
up the ghost.*

This was not the end. This was the completion of the
demonstration of God's heart—*as it really is.* Nothing
could be added. And the demonstration was there for every
man to see and to believe. Jesus was free at last to die, and
he did, so that we might live.

vv. 32 through 37
*Then came the soldiers, and brake the legs of the
first, and of the other which was crucified with him.
But when they came to Jesus, and saw that he was
dead already, they brake not his legs: But one of the
soldiers with a spear pierced his side, and forthwith
came there out blood and water. And he that saw it
bare record, and his record is true: and he knoweth
that he saith true, that ye might believe. For these
things were done, that the scripture should be fulfilled, A bone of him shall not be broken. And again
another scripture saith, They shall look on him whom
they pierced.*

Dear John, writing his story of Jesus, remains to the end,
so eager, so hopeful "that ye might believe."

Chapter 20
vv. 10 through 14
*Then the disciples went away again unto their own
home. But Mary stood without at the sepulchre weep-*

*ing: and as she wept, she stooped down, and looked
into the sepulchre, And seeth two angels in white sitting, the one at the head, and the other at the feet,
where the body of Jesus had lain. And they say unto
her, Woman, why weepest thou? She saith unto them,
Because they have taken away my Lord, and I know
not where they have laid him. And when she had thus
said, she turned herself back, and saw Jesus standing
and knew not that it was Jesus.*

Mary of Magdala was, according to John's Gospel account, the first one there on that first day of the week—
"when it was yet dark." She could not stay away even from
the place where they had laid him, so great was her grief,
so great was her love. It was she who ran to tell Peter and
John that the tomb was empty, the stone rolled away. Both
men came running, examined the visible evidence, found
the empty sepulcher, the folded-up grave cloths, "believed"
at least, that Jesus was not there, but evidently just turned
around and went home. Not Mary. Mary stood outside the
empty tomb, weeping, and once more stooped down and
looked inside. Her perseverance and her determination and
her love were rewarded: Two angels asked her why she
wept. Her answer is the profoundly simple reply of a
woman with a broken heart: "I'm weeping," she said, "because they have taken away my Lord, and I don't know
where they have laid him." (My interpolation.) Still no one
suspected he was not dead. Even Mary's grief was unbroken. Was still unbroken, when she turned and saw him
standing beside her, because she did not recognize him. She
was there, for love of him, but her *grief* had her attention.

vv. 15, 16
*Jesus saith unto her, Woman, why weepest thou?
whom seekest thou? She, supposing him to be the gar-
dener, saith unto him, Sir, if thou have borne him
hence, tell me where thou hast laid him, and I will
take him away. Jesus saith unto her, Mary. She turned
herself, and saith unto him, Rabboni; which is to say,
Master.*

She wanted only his body, so that she could "take him

away" and care for him. Her sights were no higher than
that. And she still did not recognize him until he spoke her
name, "Mary." No one else had ever spoken her name as
he did.

v. 18
  Mary Magdalene came and told the disciples that
  she had seen the Lord, and that he had spoken these
  things unto her.

Once more Mary ran to tell the disciples that she had
seen him! That he had spoken to her. There is no evidence
that they believed her this time either.

vv. 19, 20
  Then the same day at evening, being the first day of
  the week, when the doors were shut where the disci-
  ples were assembled for fear of the Jews, came Jesus
  and stood in the midst, and saith unto them, Peace be
  unto you. And when he had so said, he shewed unto
  them his hands and his side. Then were the disciples
  glad, when they saw the Lord.

Jesus knew they were locked up in a room, filled with
fears and anxieties and confusion. He also knew they
hadn't believed Mary or any of the women who had told
them their Lord was risen. He knew this, and so he did
what he had to do: he came to them personally, showing
his hands and his pierced side, saying: "Peace to you. . . ."
(He has come to me, as I write this, because he understands why I am confused and bewildered over a certain set
of circumstances in my life right now. He has come, reminding me of his hands and his pierced side and he has
brought peace with him—as he always does.)

vv. 24 through 28
  But Thomas, one of the twelve, called Didymus,
  was not with them when Jesus came. The other disci-
  ples therefore said unto him, We have seen the Lord.
  But he said unto them, Except I shall see in his hands
  the print of the nails, and put my finger into the print
  of the nails, and thrust my hand into his side, I will

not believe. And after eight days again his disciples were within, and Thomas with them: then came Jesus, the doors being shut, and stood in the midst, and said, Peace be unto you. Then saith he to Thomas, Reach hither thy finger, and behold my hands; and reach hither thy hand, and thrust it into my side: and be not faithless, but believing. And Thomas answered and said unto him, My Lord and my God.

Thomas happened not to be in the tightly barred room with the other disciples when Jesus came the first time, bringing his peace and assurance that all was well. And knowing Thomas, as only Jesus knew him, he came again —*just for Thomas*, the man with the inquiring, doubting mind. The man Jesus knew needed personal attention in order to quiet his doubts. Jesus always comes according to *our* needs. And he always comes according to our *realistic* needs, not our imagined ones. Thomas was not a weak soul. Jesus knew this. He simply had the kind of mind that demands logical answers. Once Thomas saw for himself, he fell to his knees saying: "My Lord and my God!" Jesus had not expected Thomas to accept a secondhand theological premise, a broad generality. Thomas needed a personal Lord, and a personal God and Jesus came in person—the second time, *just for Thomas*. The Master has not changed in these almost two thousand years.

v. 29
Jesus saith unto him, Thomas, because thou hast seen me, thou hast believed: blessed are they that have not seen, and yet have believed.

He was thinking of us too, even then. I do not feel he was belittling Thomas at all.

vv. 30, 31
And many other signs truly did Jesus in the presence of his disciples, which are not written in this book: But these are written, that ye might believe that Jesus is the Christ, the Son of God; and that believing ye might have life through his name.

John is again assuring and reassuring us—this time that there were many more signs of Jesus' resurrection, not recorded. I realize it is considered better literary form to remain objective. But when one is writing about the Lord God himself, it becomes urgent at times, to add a personal word. A witness. A firsthand testimony to what one knows from having experienced or from having seen with one's own eyes. John's eagerness that *we* find it possible to believe touches me.

CHAPTER 21
vv. 7, 8

Therefore that disciple whom Jesus loved saith unto Peter, It is the Lord. Now when Simon Peter heard that it was the Lord, he girt his fisher's coat unto him, (for he was naked,) and did cast himself into the sea. And the other disciples came in a little ship; (for they were not far from land, but as it were two hundred cubits,) dragging the net with fishes.

The men went back to Galilee, as he instructed. (John calls it the Sea of Tiberias since he was writing for Jewish readers. It is the same as the Sea of Galilee, where they had spent so many good hours with Jesus.) They were waiting for him to come to them, as he said he would. And being restless outdoor men, they grew fidgety. Finally, Peter said he was going fishing, and the others decided they'd go along. As on another night, before they crucified Jesus, the men caught nothing (Luke 5:5). And just at dawn, the Lord himself stood on the shore and asked them if they'd had any luck. None of the men recognized him, even when he called: "Cast the net on the right side of the ship and ye shall find!" Being Jesus, understanding them all as he did, he chose this time to come to them. It was a familiar scene. Almost literally, it had all happened before. Still, they were blind to who he really was standing there shouting instructions to them over the misty waters. When they cast their nets on the right side, they were suddenly so heavy with fish it was more than the men could manage to draw back over the side of the boat! Then it dawned on John, the beloved disciple, that this had all happened before. He peered across the expanse of water and cried: "It is the Lord!"

Peter, impetuous as ever, jumped overboard and began to swim toward his Master. The others followed quickly in the ship, with their enormous load of fish. Jesus did not meet them after his resurrection in an overwhelming majestic circumstance. He came to them in a situation where he knew *they* would feel at home.

vv. 9 through 13

As soon then as they were come to land, they saw a fire of coals there, and fish laid thereon, and bread. Jesus saith unto them, Bring of the fish which ye have now caught. Simon Peter went up, and drew the net to land full of great fishes, an hundred and fifty and three: and for all there were so many, yet was not the net broken. Jesus saith unto them, Come and dine. And none of the disciples durst ask him, Who are thou? knowing that it was the Lord. Jesus then cometh, and taketh bread, and giveth them, and fish likewise.

He was not only waiting for them on the shore, he had a fire built, bread ready and with the fish they had caught, *he cooked their breakfast for them.* "Come and dine!" "Breakfast's ready!"

v. 17

He saith unto him the third time, Simon, son of Jonas, lovest thou me? Peter was grieved because he said unto him the third time, Lovest thou me? And he said unto him, Lord, thou knowest all things; thou knowest that I love thee. Jesus saith unto him, Feed my sheep.

It is helpful here to know the J. B. Phillips translation of this provocative and sometimes confusing passage:

"When they had finished breakfast Jesus said to Simon Peter, 'Simon, son of John, do you love me more than these others?'

" 'Yes, Lord,' he replied. 'You know that I am your friend.'

" 'Then feed my lambs,' returned Jesus. Then he said for the second time,

" 'Simon, son of John, do you love me?'

" 'Yes, Lord,' returned Peter. 'You know that I am your friend.'

" 'Then care for my sheep,' replied Jesus. Then for the third time, Jesus spoke to him and said,

"'Simon, son of John, *are* you my friend?'

"Peter was deeply hurt because Jesus' third question to him was 'Are you my friend?' and he said: 'Lord, you know everything. You know that I am your friend!'

" 'Then feed my sheep,' Jesus said to him."

It seems important to me that Jesus did not call him Peter, the new name he had given him. The rock. After all, Peter had not acted like a rock during Jesus' passion and suffering. He had reverted to form—he had acted like Simon, the son of John. Not Peter, the son of God. I am also interested in the fact that Jesus kept asking Peter (using the word for love that denotes friendship) if he was really his *friend*. He did not ask him if he was his *servant*. Jesus was not starting at the wrong place. If Peter was going to be his true friend, then he would automatically "feed the sheep and the lambs." He would serve *naturally*. Friends do this. True friends always rejoice in serving each other. The sequence of questioning which Jesus used springs from divine wisdom. Divine wisdom is startlingly practical and always realistic.

Another thing that strikes me is that Jesus *kept asking*. Giving Peter ample time to see the point. That Peter didn't, that he only got his feelings hurt, should give us plenty of grounds for identification with the big disciple.

vv. 18, 19

Verily, verily, I say unto thee, When thou wast young, thou girdedst thyself, and walkedst whither thou wouldest: but when thou shalt be old, thou shalt stretch forth they hands, and another shall gird thee, and carry thee whither thou wouldest not. This spake he, signifying by what death he should glorify God. And, when he had spoken this, he saith unto him, Follow me

Jesus knew what lay up ahead for Peter: They were going to crucify him, too, as they had crucified his Lord.

And Jesus was lovingly warning him—emphasizing once more the cost of discipleship. Because after he had told Peter of his death, he said: "Follow me." In other words, "Up ahead is trouble, my child, but follow me anyway."

vv. 20 through 22

Then Peter, turning about, seeth the disciples whom Jesus loved following; which also leaned on his breast at supper, and said, Lord, which is he that betrayeth thee? Peter seeing him saith to Jesus, Lord, and what shall this man do? Jesus saith unto him, If I will that he tarry till I come, what is that to thee? follow thou me.

Peter looked around and saw John, the beloved disciple, nearby. And being Peter, he wanted to know what John's end would be. To the very close of John's Gospel, we have the chance to learn the meaning the cost of true discipleship: Jesus said to Peter, in effect, that if John lived forever, that would be nothing to Peter. In short, none of his business. That would be strictly the business of God. Just as Jesus knew Peter *as Peter really was inside,* knew him to be *unlike any other man,* so Peter would have to settle (as do we all) for a unique walk with God. I do not see Jesus as critical of Peter here. He is *clarifying.* God's plan for one of us is not necessarily his plan for anyone else. Peter was merely to follow Jesus as he had during the earthly ministry—no matter where he led him. John also, was to follow Jesus, no matter where he led.

v. 23

Then went this saying abroad among the brethren, that that disciple should not die: yet Jesus said not unto him, He shall not die; but, If I will that he tarry till I come, what is that to thee?

John ends the incident with a touch of wry humor. The gossips among the disciples were hard at it then, as they are hard at it now. "Then went this saying abroad" that John was not going to die! No doubt it was partly jealousy, because John and Jesus had been humanly very close. Whatever caused it, the end result was humor. It was plain old gossip. Thank heaven, Jesus died for the "plain old gossips," too.

vv. 24, 25

This is the disciple which testifieth of these things, and wrote these things: and we know that his testimony is true. And there are also many other things which Jesus did, the which, if they should be written every one, I suppose that even the world itself could not contain the books that should be written. Amen.

Once more, at the very close of his account, John is reaching a hand toward us to strengthen our faith. It may be true, as some scholars believe, that John, the beloved disciple, did not write this Gospel. But he seems to me to say here: "I, the disciple Jesus loved, am the witness to these things and I wrote them down." Either way, it is all right. John is not the central issue. *Jesus is.* And along with his beloved friend, John, I too, "suppose that even the world itself could not contain the books that should be written" about the life and love and wonderful deeds of this Jesus Christ, the God we follow.

Learning to Live
from the Acts

PREFACE

Even in our technological era, there is no way to cope
with the content of the book called the Acts of the Apostles
if the reader rejects the fact that there is a living, energeti-
cally active Holy Spirit. The men and women written about
in this lively New Testament book simply could not have
acted as they did on their own. Something happened to
them on the Day of Pentecost that turned them and their
world upside down by pragmatic standards. Grieving, nervous, discouraged men who had, only days before, been
hiding in a locked room, afraid for their lives, moved at
once out into the streets of Jerusalem, full of courage, balance, spirit—their sorrowing at an end, life suddenly worth
living.

Consider their grief by itself for a moment. The Man
whom they had loved and trusted enough to desert their
families and their jobs to follow, the Master in whom they
believed as children believe in a good father, their King
who was going to re-establish the throne of David and put
them all in important positions in it was gone—crucified
like a criminal between two thieves. Their hopes for their
own futures lay in the blood and the dust at the foot of that
now empty cross; but, more important than that, their
dearest Friend was dead.

How, then, could some concentrated kind of psycholog-
ical phenomenon on the Day of the Jewish Feast of Pentecost have caused those grieving, broken hearts to mend in a
matter of minutes? If God had not kept his word given to
them through Jesus to send a Comforter—the Holy Spirit
—how did they become the men and women whose grief
ended suddenly and never returned? This is not the way of
grief for human beings. Real grief seldom ends. The
healthy mind, fixed on God, can learn to live with it, but
not instantly. It often takes years.

The men and women who entered the Upper Room to
wait "in one accord" for the promised Comforter were

wearing the same clothes when they poured out into the
streets on Pentecost; they looked the same physically, but
they were not the same. They had heard no sermons on
how to handle grief and fear; they had read no books; they
had merely waited together until the One whom they loved
and believed in—and mourned—came back to them! The
dear, familiar voice was still; the loved, familiar figure
no longer walked up ahead, leading them—but in a way
only God can explain, their Master was suddenly back.
Back, living his life in the person of the Holy Spirit—
not with them, as he had been before, but *in* them: in
their very bodies and minds and hearts. They were no
longer on their own. The very Spirit of the God who created them and redeemed them in Jesus Christ was available
to these simple people as Jesus had never been available to
them. When he had walked the dusty roads and climbed
the barren hills with them during their three years together,
he had taught and inspired and encouraged them, but then
he had had no means of energizing them from within, no
way to enlighten their minds from within, no way to
strengthen their hearts. Now, suddenly, he could, and the
riotous, joy-filled, sometimes tragic, but always triumphant
story of the early Church began to "happen."

The Acts of the Apostles is not a complete biography of
Paul or even a partial one, although a generous part of the
adventure is Paul's. Neither is it Peter's story, or Stephen's,
or Barnabas', or John's. It is as though the writer, Luke,
felt it quite sufficient merely to give us a glimpse of the
continuing difference it made in each life, detailed enough
and covering just enough time to make it perfectly clear
that these things can go on happening—that life can go on
being this way for anyone who follows Jesus Christ and
obeys the promptings of his Spirit within. The short account is uneven, minutely descriptive in parts, swift and
merely outlined in others. Rather than writing a carefully
planned treatise, Luke has seemed to flash a bright light on
what he felt should be an example of the daily lives of all
believers in the risen Lord he followed. Here and there in
the first conflict-torn, joy-filled days of the early Church,
we are permitted to see for ourselves how it was meant to
be for us who call ourselves Christians.

Why it is not this way for us now, or why it is, at best,

only this way now and then, I feel we must decide. I find little or no doctrine in the Acts, but I do find life, and great and simple helps in learning to live it.

The people whose lives we glimpse in these pages were not spiritual giants—not even Paul. They were just people with personality and disposition defects like our own, with needs and problems and weaknesses we can all recognize. Even Paul did not eventually become a perfect man—no one did. No one does. But they all *grew* if they obeyed the promptings of the very real, living Spirit within them. I once heard a young lady exclaim: "Well, if those people in that group at our church are filled with the Holy Spirit and are still as unattractive as they are, I don't want to be!" An older, wiser man smiled at her and replied: "But, my dear, just think how repulsive they must have been without Him!"

I thought of this little true story as I worked through the Acts of the Apostles and rejoiced that God didn't have to limit himself to spiritually superior people. There aren't any, really, and so we are the ones who are blessed, because he limited himself to us and then figured out a way through the Holy Spirit to make our potentials limitless.

EUGENIA PRICE

St. Simons Island, Georgia
February, 1970

THE ACTS OF THE APOSTLES

CHAPTER 1
vv. 1 and 2

The former treatise have I made, O Theophilus, of all that Jesus began both to do and teach, Until the day in which he was taken up, after that he through the Holy Ghost had given commandments unto the apostles whom he had chosen:

Most authorities agree that Luke had not yet completed certain portions of his Gospel, but at least he had written enough to be convinced that, as always, Jesus was taking every precaution to be sure His followers understood at least something of the strange events of the past days. Until the day of his return to the Father, Jesus patiently instructed them. He has not changed,

v. 3

To whom also he shewed himself alive after his passion by many infallible proofs, being seen of them forty days, and speaking of the things pertaining to the kingdom of God:

The Master was not only infinitely careful with his chosen ones, mindful that they were not yet filled with the Spirit; he stayed on earth in his resurrected body for forty days, giving them "many infallible proofs" that his Resurrection was a true resurrection—not a theory, not a rumor. The Biblical account does not tell us about everyone he visited during these forty days, but it does say that he was "seen of them forty days." He must have covered a lot of ground, must have spent the entire forty days making certain that none of his own doubted that the Father *had* literally brought him from the grave. And daily he kept talking to them about the true kingdom of God—as always, doing all he could to protect them from confusion.

177

v. 4

And, being assembled together with them, commanded them that they should not depart from Jerusalem, but wait for the promise of the Father, which, saith he, ye have heard of me.

At this particular meeting, Jesus gave them the central instruction, the specific commandment: They were not to leave Jerusalem, but wait for the Father's promise. His Father had never let Jesus down, even when he was on the cross. There was to be no questioning of the promise now. Their problem would be waiting. Our timing is seldom on schedule with God's, but waiting can be a far stronger faith-builder than quickly answered prayer.

v. 5

For John truly baptized with water; but ye shall be baptized with the Holy Ghost not many days hence.

Even now, Jesus did not minimize the work of John the Baptist. This is a stunning example of God's willingness to enter into the limitations of time with us. Living in the *eternal now* as he does, he was (and is) still acting in the concept of time which human beings can understand. First, John the Baptist, who "truly baptized with water." Now the next step was coming: In a few days, these people who believed were going to be baptized with the Holy Spirit. God does not need to do one thing and then the next for us in that timebound sequence—like a ribbon stretched out—except for our sakes. And we are still his first concern.

v. 6

When they therefore were come together, they asked of him, saying, Lord, wilt thou at this time restore again the kingdom to Israel?

They simply did not understand and could not be expected to understand. Their understanding would be opened only *after* the Holy Spirit entered their very lives. Like many of us, they asked a stupid question—a superficial question—a self-centered, self-seeking question—a human question. Their concern was still not outward, but inward. How will all this help those of us who are Israelites? they asked.

v. 7
And he said unto them, It is not for you to know the times or the seasons, which the Father hath put in his own power.

This was not a divine "put-down." Jesus is simply helping them get a perspective.

v. 8
. . . ye shall receive power . . . and ye shall be witnesses unto me. . . .

If we miss this, we miss everything. No one is to seek "power from on high" in order to experience a spiritual excitement, or to perform miracles, or to be considered "advanced in the things of God." We are to receive power for only one purpose: to be witnesses unto Jesus Christ himself. Not to the organized Church or to our own holiness, but to Christ.

vv. 9 through 14
And when he had spoken these things . . . he was taken up . . . out of their sight. And while they looked . . . two men stood by them in white apparel; Which also said, Ye men of Galilee, why stand ye gazing up into heaven? this same Jesus . . . shall so come in like manner as ye have seen him go. . . . Then returned they unto Jerusalem . . . went up into an upper room, [and] continued with one accord in prayer and supplication. . . .

At the moment Jesus disappeared out of their sight, God caused them to see two Messengers who, for that moment, told them all they needed to know. The result? They did as Jesus had instructed. Peter and James and John and Andrew and Philip and Thomas and Bartholomew and Matthew and James the son of Alpheus and Simon the zealot and James' brother, Judas, along with the faithful women and Mary, Jesus' mother, and his brothers, began the waiting time. Suddenly they could wait. Their questions were stilled. One hundred and twenty people of one mind makes for quiet.

vv. 24a and 26a (Read vv. 15 through 26.)
And they prayed. . . . And they gave forth their lots; and the lot fell upon Matthias. . . .

As with the little girl who "prayed and crossed her fingers," the disciples mixed faith with expediency here. The Holy Spirit had not yet come, and so we can't blame them for using their wits instead of waiting for guidance from God. Peter evidently grew impatient and decided that he might as well get some business transacted while they waited, so he prayed and then instructed his brothers to cast lots to determine who among them would take Judas' place. Matthias must have been well liked—they had nominated him for the position. He was undoubtedly loyal, but evidently he was not God's choice. Their waiting was faulty. God, as he always does, did the best he could with Matthias until his own choice was made in Paul some months later.

CHAPTER 2
v. 1
And when the day of Pentecost was fully come, they were all with one accord in one place.

Though still powerless, except for the use of human devices, at least the one hundred and twenty were *there* where Jesus had told them to be and they were "with one accord." Their faith, sincere as it surely was, had reached out to act in the choosing of the twelfth disciple, but it had acted on merely human wisdom. The promised power had not yet come. They were doing their best, but their best had never been enough. It could not be expected to be enough now. Nine long days and nights had dragged by, but the followers of Christ were still acting on a strictly human level. Their "chosen committee" was in session, but only human power was available.

vv. 2 through 5

And suddenly there came a sound from heaven as
of a rushing mighty wind, and it filled all the house
where they were sitting. And there appeared unto
them cloven tongues like as of fire, and it sat upon
each of them. And they were all filled with the Holy
Ghost, and began to speak with other tongues, as the
Spirit gave them utterance. And there were dwelling at
Jerusalem Jews, devout men, out of every nation
under heaven.

Jerusalem was thronging with visitors on the Jewish
Feast of Pentecost, and when the sudden wind struck the
Holy City a little before nine, the narrow streets were
crowded with terrified, jostling people, crowding, elbowing
their way into shops and inns—anywhere to escape the
blowing dust and debris. In Jerusalem that day were Par-
tians, Medes, Elamites, Mesopotamians, Judeans, Cappa-
docians, travelers from Pontus, Asia, Phrygia, Pamphylia,
Egypt, Cyrene, Rome, Crete and Arabia. Almost every
known language was represented that day. When people
from the same locales met, crowding into any kind of
shelter against the driving wind, they lapsed into their own
native tongues.

There was no darkness, no rain—only the great roaring
from heaven as the people stared into the now empty
streets in wonder at what was happening. Suddenly the
wind stopped, and before the confused visitors to Jerusalem
began to pour back into the streets, down the narrow stair
from the upper room where the one hundred and twenty
had waited, the disciples of Jesus came, praising God and
clapping their hands with joy—shouting their praises in
tongues familiar to every visitor in the city. They were not
speaking in *unknown tongues.* They spoke in tongues
known to all of Jerusalem's visitors.

vv. 6 through 8

Now when this was noised abroad, the multitude
came together, and were confounded, because that
every man heard them speak in his own language.
And they were all amazed and marvelled, saying one
to another, Behold, are not all these which speak Gali-

*laeans? And how hear we every man in our own
tongue, wherein we were born?*

In the land of disciples were housewives, seamstresses,
farmers, fishermen, carpenters—not an intellectual among
them—all Galileans who, as everyone knew, spoke collo-
quial Aramaic. How could this odd assortment of country
folk suddenly begin to speak intelligently and plainly in
every language known to man? And how was it that what
they said was all in praise of the living God?

vv. 12, 13
*And they were all amazed, and were in doubt, say-
ing one to another, What meaneth this? Others mock-
ing said, These men are full of new wine.*

The glib explanation of this strange, surprising behavior
of the disciples is most understandable, especially among
those who turn first, in any emotional emergency, to scorn.
When in doubt, just say "They're drunk!" The disciples
were full of a "new wine"—the wine of the Kingdom of
God, the very life of God Himself in the person of his Holy
Spirit.

v. 14
*But Peter, standing up with the eleven, lifted up his
voice, and said unto them . . .*

Peter did not take over on his own and do the deciding
this time. He stood up "with the eleven." His very life had
been invaded by the life of God, and he could now both
lean on and support his brothers, with far less thought for
his own prestige.

vv. 29 through 32 (Read vv. 15 through 28.)
*Men and brethren, let me freely speak unto you of
the patriarch David, that he is both dead and buried,
and his sepulchre is with us unto this day. Therefore
being a prophet, and knowing that God had sworn
with an oath to him, that of the fruit of his loins, according to the flesh, he would raise up Christ to sit on
his throne; He seeing this before spake of the resurrec-*

tion of Christ, that his soul was not left in hell, neither his flesh did see corruption. This Jesus hath God raised up, whereof we all are witnesses.

Now Peter saw it all as he had never been able to see before. And as he preached his first sermon in the power of the Holy Spirit on the streets of Jerusalem that day, he bore down on dead center—Jesus had risen from the dead! His body had not been stolen and hidden from sight to make it seem as though he had been resurrected from the dead; *he had gotten up* and walked out of that tomb and, at the very moment Peter spoke, was alive in the presence of the Father. And Peter was being obedient to this living Lord by witnessing—not unto his own "emotional high" of the moment, not unto the spiritual thrill of speaking in a tongue he had never used before, but unto "this Jesus" whom God had "raised up."

vv. 40 and 41

And with many other words did he testify and exhort, saying, Save yourselves from this untoward generation. Then they that gladly received his word were baptized: and the same day there were added unto them about three thousand souls.

From one hundred and twenty, their number jumped to three thousand, one hundred and twenty—all because Peter spoke on the one essential, the bodily resurrection from the dead of Jesus Christ. Daily more continued to be added to their number, and "many wonders and signs were done by the apostles. And all that believed were together, and had all things common." Harmony and peace were there among them because they were united around the *single event in history* powerful enough to make them one: This Jesus had been God himself visiting their earth, and now his Spirit lived within them. He was no longer gone. He was back. They could stop grieving. Their Master could help them now, strengthen them from within, as even he had not been able to do when he walked with them as a Man. There among these simple people was a bond which had come *not* because they had "spoken in tongues" together—this had been done by God simply so that those still in darkness in

Jerusalem that day could understand. They were not one because of a shared emotional ecstasy. These people were one because at this point in their young church life together they were still on center—Jesus Christ was still their Lord. They "had favor with all the people" because Christ lived in them. He was, as he had said, drawing people to himself because he was being "lifted up." It takes no profound thinker to discover what is missing today.

CHAPTER 3
vv. 1 through 6

Now Peter and John went up together into the temple at the hour of prayer. . . . And a certain man lame from his mother's womb was carried, whom they laid daily at the gate of the temple which is called Beautiful, to ask alms of them that entered into the temple; Who seeing Peter and John about to go into the temple asked an alms. And Peter, fastening his eyes upon him with John, said, Look on us. And he gave heed unto them, expecting to receive something of them. Then Peter said, Silver and gold have I none; but such as I have give I thee: In the name of Jesus Christ of Nazareth rise up and walk.

Peter had lost his shyness. The very life of God was in him, and that left no more need for denials, for slinking away by night pretending that he did not know Jesus. Peter had lost his need for wasted motion. He could now go straight to the point without fear, without hedging, with the inner strength of the Master himself.

v. 7

And he took him by the right hand, and lifted him up: and immediately his feet and ankle bones received strength.

Peter did not think of pleading with God to heal this man. He expected it to happen. The years had not dimmed his memory of the Master's touch on crippled legs. Without a single course at the seminary, Peter had the sure knowledge that the same power had now come to indwell his own being.

vv. 8 and 9

And he leaping up stood, and walked, and entered with them into the temple, walking, and leaping, and praising God. And all the people saw him walking and praising God:

It is our *walk* that people watch.

vv. 11 and 12

And as the lame man which was healed held Peter and John, all the people ran together unto them in the porch that is called Solomon's, greatly wondering. And when Peter saw it, he answered unto the people, Ye men of Israel, why marvel ye at this? or why look ye so earnestly on us, as though by our own power or holiness we had made this man to walk?

Peter had already begun to make use of every opportunity to turn the people's attention to Jesus.

vv. 13 through 15

The God of Abraham, and of Isaac, and of Jacob, the God of our fathers, hath glorified his Son Jesus; whom ye delivered up, and denied him in the presence of Pilate, when he was determined to let him go. But ye denied the Holy One and the Just, and desired a murderer to be granted unto you; And killed the Prince of life, whom God hath raised from the dead; whereof we are witnesses.

Peter spoke directly to the central issue. "Ye are to be witnesses unto me." Not unto a healing—unto *me*.

v. 17

[But] now, brethren, I wot that through ignorance ye did it, as did also your rulers.

Peter had really been changed! It had always been his nature to jump to conclusions. He was balanced now that the Spirit of the God of balance lived in him. He showed clearly not merely the kindness of God, but God's very understanding of people. He was not thumping a pulpit, shouting accusations at the men who listened to him that day. He pointed no fingers, screaming that they would all be damned in their sins. He began by calling them "brothers"—no hint of spiritual superiority. These people who stood hearing Peter did not agree with him yet, but he called them his brothers. As his Master had always done, Peter was reaching toward them with an open hand. And then, he showed God's understanding. Quite simply, he told them he realized that they had "killed the Prince of life" out of ignorance of who He was. Peter even included the silk-robed Pharisees and rulers in his sweeping invitation to forgiveness. He had heard this done before. He had heard John tell of the familiar voice crying out: "Father, forgive them; for they know not what they do." The same Spirit lived in Peter now and in John. They could be open, receptive, welcoming, understanding. They could be as gentle as they were strong in the power of the crucified and risen Lord they loved.

CHAPTER 4
vv. 1 through 4

And as they spake unto the people, the priests, and the captain of the temple, and the Sadducees, came upon them, Being grieved that they taught the people, and preached through Jesus the resurrection from the dead. And they laid hands on them, and put them in hold unto the next day: for it was now eventide. Howbeit many of them which heard the word believed; and the number of the men was about five thousand.

Suddenly it was all right with Peter and John to be thrown in prison. The fear that had driven them both to desert Jesus on the dark night of his crucifixion had been pushed out by the entrance of the same Spirit that kept their Master strong and unafraid. It was of very fleeting importance to them now that they were tossed into jail for the night. The important thing had taken place: Five thousand new believers had been added to their number. They could rejoice over that in jail as well as they could have at home.

vv. 5 through 8

And it came to pass on the morrow, that their rulers, and elders, and scribes, And Annas the high priest, and Caiaphas, and John, and Alexander, and as many as were of the kindred of the high priest, were gathered together at Jerusalem. And when they had set them in the midst, they asked, By what power, or by what name, have ye done this? Then Peter, filled with the Holy Ghost, said unto them . . .

The important fact here was not what might happen to Peter and John before this mighty array of rulers who would decide their punishment; the thing that mattered was that here was another unexpected opportunity for Peter to preach a sermon about Jesus Christ. And preach it he did (verses 9 through 12).

v. 13

Now when they saw the boldness of Peter and John, and perceived that they were unlearned and ignorant men, they marvelled; and they took knowledge of them, that they had been with Jesus.

Peter and John had accomplished the ultimate: showing, even to their enemies, that "they had been with Jesus."

v. 14

And beholding the man which was healed standing with them, they could say nothing against it.

The rulers sent Peter and John outside while they conferred, but there stood the man who had been healed—what could even they say against a thing like that? Oh, the two disciples were warned never to speak in the name of Jesus again, but Peter and John had been given the holy boldness of God along with his spirit, and they merely went back to the other disciples and prayed for still more courage to speak the truth.

vv. 31 and 32

And when they had prayed, the place was shaken where they were assembled together; and they were all filled with the Holy Ghost, and they spake the word of God with boldness. And the multitude of them that believed were of one heart and of one soul: neither said any of them that ought of the things which he possessed was his own; but they had all things common.

With the prayer to speak the truth with boldness even in the face of imprisonment and flogging, there came to the band of believers a new kind of naturalness together. There is no record that anyone laid down the law about communal living, but suddenly, with that fresh visitation of the Spirit, all personal possessiveness came to an abrupt end: ". . . neither said any of them that ought of the things which he possessed was his own." Now, this is *not* natural with man, but it brought a new *naturalness* among them: the *naturalness* of the Kingdom of God. If God is love, then it is his very nature to love. If this nature indwells us by the Holy Spirit, then it becomes natural for us to love. Love does not possess. Love gives. The disciples began to live by *giving love.*

v. 37
Having land, [they] sold it, and brought the money, and laid it at the apostles' feet.

Again, there seem to have been no rules laid down. This act was spontaneous. Love had happened to them.

CHAPTER 5
vv. 1 through 5
But a certain man named Ananias, with Sapphira his wife, sold a possession, And kept back part of the price, his wife also being privy to it, and brought a certain part, and laid it at the apostles' feet. But Peter said, Ananias, why hath Satan filled thine heart to lie to the Holy Ghost, and to keep back part of the price of the land? Whiles it remained, was it not thine own? and after it was sold, was it not in thine own power? why hast thou conceived this thing in thine heart? thou hast not lied unto men, but unto God. And Ananias hearing these words fell down, and gave up the

*ghost: and great fear came on all them that heard
these things.*

I would be utterly presumptuous if I attempted an explanation of why Ananias (and later, in verse 10, his wife,
Sapphira) dropped dead after their acts of trickery. I do
not believe that God arbitrarily kills those who disobey
him. If he did, none of us would be alive today. If he acted
in this way, think how short Jacob's life would have been! I
see nothing arbitrary in the nature of Jesus Christ, and a
Christian forms his concept of God by Jesus. The only explanation of the sudden deaths of this deceitful couple
which has any meaning for me is that the atmosphere in
this first Christian community was so rarefied, so pure in
love, that deceit in the heart of anyone literally stopped
that heart. If we believe that Jesus was right when he said
"the Kingdom is within," this is an acceptable explanation,
although it may be partial. Actually, beyond normal curiosity, I need no explanation of the deaths. I am willing, as
with so many passages from Scripture, to wait until I am
mature enough in Christ to comprehend more fully. For
now, what I do understand of this dramatic incident is
quite enough to think about. Whether it was actually
Peter's duty or whether he was being impulsive when he
accused Ananias and his wife is a moot question. But what
strikes me is this: "thou hast not lied unto men, but unto
God." Peter may have been taking things into his own
hands by condemning Ananias and Sapphira, but what he
said gives me pause. I may get by with fooling you, but
God's understanding of why I even tried to fool you is so
complete that it might knock me dead if I glimpsed even a
part of it.

At the end of verse 5, there is another stopper: "and
great fear came on all them. . . ." Up to then, perfect love
had kept away fear. The believers enjoyed their new life.
Now, suddenly, they were afraid. The community structure
had been weakened.

v. 14
*And believers were the more added to the Lord,
multitudes both of men and women.*

For a brief time, love reigned, and then fear, and this is the last mention in the Acts of this communal life of sharing. What happened did not stop God, though—as our fears and prejudices and irregularities do not stop him now. We may slow him down, cause him to have to seek other channels through which to work, but he is God. He will remain in motion toward his children. "Believers *were . . .* added" anyway.

v. 24 (Read vv. 15 through 23).
Now when the high priest and the captain of the temple and the chief priests heard these things, they doubted of them whereunto this would grow.

The last word in this verse is the key: *grow.* I am reminded by name of certain politicians who tremble as they look about them *seeing* the redefinition of freedom abroad in the world. *Seeing* some of us who have always been free joining forces with those who have been crippled by bondage. *Seeing* their precious political bases shake and crumble. *Seeing* love begin to *grow* across the world. God still permits his people to go to prison, but he also still knows how to open those doors which have been "shut with all safety."

vv. 25 through 28
Then came one and told them, saying, Behold, the men whom ye put in prison are standing in the temple, and teaching the people. Then went the captain with the officers, and brought them without violence: for they feared the people, lest they should have been stoned. And when they had brought them, they set them before the council: and the high priest asked them, Saying, Did not we straitly command you that ye should not teach in his name? and, behold, ye have filled Jerusalem with your doctrine, and intend to bring this man's blood upon us.

The account of the Acts of the Apostles is stunningly contemporary. Think back through the years since the school desegregation decision in 1954 by the United States Supreme Court. Like the early Christians, once fear and violence shattered their perfect communion twentieth-century apostles of equality and love have made mistakes; but prison doors still swing open, and the "captains of the temple" still rage when the courageous men and women walk the streets again preaching brotherhood and love.

vv. 29 through 33

Then Peter and the other apostles answered and said, We ought to obey God rather than men. The God of our fathers raised up Jesus, whom ye slew and hanged on a tree. Him hath God exalted with his right hand to be a Prince and a Saviour, for to give repentance to Israel, and forgiveness of sins. And we are his witnesses of these things; and so is also the Holy Ghost, whom God hath given to them that obey him. When they heard that, they were cut to the heart, and took counsel to slay them.

It is a painful thing to me that so many persons in the twentieth century who call themselves Christians do not believe that we "ought to obey God rather than man" when injustice is involved. I do not refer to the actions of violence-prone militants. I refer to such authentic exponents of Christian love and nonviolence as the late Martin Luther King, who spoke and acted as did Peter and the early apostles. And yet I have heard hundreds of contemporary Christians condemn Dr. King for civil disobedience. Peter thought of it first. Ultimately they killed him too.

vv. 34, 38 and 39

Then stood there up one in the council, a Pharisee, named Gamaliel, a doctor of the law, had in reputation among all the people, and commanded to put the apostles forth a little space. . . . And now I say unto you, Refrain from these men, and let them alone: for if this counsel or this work be of men, it will come to nought: But if it be of God, ye cannot overthrow it; lest haply ye be found even to fight against God.

We can be thankful for the Gamaliels today, who choose to act by their innate wisdom and not by their emotions or their prejudices or their political prospects. They may not all be believers in Christ, as Gamaliel was not, but God can use them to keep love moving.

vv. 40 through 42

And to him, [Gamaliel] they agreed: and when they had called the apostles, and beaten them, they commanded that they should not speak in the name of Jesus, and let them go. And they departed from the presence of the council, rejoicing that they were counted worthy to suffer shame for his name. And daily in the temple, and in every house, they ceased not to teach and preach Jesus Christ.

When men believe they are in God's will, even when they are afraid, they cannot be stopped. Their work will go on, and so will their rejoicing. Shame becomes glory.

CHAPTER 6
vv. 1 through 3 and 5a

And in those days, when the number of the disciples was multiplied, there arose a murmuring of the Grecians against the Hebrews, because their widows were neglected in the daily ministration. Then the twelve called the multitude of the disciples unto them, and said, It is not reason that we should leave the word of God, and serve tables. Wherefore, brethren, look ye out among you seven men of honest report, full of the Holy Ghost and wisdom, whom we may appoint over this business. . . . And the saying pleased the whole multitude: and they chose Stephen. . . .

They chose six other worthy men too, but Stephen was the one of the seven so filled with God that, while he ministered fully to the widows and the poor, he could not be confined to menial work. This is no indictment of humble service—Stephen had been chosen to serve tables—but his spirit and his faith overflowed his appointed task. We should note here, also, that this is the first committee meeting of the organized Church. The Greeks among the Christian believers felt slighted. Something had to be done, so the brothers called a meeting and made appointments. As long as there is a Stephen appointed now and then, the organized Church will live, because Stephen, "full of faith and power, did great wonders and miracles among the people." He was not just a worthy servant; he resembled his Master.

v. 9
Then there arose certain of the synagogue . . . disputing with Stephen.

It never fails. Stephen was "living God" among them, and they couldn't bear it. The confrontation was too direct.

vv. 10 through 15
And they were not able to resist the wisdom and the spirit by which he spake. Then they suborned [secretly incited] men, which said, We have heard him speak blasphemous words against Moses, and against God. And they stirred up the people, and the elders, and the scribes, and came upon him, and caught him, and brought him to the council. And set up false witnesses. . . . And all that sat in the council, looking stedfastly on him, saw his face as it had been the face of an angel.

Stephen's persecutors managed to get some men to bear false witness against him. Stephen was called on the carpet before the self-righteous of the temple and accused of blasphemy—as his Saviour had been accused of it. What did Stephen do? He stood there with an expression on his face that made even these men think of an angel. Apparently, Stephen felt no need to say anything in his own defense. He just looked like Jesus.

CHAPTER 7
v. 1 (Read vv. 2 through 54.)
Then said the high priest, Are these things so?

The whole of Chapter 7 has been called Stephen's defense. I do not see it as a defense. When the high priest asked him to speak, he did—eloquently, in marvelous order, covering Jewish history and the coming of the Messiah skillfully, clearly until his words so accused his accusers that they began to gnash their teeth in fury. One young intellectual named Saul of Tarsus stood back from the others as they rushed at Stephen, but his face was distorted with anger against the disciple.

vv. 55 and 56
But he [Stephen], being full of the Holy Ghost, looked up stedfastly into heaven, and saw the glory of God, and Jesus standing on the right hand of God, And said, Behold, I see the heavens opened, and the Son of man standing on the right hand of God.

Stephen did not see the angry mob rushing toward him with stones in their hands. He did not see Saul's hatred. Stephen was seeing, perhaps for the first time, that this Jesus whom he loved was more than merely the Jewish Messiah. He saw him as the Son of man—the Saviour of all men, universal, triumphant, "standing on the right hand of God." Jesus was not sitting down. He was *standing*, cheering Stephen on to act, even unto the moment of brutal death, in love. No wonder Stephen felt secure.

v. 57
Then they cried out with a loud voice, and stopped their ears, and ran upon him with one accord.

Why did they "stop their ears"? If I were in the process of stoning a man to death, I wouldn't want to hear his voice praising God either.

vv. 58 through 60
[They] cast him out of the city, and stoned him: and the witnesses laid down their clothes at a young man's feet, whose name was Saul. And they stoned Stephen, [he] calling upon God, and saying, Lord Jesus, receive my spirit. And he kneeled down, and cried with a loud voice, Lord, lay not this sin to their charge. And when he had said this, he fell asleep.

The young man, Saul of Tarsus, would find out for himself in a short time that Stephen was able to die forgiving his murderers, because *in Stephen* lived the same Spirit as in Christ. Stephen was filled with the Holy Spirit—the very Spirit of Jesus, whom he followed, the Spirit who never contradicts himself. Christ in Stephen would act no differently under the barrage of stones and curses than he had acted on the cross.

CHAPTER 8
v. 1 (a)
And Saul was consenting unto his death.

This short, dramatic verse ends Chapter 7 in most of the newer translations. Wherever it is placed, I feel guilt well up within me when I read it. Saul stood by and held the coats of those who threw the stones; but like us when we stand by and do nothing but hate, he was a murderer too.

vv. 1 (b) through 4
And at that time there was a great persecution against the church which was at Jerusalem; and they were all scattered abroad throughout the regions of Judaea and Samaria, except the apostles. And devout men carried Stephen to his burial, and made great lamentation over him. As for Saul, he made havock of the church, entering into every house, and haling men and women committed them to prison. Therefore they that were scattered abroad went every where preaching the word.

The same Spirit was living in the believers who were scattered by the persecutions. They "went every where preaching the word." What is eternally alive cannot be killed. Saul had watched Stephen die as Christ had died— praying for the forgiveness of his enemies. It incensed the young man, Saul, Gamaliel's student, and his hatred of the followers of the Crucified drove him to a special, scalding persecution of his own. This happens. Saul was not changed at once. He became worse first. But he had *watched* Stephen die. God's pursuit of Saul had begun.

vv. 5 through 13
Then Philip went down to the city of Samaria, and preached Christ unto them. And the people with one

accord gave heed unto those things which Philip
spake, hearing and seeing the miracles which he
did, . . . But there was a certain man, called Simon,
which beforetime in the same city used sorcery, and be-
witched the people of Samaria, giving out that himself
was some great one: To whom they all gave heed,
great power of God. . . . But when they believed Philip
from the least to the greatest, saying, This man is the
preaching the things concerning the kingdom of God,
and the name of Jesus Christ, they were baptized, both
men and women. Then Simon himself believed also:
and when he was baptized, he continued with Philip,
and wondered, beholding the miracles and signs which
were done.

It is interesting and hopeful that Simon "believed . . .
was baptized [and] continued with Philip." All of these
are good signs. At the same time he "wondered, beholding
the miracles and signs which were done." Now, there is
surely nothing wrong with Simon's being impressed with
the miracles Philip performed. After all, this had been Simon's profession too. There is nothing unusual in the fact
that the miracle-working would have intrigued him more
than any other aspect of his new faith. It would intrigue
anyone so new in the kingdom. It is no indication to me of
any lack of sincerity on Simon's part—merely an indication
of his conditioning. But the remainder of the story about
Simon indicates that he was still in some darkness.

vv. 14 through 19
Now when the apostles which were at Jerusalem
heard that Samaria had received the word of God,
they sent unto them Peter and John: Who, when they
were come down, prayed for them, that they might re-
ceive the Holy Ghost: (For as yet he was fallen upon
none of them: only they were baptized in the name of
the Lord Jesus.) Then laid they their hands on them,
and they received the Holy Ghost. And when Simon
saw that through laying on of the apostles' hands the
Holy Ghost was given, he offered them money, Say-
ing, Give me also this power, that on whomsoever I
lay hands, he may receive the Holy Ghost.

There is no doubt here that Simon, although he had "believed" and was baptized by Philip, was still in hot pursuit of glory for himself—power for his own use. He had barely set his foot on the Way. As many today, after years of "believing" and years after baptism, have merely set their feet on the Way. Simon, as I see him, had made an intellectual decision to follow Christ, but was still just standing there. He had not begun to walk.

vv. 20 through 23

But Peter said unto him, Thy money perish with thee, because thou hast thought that the gift of God may be purchased with money. Thou hast neither part nor lot in this matter: for thy heart is not right in the sight of God. Repent therefore of this thy wickedness, and pray God, if perhaps the thought of thine heart may be forgiven thee. For I perceive that thou art in the gall of bitterness, and in the bond of iniquity.

Let us glance away from Simon for a moment in order to take a quick look at how Peter handled this new believer. What he said to Simon is true. The man had missed the point entirely. But to me it is interesting to note that even though he had been filled with the Spirit, Peter could still revert to his old impetuous manner. He spoke the truth, but this time he did not speak it in anything resembling tenderness or gentleness. There is always the possibility, of course, that Peter had learned that Simon, the sorcerer, only responded to plain talk—brusqueness. Yet it is fascinating to me that God does not always completely alter human personality. I think he seldom alters it entirely. He is not about the business of making us carbon copies of what we think of as "saints." God is about the eternal business of living his life in us through his Holy Spirit so that we can begin to be the very best we can be within our human limitations.

v. 24

Then answered Simon, and said, Pray ye to the Lord for me, that none of these things which ye have spoken come upon me.

Simon is still thinking of Simon, but at least he had the grace and humility to ask for prayer. We are not told what eventually happened to Simon's faith, but because I can so easily identify with his mixed motives, I have to be hopeful about him.

v. 25
And they, when they had testified and preached the word of the Lord, returned to Jerusalem, and preached the gospel in many villages of the Samaritans.

It is well to remember, in view of our race-relations problems of today, that the Samaritans hated the Jews. The members of the early Church must have shown love, or they would not have been received. Their Master had preceded them into Samaria, and John and Peter and the other Twelve were with him there. The Samaritans must have seen Christ's love in them by his Spirit which had invaded their lives.

v. 26
And the angel of the Lord spake unto Philip, saying, Arise, and go toward the south unto the way that goeth down from Jerusalem unto Gaza, which is desert.

Does God speak to us directly? So directly that we would change our route and go by another road—a road seldom used by other travelers? Is it really possible that a mere human being filled with the Spirit of God can be guided in this specific way? Frequently I receive—out of the blue— entire manuscripts from would-be writers who insist that God has "told" them to write. Of course, editing is not my profession, but when there is time to scan a page or two, this is enough to let me know that God simply could not have "told" the person to write because ninety-nine times out of a hundred he or she is no writer. God has no need for any more inferior efforts. Often the subject matter, while it may be sprinkled with religious terminology, is off-center, marginal, fanatic in its emphasis. Or it is so totally self-centered as to be neurotic. I also receive letters from persons who need a speaker for some particularly important meeting—one they obviously look forward to with great eagerness. They have been assigned the job of getting a speaker, and "The Lord has told us specifically that you are the one. I feel sure, Miss Price, that if you pray about it, you will come to us." In other words, if I am writing and can't come or if I am already committed elsewhere on that date, I *must* be disobeying God. This is a ticklish thing. We need to be very realistic and honest when we attempt to get our guidance from on high. Actually, after more than twenty years as a follower of Jesus Christ, who indwells me by his Spirit too, I have become convinced that if a human heart is surrendered to his heart, God doesn't mind whether that disciple goes about being God's friend in Africa or Germany or New York. It seems more logical and more like Jesus Christ to conclude that *wherever we are,* he wants to teach us particularized love for those whom our lives touch.

None of this means that I believe he never gives us detailed directions. He does. There are certain circumstancs where he must. But we weaken our own spirits when we fool around waiting for handwriting on the wall. God makes marvelously creative use even of our mistakes. His main interest is the condition of our hearts—not the route number of the road on which we drive our cars.

Still, I believe the circumstance of Philip's encounter with the Ethiopian authority was such that God did speak plainly to him. A few times in my years with Christ, he has guided me specifically. Mainly, he guides by the measure of our friendship with him.

Our part is to stay in open fellowship with the Source of all wisdom—learning, learning daily how to be natural with God, learning how to be his friend. We are never on a hot seat with a real friend, chewing our nails wondering what will please him and what will displease him. We are comfortable with our real friends because we know them. If you are agitating because you haven't received your "guidance" for something, put it aside for the time being and concentrate on learning more of what Jesus Christ is really like. As with Philip, there is at certain times definite direction, but I believe that God has a right to expect us to learn to use our Spirit-enlightened intelligence.

vv. 27 through 31

And he [Philip] arose and went: and, behold, a man of Ethiopia, an eunuch of great authority under Candace queen of the Ethiopians, who had the charge of all her treasure, and had come to Jerusalem for to worship, Was returning, and sitting in his chariot read Esaias the prophet. Then the Spirit said unto Philip, Go near, and join thyself to this chariot. And Philip ran thither to him, and heard him read the prophet Esaias, and said, Understandest thou what thou readest? And he said, How can I, except some man should guide me? And he desired Philip that he would come up and sit with him.

Now undoubtedly the Spirit of God guided Philip specifically that day. Being God, he knew that the Ethiopian was on that particular road. Being God, he also knew that the man's heart was open and receptive. (There would be no need for Philip to behave like a heavy-handed "personal worker!") God also knew about the wide sphere of influence this man held in his own country. He needed the Ethiopian. The Ethiopian needed God. He guided Philip to him.

vv. 32 through 35

The place of the scripture which he read was this, He was led as a sheep to the slaughter; and like a lamb dumb before his shearer, so opened he not his mouth: In his humiliation his judgment was taken away: and who shall declare his generation? for his life is taken from the earth. And the eunuch answered Philip, and said, I pray thee, of whom speaketh the prophet this? of himself, or of some other man? Then Philip opened his mouth, and began at the same scripture, and preached unto him Jesus.

This encounter must have been one of the happiest and most exciting of Philip's life. He was one of the seven chosen with Stephen to be a servant to the widows and the poor. For his willingness to serve, to handle food supplies and other necessary provisions, to help keep the peace among the faithful by seeing to it that the Grecian widows were treated as well as the Hebrew widows—for being willing to be all things to all men, even to preaching and traveling and healing when the occasion arose—God gave Philip this beautiful encounter with the Ethiopian. I can't think of any kind of experience that would bring more joy to a disciple than this: A learned man, with influence among his own people, a hungry heart and his scroll open to the fifty-third chapter of Isaiah! The eunuch's question went straight to the heart of the Christian faith: "Who is this? Tell me the name of this man who was led as a sheep to the slaughter? What is his name?"

"Then Philip . . . preached unto him Jesus." Quite probably this man took true Christianity to his native Africa because Philip met him that day. But to me, the beauty of the incident lies in the amazing, God-ordered symmetry of the encounter: an intelligent, inquiring mind, open to truth, reading truth without knowing it, but wanting to know; matched with this, a God-guided messenger with an open, uncondemning heart, time to talk and the truth to unfold. The influential Ethiopian and Philip and God. The meeting of these three on that little-traveled desert road rivals any art piece, any music, any literature in the pure form and symmetry of the Spirit. There was nothing off-key, nothing out of balance. It was all there.

vv. 36 and 37

And as they went on their way, they came unto a certain water: and the eunuch said, See, here is water; what doth hinder me to be baptized? And Philip said, If thou believest with all thine heart, thou mayest. And he answered and said, I believe that Jesus Christ is the Son of God.

It was all there, the central truth: Jesus is God, the articulated faith, the act.

vv. 38 and 39

And he commanded the chariot to stand still: and they went down both into the water, both Philip and

*the eunuch; and he baptized him. And when they were
come up out of the water, the Spirit of the Lord
caught away Philip, that the eunuch saw him no
more: and he went on his way rejoicing.*

It was all there—and the rejoicing.

CHAPTER 9
vv. 1 and 2
*And Saul, yet breathing out threatenings and
slaughter against the disciples of the Lord, went unto
the high priest, And desired of him letters to Damascus to the synagogues, that if he found any of this
way, whether they were men or women, he might
bring them bound unto Jerusalem.*

As the rulers of the temple who stood at Jesus' cross
watching him die grew more and more enraged, so did
Saul, who had watched Jesus' disciple, Stephen, die. The
King James Version cannot be improved upon here: "Saul,
yet breathing out threatenings and slaughter. . . ." To destroy the believers in Christ had become his very breath.

vv. 3 through 5
*And as he [Saul] journeyed, he came near Damas-
cus: and suddenly there shined round about him a
light from heaven: And he fell to the earth, and heard
a voice saying unto him, Saul, Saul, why persecutest
thou me? And he said, Who art thou, Lord? And the
Lord said, I am Jesus whom thou persecutest: it is
hard for thee to kick against the pricks.*

The impact of that sudden Presence of love against the
hate in Saul was enough to knock a man to the ground. Saul
was a religionist. He believed himself to be serving the
Lord God of Israel when he persecuted the disciples of
Jesus. His service had become an obsession. Now, in that
terrible moment of light, the proud spirit cracked. The brilliant, highly educated student of Gamaliel did not take time
for reason or for logic. On his knees in the dusty road, he
heard himself call this Jesus "Lord": "Who art thou,
Lord?"

Most of the modern translations omit the line the King James Version indicates Jesus spoke: "it is hard for thee to kick against the pricks." This line, whether it was in the original writings or not, has meaning for me. It is like Jesus. He is, even at this stunning moment of encounter with the hate-filled Saul, showing Saul that he understands how destructive this pursuit of violence has been for a sensitive man to follow. Without knowing it, Saul had been persecuting the God he meant to be serving. It was tearing him apart inwardly, destroying him. The Lord knew this, and he let Saul know that he knew.

vv. 6 through 9

And he trembling and astonished said, Lord, what wilt thou have me to do? And the Lord said unto him, Arise, and go into the city, and it shall be told thee what thou must do. And the men which journeyed with him stood speechless, hearing a voice, but seeing no man. And Saul arose from the earth; and when his eyes were opened, he saw no man: but they led him by the hand, and brought him into Damascus. And he was three days without sight, and neither did eat nor drink.

Saul not only instantly called Jesus "Lord"; he immediately obeyed Jesus' command to "go into the city"—obeyed and, obviously as suddenly, *believed.* The shock of discovering who it was he had been persecuting blinded the young man, but he permitted himself to be led by the hand in total obedience with what Jesus had said to him.

It has always been a fascination to me to try to imagine what Paul *thought* during the three days he was "without sight" or food or drink. Having experienced a definite moment of conversion myself (and not all do, of course), I can comprehend something of the wonder, the mystery, the altogether new sense of worship which must have filled his mind. In a definite sense, Saul *lived* on the new awareness of God's identity. There were surely moments of deep remorse and repentance, but I doubt that he suffered only the pain of actual guilt during those first three days. I believe the wonder was too great.

vv. 10 through 12
*And there was a certain disciple at Damascus,
named Ananias; and to him said the Lord in a vision,
Ananias. And he said, Behold, I am here, Lord. And
the Lord said unto him, Arise, and go into the street
which is called Straight, and enquire in the house of
Judas for one called Saul, of Tarsus: for, behold, he
prayeth, And hath seen in a vision a man named Ananias coming in, and putting his hand on him, that he
might receive his sight.*

The interesting line here is "for, behold, he prayeth."
Jesus knew that Ananias, no matter how deep his loyalty,
would be afraid of Saul, the persecutor of Christians. And
it would seem that the fear should drop away if Ananias
saw Saul praying. This was not true then, and it is not true
now. Prayer still serves too many purposes for man. Saul
was known to be religious. To see him at prayer would not
quiet Ananias' anxiety.

vv. 15 and 16
*But the Lord said unto him, Go thy way: for he is a
chosen vessel unto me, to bear my name before the
Gentiles, and kings, and the children of Israel: For I
will shew him how great things he must suffer for my
name's sake.*

Ananias (in verses 13 and 14) explained his fears to the
Lord, and then Jesus did what he so often does: He gave
the anxious disciple a specific explanation: "for he [Saul]
is a chosen vessel unto me, to bear my name. . . ." Up to
that point, Ananias had been thinking (quite naturally) in
terms of his own service and safety. But the Lord got down
to particulars, reminding him that He needed this man,
Saul, for His own purposes. This shifted Ananias' attention
from himself to God and (verse 17) he went on his way,
and laid his hands on Saul, praying for him to receive his
sight and to be filled with the Holy Spirt.

vv. 18 and 19
*And immediately there fell from his eyes as it had
been scales: and he received sight forthwith, and*

arose, and was baptized. And when he had received meat, he was strengthened. Then was Saul certain days with the disciples which were at Damascus.

It is interesting to me that, when no disciple was available, Jesus appeared personally to Saul and to Ananias. But when possible, God uses a human intermediary. It is also interesting and (with simple believers, *natural*) to do what Saul did once he could see again and once he was filled with the Spirit: He looked up other Christians, the very men he was on his way to Damascus to persecute!

v. 20
And straightway he preached Christ in the synagogues, that he is the Son of God.

This to me is the most dynamic verse in the entire story of Saul's conversion. He started out on center with Christ only, and throughout his entire life the great Apostle stayed on center. He began "straightway" to preach that Jesus Christ is the Son of God, and nothing moved Saul (Paul) from this one Absolute. He treated the marginal issues in his teaching programs with the young churches, but inevitably he returned to the only essential: Jesus Christ himself.

vv. 23 through 25
And after that many days were fulfilled, the Jews took counsel to kill him: But their laying await was known to Saul. And they watched the gates day and night to kill him. Then the disciples took him by night, and let him down by the wall in a basket.

Of course, the non-Christian Jews wanted Saul out of the way. He was more than just another disciple causing trouble by his preaching that Jesus was the Son of God; he was, to them, an out-and-out traitor.

Here again, God never uses visions and miracles if he can make use of the ordinary: Saul escaped death by way of a basket on the end of a rope.

v. 26

*And when Saul was come to Jerusalem, he assayed
to join himself to the disciples: but they were all
afraid of him, and believed not that he was a disciple.*

Saul even had to prove himself to those who already followed Christ. This, however, is not so unusual as it may
appear at first glance. Even relatively new believers, mainly
because of what to long-time Christians is "strange" conditioning, still must do this now and then. After twenty years
of following Christ publicly, I still have to answer letters
from those who are suddenly "suspicious" of me. "I no
longer consider you a disciple of Jesus Christ after reading
your novel, *New Moon Rising*," a lady wrote. The book
ends with what to me is a conversion, but it sounded
strange to her. Christians today are no different from the
Christians Saul knew.

vv. 27 through 31

*But Barnabas took him, and brought him to the
apostles, and declared unto them how he had seen the
Lord in the way, and that he had spoken to him, and
how he had preached boldly at Damascus in the name
of Jesus. And he was with them coming in and going
out at Jerusalem. And he spake boldly in the name of
the Lord Jesus. . . . Then had the churches rest
throughout all Judaea and Galilee and Samaria, and
were edified; and walking in the fear of the Lord, and
in the comfort of the Holy Ghost, were multiplied.*

One of their own, Barnabas, had to come to Saul's rescue. Apparently, even with the Twelve, Saul had to be
vouched for. As with some of us, they seemed to have a
hard time believing that Jesus Christ can change a man as
much as he had obviously changed Saul.

vv. 36 through 40 (Read through v. 43.)

*Now there was at Joppa a certain disciple named
Tabitha, which by interpretation is called Dorcas: this
woman was full of good works and almsdeeds which
she did. And it came to pass in those days, that she
was sick, and died: . . . And forasmuch as Lydda was*

nigh to Joppa, and the disciples had heard that Peter was there, they sent unto him two men, desiring him that he would not delay to come to them. Then Peter arose and went with them. When he was come, they brought him into the upper chamber: and all the widows stood by him weeping, and shewing the coats and garments which Dorcas made, while she was with them. But Peter put them all forth, and kneeled down, and prayed; and turning him to the body said, Tabitha, arise. And she opened her eyes: and when she saw Peter, she sat up.

I do not believe that the Lord raised Dorcas from the dead through Peter merely because she had worked hard to make a lot of coats and garments for the poor. Millions of women in the history of Christianity have been as faithful and unselfish as Dorcas and were not raised from the dead. We err when we attempt to pin God down in this superficial manner by some pat explanation man can accept. I have no theory as to why they did not have to bury Dorcas that day, other than the fact that so often, when one of the disciples permitted God to perform a miracle through him, numbers began to believe. There was no better way to convince the skeptic then. God is not unmindful of what methods are effective at a given time in the stubborn history of his loved ones.

CHAPTER 10
vv. 1 through 8
There was a certain man in Caesarea called Cornelius . . . A devout man, and one that feared God with all his house, which gave much alms to the people, and prayed to God alway. He saw in a vision evidently about the ninth hour of the day an angel of God coming in to him, and saying unto him, Cornelius. And when he looked on him, he was afraid, and said, What is it, Lord? And he said unto him, Thy prayers and thine alms are come up for a memorial before God. . . . send men to Joppa, and call for one Simon, whose surname is Peter: He lodgeth with one Simon a tanner, whose house is by the sea side: he shall tell thee what thou oughtest to do. And when the angel . . . was

*departed, he called two of his household servants, and
a devout soldier of them that waited on him continually; And when he had declared all these things unto
them, he sent them to Joppa.*

Contrary to the point of view of many rigid Christians,
God can and does "get through" to men and women whose
hearts are open to him, but who may not have total New
Testament light on their paths. Cornelius truly worshiped
all he knew of the Lord God. As far as he saw, he acted.

Here again, because there were no enlightened disciples
around, God had to resort to supernatural means of com-
municating with Cornelius. But He was sending him to talk
to Peter.

v. 9
*On the morrow, as they went on their journey, and
drew nigh unto the city, Peter went up upon the house-
top to pray about the sixth hour:*

As he is now, God was then acting, directing, prompting
men within their familiar framework of *time.* He lives in
the *eternal now,* but he never forgets that we are timebound.

vv. 10 through 16
*And he [Peter] became very hungry, and would
have eaten: but while they made ready, he fell into a
trance, And saw heaven opened, and a certain vessel
descending unto him, as it had been a great sheet knit
at the four corners, and let down to the earth:
Wherein were all manner of fourfooted beasts of the
earth, and wild beasts, and creeping things, and fowls
of the air. And there came a voice to him, Rise, Peter;
kill, and eat. But Peter said, Not so, Lord; for I have
never eaten any thing that is common or unclean. And
the voice spake unto him again the second time, What
God hath cleansed, that call not thou common. This
was done thrice: and the vessel was received up again
into heaven.*

The first thing that strikes me here is that God knew Peter through and through. He chose a time when Peter was his most vulnerable—early in the morning, before breakfast (while breakfast was being prepared), to begin teaching him the central Christian lesson of brotherhood. So conditioned by his early training, which centered around the superiority of the Jews as God's chosen people, Peter needed some means which would strike him "where he lived" to crack this patronizing shell of hereditary righteousness. God picked out a time when Peter's mind was on food and let down the big sheet full of things to eat. Of course, when Peter refused, he felt utterly "spiritual." Until this moment, he had been convinced that God agreed with his ancestors concerning their superiority to Gentiles and all other races. Being God, He patiently repeated the command three times. And then the vision vanished, and Peter had a few minutes to think it through.

vv. 17 through 20

Now while Peter doubted in himself what this vision . . . should mean, behold, the men which were sent from Cornelius had made enquiry for Simon's house, and stood before the gate, And called, and asked whether Simon, which was surnamed Peter, were lodged there. While Peter thought on the vision, the Spirit said unto him, Behold, three men seek thee. Arise therefore, and get thee down, and go with them, doubting nothing: for I have sent them.

God knew exactly where the messengers from Cornelius were on the way, and he knew exactly where Peter was—in his confusion. He gave Peter what he still gives us: the chance to learn a truth by acting on it in blind faith in the nature of God. I am learning, as the years go by, to go ahead whether I understand God's reasoning or not. Authentic faith is based not on our understanding of God's directions, but on our understanding of what he is really like. This, of course, is the reason no one lives adequately unless he or she is concentrating on the continuous discovery of the nature of God in Jesus Christ. There is no other specific way to learn God's nature. This is why Jesus came to earth.

v. 21

*Then Peter went down to the men which were sent
unto him from Cornelius; and said, Behold, I am he
whom ye seek: what is the cause wherefore ye are
come?*

Peter was acting on what he knew of the very nature of
the God who had been trying to teach him such a surprising facet of truth. I like Peter because obviously he was no
spiritual giant. He was just plain "people" like us. But he
had lived with Jesus of Nazareth during his time on earth,
had been the first to catch on to the central truth that "thou
art that Christ, the Son of the living God"—and so, because of what Peter knew of the nature of this God, he
obeyed His command, though still doubting, still mostly in
the dark as to what God was up to. In verses 22 and 23, the
men explained about Cornelius and their mission, Peter
took them in for the night, called for a few of the brothers
who lived in Joppa to go with him on the strange journey,
and set out for Caesarea.

vv. 24 through 26

*And the morrow after they entered into Caesarea.
And Cornelius waited for them, and had called together his kinsmen and near friends. And as Peter was
coming in, Cornelius met him, and fell down at his
feet, and worshipped him. But Peter took him up, saying, Stand up; I myself also am a man.*

Peter had this much straight. A tiny crack in his ancient
concept of the superiority of his own race had been made
the day he was shown on the road to Philippi with Jesus
that his Master *was* God in the flesh. This freed Peter of at
least some of his exclusiveness. We are all born to worship,
not to be worshiped. He had found a Master who satisfied
his normal human desire to adore another. He discovered,
as anyone can in that moment of realization about Jesus,
that we are merely human, as is any other mortal. Nothing
could have been more out of line to Peter than to have a
man worship him. Peter was a believer in the Godship of

Jesus Christ. He would never again be able to worship a great man, even a human king. The first crack in Peter's hereditary armor had been made: "Stand up, man! I am only a man too."

vv. 27 through 29
And as he talked with him, he went in, and found many that were come together. And he said unto them, Ye know how that it is an unlawful thing for a man that is a Jew to keep company, or come unto one of another nation; but God hath shewed me that I should not call any man common or unclean. Therefore came I unto you without gainsaying, as soon as I was sent for: I ask therefore for what intent ye have sent for me?

Peter grew a hundred cubits in that moment. Even if perhaps he was secretly hoping that Cornelius and his friends might think him a bighearted fellow for being so humble as to walk right into their Gentile house, still Peter spoke what for him was an entirely new, earthshaking truth. And he spoke it *after* he had acted upon it. "Therefore came I unto you." He didn't go about "preaching brotherhood" and spouting off about his special vision from God. He acted first and then articulated what God had just taught him. At that moment, Peter was indeed being God's friend—far more than a servant, a friend. Addressing men and women who had up to *yesterday* been unclean and common to him, Peter actually stood inside their house asking, "What may I do for you?"

In the remaining verses of Chapter 10, truth, the whole truth about God's visit to the earth in Jesus, broke over the roomful of people because another facet of that Truth had broken over Peter that day. Historically, it was an important moment in the life of the Church, but to me the dynamic of the story is that God chose the most headstrong Apostle, Peter, to begin to move love abroad in the world. Peter could well have been like some headstrong segregationists today—not a cruel man, but so certain of his own racial superiority that God knew to convince Peter would be ultimately to convince a world.

CHAPTER 11
vv. 1 through 3

*And the apostles and brethren that were in Judaea
heard that the Gentiles had also received the word of
God. And when Peter was come up to Jerusalem, they
that were of the circumcision contended with him,
Saying, Thou wentest in to men uncircumcised, and
didst eat with them.*

This is so familiar to this day as to call forth a loud "Ho
hum." The "apostles and brethren" didn't want any new
"brothers" who deviated one iota from what they believed.
No one could congratulate Peter on his new insight because
all of them were in too much darkness themselves to recognize it as such. Rather, they jumped on him for eating with
"unclean" people.

"I can't possibly have fellowship with *him*—he drinks or
smokes or was baptized the wrong way! No man is *my*
brother until he holds exactly the same doctrine about the
Lord Jesus Christ that I hold!" Sound familiar? A com-
plaint still repeating itself down through the years from the
day Peter was attacked by those who professed to believe in
the heart that broke on Calvary, who professed to believe
in the stretched-out arms—stretched out on a cross to en-
compass and welcome the world which "God so loved."

I can only thank this One of the stretched-out arms and
the torn-open heart that the complainer's half-truth about
him is just that—half truth, minus his mercy and his patience and his understanding.

vv. 4, 17 and 18

*But Peter rehearsed the matter from the beginning,
and expounded it by order unto them, saying [in sum-
mary] . . . Forasmuch then as God gave them the like
gift as he did unto us, who believed on the Lord Jesus
Christ; what was I, that I could withstand God? When
they heard these things, they held their peace, and
glorified God, saying, Then hath God also to the Gentiles granted repentance unto life.*

Hurray for those "apostles and brethren"! And hurray, I
say, for Peter. He must have lived well before them be-

cause once he told them, step by step, exactly what had happened on the rooftop in his vision and at Cornelius' house, they believed him. Peter told them that he saw these Gentiles filled with the same familiar Spirit. Peter's word held. He did not compromise in the telling. He made no effort to be falsely "humble." He didn't say, "Now, I'm not altogether sure about these people—we'll have to watch them for a while and see." He put no one on trial. He had no reservations. He had seen with his own eyes and he told them what he knew to be true. Shocking as it must have been to them all—as it was to Peter—the big fisherman had seen God in Gentiles. "Who was I, then, to try to stop God?" (*Good News for Modern Man*)

vv. 22, 24 and 25

Then tidings of these things came unto the ears of the church which was in Jerusalem: and they sent forth Barnabas, that he should go as far as Antioch. . . . For he was a good man, and full of the Holy Ghost and of faith: and much people was added unto the Lord. Then departed Barnabas to Tarsus, for to seek Saul: And when he had found him, he brought him unto Antioch. And it came to pass, that a whole year they assembled themselves with the church, and taught much people. And the disciples were called Christians first in Antioch.

Once Peter saw that God loved Gentiles too, the early Church began to spread like wildfire, not only because including Gentiles increased the "harvest field," but because the full operative power of love had been set free in the world.

I am fascinated by the special mention of the kind of man Barnabas was: "a good man, and full of the Holy Ghost and of faith." The Holy Ghost is God's life in us, and surely Barnabas was filled with the very perception of God. Remember (Chapter 9, verse 27) that it was Barnabas who, seeing in Saul of Tarsus a man filled with God— even a few days after his conversion—took him to the skeptical Apostles and convinced them that he was a true believer. Saul must have made a deep impression on Barnabas then. It is obvious that a deep friendship sprang up between the two men, because now that the need for active disciples was so great, Barnabas went to Tarsus to get Saul to help him in Antioch.

And, I think, most appropriately—because of the new believer, Saul, and the "good man," Barnabas—it was at Antioch that followers of the Way began to be called Christians.

vv. 27 through 30

And in these days came prophets from Jerusalem unto Antioch. And there stood up one of them named Agabus, and signified by the Spirit that there should be great dearth throughout all the world: which came to pass in the days of Claudius Caesar. Then the disciples, every man according to his ability, determined to send relief unto the brethren which dwelt in Judaea: Which also they did, and sent it to the elders by the hands of Barnabas and Saul.

It is appropriate also that these two friends (Saul and Barnabas) were the first Christian caseworkers.

CHAPTER 12
vv. 1 and 2

Now about that time Herod the king stretched forth his hands to vex certain of the church. And he killed James the brother of John with the sword.

Until now, I hadn't thought about John, the beloved disciple, in connection with the murder of his brother, James. Both men were Jesus' first cousins—their mothers were sisters. And all through their ministry with Jesus before his death, these brothers were always mentioned together in one breath. Jesus thought of them that way, even to the amusing nickname he gave them: sons of thunder. John's grief must have been inexplicable, and undoubtedly, as grief can do for those who know Christ, it helped prepare him to write his simple, loving Gospel and the short letters so filled with the love of God himself.

vv. 3 through 8

And because he [Herod] saw it pleased the Jews,

he proceeded further to take Peter also . . . he put him in prison, and delivered him to four quaternions of soldiers [sixteen] to keep him; intending after Easter to bring him forth to the people. Peter therefore was kept in prison: but prayer was made without ceasing of the church unto God for him. And when Herod would have brought him forth, the same night Peter was sleeping between two soldiers, bound with two chains: and the keepers before the door kept the prison. And, behold, the angel of the Lord came upon him, and a light shined in the prison: and he smote Peter on the side, and raised him up, saying, Arise up quickly. And his chains fell off from his hands. And the angel said unto him, Gird thyself, and bind on thy sandals. And so he did. And he saith unto him, Cast thy garment about thee, and follow me.

The wonder here to me has always been not that God managed Peter's escape from prison—God can do anything —but that he once more proved himself to be minutely loving, caring for the smallest detail of Peter's welfare. "Gird thyself, and bind on thy sandals. . . . Cast thy garment about thee. . . ." Get dressed, Peter, my son. Put on your shoes and don't forget your coat. God's tenderness is far more transforming than what we think of as power.

vv. 9 through 11

And he went out, and followed him; and wist not that it was true which was done by the angel; but thought he saw a vision. When they were past the first and the second ward, they came unto the iron gate that leadeth unto the city; which opened to them of his own accord: and they went out, and passed on through one street; and forthwith the angel departed from him. And when Peter was come to himself, he said, Now I know of a surety, that the Lord hath sent his angel, and hath delivered me out of the hand of Herod. . . .

Understanding Peter, God's angel walked with him not only all the way out of the prison, but up one familiar street, making sure that Peter knew it was not a dream.

Again, we can find easy affinity with Peter who, in spite of all he had seen the Lord do before, still thought he must be dreaming this time.

v. 12
And when he had considered the thing, he came to the house of Mary the mother of John, whose surname was Mark: where many were gathered together praying.

As soon as Peter realized the predicament he was in, he knew he needed to find a safe place. God used an angel to do what the praying disciples at Mark's mother's house could not do—open the doors of the prison. But now Peter knew God well enough to begin to act on his own human intelligence. He was not safe from the authorities just because God had let him out into the streets.

vv. 13 and 14
And as Peter knocked at the door of the gate, a damsel came to hearken, named Rhoda. And when she knew Peter's voice, she opened not the gate for gladness, but ran in, and told how Peter stood before the gate.

In *The Unique World of Women* I have written at length about Rhoda, the slave girl of Mary, Mark's mother, and I concluded that Rhoda was not stupid—just young and somewhat scatterbrained—and so excited to recognize Peter's voice that she simply didn't use her head enough to let him come inside to safety. She had to tell her news first. I think this is really all that's here, except that it is obvious that Rhoda had a real capacity for joy and excitement—a capacity we all need.

vv. 15 and 16
And they said unto her [Rhoda], Thou art mad. But she constantly affirmed that it was even so. Then said they, It is his angel. But Peter continued knocking: and when they had opened the door, and saw him, they were astonished.

Silly girl! She's crazy! Even God could not manage to have Peter out of prison and knocking on their door. It *has* to be his angel standing there. It can't be Peter!

v. 17
But he [Peter], beckoning unto them with the hand to hold their peace, declared unto them how the Lord had brought him out of the prison. And he said, God shew these things unto James, and to the brethren. And he departed, and went into another place.

Peter had not run to Mary's house only for safety, but to let the disciples know their prayers had been answered—and to send word to James, the brother of Jesus, who now headed the church in Jerusalem. James had not believed that his elder brother, Jesus, had come from God during Jesus' earthly lifetime, but when the Lord made a point of appearing to James (I Corinthians 15:7) after His Resurrection, James believed and now had become a leader in his brother's church. Peter wanted it known that God had once more protected his own. Only after that did he go "into another place" to preach where it would be safer—at least until the present trouble blew over.

v. 25
And Barnabas and Saul returned from Jerusalem, when they had fulfilled their ministry, and took with them John, whose surname was Mark.

Here, in the action-packed story of the new Church, is where Saul—soon to be renamed Paul—came into his own. He was already a leader in need of an assistant. He chose Barnabas' nephew, John Mark.

CHAPTER 13
vv. 1 through 3
Now there were in the church that was at Antioch certain prophets and teachers; as Barnabas, and Simeon that was called Niger, and Lucius of Cyrene, and Manaen . . . and Saul. As they ministered to the Lord, and fasted, the Holy Ghost said, Separate me Barnabas and Saul for the work whereunto I have

*called them. And when they had fasted and prayed,
and laid their hands on them, they sent them away.*

The bond was already there, humanly speaking, between
Barnabas and Saul. It is the same whether God caused their
friendship to spring up knowing he would send them out
together, or whether he sent them to work as a team because he knew of their close relationship.

vv. 4 and 5

*So they, being sent forth by the Holy Ghost, depart-
ed unto Seleucia; and from thence they sailed to Cyprus. And when they were at Salamis, they preached
the word of God in the synagogues of the Jews: and
they had also John to their minister.*

This rather awkward wording in the King James, "and
they had also John to their minister," simply means that
Mary's young son, John Mark, went along to minister to
Barnabas and Saul and to help in the work in any way he
might be needed. John Mark was quite young, perhaps still
a teen-ager. His mother, Mary of Jerusalem, must have
been happy to see her son under the influence of two men
like Paul and Barnabas.

vv. 6 through 12

*And when they had gone through the isle unto Pa-
phos, they found a certain sorcerer, a false prophet, a
Jew, whose name was Bar-jesus: Which was with the
deputy [Governor] of the country, Sergius Paulus, a
prudent man; who called for Barnabas and Saul, and
desired to hear the word of God. But Elymas the sorcerer [his name in Greek] withstood them, seeking to
turn away the deputy from the faith. Then Saul, (who
also is called Paul,) filled with the Holy Ghost, set his
eyes on him, And said, O full of all subtilty and all
mischief, thou child of the devil, thou enemy of all
righteousness, wilt thou not cease to pervert the right
ways of the Lord? And now, behold, the hand of the
Lord is upon thee, and thou shalt be blind, not seeing
the sun for a season. And immediately there fell on*

*him a mist and a darkness; and he went about seeking
some to lead him by the hand.*

This passage is one of the many in the Bible (more in
the Old Testament, of course, than in the New) where I
cannot reconcile what I read with what I have learned
about the nature of God in Jesus Christ from the same
New Testament. The Scriptures say that Paul was filled
with the Holy Ghost when he lashed out at the sorcerer.
Well, as I see it, the Holy Ghost is not likely to do anything
that Jesus wouldn't do. Jesus did say (John 16:8a) that
when the Holy Ghost came, he would "reprove the world
of sin. . . ." Paul was not acting in a contradictory way
when he informed Elymas of his sinful behavior. But
would Jesus have struck a man blind? Did he blind Saul?
Didn't he go about bringing sight to blind eyes? Some will
say, "But God must have done it through Paul—a mere
man cannot cause another man to go suddenly blind." I
don't know.

Sorcerers, those who dabble in the occult either as a
hobby or professionally, are much in the news these days.
People are buying their books in far greater quantities than
they buy books about Jesus Christ. And surely some of
those who operate in the world of the occult are—or at
least seem to be—evil people. Some, of course, are not. I
feel that the occult is often a substitute for faith and, for
that reason, it is dangerous. Yet one of America's most famous soothsayers, Jeanne Dixon, is a Christian. There is
no point in arguing the wrong or the right of the use of the
occult here. My thoughts are quite open-end on it, anyway
at this point. And this is one of the new freedoms I am
finding in God. I no longer need to have it all decided. I no
longer need to fear the criticism of God's people if I don't
happen to be as certain of someone's sinful pursuits as they
are. I need only fear God, and he is going right along with
me on my pilgrimage toward deeper understanding, ap-
proving the fact, I believe, that I am never again going to
be satisfied with pat answers.

So I do not disagree with Paul for telling the man off. I
have to admit that I am puzzled by the "punishment,"
though it is possible that the man suffered sudden (and
commonplace) hysterical blindness—as perhaps occurred

to Saul on the Damascus road. I can only say that this
strange happening strikes me as more like Paul's opinion of
what the man deserved than God's. After all, Paul was an
intense, once utterly self-righteous, man. I've never known
a conversion to change anyone entirely, just like that. If
Paul lost all his overriding, opinionated, violent characteristics overnight, I think he must have been the first one.
The great Apostle (to me the greatest) is a favorite of mine
for this reason: He remained the honed intellectual, and it
would have been a miracle indeed if he had become a pa-
tient saint in a flash.

v. 12
*Then the deputy [Governor], when he saw what
was done, believed, being astonished at the doctrine of
the Lord.*

At any rate, Paul got his man, the Governor. I'm frankly
confused at the fact that seeing a man go blind should clear
up the "doctrine of the Lord," but any passage such as this
which forces us to get down to the nitty-gritty where God's
character is concerned is cause for joy—as is any passage
that *dares* us to think.

v. 13
*Now when Paul and his company loosed from Pa-
phos, they came to Perga in Pamphylia: and John
[Mark] departing from them returned to Jerusalem.*

I am terribly curious as to what really happened between
Paul and John Mark, but of two things we can be sure:
John Mark was young and impulsive, and Paul *was* a new
Christian still. It is not at all farfetched to observe that
Paul must have been like most of the rest of us when that
first Light breaks suddenly: almost obnoxious in our certainty, our desire to convince—fast. I do not worship Paul.
Some almost seem to, simply because he wrote so many of
the Scriptures. This would have broken his heart—he
whose very life was not his own spiritual experience, but
Jesus Christ. "To me to live is Christ." A man who could
write that would loathe being worshiped as a perfect
human being. He never forgot that he felt he was "the chief-

est of sinners." Of course, he wasn't. No one is. Or is everyone? But as I see it, this is Paul admitting that he got his own way often, and this could have had a lot to do with John Mark's going home to Jerusalem.

v. 49 (Read Paul's sermons at Antioch, vv. 14 through 47.)
And the word of the Lord was published throughout all the region.

Paul's expositions were so learned, so lucid, so filled with the very light of God that his message began to be talked about far and wide.

vv. 50 through 52
But the Jews stirred up the devout and honourable women, and the chief men of the city, and raised persecution against Paul and Barnabas, and expelled them out of their coasts. But they shook off the dust of their feet against them, and came unto Iconium. And the disciples were filled with joy, and with the Holy Ghost.

Wherever the whole truth of God in Christ is preached, some people always grow angry and begin to stir up trouble. If men are still running their own lives, confrontation with the truth of God can appear as an outright attack. They can become self-defensive, even violent. Here the full momentum of God through his Holy Spirit was active, so Paul and Barnabas were kicked out of the area. Did they leave depressed, feeling failures, certain they had let God down? Not at all. They shook the dust from their feet and went on to another town. And the holy hilarity of God possessed them as they went: "the disciples were filled with joy. . . ."

CHAPTER 14
vv. 4 through 8
[In Iconium] the multitude of the city was divided: and part held with the Jews, and part with the apostles. And when there was an assault made both of the Gentiles, and also of the Jews with their rulers, to use

*them despitefully, and to stone them, They were ware
of it, and fled unto Lystra and Derbe, cities of Lycaonia, and unto the region that lieth round about: And
there they preached the gospel.*

One place was as good as another to these men. They
had something to say! Creativity was upon them and within them.

vv. 8 through 11

*And there sat a certain man at Lystra, impotent in
his feet, being a cripple from his mother's womb, who
never had walked: The same heard Paul speak: who
stedfastly beholding him, and perceiving that he had
faith to be healed, Said with a loud voice, Stand
upright on thy feet. And he leaped and walked. And
when the people saw what Paul had done, they lifted
up their voices, saying in the speech of Lycaonia, The
gods are come down to us in the likeness of men.*

It is more than interesting that these Greek worshipers of
pagan gods found it simple to believe their gods *could*
come down to them in the likeness of men! No one taught
them a "doctrine" that said Paul and Barnabas were "gods
come down" as men. They found this the most logical thing
to believe when they saw the healing. Why has it become so
difficult for us to realize that God did a "natural," believable thing when he visited our earth in Jesus of Nazareth?

vv. 12 and 13

*And they called Barnabas, Jupiter; and Paul, Mer-
curius, because he was the chief speaker. Then the
priest of Jupiter, which was before their city, brought
oxen and garlands unto the gates, and would have
done sacrifice with the people.*

Our society has done its best to gloss over man's deepest
needs, but they are still just what they were then—including the need to worship.

vv. 14 through 18

Which when the apostles, Barnabas and Paul, heard

*of, they rent their clothes, and ran in among the peo-
ple, crying out, And saying, Sirs, why do ye these
things? We also are men of like passions with you, and
preach unto you that ye should turn from these vani-
ties unto the living God, which made heaven, and
earth, and the sea, and all things that are therein:
Who in times past suffered all nations to walk in their
own ways. Nevertheless he left not himself without
witness, in that he did good, and gave us rain from
heaven, and fruitful seasons, filling our hearts with
good and gladness. And with these sayings scarce re-
strained they the people, that they had not done sacrifice unto them.*

Paul had a genius for speaking to people where they
were. The only thing he attempted with those worshipers of
many gods was to convince them that there was but one
living God. He did not preach the death and Resurrection
of Christ here. In his wisdom from God, he met these people with what they could understand. They were all set to
worship him and Barnabas. His job at the moment was to
turn them from this, and he did it by telling them of the
goodness and love and mercy of the one God who, in spite
of the history of nations going their own ways ignoring
him, he "left not himself without witness." In his caring,
God kept the rain falling and the fruit and grain growing
and, in all the ways the people would permit, he filled their
"hearts with food and gladness."

As with the gospel of Christ, even this much must have
seemed too good to be true to Paul's pagan listeners. Also
as with the gospel of Christ, though, it was too good not to
be true. It stopped their attempted worship of Paul and
Barnabas. Just barely, but it did stop it.

vv. 19 and 20

*And there came thither certain Jews from Antioch
and Iconium, who persuaded the people, and, having
stoned Paul, drew him out of the city, supposing he
had been dead. Howbeit, as the disciples stood around
about him, he rose up, and came into the city: and the
next day he departed with Barnabas to Derbe.*

Paul must have been horribly injured. His enemies meant to kill him, and it isn't likely that they would have left their mission unfinished had they known he was not dead. After all, they had tracked him down at Lystra, from Antioch and Iconium. Still, the Spirit of life was so concentrated as the disciples stood around their fallen leader that "he rose up," went back into Lystra and was able to leave the next day for Derbe. This man, Paul, had been set in motion.

vv. 21 through 22

And when they had preached the gospel to that city [Derbe], and had taught many, they returned again to Lystra, and to Iconium, and Antioch, Confirming the souls of the disciples, and exhorting them to continue in the faith, and that we must through much tribulation enter into the kingdom of God.

Paul was not only a man set in motion; he was a man *enabled* by the Holy Spirit within him to move about without fear—even back into the very towns of Iconium and Antioch, the hometowns of the men who traveled to Lystra to stone him to death. It was not Paul's own "perfect love" which cast out his fear; it was the love of God in him. This is a tremendous relief and one which must be remembered when we are afraid.

v. 23

And when they had ordained them elders in every church, and had prayed with fasting, they commended them to the Lord, on whom they believed.

Paul and Barnabas seem to have been practical men. It is true that Paul, at times especially, was an eloquent speaker, but he did not stop here. In every town where they had won disciples to Christ, they handled the business of forming the new churches for local rule after they were gone. Both men did what they had to do, but then had the humility to move on, commending the young church members "to the Lord, on whom they believed."

v. 24 through 26 and 28

And after they had passed through Pisidia, they came to Pamphylia. And when they had preached the word in Perga, they went down into Attalia: And thence sailed to Antioch, from whence they had been recommended to the grace of God for the work which they fulfilled. . . . And there they abode long time with the disciples.

Paul and Barnabas had completed their first missionary journey. They were back again in Antioch where, so many miles and months and experiences ago, they had been waved off by the disciples. Now they stayed a long time with these disciples. When Paul was in action, he kept going, but I am impressed with his balance, especially in a man so intense and energetic and full of purpose. In spite of his intellect and seriousness of mind, he seemed, much of the time, to be a man almost driven by joy. And yet, now he was staying in Antioch to be a part of the new church there—to strengthen the others, but also to be strengthened by them. He was never a "traveling religioso" staying on the go, missing both the heartache and the inspiration of seeing people through their problems. To travel constantly is exhausting, but it is one thing to preach a sermon and move on. It is quite another thing to have the patience and wisdom to counsel and suffer with troubled people. Paul could do both.

CHAPTER 15
v. 1

And certain men which came down from Judaea taught the brethren, and said, Except ye be circumcised after the manner of Moses, ye cannot be saved.

This was bound to happen sooner or later.

v. 2

When therefore Paul and Barnabas had no small dissension and disputation with them, they determined that Paul and Barnabas, and certain other of them, should go up to Jerusalem unto the apostles and elders about this question.

This, of course, was the first Christian Church Con-
clave, and it is well, I think, to note that there was a specific need for it. The young church, whatever its faults, was at
least not overorganized. When they had a real problem,
they got together to settle it. There were no planned com-
mitteee meetings or conventions just because a date had
come up on the calendar.

vv. 4 through 6
*And when they were come to Jerusalem, they were
received of the church, and of the apostles and elders,
and they declared all things that God had done with
them. But there rose up certain of the sect of the
Pharisees which believed, saying, That it was needful
to circumcise them, and to command them to keep the
law of Moses. And the apostles and elders came together for to consider of this matter.*

There was really one matter and one only to decide
upon: Would Christianity break free of the laws of Judaism and become a complete faith on its own, based solely
on confidence in the risen Lord, Jesus Christ? Or would it
remain a Jewish sect within the Mosaic framework, made
up of those who believed that the Messiah had come in
Jesus, but who continued to obey the Law of Moses? Still
more simply: Can a man be a Christian (whether he is Jew
or Gentile) and not follow the Mosaic Law?

vv. 7 through 11
*And when there had been much disputing, Peter
rose up, and said unto them, Men and brethren, ye
know how that a good while ago God made choice
among us, that the Gentiles by my mouth should hear
the word of the gospel, and believe. And God, which
knoweth the hearts, bare them witness, giving them
the Holy Ghost, even as he did unto us; And put no
difference between us and them, purifying their hearts
by faith. Now therefore why tempt ye God, to put a
yoke upon the neck of the disciples, which neither our
fathers nor we were able to bear? But we believe that*

*through the grace of the Lord Jesus Christ we shall be
saved, even as they.*

Of course they disputed hotly, and of course Peter stood
up. Even though much of the work among the Gentiles had
been given to Paul by now, it had been Peter to whom the
Lord gave the first hint of His love for Gentiles as well as
Jews. No one could have been more shocked when the
Spirit told him to go to the house of the Gentile Cornelius.
But Peter went, and there he was convinced. A very high,
ancient wall fell down for Peter that day as he stood among
the members of Cornelius' family, seeing with his own eyes
that God meant to include them too. He had been convinced once and for all, and so naturally he got up to speak
now. And he spoke plainly, concisely, to the one point of
trouble—either a man found salvation only through the
grace of the Lord Jesus Christ, or he didn't. Peter knew for
a fact that God "put no difference between us and them,
purifying their hearts by faith." Not by obedience to this
law and that—by faith.

v. 12
*Then all the multitude kept silence, and gave audi-
ence to Barnabas and Paul, declaring what miracles
and wonders God had wrought among the Gentiles by
them.*

Like Peter, Paul and Barnabas simply witnessed to what
they had seen, experienced and knew to be fact. The evidence piled very high.

vv. 13, 19, 20 (Read vv. 13 through 20.)
*And after they had held their peace, James an-
swered, saying, Men and brethren, hearken unto me:
. . . Wherefore my sentence is, that we trouble not
them, which from among the Gentiles are turned to
God: But that we write unto them, that they abstain
from pollutions of idols, and from fornication, and
from things strangled, and from blood.*

James, the head of the church at Jerusalem and Jesus'
own brother, set the precedent. He quoted from the Old

Testament and made a loving, inclusive, New Testament-tempered suggestion: Let us not trouble these Gentiles whose hearts have turned to God. We will write them a letter giving them four rules to obey—and all of these four are for their good in the pagan society in which we Christians now live.

To some, it may seem that James was simply being expedient, forcing onto the Gentile believers just enough Judaism "to get by." This is not what he did at all. The four Christian abstinences were then beneficial ones, and they were, from that time on, to apply to Jewish Christians too.

vv. 22, 23, 30, 31

Then pleased it the apostles and elders, with the whole church, to send chosen men of their own company to Antioch with Paul and Barnabas; namely, Judas surnamed Barsabas, and Silas, chief men among the brethren: And they wrote [sent] letters by them. . . . So when they were dismissed, they came to Antioch: and when they had gathered the multitude together, they delivered the epistle: Which when they had read, they rejoiced for the consolation.

Indeed, it must have been a real "consolation." These Gentile Christians had been drawn to the faith by the Spirit of liberty, of love, of grace. They had become believers because of Jesus Christ. They had not been looking, within the context of Judaism, for a Messiah. They had been seeking the peace that comes from the forgiveness of their sins. That peace had come to them when they placed their faith in the resurrected Lord. His Resurrection was not a Jewish dogma to them—it was fact. Suddenly, to have been told by other legalistic Christians that they must now begin to obey certain laws in order to be saved must have distressed them deeply. Once all fears and anxieties had been stilled, Judas returned to Jerusalem, but Silas stayed in Antioch (verses 32-34). We are told that "it pleased Silas to abide there still." He must have had a particular affinity for these Gentiles who needed to learn now how to grow up in this new thoroughly *Christian* liberty.

vv. 35 and 36

Paul also and Barnabas continued in Antioch, teaching and preaching the word of the Lord, with many others also. And some days after Paul said unto Barnabas, Let us go again and visit our brethren in every city where we have preached the word of the Lord, and see how they do.

Paul was not content with the "victories" of the first missionary journey. The "numbers" he and Barnabas reported back to the disciples and the Apostles did not content him. He wanted to "see how they do" by now. And this was no small, easily made decision. Travel in those days was difficult. There were ships when the routes could be covered by sea, but they were small, cramped, stocked with the bare necessities. Portions of the trip would be made on foot mile after mile along hot, dusty roads in constant danger of bandits who killed when they robbed. Paul was not suggesting a vacation from the church at Antioch. He was wholeheartedly about his Master's business. Jesus Christ still filled Paul's horizons. Christ's concerns for the new converts along the route of that first difficult journey were Paul's too.

vv. 37 through 41

. . . Barnabas determined to take with them John, whose surname was Mark. But Paul thought not good to take him with them, who departed from them from Pamphylia, and went not with them to the work. And the contention was so sharp between them, that they departed asunder one from the other: and so Barnabas took Mark, and sailed unto Cyprus: And Paul chose Silas, and departed, being recommended by the brethren unto the grace of God. And he went through Syria and Cilicia, confirming the churches.

This story has always been a heartbreak to me. After what Paul and Barnabas had been through together—after what they had accomplished as a team—to read that the two Christian leaders contended so sharply with each other that they separated is sad. Where was God's will in this purely human dispute? Just where it always is, on the side of love. God's love, of course, since neither brother showed exactly what one could call "love" toward the other. Still, each undoubtedly had a point. After all, John Mark was Barnabas' nephew. Barnabas felt a certain responsibility toward him, I'm sure. And Paul was so intent upon a successful journey that he simply did not want a temperamental young man along to add, perhaps, to the already burdensome time ahead. Both men were probably right in their decisions—even to separate. But the heartbreak comes with the words "the contention was so sharp between them." Evidently they separated in anger.

CHAPTER 16
vv. 1 through 3

Then came he [Paul] to Derbe and Lystra: and behold, a certain disciple was there, named Timotheus, the son of a certain woman, which was a Jewess, and believed; but his father was a Greek: Which was well reported of by the brethren that were at Lystra and Iconium. Him would Paul have to go forth with him; and took and circumcised him because of the Jews which were in those quarters: for they knew all that his father was a Greek.

In place of John Mark, Paul found "his son" Timothy, and here began one of the tenderest, closest relationships in the New Testament. Paul, as we have seen, because of his own clear light on the pure grace of God through Jesus Christ, was not a legalist. His obedience was strict, but it was motivated by love for the Lord Christ who, in spite of the disposition problems Paul might have had, did fill the Apostle's life. And so Paul did not circumcise Timothy from convictions of his own. He had seen too many works of grace among uncircumcised Gentiles by now ever to feel that circumcision was necessary, but he was using his balanced intelligence. Hundreds of Jews where he would be traveling with young Timothy knew the boy's father was a Greek. It would be best not to upset them unnecessarly—perhaps prevent their hearing a more important part of Paul's message.

vv. 8 through 10 (Read vv. 4 through 7.)

And they passing by Mysia came down to Troas.
And a vision appeared to Paul in the night; There
stood a man of Macedonia, and prayed him, saying,
Come over into Macedonia, and help us. And after he
had seen the vision, immediately we endeavoured to
go into Macedonia, assuredly gathering that the Lord
had called us for to preach the gospel unto them.

The first thing to notice here is that the narrator quite
suddenly begins to use the first person pronoun. Since Luke
is the author of the Acts of the Apostles, it is almost certain
that the gentle, sensitive physician joined Paul's party at
Troas, where the sea had stopped them temporarily. In
verses 6 and 7, Paul's original plans to revisit the towns
along the route of his first journey are changed at every
turn. And at Troas, God redirected him in a most definite
way—sending, for the first time, the message of Jesus
Christ into Europe.

vv. 11 and 12

Therefore loosing from Troas, we came with a
straight course to Samothracia, and the next day to
Neapolis; And from thence to Philippi, which is the
chief city of that part of Macedonia . . . and we were
in that city abiding certain days.

Paul had done well on his first missionary journey, mainly to the Jews, but now God was centering down on His
major purpose for His uniquely dedicated Apostle. He had
to convince Paul through a vision, but at last the Christian
gospel was to be heard on the continent of Europe. The
momentous voyage took only a few days. The travelers—
Paul, Timothy, Silas and now Luke, the doctor—landed at
Neapolis and crossed the mountains to Philippi, ten miles
away. On the plains of Philippi, nearly a century before,
the fate of the world had been determined when Augustus
and Antony had defeated Brutus and Cassius. Philippi was
a military colony filled with sophisticated people—a minia-
ture Rome. Paul and his friends saw there a clear picture
of the moral and spiritual needs of the successful, cultivated citizens of their world. The people with whom they

spent their time, both Greek and Jew, were not ordinary. Even the women of Philippi enjoyed privileges seldom experienced in the ancient East. Every citizen of Philippi was proud of both his city and his unique Roman privileges. God was seeking to show himself as he really is to the privileged class in Europe—and he had wisely chosen Paul.

vv. 13 through 15

And on the sabbath we went out of the city by a river side, where prayer was wont to be made; and we sat down, and spake unto the women which resorted thither. And a certain woman named Lydia, a seller of purple, of the city of Thyatira, which worshipped God, heard us: whose heart the Lord opened, that she attended unto the things which were spoken of Paul. And when she was baptized, and her household, she besought us, saying, If ye have judged me to be faithful to the Lord, come into my house, and abide there. And she constrained us.

I have always liked Lydia, although to me she seems to be a little domineering. I know businesswomen like Lydia —lovable, middle-aged, successful, their faces showing the strain of having made it on their own—and they are forever deciding just what other people should do. Lydia was a successful businesswoman. She dealt in the famous purple dye made from the secretion of a native shellfish. Lydia had all she needed materially; evidently she had a large household. But her heart was empty and, although she was a Gentile, she had begun to join a small group of Jewish women by the river for prayer. By the time Paul and his friends reached Philippi, Lydia had come to believe in the Lord God of the Jews. She was not a scoffer at religion. She prayed; she worshiped God. And her heart was so open that she seems to have been the first person in the entire city to begin to believe Paul's message about the risen Lord. Domineering, strong-minded people are difficult to get along with at times; but when they make up their minds, they act. Lydia did both. She lost no time in being baptized and in seeing to it that her entire household was baptized too, and then she immediately "got Paul's guidance" for him! "If you really believe I have become a

Christian, then I insist that you and your party move into my house to live!" I think it's quite likely that they were already comfortably settled elsewhere. Otherwise why would Luke have emphasized that Lydia "besought"—persuaded —them? Finally she "constrained" them—gave them no choice but to accept her enforced hospitality. Those of you who, like me, live even a partially public life know the type of hostess Lydia must have been. But from Paul's first day in Europe her heart was filled with the Spirit of Christ. If Lydia permitted it, God would soon begin to melt away the rough edges of her personality.

vv. 16 through 18

And it came to pass, as we went to prayer, a certain damsel possessed with a spirit of divination met us, which brought her masters much gain by soothsaying: The same followed Paul and us, and cried, saying, These men are the servants of the most high God, which shew unto us the way of salvation. And this did she many days. But Paul, being grieved, turned and said to the spirit, I command thee in the name of Jesus Christ to come out of her. And he came out the same hour.

I may be criticized for even intimating that not all persons who have a "spirit of divination"—or who can foresee future events—are evil people. I merely feel that I am not the judge of these people. That many do have certain powers of foretelling has long been a proved fact. For years it has been, and still is, a subject for calm, scientific, careful study at Duke University and other schools. One thing seems certain here: This poor girl *could* both *see* and *foresee*, because she recognized Paul and Timothy and Silas and Luke as "servants of the most high God" and she knew not only that the people of Philippi had need of salvation, but that Paul and his friends could show them the way to find it.

What does seem equally apparent is that she *was* possessed of at least enough of the spirit of fear so that the men who were "making it big" by using her occult power were able to keep her chained to them in slavish obedience. Paul watched her pathetic tagging along, listened to her

shrill, girlish voice shouting day after day; and when he
could stand it no longer, he cast out the spirit which bound
her to these men. I wish Luke had told us what happened
to her after that. It is not likely that she changed her mind
about Paul's message.

vv. 19 through 24

*And when her masters saw that the hope of their
gains was gone, they caught Paul and Silas, and drew
them into the marketplace unto the rulers, And
brought them to the magistrates, saying, These men,
being Jews, do exceedingly trouble our city, And teach
customs, which are not lawful for us to receive, neither to observe, being Romans. And the multitude
rose up together against them: and the magistrates
rent off their clothes, and commanded to beat them.
And when they had laid many stripes upon them, they
cast them into prison, charging the jailor to keep them
safely: Who, having received such a charge, thrust
them into the inner prison, and made their feet fast in
the stocks.*

Apparently Luke and Timothy were not jailed. Paul and
Silas, I imagine, did all the preaching and teaching. There
was no trial, and of course the charges were false. Both
Paul and Silas were Roman citizens too, but they were
given no chance to say so.

v. 25

*And at midnight Paul and Silas prayed, and sang
praises unto God: and the other prisoners heard them.*

The two friends could not have been comfortable; their
backs burned from the lashes which had been laid across
them time and time again. There were no soothing oint-
ments and no clean beds—only dried, caked blood and a
damp stone floor. Their feet were chained to the wooden
stocks, so that their stiff shoulders and backs could not
even be rested by a shift in position. They had to sit up,
their raw backs against a wall. But they praised God and
sang songs! When we can sing while we suffer, someone is
always going to "hear." When we can praise God after an

unjust treatment of any kind, other "prisoners" will always "hear." The natural reaction under these circumstances would have been loud complaints and cursing. These men reacted *supernaturally*—they sang.

vv. 26 through 28

And suddenly there was a great earthquake, so that the foundations of the prison were shaken: and immediately all the doors were opened, and every one's bands were loosed. And the keeper of the prison awaking out of his sleep, and seeing the prison doors open, he drew out his sword, and would have killed himself, supposing that the prisoners had been fled. But Paul cried with a loud voice, saying, Do thyself no harm: for we are all here.

Whether God sent the earthquake is beside the point. Far more important is that he made such marvelous, creative, redemptive *use* of the quake (common in that region) to bring about an even greater miracle—the salvation of the jailer. At this point on my pilgrimage, above all things I see God as a redeemer—even of such dreadful natural catastrophes as earthquakes. He permitted it, of course, because deep within the earth creation is continuing, but the quake merely gave Paul a chance to *act like a Christian*. When God wanted Peter out of jail, he sent a messenger, making it perfectly clear that Peter should leave. This time, God *wanted* Paul and Silas to stay. And these two friends of God knew him well enough to know this. They had not been legally freed, and so Paul comforted the terrified jailer, assuring him that they were all still there. Notice that the other prisoners did not break and run either. They had heard Paul and Silas singing praises to God in the midst of their suffering. They found two men they could trust, and so they did what Paul and Silas did.

vv. 29 through 31

Then he [the jailer] called for a light, and sprang in, and came trembling, and fell down before Paul and Silas, And brought them out, and said, Sirs, what must I do to be saved? And they said, Believe on the Lord Jesus Christ, and thou shalt be saved, and thy house.

It *is* as simple as that. Why do we go on complicating God's magnificent simplicity?

vv. 32 through 34
And they spake unto him the word of the Lord, and to all that were in his house. And he took them the same hour of the night, and washed their stripes; and was baptized, he and all his, straightway. And when he had brought them into his house, he set meat before them, and rejoiced, believing in God with all his house.

The jailer was an abrupt, straightforward man. He entered the kingdom the same way—abruptly. God has no formula. He moves toward us at exactly the pace he knows we can accept. There is no doubt that the jailer was changed. His persecuting stopped at once, and he began to minister.

vv. 35 and 36
And when it was day, the magistrates sent the serjeants, saying, Let those men go. And the keeper of the prison told this saying to Paul, The magistrates have sent to let you go: now therefore depart, and go in peace.

After the ceremonies and the ministrations at the jailer's house during the night, Paul and Silas evidently went back to their cells. First thing the next morning, the jailer, wanting to show gratitude to his new brothers in Christ, used his "clout" with the magistrates to set his prisoners free.

vv. 37 through 39
But Paul said unto them, They have beaten us openly uncondemned, being Romans, and have cast us into prison; and now do they thrust us out privily? nay verily; but let them come themselves and fetch us out. And the serjeants told these words unto the magistrates: and they feared, when they heard that they were Romans. And they came and besought them, and

brought them out, and desired them to depart out of the city.

Paul waited until just the right time to let it be known that he and Silas were Romans too. This is one of the many reasons God could send Paul among the Europeans.

v. 40
And they went out of the prison, and entered into the house of Lydia: and when they had seen the brethren, they comforted them, and departed.

The two friends walked out of the prison in dignity, escorted by the magistrates themselves; but before they left Philippi, they took time to call a meeting at Lydia's house for the encouragement of the members of the new Philippian church. What had happened to Paul and Silas did *not* depress them; rather, they were encouraged and emboldened by it.

CHAPTER 17
vv. 1 through 3
Now when they had passed through Amphipolis and Apollonia, they came to Thessalonica, where was a synagogue of the Jews: And Paul, as his manner was, went in unto them, and three sabbath days reasoned with them out of the scriptures. Opening and alleging, that Christ must needs have suffered, and risen again from the dead; and that this Jesus, whom I preach unto you, is Christ.

There had not been enough Jews in Philippi for a synagogue, and so the handful had held their prayers by the river where Paul met Lydia. There was a synagogue in Thessalonica and, knowing full well what could happen eventually when the nonbelieving Jews in town learned that the Thessalonians were becoming Christians, Paul stood and preached Christ in sharp, definite, concise words. He left no doubt in anyone's mind that Jesus was the awaited Messiah. As Paul knew would happen, because he knew the drawing power of the Lord he followed, many Greek men and women began to follow the risen Jesus too (verse 4).

v. 5

But the Jews which believed not, moved with envy, took unto them certain lewd fellows of the baser sort, and gathered a company, and set all the city on an uproar, and assaulted the house of Jason, and sought to bring them out to the people.

". . . lewd fellows of the baser sort"—ne'er-do-wells—have not changed. They may still be "gathered" into "a company" for causing uproars in cities at the drop of the proverbial hat. It's human nature to relish disturbances in public—either as participants or observers. Mobs have not changed, but neither have the agitators who "gather a company." I do not speak of the cause here—merely of those who make the commotion, both behind the scenes and out front.

This mob, with no notion of why they were doing it, tracked Paul and Silas and Timothy and Luke down to the home of Jason, a believer, who had offered them his hospitality during their stay in Thessalonica. The members of the mob did not knock politely on the door, either. They "assaulted the house."

vv. 6 through 9

And when they found them not, they drew Jason and certain brethren unto the rulers of the city, crying, These that have turned the world upside down are come hither also; Whom Jason hath received: and these all do contrary to the decrees of Caesar, saying that there is another king, one Jesus. And they troubled the people and the rulers of the city, when they heard these things. And when they had taken security of Jason and of the other, they let them go.

After all the trouble, the authorities ended up with only a little bail money from Jason and the other disciples. They did not find Paul and his friends. Of course, Paul's work in Thessalonica was cut short, but one shining truth was uttered inadvertently by a Jew who helped drag Jason before

the rulers of the city: "These that have turned the world
upside down. . . ." The Spirit-filled Christians of the early
Church were doing just that—in a redemptive way. Everything authentically Christian is looked at through the opposite end of the telescope from the view the world takes.
Paul and his friends had learned so well how to rejoice in
hardship—to make creative, redemptive use of every tragedy and every setback—that to those still in darkness they
must have seemed to be living in an upside-down world.

vv. 10 through 15
*And the brethren immediately sent away Paul and
Silas [apparently not Luke and Timothy] by night
unto Berea . . . [where] many . . . believed; also of
honourable women which were Greeks, and of men,
not a few. But when the Jews of Thessalonica had
knowledge that the word of God was preached of Paul
at Berea, they came thither also, and stirred up the
people. And then immediately the brethren sent away
Paul to go as it were to the sea: but Silas and Timotheus abode there still. And they that conducted Paul
brought him unto Athens: and receiving a commandment unto Silas and Timotheus for to come to him
with all speed, they departed.*

Paul *had* truly been set in motion by the Spirit. One
troubled time followed another, but his course was set. He
was fighting "the good fight" and he knew it. Still, Paul was
quick to confess his own personal needs. Before he said
good-bye to the Berean disciples who went with him as far
as Athens, he asked them urgently to tell Timothy and Silas
to come to him as quickly as possible. He needed them. His
sufficiency in God left him free, as it always does, to need
other people, as well as to be needed.

v. 16
*Now while Paul waited for them at Athens, his
spirit was stirred in him, when he saw the city wholly
given to idolatry.*

I can see the brilliant Apostle walking the wide streets of
Athens—moving from one temple to another, from one

altar to another; reading the inscriptions to pagan gods; turning to look at the Athenians strolling the wide streets in spiritual darkness, his weathered, sensitive face frowning; troubled to the depths of his heart. Paul knew the truth of eternal life in Christ—knew it well enough to be the leader in the new movement that was turning the world upside down. He knew Christ so well, loved him so wholly, that he could write in a later letter to his friends back in Philippi: "To me to live is Christ." Paul knew and with his fine mind sensed the spiritual hunger in these intellectually inclined Athenians—a hunger not met. And he grieved as he walked the streets of the beautiful city, waiting for his friends to join him.

v. 17

Therefore disputed he in the synagogue with the Jews, and with the devout persons, and in the market daily with them that met with him.

Paul had not been sent by the Spirit to Athens. He was just waiting there for Silas and Timothy and Luke. But so deeply was he troubled about the people of this city filled with monuments and altars to pagan gods that he simply could not restrain himself any longer. He went first to the synagogue to discuss his faith with devout Jews; and before he knew it, he was speaking on the streets and in the marketplace—anywhere he could get people to listen.

Of course, this was not the same then as with street-corner preachers now. In Paul's time, this was the normal means of sharing ideas. There were no printed books, no telephones or other electronic means of communication. The wonder is not that he discussed Christ with the men in the streets; the wonder is that, even when he had this brief chance to rest, he couldn't. His heart was so stirred toward the people.

vv. 18 through 21

Then certain philosophers of the Epicureans, and of the Stoicks, encountered him. And some said, What will this babbler say? other some, He seemeth to be a setter forth of strange gods: because he preached unto them Jesus, and the resurrection. And they took him,

*and brought him unto [the] Areopagus, saying, May
we know what this new doctrine, whereof thou speak-
est, is? For thou bringest certain strange things to our
ears: we would know therefore what these things
mean. (For all the Athenians and strangers which
were there spent their time in nothing else, but either
to tell, or to hear some new thing.)*

Paul's spirit was stirred toward these men, but his intellect should have told him they were not really interested—only curious about what he believed. To argue ideas,
to listen to others, or to express one's own theories consti-
tuted the most enjoyable kind of leisure hours for the men
of Athens. Perhaps Paul was too weary to think clearly;
perhaps by now he was moving slightly toward the common trap of those whose profession is to win people to
Jesus Christ. Perhaps Paul, like so many faithful disciples
now, had forgotten how to be "just people." He just *had* to
preach.

The Areopagus (City Council) met for some of its ses-
sions on Mars Hill. It met there when Paul stood up that
day.

vv. 22 and 23
    *. . . Ye men of Athens, I perceive that in all things
ye are too superstitious [very religious]. For as I
passed by, and beheld your devotions, I found an altar
with this inscription, TO THE UNKNOWN GOD.
Whom therefore ye ignorantly worship, him declare I
unto you.*

I wonder what might have happened if Paul had either
stopped here to permit their questions, or if he had leaped
from this loving, inclusive, sensitive introduction into his
clear statements about Christ. "I sense your religious interest, gentlemen," he might have said. "You are, by nature,
religious people. As I walked through your city, I even saw
an altar which you have inscribed TO THE UNKNOWN
GOD. Men of Athens, let me tell you his real name!"
But he didn't. I urge you to read Paul's speech to the
Athenians that day (verses 24 through 31). It is beautifully
worded. It shows Paul's broad knowledge of Greco-Roman

philosophy, poetry, sculpture, architecture and religion. He brushed them all knowingly, delighting the intellects of his hearers; but he touched very few hearts, moved very few wills. As he went on to Corinth, the zealous Apostle vowed never to speak that way again. From that time on, he would "preach Christ and him crucified." He would try with all his heart to meet the real needs of his hearers, not merely to titillate their minds. All that Paul said on Mars Hill was true. He just didn't go far enough.

v. 33
So Paul departed from among them.

Timothy and Luke and Silas had not come yet, but Paul left anyway—alone. I love him here in his partial failure— his utter humanity—more than at any other time.

CHAPTER 18
vv. 1 through 4
After these things Paul departed from Athens, and came to Corinth; And found a certain Jew named Aquila, born in Pontus, lately come from Italy, with his wife Priscilla; (because that Claudius had commanded all Jews to depart from Rome:) and came unto them. And because he was of the same craft, he abode with them, and wrought: for by their occupation they were tentmakers. And he reasoned in the synagogue every sabbath, and persuaded the Jews and the Greeks.

This is a fascinating period in Paul's life. He had always been mainly a scholar. In those days scholars were supported by friends or relatives while they traveled and taught. Still, he did have a trade. Paul had, at some time in his life, been a tentmaker. And now, after his new resolve to preach Jesus Christ and him only, following the Mars Hill episode, he seems to be determined to simplify his daily life too. Something new seems to me to be stirring in Paul here. He needed, perhaps, a closer bond with people. Possibly he recognized his need for routine work for a while, for rest from the exhausting travel and preaching. Also, he must have been lonely. His friends had not yet been able to join him, and so he made two new friends—Aquila and Priscilla—who invited him to live in their home. On the sabbath, Paul could still continue his reasoning and preaching about Christ. This is a quieter, possibly deeper period for him in Corinth.

vv. 5 and 6

And when Silas and Timotheus were come from Macedonia, Paul was pressed in the spirit, and testified to the Jews that Jesus was Christ. And when they opposed themselves, and blasphemed, he shook his raiment, and said unto them, Your blood be upon your own heads; I am clean: from henceforth I will go unto the Gentiles.

By the time Timothy and Silas rejoined Paul in Corinth, he had dropped all nonessentials and was concentrating only upon preaching the one central truth—that the risen Jesus was the Christ, their Messiah. It is as though Paul were making one last effort to get through to his own people. He was down to bedrock. He had been working with his hands, perhaps spending more time alone, resting physically from his exhausting travels, and God had "centered him down" on the one absolute. I feel that in an entirely new way Christ was filling Paul's horizons. In spite of his new friends, Aquila and Priscilla, Paul must have felt lonely at times without Timothy and Silas. As he always does in the midst of loneliness if we let him, God became still more real to the Apostle. And when God grows more real to us, we invariably begin to drop the nonessentials. Everything becomes clarified. Decisions are simpler to make. Paul made his decision: He would stop trying to persuade his fellow Jews because they were paying no attention to him whatever. If he acted realistically (and this is what we do when God is central), he would simply stop trying and turn to the Gentiles. His conscience was free and clear. Paul's statement: "Your blood be upon your own heads; I am clean . . ." is translated in *Good News for Modern Man* as: "If you are lost, you yourselves must take the blame for it! I am not responsible." Such strong words show Paul's haunted mind where his own people were concerned. He loved them, he longed to see them living in the fulfillment of the Scriptural prophecies, but he came to the place where he felt that he had done all he could do. The Jews who did not accept Jesus as their Messiah were not evil people; they were just unteachable—too sure *they* were right. Their minds were closed.

vv. 7 and 8
> *And he departed thence, and entered into a certain man's house, named Justus, one that worshipped God, whose house joined hard to the synagogue. And Crispus, the chief ruler of the synagogue, believed on the Lord with all his house; and many of the Corinthians hearing believed, and were baptized.*

Almost as soon as Paul decided to leave the Jews to their own fate, Crispus, a ruler of the synagogue, became a believer. Does this mean that Paul had made the wrong decision? I don't think so. What God is always trying to get us to do is to stay open—to keep his fresh air blowing through our minds. Paul may have needed to be reminded that Christ came for all people, not just Jews or just Gentiles. There are devout Christians today who seem to see need only among Jews or alcoholics or drug addicts or athletes or actors. Need is everywhere there is a human heart beating. We know this—even those who feel "called" to specialize in reaching one group or another—and yet our conditioning, our egos, our pride can get involved and God is the loser. Don't think for one minute that Paul had no pride, no ego operating overtime as our egos do. The great Apostle *was* an opinionated man. His mind was a good one; he respected his own thinking and was just as susceptible to getting his strong head confused with God's will as we are. Whether Paul made a right or a wrong decision when "he shook his raiment" at the Jews is not really relevant to what God seems to be saying in this incident. What appears to be important is that we are to stay open. Paul went right out and won a Jewish leader!

So many people exhaust themselves emotionally and spiritually by fretting over whether or not they have caught God's highest will in something. I've found that when I make my biggest mistakes, God sometimes makes his biggest gains—not only with me in the lessons I learn but, any time redemption is set free to operate, with everyone. God knows when we have made an honest mistake in judgment. If our error has been honestly made or innocently made or even ignorantly made, he goes immediately to work redeeming it.

vv. 9 through 11
Then spake the Lord to Paul in the night by a vision, Be not afraid, but speak, and hold not thy peace: For I am with thee, and no man shall set on thee to hurt thee: for I have much people in this city. And he continued there a year and six months, teaching the word of God among them.

Even in the vision, God didn't clarify exactly whether Paul had made the right decision. He just reassured him and told him to go ahead without wasting any time on perplexity or fear. Most of us want God to be more specific. Nine times out of ten he won't be. He loves us too much. If he were in the habit of putting things down in black and white for us, we would depend on that, and nothing could weaken faith more surely. He said to Paul all Paul or anyone ever needs to hear specifically: "Be not afraid . . . I am with thee."

vv. 12 through 17
And when Gallio was the deputy of Achaia, the Jews made insurrection with one accord against Paul, and brought him to the judgment seat, Saying, This fellow persuadeth men to worship God contrary to the law. And when Paul was now about to open his mouth, Gallio said unto the Jews, If it were a matter of wrong or wicked lewdness, O ye Jews, reason would that I should bear with you: But if it be a question of words and names, and of your law, look ye to it; for I will be no judge of such matters. And he drave them from the judgment seat. Then all the Greeks took Sosthenes, the chief ruler of the synagogue, and beat him before the judgment seat. And Gallio cared for none of those things.

Gallio has always interested me as a human being. He would be a strong central character for a novel. Even the exact date of Gallio's proconsularship is fixed now by an inscription in Delphi which was discovered in 1905. Paul was dragged by the Jews before Gallio in A.D. 52. Gallio, the brother of the philosopher Seneca, who called him "sweet Gallio," must have been an attractive, charming—certainly, a wise—ruler, the epitome of religious tolerance. In fact, he was so just, so quick to shut off the complaints of the nonbelieving Jews, that he may have blocked God a little. It is quite possible for God to use a nonbeliever to protect a Christian as he used Gallio to set Paul free that day in Corinth; but if Paul had been permitted to speak, some might have believed. No one knows if this would have happened, of course. At any rate, Gallio let Paul go and made it possible for him to finish his Corinthian work before he left for Syria with Priscilla and Aquila, to begin what has come to be known as his third missionary journey (verse 18).

vv. 24 through 28 (Read vv. 19 through 23.)

And a certain Jew named Apollos, born at Alexandria, an eloquent man, and mighty in the scriptures, came to Ephesus. This man was instructed in the way of the Lord; and being fervent in the spirit, he spake and taught diligently the things of the Lord, knowing only the baptism of John. And he began to speak boldly in the synagogues whom when Aquila and Priscilla had heard, they took him unto them, and expounded unto him the way of God more perfectly. And when he was disposed to pass into Achaia, the brethren wrote, exhorting the disciples to receive him: who, when he was come, helped them much which had believed through grace: For he mightily convinced the Jews, and that publickly, shewing by the scriptures that Jesus was Christ.

Apollos is a fascinating character too. Brilliant, eloquent, fervent, he must also have been an almost uniquely humble man. Most leaders with followings as large as those of Apollos would not have accepted the teaching of two tentmakers. He did. Apollos had all the truth except the one, central freeing fact of the deity of Jesus Christ. When he had that, he was free to be still greater.

CHAPTER 19
vv. 24 through 29a

For a certain man named Demetrius, a silversmith, which made silver shrines for Diane, brought no small gain unto the craftsmen; Whom he called together with the workmen of like occupation, and said, Sirs, ye know that by this craft we have our wealth. Moreover ye see and hear, that not alone [here] at Ephesus, but almost throughout all Asia, this Paul hath persuaded and turned away much people, saying that they be no gods, which are made with hands: So that not only this our craft is in danger . . . but . . . the temple of the great goddess Diane. . . . And when they heard these sayings, they were full of wrath, and cried out saying, Great is Diana of the Ephesians. And the whole city was filled with confusion. . . .

There is never a letdown in the genuine drama of the Acts of the Apostles. Wherever Paul went, conflict inevitably resulted—not because he tried to stir it up, but because he held up Jesus Christ and man slammed himself invariably against His purity. In Ephesus, after long months of success, Paul was caught again between the evil of man and the purity of Christ—at the point where the drama takes place. Here, the Apostle stood to hurt business. A riot resulted. There isn't always the noisy melodrama of the outbreak in the temple at Ephesus. More often the truth of Christ causes inner rebellion, but there is the drama just the same; and there always will be when man's selfish motives smash against the pure heart of Christ.

CHAPTER 20
vv. 1 through 6

And after the uproar [in Ephesus] was ceased, Paul called unto him the disciples, and embraced them, and departed for to go into Macedonia. And when he had gone over those parts, and had given them much exhortation, he came into Greece. And there abode three months. And when the Jews laid wait for him, as he was about to sail into Syria, he purposed to return through Macedonia. And there accompanied him into Asia Sopater of Berea; and of the Thessalonians, Aristarchus and Secundus; and Gaius of Derbe, and Timotheus; and of Asia, Tychicus and Trophimus. These going before tarried for us at Troas.

In verse 6, Luke lets us know that he rejoined Paul on the journey. In his absence, Luke has reported by way of research and interviews with those who were with Paul— probably interviews with Paul himself. From this point on, there is far more detail. Luke is seeing it all happen first-hand.

vv. 7 through 10

And upon the first day of the week, when the disciples came together to break bread, Paul preached unto them, ready to depart on the morrow; and continued his speech until midnight. And there were many lights in the upper chamber, where they were gathered together. And there sat in a window a certain young man named Eutychur, being fallen into a deep sleep: and as Paul was long preaching, he sunk down with sleep, and fell down from the third loft, and was taken up dead. And Paul went down, and fell on him, and embracing him said, Trouble not yourselves; for his life is in him.

In a daily devotional book* I once wrote:

What might have happened had Paul been insulted at the boy's falling asleep in the middle of his lengthy sermon? God would still have had the power to bring the boy to life, but could that power have gotten through Paul if he had been suddenly filled up with wounded pride? A tragedy might have been left a tragedy.

Paul evidently wasn't insulted and, instead of ending in

---

* *Share My Pleasant Stones* (Grand Rapids: Zondervan Publishing House, 1957).

tragedy and turmoil, the meeting ended in joy. The Apostle even went back upstairs and finished his sermon, talking until daybreak (verse 11).

v. 16

For Paul had determined to sail by Ephesus, because he would not spend the time in Asia: for he hasted, if it were possible for him, to be at Jerusalem the day of Pentecost.

One is reminded here of Jesus' determination to take one and then another step along the way to Jerusalem. Paul knew, as his Master had known, that the ultimate trial could come there. All through the third missionary journey, his enemies among the Jews had plagued him. He had no reason to think he might escape them in the Holy City, and yet he pushed on. For months he had been carrying money from the other churches for the mother church in Jerusalem. Paul wanted to deliver the gifts at Pentecost.

vv. 22 and 23 (Read vv. 17 through 21.)

And now, behold, I go bound in the spirit unto Jerusalem, not knowing the things that shall befall me there: Save that the Holy Ghost witnesseth in every city, saying that bonds and afflictions abide me.

In Miletus, after having called the faithful believers from Ephesus to meet with him, Paul makes no effort to hide either his Christian tenderness and concern for them or his sure knowledge that trouble lies ahead.

v. 24

But none of these things move me, neither count I my life dear unto myself, so that I might finish my course with joy, and the ministry, which I have received of the Lord Jesus, to testify the gospel of the grace of God.

Aside from his line from the Philippian letter in which Paul wrote "To me to live is Christ," the first line of verse 24 is for me the most important in all the Pauline literature: "None of these things move me. . . ." Perhaps, if we are honest, this testimony of Paul's inner steadiness, if it has released us at all, has released us from some form of fear. We fear death, the death of a loved one—the grief and empty hours that follow. We fear criticism, the sting of it, the anxiety from it. We fear failure and illness and loneliness. We fear for our jobs, for our old age. We fear depending on someone other than ourselves. We fear not being liked. At the bottom of most of our troubles lies some kind of fear. Paul was not saying that he was full of courage and fearless. He simply said, in effect, that whatever lay ahead, none of it would change his love for Jesus Christ. He would not be moved from living by that love.

I used to fear criticism from God's people. I don't any more, and Paul has helped me enormously. When he began to speak to the Ephesians at this last sad farewell, he said (verse 18): "Ye know, from the first day that I came into Asia, after what manner I have been with you at all seasons." Paul had made mistakes and hasty judgments, as we do, but they knew his life. He had kept his accounts clear with God. If being his best self in Christ was going to bring down persecution when he reached Jerusalem, so be it. "None of these things move me." We will always feel fears —I'm sure Paul did. But no matter what happens, we need not be "moved" from our course. If we have "fought the good fight" as he felt he had, we need not be unduly moved by trouble up ahead. After all, trouble is up ahead for everyone. No one escapes. It is clear that Paul was not seeking sympathy from the Ephesians gathered around him to say good-bye. Nor was he seeking to appear spiritual. He was merely stating a fact. And perhaps a clue to the way he achieved this kind of inner calm "in the midst of" lies in his use of the word "joy" instead of courage or bravery. "But none of these things move me, neither count I my life dear unto myself, so that I might finish my course with joy. . . ." As Oswald Chambers once said, "Joy is God in your blood." No amount of trouble can rob a Christian of the joy Jesus left us.

v. 32 (Read vv. 25 through 31.)
And now, brethren, I commend you to God, and to the word of his grace, which is able to build you up,

*and to give you an inheritance among all them which
are sanctified.*

Only God is able to "build us up" through grace. I have
yet to learn an adequate definition of grace, but I have
learned the hard way that only grace can add to my inner
being. If only we could begin to see the difference between
self-effort in God's behalf and cooperation with him as he
does the work in us!

vv. 36 through 38

*And when he had thus spoken, he kneeled down,
and prayed with them all. And they all wept sore, and
fell on Paul's neck, and kissed him. Sorrowing most of
all for the words which he spake, that they should see
his face no more. And they accompanied him unto the
ship.*

Little needs to be said here, except that these early
Christians were not afraid to express their feelings of genuine affection. What would we say now if two Christian men
wept and kissed each other good-bye?

CHAPTER 21
vv. 8 through 12

*And the next day we that were of Paul's company
departed, and came unto Caesarea: and we entered
into the house of Philip the evangelist, which was one
of the seven; and abode with him. And the same man
had four daughters, virgins, which did prophesy. And
as we tarried there many days, there came down from
Judaea a certain prophet, named Agabus. And when
he was come unto us, he took Paul's girdle, and bound
his own hands and feet, and said, Thus saith the Holy
Ghost, So shall the Jews at Jerusalem bind the man
that owneth this girdle, and shall deliver him into the
hands of the Gentiles. And when we heard these
things, both we, and they of that place, besought him
[Paul] not to go up to Jerusalem.*

Paul was not going to be taken by surprise in Jerusalem.
The Holy Spirit was seeing to that. The disciples in Tyre

(though the Spirit) had warned him. Here was another
graphic warning. I do not think that God gave Paul all
these definite warnings so much for Paul's sake as for the
sake of the people to whom Paul spoke along the way. By
this time, one warning to the faithful Apostle would have
been enough. God knew this. The repeated warnings must
have been so that Paul would have a chance every place he
stopped to *demonstrate*—by his words as well as by his
steady demeanor—that "none of these things moved" him.

vv. 13 through 15
*Then Paul answered, What mean ye to weep and to
break mine heart? for I am ready not to be bound
only, but also to die at Jerusalem for the name of the
Lord Jesus. And when he would not be persuaded, we
ceased, saying, The will of the Lord be done. And
after those days we took up our carriages, and went
up to Jerusalem.*

The disciples (Luke among them) tried everything.
When Paul would not turn back from Jerusalem, they
turned the whole problem over to God. Paul had done it
long before that.

vv. 18 through 22
*And the day following Paul went in with us unto
James; and all the elders were present. And when he
. . . declared particularly what things God had
wrought among the Gentiles by his ministry . . . they
glorified the Lord, and said unto him [Paul], Thou
seest, brother, how many thousands of Jews there are
which believe; and they are all zealous of the law:
And they are informed of thee, that thou teachest all
the Jews which are among the Gentiles to forsake
Moses, saying that they ought not to circumcise their
children, neither to walk after the customs. What is it
therefore? the multitude must needs come together:
for they will hear that thou art come.*

Paul had been in the field so long—had lived the life of
liberty in Christ away from the organized church, watching
the direct work of the Holy Spirit—that he may have for-

gotten the feel of the restrictions of the mother church in Jerusalem. If he had forgotten, by this time in James' little speech it had all come back to him. But Paul had been truly liberated—he was free from within where it counted. Whatever James had to say, he could meet the request in love. He waited quietly, and James went on.

vv. 23 and 24

Do therefore this that we say to thee: We have four men which have a vow on them; Them take, and purify thyself with them, and be at charges with them, that they may shave their heads: and all may know that those things, whereof they were informed concerning thee, are nothing; but that thou thyself also walkest orderly, and keepest the law.

Paul was free of the law in Christ, but he was not outside it, as Christ was not. Jerusalem would be thronging with people. It was the Jewish Feast of Pentecost. No one knew better than Paul how he had been criticized by the unbelieving Jews. The brethren in the Jerusalem church were right. He would not be acting in love if he refused to do what he could to keep peace and harmony in the church. The Nazarite vow he had been asked to take required four weeks, but a man who had purified himself could attach himself to three other men already entered into the rituals of the vow. The Christian Jewish brothers in Jerusalem had anticipated the need for Paul to make some outward show that he was still orthodox in order to quiet the gossip of the Jews who had not accepted Christ. Three men had already made the Nazarite observance for three weeks. Seven days remained.

vv. 26 through 28

Then Paul took the men, and the next day purifying himself with them entered into the temple, to signify the accomplishment of the days of purification, until that an offering should be offered for every one of them. And when the seven days were almost ended, the Jews which were of Asia, when they saw him in the temple, stirred up all the people, and laid hands on

him, Crying out, Men of Israel, help: This is the man,
that teacheth . . . against the people, and the law, and
this place: and [has] further brought Greeks also into
the temple, and hath polluted this holy place.

Paul's attempt to pacify his critics did not work. The
non-Christian Jews who had come to Jerusalem for Pentecost from Asia were already convinced of Paul's lack of
orthodoxy. Nothing he could have done would have
changed their attitude toward him. They had seen him with
Greeks in Asia (verse 29), and that's what they "saw" in
Jerusalem.

vv. 30 through 36
And all the city was moved, and the people ran to-
gether: and they took Paul, and drew him out of the
temple: and forthwith the doors were shut. And as
they went about to kill him, tidings came unto the
chief captain of the band, that all Jerusalem was in an
uproar. Who immediately took soldiers and centuri-
ons, and ran down unto them: and . . . they left beat-
ing of Paul. Then the chief captain . . . took him, and
commanded him to be bound with two chains; and de-
manded who he was, and what he had done. And
some cried one thing, some another, among the multi-
tude: and when he [the captain] could not know the
certainty for the tumult, he commanded him [Paul]
to be carried into the castle. . . . the multitude of the
people followed after, crying, Away with him.

A not too distant echo must have run in Paul's ears:
Crucify him! Crucify him! Like his Master, Paul had been
judged by what the people chose to think of him—not for
what he was. In the midst of an act of love toward his Jewish persecutors, God permitted Paul to be attacked and
beaten. The Apostle was trying to make a bridge to the
Jews, and seemingly his effort had failed. But had it? God's
ultimate purpose is always love, but he knew he could trust
Paul to allow him to include even Paul's enemies in that
love. If they had not tried to kill Paul, his ritual of love in
the temple might have gone unnoticed. God did not prompt

the attack; he *used* it. He did not protect Paul because He needed him to be as He knew Paul would be in the midst of suffering and attack.

vv. 37, 39, 40a

And as Paul was to be led into the castle, he said unto the chief captain, May I speak unto thee? Who said, Canst thou speak Greek? . . . [And] Paul said, I am a man which am a Jew of Tarsus, a city in Cilicia, a citizen of no mean city: and, I beseech thee, suffer me to speak unto the people. And when he had given him licence, Paul stood on the stairs, and beckoned with the hand unto the people.

By now Paul knew God's ways. Paul was ready to let Him work through his suffering in order to reach the people who hated him, but whom he knew God loved. Standing on the palace stairs, Paul, bound by two chains, his back and face bleeding from the beating, began to speak to the people in Hebrew.

CHAPTER 22
vv. 1 through 3

Men, brethren, and fathers, hear ye my defence which I make now unto you. (And when they heard that he spake in the Hebrew tongue to them, they kept the more silence: and he saith,) I am verily a man which am a Jew, born in Tarsus, a city in Cilicia, yet brought up in this city at the feet of Gamaliel, and taught according to the perfect manner of the law of the fathers, and was zealous toward God, as ye all are this day.

With all his being, Paul is trying to identify with his listeners, by speaking in their Hebrew tongue and by assuring them that, in spite of their drastic differences, he knows they too are "zealous toward God."

v. 4
*And I persecuted this way unto the death, binding
and delivering into prisons both men and women.*

"And I persecuted *this way.*" Paul may have gestured toward his own wounds and chains as he struggled to let
them know that he knew how they felt toward him. He had
done to other Christians what they were doing to him now.

vv. 5 through 8
*As also the high priest doth bear me witness, and all
the estate of the elders: from whom also I received
letters unto the brethren, and went to Damascus, to
bring them which were there bound unto Jerusalem,
for to be punished. And it came to pass, that, as I . . .
was come nigh unto Damascus about noon, suddenly
there shone from heaven a great light round about me.
And I fell unto the ground, and heard a voice saying
unto me, Saul, Saul, why persecutest thou me? And I
answered, Who art thou, Lord? And he said unto me,
I am Jesus of Nazareth, whom thou persecutest.*

Apparently, even the mention of the hated name of Jesus
did not break the attentiveness of Paul's audience. After
all, this was a highly dramatic story and the Apostle was a
dynamic speaker. He still had their attention.

vv. 9 through 11
*And they that were with me saw indeed the light,
and were afraid; but they heard not the voice of him
that spake to me. And I said, What shall I do, Lord?
And the Lord said unto me, Arise, and go into Damascus; and there it shall be told thee of all things which
are appointed for thee to do. And when I could not
see for the glory of that light, being led by the hand of
them that were with me, I came into Damascus.*

Paul did not say that he was blind. He said he could not
see "for the glory of that light." So real was his encounter
with the living Jesus Christ that day on the Damascus road
that even sudden blindness was like a great light. Paul's
very being was so filled with the "glory of that light" that

the fact he had to be led by the hand would have seemed secondary.

vv. 12 through 14

And one Ananias, a devout man according to the law, having a good report of all the Jews which dwelt there, Came unto me, and stood, and said unto me, Brother Saul, receive thy sight. And the same hour I looked up upon him. And he said, The God of our fathers hath chosen thee, that thou shouldest know his will, and see that Just One, and shouldest hear the voice of his mouth. For thou shalt be his witness unto all men of what thou hast seen and heard.

As Paul spoke from the palace stairs in chains, he was *being* the "voice of his mouth." He used no embellishments. He was not preaching a sermon. What he had to say was a simple, unadorned witness to the God of their fathers. "I met that God on the road to Damascus that day," he was saying, "and He changed me."

vv. 16 through 18

And now [Ananias said] why tarriest thou? arise, and be baptized, and wash away thy sins, calling on the name of the Lord. And it came to pass, that, when I was come again to Jerusalem, even while I prayed in the temple, I was in a trance; And saw him saying unto me, Make haste, and get thee quickly out of Jerusalem: for they will not receive thy testimony concerning me.

Still the Jews in Paul's audience did not begin to shout. Even with this reference to them, they held their silence.

vv. 19 through 22

And I said, Lord, they know that I imprisoned and beat in every synagogue them that believed on thee: And when the blood of thy martyr Stephen was shed, I also was standing by, and consenting unto his death, and kept the raiment of them that slew him. And he said unto me, Depart: for I will send thee far hence unto the Gentiles. And they gave him audience unto

this word, and then lifted up their voices, and said,
Away with such a fellow from the earth: for it is not
fit that he should live.

"And they gave him audience unto this word": *Gentiles.*
Somehow Paul had held the Jews through his clear, unmistakable witness to Jesus Christ as the Messiah. He had crossed their theological beliefs and they listened without interrupting him; but when he spoke the word "Gentiles," bedlam broke out. The Jews would do business with the Gentiles, would even obey their government officials up to a point; but it must be remembered that to be a Jew in those days meant far more to the Jew than merely having someone agree with him theologically. To have been born a Jew was to have been born privileged, chosen of God. Their hatred of Paul's insistence that God included Gentiles in his love and his redemptive plan raised more than a doctrinal issue; it was also a red-hot social issue. Gentiles were unclean people. Gentiles were inferior people. Jews would neither worship nor eat with them. Even Gentile dishes were unclean. Does this sound familiar? These Jews were respectable, cultivated, educated. But they were convinced of their superiority to Gentiles, and even Paul's straightforward witness to the all-inclusive love of God could not sway them. He raised the one social issue that raised hackles, as it does among some now when integration of the races is mentioned. To the angered Jews who heard Paul that day, Gentiles were all right—in their places. In the marketplace, on the streets, but not at Jewish tables or in the Jewish temple. Recently I spoke in churches and at luncheons and dinners from California to South Carolina and not one black face did I see. I missed them. So did God. Bedlam broke loose when Paul said the unacceptable word: Gentiles.

vv. 23 through 25

And as they cried out, and cast off their clothes, and
threw dust into the air, The chief captain commanded
him to be brought into the castle, and bade that he
should be examined by scourging; that he [the captain] might know wherefore they cried so against him.
And as they bound him with thongs, Paul said unto

the centurion that stood by, Is it lawful for you to scourge a man that is a Roman, and uncondemned?

God had a steady disciple in Paul. Not once during all the maltreatment did the Apostle stop using his Spirit-enlightened mind. It is no wonder he wrote that we are to "let this mind be in you which was in Christ Jesus." Paul could write that. He had "let" that mind invade his.

vv. 26 through 30
When the centurion heard that [Paul's question], he went and told the chief captain, Take heed . . . this man is a Roman. Then the chief captain came, and said unto him [Paul], Tell me, art thou a Roman? He said, Yea. And the chief captain answered, With a great sum obtained I this freedom [this Roman citizenship]. And Paul said, But I was free born. Then straightway they departed from him . . . and the chief captain also was afraid. . . . On the morrow, because he would have known the certainty wherefore he [Paul] was accused of the Jews, he loosed him from his bands, and commanded the chief priests and all their council to appear, and brought Paul down, and set him before them.

Paul knew the law as intimately as he knew grace. And as he was led before the council, which he knew to be made up of both Pharisees and Sadducees, he was on familiar ground. He must have welcomed still another chance to witness as he stood up to speak in his own defense before these rulers.

CHAPTER 23
vv. 1 and 2
And Paul, earnestly beholding the council, said, Men and brethren, I have lived in all good conscience before God until this day. And the high priest Ananias commanded them that stood by him to smite him on the mouth.

Paul found less courtesy with the rulers than he had found with the angry mob the day before.

vv. 3 through 5

Then said Paul unto him, God shall smite thee, thou whited wall: for sittest thou to judge me after the law, and commandest me to be smitten contrary to the law? And they that stood by said, Revilest thou God's high priest? Then said Paul, I wist not, brethren, that he was the high priest: for it is written, Thou shalt not speak evil of the ruler of thy people.

The blow on the mouth must have starled Paul. After all, he was just beginning his defense. He had spoken only one sentence. The great Apostle was human. A sudden blow can bring a quick, spiteful reaction from anyone. Paul lashed out, but as quickly recanted when he realized that he had been caustic with the high priest himself. His Christianity came to the fore, even to quoting the Scripture that proved him wrong to have said what he said to Ananias.

vv. 6 through 10

But when Paul perceived that the one part were Sadducees, and the other Pharisees, he cried out in the council, Men and brethren, I am a Pharisee, the son of a Pharisee: of the hope and resurrection of the dead I am called in question. And when he had so said, there arose a dissension between the Pharisees and the Sadducees: and the multitude was divided. For the Sadducees say that there is no resurrection, neither angel, nor spirit: but the Pharisees confess both. And there arose a great cry . . . and . . . a great dissension, [and] the chief captain, fearing lest Paul should have been pulled in pieces of them, commanded the soldiers to go down, and to take him by force from among them, and to bring him into the castle.

Wise Paul merely used a bit of psychology here—and it worked.

v. 11

And the night following the Lord stood by him, and said, Be of good cheer, Paul: for as thou hast testified of me in Jerusalem, so must thou bear witness also at Rome.

God always knows when, in spite of the fact that we may appear to be doing rather well, we need further reassurance. He not only came to Paul that night in prison; he added comfort by calling the harassed disciple by his name. "Be of good cheer, Paul."

v. 12
And when it was day, certain of the Jews banded together, and bound themselves under a curse, saying that they would neither eat nor drink till they had killed Paul.

The pure life of Christ within Paul was driving his enemies to further deeds of evil just as surely as Christ's life drove His enemies a few years before.

v. 16
And when Paul's sister's son heard of their lying in wait, he went and entered into the castle, and told Paul.

Nothing has been said before and nothing is said following this incident of Paul's nephew. We aren't even told the boy's name, but God obviously used the young man to save his uncle's life.

vv. 17 through 22
Then Paul called one of the centurions unto him, and said, Bring this young man unto the chief captain: for he hath a certain thing to tell him. So he took him. . . . [And] the chief captain took him by the hand, and went with him aside privately, and asked him, What is that thou hast to tell me? And he said, The Jews have agreed to desire thee that thou wouldest bring down Paul to morrow into the council, as though they would enquire somewhat of him more perfectly. But do not thou yield unto them: for there lie in wait for him of them more than forty men, which have bound themselves with an oath, that they

*will neither eat nor drink till they have killed him: and
now are they ready, looking for a promise from thee.
So the chief captain then let the young man depart,
and charged him, See thou tell no man that thou hast
shewed these things to me.*

We are told so little—almost nothing of Paul's family—
but even without a known name, this young man stands
out. He must have shown genuine integrity, or the chief
captain would not have trusted his story. The boy impressed the chief captain because he lost no time in acting.

vv. 23 and 24
*And he called unto him two centurions, saying,
Make ready two hundred soldiers to go to Caesarea,
and horsemen threescore and ten, and spearmen two
hundred, at the third hour of the night; And provide
them beasts, that they may set Paul on, and bring him
safe unto Felix the governor.....*

The chief captain, whose name we now know to be
Claudius Lysius (verse 26), saw to it that Paul arrived in
Caesarea safely and swiftly. God meant it when He told
was on his way. A letter of explanation of Paul's predicament accompanied him, written by Claudius Lysius to
Felix, the Caesarean governor. (Read verses 26 through
30.) The letter's tone implies that Claudius had come to
believe Paul's innocence of the nebulous charges.

vv. 33 through 35
*Who, when they came to Caesarea, and delivered
the epistle to the governor, presented Paul also before
him. And when the governor had read the letter, he
asked of what province he was. And when he understood that he was of Cilicia; I will hear thee, said he,
when thine accusers are also come. And he commanded him to be kept in Herod's judgment hall.*

Paul's thoughts as he waited in Herod's judgment hall—
still a prisoner in chains—must have been anxious ones. He
knew that the Jews who refused the Messiah he proclaimed
would come prepared. They were well able to afford the

best legal counsel. They would have it. The wait must have seemed long indeed.

CHAPTER 24
vv. 1 and 5 through 9

And after five days Ananias the high priest descended with the elders, and with a certain orator named Tertullus, who informed the governor against Paul. . . . For we have found this man a pestilent fellow, and a mover of sedition among all the Jews throughout the world, and a ringleader of the sect of the Nazarenes: Who also hath gone about to profane the temple: whom we took, and would have judged according to our law. But the chief captain Lysias came upon us, and with great violence took him away out of our hands, Commanding his accusers to come unto thee. . . . And the Jews also assented, saying that these things were so.

The old boys really meant to silence Paul one way or another. The journey from Jerusalem to Caesarea was sixty-four long miles, but they did not rest at merely having Paul out of Jerusalem. They wanted him dead. Even the high priest Ananias came along.

vv. 10 through 13 and 21

Then Paul, after that the governor had beckoned unto him to speak, answered, Forasmuch as I know that thou hast been of many years a judge unto this nation, I do not mere cheerfully answer for myself: Because that thou mayest understand, that there are yet but twelve days since I went up to Jerusalem for to worship. And they neither found me in the temple disputing with any man, neither raising up the people, neither in the synagogues, nor in the city: Neither can they prove the things whereof they now accuse me. . . . Except it be for this one voice, that I cried standing among them, Touching the resurrection of the dead I am called in question by you this day.

Paul minced no words. Categorically, he denied all their accusations as stated by their lawyer, Tertullus, but added

that he was "guilty" of believing in the resurrection of the
dead. Once more, Paul turned a defense into a witness.

vv. 23, 23
*And when Felix heard these things, having more
perfect knowledge of that way, he deferred them, and
said, When Lysias the chief captain shall come down,
I will know the uttermost of your matter. And he
commanded a centurion to keep Paul, and to let him
have liberty, and that he should forbid none of his ac-
quiantance to minister or come unto him.*

Felix passed the buck—at least in part. His decision was
to keep Paul a prisoner, but with many liberties, even visits
by his friends. There is no indication that Felix sent for Lysius to come down to Caesarea. Somehow the governor
had been exposed to The Way of the early Christians and,
although he didn't have the courage to free Paul for fear of
more trouble from the Jews, he imprisoned him as lightly
as possible. He seemed more interested in the quick depar-
ture of Paul's accusers than in justice. Felix was not anti-
Christian or pro-Christian. He was merely being expedient.

vv. 24 through 26
*And after certain days, when Felix came with his
wife Drusilla, which was a Jewess, he sent for Paul,
and heard him concerning the faith in Christ. And as
he reasoned of righteousness, temperance, and judgment to come, Felix trembled, and answered, Go thy
way for this time; when I have a convenient season, I
will call for thee. He hoped also that money should
have been given him of Paul, that he might loose him:
wherefore he sent for him the oftener, and communed
with him.*

I have heard sermons on this passage telling of Felix' relationship with Paul which argued that Felix was near the
kingdom—the point of the sermons being that no one
should put God off until a more "convenient season." I
doubt that we can really know about Felix, the governor of
the sophisticated city of Caesarea. Furthermore, I doubt
that Felix knew all his own motives in taking his wife, Dru-

silla, to hear Paul speak about Christ. I'm sure Felix was hoping for a bribe from Paul, and this explains the frequency of the visits the governor permitted Paul to make to his quarters. Felix did tremble when Paul spoke of "righteousness, temperance, and judgment to come"—and it is, of course, altogether possible that Felix was both expedient *and* "under conviction" as the old-fashioned preachers said. We are like this as human beings. Our motives are almost always mixed.

v. 27

But after two years Porcius Festus came into Felix' room: and Felix, willing to shew the Jews a pleasure, left Paul bound.

Felix' ultimate recorded act when he left office was pure expediency. Two years in semiconfinement is a long time. The added wait must have been the most difficult of all for Paul.

CHAPTER 25

vv. 1 through 3

Now when Festus was come into the province, after three days he ascended from Caesarea to Jerusalem. Then the high priest and the chief of the Jews informed him against Paul, and besought him, And desired favour against him, that he would send for him to Jerusalem, laying wait in the way to kill him.

Poor old hate-filled men! Two years had passed since they had appeared before Felix in an effort "to get" Paul, and still they were hard at it. What is it about hate that often seems to cause it to outlast love? Is it because hate feeds the human ego—turns one in on oneself—while love, if it is real love, always turns outward toward the loved one?

vv. 4 and 5

But Festus answered, that Paul should be kept at Caesarea, and that he himself would depart shortly thither. Let them therefore, said he, which among you are able, go down with me, and accuse this man, if there be any wickedness in him.

I feel now like saying "Poor Festus." Here is another Roman governor caught in the squeeze of Paul's righteousness and the hatred of his enemies. Every Roman ruler wanted to please the Jews enough to keep peace but, as with Felix, Festus couldn't have cared less about their Law—or Paul. He was simply in the same political bind in which Felix served out his term as governor.

v.11

For if I be an offender [said Paul], or have committed any thing worthy of death, I refuse not to die: but if there be none of these things whereof these accuse me, no man may deliver me unto them. I appeal unto Caesar.

Festus stalled around Jerusalem for ten days, then went down to Caesarea, the Jews right with him. Once more they made their stereotyped accusations against the Apostle, once more he denied them; but this time he asked to be heard by Caesar under his right as a Roman citizen. Again the disgruntled Jews went back to Jerusalem, and again Paul continued his semi-imprisonment at Caesarea. He didn't have to twist Festus' arm at all. Like Felix, Festus was glad for any "legal" reason to send the Jews home (verse 12).

vv. 13 and 14a

And after certain days king Agrippa and Bernice came unto Caesarea to salute Festus. And when they had been there many days, Festus declared Paul's cause unto the king. . . .

Paul, by then, was like a brier in Festus' finger. The governor told Agrippa the whole story of the Jews' accusations, of Paul's denial, and of his own hopefully wise handling of the case. "I asked this Christian, Paul, if he was willing to go back to Jerusalem to stand trial before the Jews themselves. He's a brilliant thinker. Immediately, he reminded me that although he was not unwilling to die, he was unwilling not to insist upon his legal rights as a Roman citizen. He appealed to Caesar. That's where things stand

now. I'm simply holding the man. It's an interesting case—
and an irritating one" (verses 14b through 21).

v. 22

*Then Agrippa said unto Festus, I would also hear
the man myself. To morrow, said he, thou shalt hear
him.*

Without a doubt, Festus was hoping for just this kind of
response from his important guest. Maybe somehow, he
thought, King Agrippa will come up with a helpful solu-
tion. He could send Paul to be heard before Caesar, but
how would he, Festus, state the case (verses 25 through
27)?

v. 23

*And on the morrow, when Agrippa was come, and
Bernice, with great pomp, and was entered into the
place of hearing, with the chief captains, and principal
men of the city, at Festus' commandment Paul was
brought forth.*

How weary Paul must have been by now of being
"brought forth" to be heard again on these nebulous,
trumped-up charges!

CHAPTER 26
vv. 1 through 8

*Then Agrippa said unto Paul, Thou art permitted to
speak for thyself. Then Paul stretched forth the hand,
and answered for himself: I think myself happy, king
Agrippa, because I shall answer for myself this day
before thee touching all the things whereof I am accused of the Jews. . . . My manner of life from my
youth, which was at the first among mine own nation
at Jerusalem, know all the Jews; Which knew me from
the beginning, if they would testify, that after the most
straitest sect of our religion I lived a Pharisee. And
now I stand and am judged for the hope of the promise made of God unto our fathers. . . . Why should it
be thought a thing incredible with you, that God
should raise the dead?*

I see Paul standing with the characteristic outstretched
hand, determined once more to restate his case. His agile
mind found a slightly new approach each time, and yet, to
me, here, he almost bogged down—not in the sense of giving up; rather, in the sense of being suddenly swamped
with the ludicrous facts of the case. His normally smooth
flow of speech broke off, and he burst out with the question: "Why should it be thought incredible that God should
raise the dead?" Why, indeed? He recouped, though, and
plunged again into his personal witness to the transforming
power of Jesus Christ.

vv. 9 through 11

I verily thought with myself, that I ought to do
many things contrary to the name of Jesus of Naz-
areth. Which thing I also did in Jerusalem: and many
of the saints did I shut up in prison, having received
authority from the chief priests; and when they were
put to death, I gave my voice against them. And I
punished them oft in every synagogue, and compelled
them to blaspheme; and being exceedingly mad
against them, I persecuted them even unto strange
cities.

I once read a brilliant treatise on Paul which argued that
whatever his experience on the road to Damascus had
been, it had surely left him warped and preoccupied with
himself, a little mad. The basis for this argument was the
above quotation from the Scriptures. Over and over, the
author maintained, Paul reveled in boasting about his past
sins. The conclusion stated that all persons who claim to
have experienced an encounter with Jesus Christ begin to
dwell unhealthily on their past sins. Some do. But I feel
that most of those who do have been unhealthily influenced
by other Christians attempting to spice up their meetings
under the guise of letting God "use" the new converts' tes-
timonies. After five years of telling the story of my own
conversion to Jesus Christ in 1949, I banged down the lid.
I have never told it again except once or twice when—to
my own surprise—I found it tumbling out. This, I reasoned, must have been God's prompting. Unless Paul was

in a predicament or before an audience where the telling of
his own meeting with Christ on the Damascus road was
relevant, he did not go over it again. The recounting
(which he does very briefly here) of his past brutality
against the followers of Jesus of Nazareth is an integral
part of the story. He was not telling it again only to Festus.
King Agrippa and his queen, Bernice, had not heard it before. Paul does repeat his past sins often in the New Testament, but always for a specific reason which even human
intelligence alone would dictate.

vv. 12 through 15

*Whereupon as I went to Damascus with authority
and commission from the chief priests, At midday, O
king, I saw in the way a light from heaven, above the
brightness of the sun, shining round about me and
them which journeyed with me. And when we were all
fallen to the earth, I heard a voice speaking unto me,
and saying in the Hebrew tongue, Saul, Saul, why persecutest thou me? it is hard for thee to kick against the
pricks. And I said, Who are thou, Lord? And he said,
I am Jesus whom thou persecutest.*

I can believe that when Paul spoke this name, King
Agrippa frowned and changed position in his chair, and
that Festus, nervous before his royal guest, began to squirm
in discomfort. But Paul would not be slowed even now.
There comes a particular inner-energizing when one is telling of the actual meeting with the living Christ.

vv. 16 through 18

*But rise [the Lord said], and stand upon thy feet:
for I have appeared unto thee for this purpose, to
make thee a minister and a witness both of these
things which thou hast seen, and of those things in the
which I will appear unto thee; Delivering thee from
the people, and from the Gentiles, unto whom now I
send thee, To open their eyes, and to turn them from
darkness to light, and from the power of Satan unto
God, that they may receive forgiveness of sins, and inheritance . . . by faith that is in me.*

Paul must have sensed Festus' anxiety because he continuously caught Agrippa's attention by using his name again as he went resolutely on with his story:

vv. 19 through 23

Whereupon, O king Agrippa, I was not disobedient unto the heavenly vision: But shewed first unto them of Damascus, and at Jerusalem, and throughout all the coasts of Judaea, and then to the Gentiles, that they should repent and turn to God, and do works meet for repentance. For these causes the Jews caught me in the temple, and went about to kill me. Having therefore obtained help of God, I continue unto this day, witnessing both to small and great, saying none other things than those which the prophets and Moses did say should come: That Christ should suffer, and that he should be the first that should rise from the dead, and should shew light unto the people, and to the Gentiles.

Paul has been accused of boasting when he reiterated how much work he had done, mentioned the places to which he had traveled. I can understand why a superficial reading might cause one to think this, but after years of reading and rereading Paul's recorded journeys, I believe firmly that he mentioned these things only to impress his hearers with his own conviction that the "heavenly vision" on the road to Damascus was *real*—that his Lord was real, that Jesus of Nazareth *was* God, and that He did rise from the dead. I do not think Paul was being only dramatic or self aggrandizing. He stood before Agrippa a convinced man. If he had spoken otherwise, he would have compromised his own integrity. I have wondered if Paul was really finished with what he had to say that day as he stood before Agrippa and Festus. We shall never know, because Festus had heard enough:

v. 24

And as he thus spake for himself, Festus said with a loud voice, Paul, thou art beside thyself; much learning doth make thee mad.

Paul had spoken more of Jesus this time than on his first defense before Festus. It was too much for Festus. He lost his poise and shouted at Paul that he was insane. There are those who contend that Festus was also "under conviction" before God. It seems more plausible that he just didn't want to be embarrassed before Agrippa by having Paul go into too much personal detail. Festus' attitude is neither right nor wrong. It is simply pagan. He is more aware of royal proprieties and his position as governor than he is of spiritual truths.

vv. 25 through 27

But he [Paul] said, I am not mad, most noble Festus; but speak forth the words of truth and soberness. For the king knoweth of these things, before whom also I speak freely: for I am persuaded that none of these things are hidden from him; for this thing was not done in a corner.

Paul knew that Agrippa had had Jewish upbringing and was aware of the promise of the Lord God. He had now decided to be direct with the king in his next statement.

v. 27

King Agrippa, believest thou the prophets? I know that thou believest.

Paul may have smiled a little when he answered his own question. The continuity between the Old and the New Testament messages was so clear to Paul that perhaps he even hoped for a moment it had been clarified for Agrippa too.

v. 28

Then Agrippa said unto Paul, Almost thou persuadest me to be a Christian.

This short reply from the king has been, and still is, a controversial verse. I fail to see any reason for actual controversy here, but I do see how it can be interpreted in two ways. The problem obviously is in the translation. The King James Version used here easily indicates that Agrippa was on the verge of believing in Jesus Christ as the promised Messiah, but the newer, more accurate translations do not read this way at all. Only Phillips tilts in the direction of Agrippa's seriousness about Paul's message: " 'Much more of this, Paul,' returned Agrippa, 'and you will be making me a Christian!' " In *Good News for Modern Man*, the American Bible Society's highly contemporary translation, verse 28 is phrased this way: "Agrippa said to Paul, 'In this short time you think you will make me a Christian?' " And in *The Amplified Bible:* "Then Agrippa said to Paul, You think it a small task to make a Christian of me—just off hand to induce me with little ado and persuasion, at very short notice." Most of the so-called controversy stems from human curiosity. I tend to believe that Agrippa was more involved in his kingly position and riches than in eternal verities, and so I find the phrasing in *Good News for Modern Man* more acceptable.

v. 29

And Paul said, I would to God, that not only thou, but also all that hear me this day, were both almost, and altogether such as I am, except these bonds.

Paul may also have smiled a little here, as one does when it is evident that the gift of truth has been overlooked. I don't think he smiled from a superior spiritual place; rather, sadly, seeing as he did that his "riches in Christ" far outshone all their worldly pomp and wealth.

vv. 30 through 32

And when he had thus spoken, the king rose up, and the governor, and Bernice, and they that sat with them: And when they were gone aside, they talked between themselves, saying, This man doeth nothing worthy of death or of bonds. Then said Agrippa unto Festus, This man might have been set at liberty, if he had not appealed unto Caesar.

Paul has been pronounced innocent, but "aside" only among Festus, Agrippa, Bernice and their official circle. The verdict did not free Paul. He had appealed to Caesar and he would be sent to Rome. God had promised that his loyal disciple would witness in Rome. Paul was on his way at last. Nowhere in the New Testament are the basic premises of Christianity more clearly explained than in Paul's words before Agrippa: At the very heart of the Christian faith is the *fact* of the resurrected Lord, Jesus Christ; and through him, and him only, comes forgiveness—both for Jews and Gentiles. The "middle wall of partition" is knocked down here once and for all. Paul did not lose. He would go on to Rome in chains, but he had fulfilled his mission. He had fulfilled the purpose of the Christ who met him on the road to Damascus: Before Agrippa and Festus, Paul was a witness to the Lord who *was* Paul's very life. The rest he could leave up to God. It is interesting that Paul did not press his argument with Agrippa. The great Apostle had learned the all-important lesson that no man, even Paul, ever needs to "play God."

CHAPTER 27
v. 1

And when it was determined that we should sail into Italy, they delivered Paul and certain other prisoners unto one named Julius, a centurion of Augustus' band.

Luke had evidently used the more than two year's imprisonment of Paul in Caesarea to gather material for his Gospel. Now he has rejoined his hero, Paul, and will sail with him to Rome. The narrative resumes in the first person, *we.*

vv. 2 and 3

And entering into a ship of Adramyttium, we launched, meaning to sail by the coasts of Asia; one Aristarchus, a Macedonian of Thessalonica, being with us. And the next day we touched at Sidon. And Julius courteously entreated Paul, and gave him liberty to go unto his friends to refresh himself.

There was no boat direct to Rome, so Paul and his guard, Captain Julius; Luke; Aristarchus, another friend of Paul's; and the other prisoners also going to Rome embarked on a ship heading toward Myra, where they hoped

to make a further connection (verse 5). Luke's attention to
Paul is touching. The "beloved physician" seems always
genuinely pleased when some courtesy is shown Paul. In
Sidon, Captain Julius, evidently an admirer of the Apostle,
had permitted him to spend some time ashore with the
Christians there "to refresh himself."

vv. 9 and 10

*Now when much time was spent, and when sailing
was now dangerous, because the fast was now already
past, Paul admonished them, And said unto them,
Sirs, I perceive that this voyage will be with hurt and
much damage, not only of the lading and ship, but
also of our lives.*

I don't think Paul was soothsaying here. He simply knew
that navigation was dependent on the winds and always difficult after September—practically impossible in No-
vember. It was already early October; the fast of the Day
of Atonement was past. They had managed to board a ship
(most likely a grain ship) at Myra, but Paul's common
sense caused him to warn them of the dangers ahead. Captain Julius admired Paul, but he chose to take the advice of
the ship's master, who wanted more than anything else to
get his cargo out of that unfit harbor before winter set in
(verse 11).

vv. 13 through 17

*And when the south wind blew softly, supposing
that they had obtained their purpose, loosing thence,
they sailed close by Crete. But not long after there
arose against it a tempestuous wind, called Eurocly-
don [a northeaster]. And when the ship was caught,
and could not bear up into the wind, we let her drive.
And running under a certain island which is called
Clauda, we had much work to come by the boat:
Which when they had taken up, they used helps, un-
dergirding the ship; and, fearing lest they should fall
into the quicksands, strake sail, and so were driven.*

At first, Paul seemed to have been overly cautious. A
soft, south wind blew and, since most of the men preferred

the dangers of a voyage to the unsafe harbor at Myra as a
winter haven, they sailed—almost straight into a gigantic
windstorm. In an effort to make the ship's wooden lifeboat
secure, they "undergirded" it; i.e., they bound the boat
round and round with strong cables so that the timbers
would not break apart. Fearing the sandbanks off the coast
of Libya, they lowered the sail and let the ship be carried
by the wind.

vv. 18 through 19
*And we being exceedingly tossed with a tempest,
the next day they lightened the ship; And the third day
we cast out with our own hands the tackling of the
ship.*

Now the storm was so severe that even the prisoners,
Paul and the others, and Luke and Aristarchus were put to
work to lighten the ship. What is referred to as "tackling"
was probably all the superfluous equipment aboard.

v. 20
*And when neither sun nor stars in many days ap-
peared, and no small tempest lay on us, all hope that
we should be saved was then taken away.*

Day after day the sky hung above them—too dark for
stars, even too dark to see the sun—and "all hope" vanished. Luke does not say that Paul alone believed they
would be saved. He simply wrote: "All hope that we
should be saved was then taken away." After all, they had
no compasses; they steered by the stars. Even Paul's hope
was gone. I am better able to lay hold of Paul's high moments when I remember his times of humanity such as this.
He was not a super-Christian; he was simply a human
being filled with the life of God.

vv. 21 through 26
*But after long abstinence Paul stood forth in the
midst of them, and said, Sirs, ye should have heark-
ened unto me, and not have loosed from Crete, and to
have gained this harm and loss. And now I exhort you
to be of good cheer: for there shall be no loss of any*

*man's life among you, but of the ship. For there stood
by me this night the angel of God, whose I am, and
whom I serve, Saying, Fear not, Paul; thou must be
brought before Caesar: and, lo, God hath given thee
all them that sail with thee. Wherefore, sirs, be of
good cheer: for I believe God, that it shall be even as
it was told me. Howbeit we must be cast upon a certain island.*

Paul, still utterly human, could not resist an "I told you
so," but with great certainty he told the men what God had
shown him of their fate. Luke doesn't say whether or not
anyone believed Paul; he just goes right on with his dramatic narrative, taking care to describe even the smallest
details. Obviously, this storm at sea was the most traumat-
ic event of Luke's life.

vv. 27 through 29

*But when the fourteenth night was come, as we
were driven up and down in Adria [the Mediterra-
nean waters], about midnight the shipment deemed
that they drew near to some country; And sounded,
and found it twenty fathoms [120 feet]: and when
they had gone a little further, they sounded again, and
found it fifteen fathoms [90 feet]. Then fearing lest
we should have fallen upon rocks, they cast four anchors out of the stern, and wished for the day.*

Luke does not say that Paul was now in command of the
ship, but the actions of the shipmen showed that at least
they had listened when Paul had declared that they would
go aground on an island. Normally anchors are dropped
from the prow of a ship, but in this case they were eager
to keep her headed toward the shore, just in case Paul
was right.

vv. 30 through 32

*And as the shipmen were about to flee out of the
ship, when they had let down the boat into the sea,
under colour as though they would have cast anchors
out of the foreship, Paul said to the centurion and to
the soldiers, Except these abide in the ship, ye cannot*

*be saved. Then the soldiers cut off the ropes of the
boat, and let her fall off.*

Evidently some of the men did not believe Paul, so great
was their fright. At least, under cover of the night, they attempted to get away in the lifeboat. But when Paul insisted
to his friend, Captain Julius, that only those who stayed
on the ship would be saved, any doubt that Paul was
theoretically in charge was gone. The men were ordered
to cut the ropes and let the boat fall into the water. The die
was cast. They would follow Paul's orders.

vv. 33 and 34

*And while the day was coming on, Paul besought
them all to take meat, saying, This day is the fourteenth day that ye have tarried and continued fasting,
having taken nothing. Wherefore I pray you to take
some meat: for this is for your health: for there shall
not an hair fall from the head of any of you.*

Paul was not a weirdo. No matter how strange his message sounded to the pagan ears of Felix and Festus, as with
any Christian centered down in Jesus Christ, Paul was
practical. He had had his word from the Lord about their
safety, but his intelligence told him to urge these starving,
frightened men to break their fast and eat. "This is for
your health," he said. God is interested in our health because it is irrevocably tied up with our spiritual lives. They
are one to Christ because he is a realist, and no one knows
better than he that "in the beginning" a whole person was
created.

vv. 35 through 38

*And when he had thus spoken, he took bread, and
gave thanks to God in presence of them all: and when
he had broken it, he began to eat. Then were they all
of good cheer, and they also took some meat. And we
were in all the ship two hundred threescore and six-
teen souls [276 people]. And when they had eaten
enough, they lightened the ship, and cast out the
wheat into the sea.*

To Paul there was no sacred and no secular. All of life was "of a piece" in God. He gave orders of a practical nature and prayed in one motion, then ate first to show the men that he held no more fears for his own life. It worked. They all ate, and "they were all of good cheer" suddenly.

vv. 39 through 44

And when it was day, they knew not the land: but they discovered a certain creek with a shore, into the which they were minded, if it were possible, to thrust in the ship. And when they had taken up the anchors, they committed themselves unto the sea, and loosed the rudder bands, and hoised up the mainsail to the wind, and made toward shore. And falling into a place where two seas met, they ran the ship aground; and the forepart stuck fast, and remained unmoveable, but the hinder part was broken with the violence of the waves. And the soldiers' counsel was to kill the prisoners, lest any of them should swim out, and escape. But the centurion, willing to save Paul, kept them from their purpose; and commanded that they which could swim should cast themselves first into the sea, and get to land: And the rest, some on boards, and some on broken pieces of the ship. And so it came to pass, that they escaped all safe to land.

I wish Luke, who had been so detailed up to now, had told us how Paul got to land; how Luke reached shore, too, and the kind centurion, and Aristarchus. At any rate, they all made it. God's promise to Paul held. And it is certainly well for us to note that Paul had to do his part too in bringing that promise to fulfillment. There was no celestial magic wand-waving performed here. God made no supernatural miracle of it. He simply told Paul that they would make it—and they did. He spared his beloved disciple no hard knocks in the process. The Almighty did not reach down and whisk Paul to shore just because he "had fought the good fight." Paul swam or splashed his way to the beach on a broken bit of ship, just like the others. Neither Paul nor God was vindicated. Neither needed to be. I believe Luke gave so much space to the story of the shipwreck because it ran so much the way most of life runs. Good advice ignored, stormy seas, frail ships, lost hope, prayer, practical action, faith, struggle—and with God, eventually the shore.

CHAPTER 28
vv. 1 and 2

And when they were escaped, then they knew that the island was called Melita [Malta]. And the barbarous people shewed us no little kindness: for they kindled a fire, and received us every one, because of the present rain, and because of the cold.

These people of the island of Melita were not "barbarians" in the sense that we use the word. "Barbarians" as Luke uses it here is merely the Greek word for all people who did not speak Greek. These islanders were not only kind and hospitable; they were cultivated and prosperous. The whole rescue operation of Melita must have been welcomed by Paul. He was overjoyed to see friendly faces and strong arms to pull them out of the icy winter sea; but more than that, Paul must have reveled in being treated like a free man again. Standing on the beach of Malta in the pouring, cold rain, Paul, I feel sure, in spite of his physical discomfort, could not help contrasting the kindness of these strange pagans with the vindictiveness of the Jews and the trickery of the Romans who had kept him in chains. So far as we know, there were no believers on Melita, but God was there in their kindness to the shipwrecked men.

vv. 3 and 4

And when Paul had gathered a bundle of sticks, and laid them on the fire, there came a viper out of the heat, and fastened on his hand. And when the barbarians saw the venomous beast hang on his hand, they said among themselves, No doubt this man is a murderer, whom, though he hath escaped the sea, yet vengeance suffereth not to live.

In the confusion of the rescue from the sea, no one had noticed Paul among the crowd until, as he worked along with the others, a snake fastened onto his hand as he threw a bundle of sticks on the hastily built fire. Even the pagan

mind has a sense of right and wrong and believes in some
manner of punishment for wrong, so Luke evidently over-
heard one of the islanders speculate that Paul must be a
murderer getting his just due in spite of the rescue from the
storm. They knew that the snake was deadly. Paul would
surely die.

vv. 5 and 6

*And he shook off the beast into the fire, and felt no
harm. Howbeit they looked when he should have
swollen, or fallen down dead suddenly: but after they
had looked a great while, and saw no harm come to
him, they changed their minds, and said that he was a
god.*

I do not see this startling episode as an indication that
God's people are cosmic pets who will be protected from
deadly vipers. In my home state of West Virginia, back in
the mountains, are religious cults called "snake handlers,"
who use this incident on the beach at Melita as their basic
doctrine. True, Jesus said that his disciples "should take up
serpents" but, he spoke often in colorful Eastern meta-
phors; and at this point on my journey I am trying to understand the Scriptures by the light of what I have come to
understand about the nature of Jesus Christ. He, as Dr. E.
Stanley Jones says, "was all sanctity, but he was also all
sanity." I live in snake country now, on an island—my
house surrounded by woods and marsh—but I see no sanity in counting on divine protection, and so I have learned
to enjoy the woods with one eye on the ground. We should
not attempt any sort of explanation as to why God did this
for Paul. He had a reason, and all manner of speculation is
possible. For one thing, a sudden act of this kind focused
attention on Paul. God had promised Paul he would witness in Rome, and they weren't there yet. What is relevant
is what happens next, and none of it could have happened
if Paul had lain on the sand dead from snakebite.

v. 7

*In the same quarters were possessions of the chief
man of the island, whose name was Publius; who received us, and lodged us three days courteously.*

Paul was "somebody" now—a "god," the people said—
and so he and Luke and Aristarchus were entertained
"courteously" at the home of the island's most important
official.

vv. 8 through 10

*And it came to pass, that the father of Publius lay
sick of a fever and of a bloody flux: to whom Paul entered in, and prayed, and laid his hands on him, and
healed him. So when this was done, others also, which
had diseases in the island, came, and were healed:
Who also honoured us with many honours; and when
we departed, they laded us with such things as were
necessary.*

God seldom has just one simple purpose in what he does.
If Paul had died, none of these people would have been
healed, none of them would have heard the Gospel of
Christ—and we may be sure they did, even though Luke
does not mention it. For Paul "to live was Christ"; he
could no more have healed those people without telling
them about the Healer than he could have lived without
breathing. This is a lovely example not only of the rhyth-
mic two-way motion of the kingdom of love, but of God's
constant concern with the total person. Paul prayed for the
Maltese and they supplied his needs. Nothing ever works
just one way in the kingdom of love, and love abounded on
Melita for the three months Paul and his party lived there.

vv. 11 through 14

*And after three months we departed in a ship of
Alexandria, which had wintered in the isle, whose
sign was Castor and Pollux. And landing at Syracuse,
we tarried there three days. And from thence we
fetched a compass, and came to Rhegium: and after
one day the south wind blew, and we came the next
day to Puteoli: Where we found brethren, and were
desired to tarry with them seven days: and so we went
toward Rome.*

Another Greek grain ship had wintered at friendly Melita, and Paul and his party secured passage to leave as soon as winter was over and navigation was again possible. Luke, the physician, seems to be quite carried away with ships and winds and the problems of sailing; he is still being rather detailed about these things. Quite probably, Luke had never sailed so much on the high seas before, and he relished it.

Paul had lived for a long time with the conviction that he would eventually die a martyr's death in Rome. "Yea, and if I be offered upon the sacrifice and service of your faith, I joy, and rejoice with you all." He had already written this in his letter to the church at Philippi. After the troubled years, death could have been no surprise to the Apostle, and he was on his way to Rome—joyfully, because God was sending him. Luke mentions only one stop with "the brethren," but he says "and so we went toward Rome." There must have been other meetings along the way to encourage and warm Paul's heart.

v. 15

And from thence, when the brethren heard of us, they came to meet us as far as Appii forum, and The three taverns: whom when Paul saw, he thanked God, and took courage.

It had been a long time—more than three years—since Paul wrote his letter to the Roman Christians telling them of his desire to visit them. "For God is my witness, whom I serve with my spirit in the gospel of his Son, that without ceasing I make mention of you always in my prayers; Making request, if by any means now at length I might have a prosperous journey by the will of God to come unto you. For I long to see you, that I may impart unto you some spiritual gift, to the end ye may be established: That is, that I may be comforted together with you by the mutual faith both of you and me. Now I would not have you ignorant, brethren, that oftentimes I purposed to come unto you, (but was let hitherto,) that I might have some fruit among you also, even as among other Gentiles." The long wait was ended at last, and Paul joyfully embraced one group after another of the Roman Christians, who couldn't wait for him to reach them, but hurried out to greet him with open arms and hearts. After what he had been through, Paul needed them as much as they needed him.

v. 16

And when we came to Rome, the centurion delivered the prisoners to the captain of the guard: but Paul was suffered to dwell by himself with a soldier that kept him.

Paul was innocent of the Jews' charges, and yet there was the legal technicality of his appearance before Caesar still ahead. He was not free, in spite of the private quarters where he was permitted to live. He was still in bonds, with a soldier to guard him.

vv. 17 through 20

And it came to pass, that after three days Paul called the chief of the Jews together: and when they were come together, he said unto them, Men and brethren, though I have committed nothing against the people, or customs of our fathers, yet was I delivered prisoner from Jerusalem into the hands of the Romans. Who, when they had examined me, would have let me go, because there was no cause of death in me. But when the Jews spake against it, I was constrained to appeal unto Caesar; not that I had ought to accuse my nation of. For this cause therefore have I called for you, to see you, and to speak with you: because that for the hope of Israel I am bound with this chain.

Paul had scarcely arrived in Rome before he called the Jews to him. With all his mind and heart Paul's faith was in Jesus, the Messiah, but he remained a Jew. Three days after he reached Rome, found a rented house and settled in, he invited the Roman Jews to visit him and once more poured out his great heart and the story of his persecution by the Jerusalem rulers. He was still in chains, not free to go to them at the synagogue, but he had to see them—had to let them hear from his own lips what had really happened.

vv. 21 and 22

*And they said unto him, We neither received letters
out of Judaea concerning thee, neither any of the
brethren that came shewed or spake any harm of
thee. But we desire to hear of thee what thou thinkest
for as concerning this sect, know that everywhere it is
spoken against.*

Paul's heart must have leapt up. They had heard no ill of
him. He could be hopeful again—hopeful of freedom, perhaps, on the charges but, more than that, hopeful that, by
some means, he might be able to help these Jews see that
their Messiah had come in Jesus Christ. At least they professed interest in finding out what Paul believed. They
would give him a fair hearing. I can almost *feel* his hope.

vv. 23 and 24

*And when they had appointed him a day, there
came many to him into his lodging; to whom he expounded and testified the kingdom of God, persuading
them concerning Jesus, both out of the law of Moses,
and out of the prophets, from morning till evening.
And some believed the things which were spoken, and
some believed not.*

From morning until evening Paul poured out his heart
and his knowledge to these men, using the Scriptures with
which they were all familiar to prove that God had already
sent the promised Messiah in Jesus of Nazareth. "And
some believed . . . and some believed not." Paul's audience
that day in his little rented house was like any church audience today—some believe and some do not. But being
Paul, he could not be satisfied with half measures. To his
Jewish mind, it was all so clear—so real, so irrefutable. In
spite of their maltreatment of him, Paul still seemed to expect more spiritual perception, more definite recognition of
the truth from his fellow Jews. Some apparently did believe
him, but when they left his house that day they were all
arguing (verse 25a).

vv. 25 through 27

And when they agreed not among themselves, they

departed, after that Paul had spoken one word, Well spake the Holy Ghost by Esaias the prophet unto our fathers, Saying, Go unto his people, and say, Hearing ye shall hear, and shall not understand; and seeing ye shall see, and not perceive: For the heart of this people is waxed gross, and their ears are dull of hearing, and their eyes have they closed; lest they should see with their eyes, and hear with their ears, and understand with their heart, and should be converted, and I should heal them.

As the men began to leave Paul's house arguing among themselves, he stopped them with one more word from Isaiah. I see in this last desperate attempt no rancor on Paul's part—disappointment, yes, but to me it is a final effort to reach them through Isaiah, their own prophet, who had accurately described the scene in Paul's house that day.

vv. 28 and 29

Be it known therefore unto you, that the salvation of God is sent unto the Gentiles, and that they will hear it. And when he had said these words, the Jews departed, and had great reasoning among themselves.

Paul had done all he knew to do to reach his brothers. He may have sat down at this point with a long, heavy sigh. "I must tell you then, that God's message is going to be given to the Gentiles. They will listen!" He had done all he knew how, and his hopes for most of his brothers faded as he watched them walk away from his house, arguing as though they had heard little more than another philosophical premise.

vv. 30 and 31

And Paul dwelt two whole years in his own hired house, and received all that came in unto him, Preaching the kingdom of God, and teaching those things which concern the Lord Jesus Christ, with all confidence, no man forbidding him.

Luke seems to have ended this gripping story of Paul rather abruptly. As I pointed out earlier, his account of the

Acts of the Apostles is not a biography of Paul. It is, as J. B. Phillips wrote, "Some acts of some apostles." It is quite probable that, when Paul seemed settled down in Rome to wait for his appearance before Caesar, Luke returned home to work on his Gospel account. Paul was content because he was not forbidden to preach Jesus Christ, the risen Lord, and long ago he had learned to be content in chains. This man, Paul, was the bond servant of Jesus Christ—iron chains could not bind him—and I can imagine that Paul urged Luke to put the finishing touches on his Gospel. Nothing would have pleased the great Apostle more than to have his beloved friend hard at work on the story of Jesus of Nazareth, the Son of God.

In two years Paul would be beheaded by the young Caesar, and Luke's Gospel would be available to us so that we, too, could be sure that Paul was right when he said that Jesus is "the Son of God with power, according to the spirit of holiness, by the resurrection from the dead. . . . and that in him should all fullness dwell."

Inspirational titles
Robert H. Schuller

Robert Schuller has shown millions of people the way to success in business, interpersonal relations, and every other aspect of life through his inspiring messages over the internationally televised program, "The Hour of Power," and through his many books.

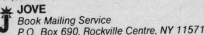